The Telling Error

Also by Sophie Hannah

Little Face
Hurting Distance
The Point of Rescue
The Other Half Lives
A Room Swept White
Lasting Damage
Kind of Cruel
The Carrier

SOPHIE HANNAH

The Telling Error

HODDER &
STOUGHTON

First published in Great Britain in 2014 by Hodder & Stoughton

An Hachette UK company

1

A CIP catalogue record for this title is available from the British Library

Hardback ISBN 978 0 340 98075 0
Trade paperback ISBN 978 0 340 98076 7
Ebook ISBN 978 1 444 73675 5

Typeset in Sabon MT Std
by Palimpsest Book Production Limited, Falkirk, Stirlingshire

Printed and bound by Clays Ltd, St Ives plc

Hodder & Stoughton policy is to use papers that are natural, renewable and recyclable products and made from wood grown in sustainable forests. The logging and manufacturing processes are expected to conform to the environmental regulations of the country of origin.

Hodder & Stoughton Ltd
338 Euston Road
London NW1 3BH

www.hodder.co.uk

For my genius editor and amazing friend Carolyn Mays, who has been the bright side of my dark side for nine years

IntimateLinks > uk > all personals
Reply: 22547652@indiv.intimatelinksUK.org
Posted: 2013-07-04, 16:17PM GMT

Looking for a Woman with a Secret

LOCATION: WHEREVER YOU ARE

Hello, females!

Are you looking on here because you're hoping to find something that stands out from all the dull one-line I-want-a-blow-job-in-my-hotel-room-type adverts? Well, look no further. I'm different and this is different.

I'm not seeking casual sex or a long-term relationship. I've had plenty of the first in my time, and I've got one of the second that I'm happy with. Actually, I'm not looking for anything sexual or romantic. So what am I doing on Intimate Links? Well, as I'm sure you're aware if you're clever (and I suspect that the woman I am looking for is very bright), there are different kinds of intimacy. There's taking off your clothes and getting dirty with an illicit stranger, there's deep and meaningful love-making with a soulmate . . . and then there's the sort of intimacy that involves two people sharing nothing more than a secret. An important secret that matters to both of them.

Perhaps these two people have never met, or perhaps they know each other but not very well. Either way, they can only establish a bond of common knowledge once the one who has the information has given it to the one who needs it. Think of the rush of relief you'd experience if you shared your burden, after the agony of prolonged silence with the secret eating away at you . . . If you're the person I'm looking for, you'll be desperate to confide in someone.

That's where I come in. I'm your confidant, ready and eager to listen. Are you the keeper of the secret I'm waiting to be told?

Let's find out by asking a question that only the person I'm looking for would be able to answer. It will make no sense to anyone else. You'll have to bear with me. Before I get to the question part, I'll need to lay out the scenario.

Picture a room in a large Victorian house: a spacious, high-ceilinged first-floor bedroom that's used as a study. There are overstuffed built-in bookshelves in this room, a pale blue and brown jukebox with curved edges that has a vintage look about it and is much more beautiful than the kind you sometimes see in pubs, an armchair, a filing cabinet, a long desk with square wooden legs and a green glass top that has a laptop computer at its centre. The computer is neither open nor closed. Its lid is at a forty-five-degree angle, as if someone has tried half-heartedly to push it shut but it hasn't gone all the way. The laptop is surrounded on all sides by cheap-looking biros, empty and half-empty coffee mugs, and scattered papers: handwritten notes, ideas jotted down.

Pushed back from the desk is a standard black office-style swivel chair, and lolling in the chair, his head leaning to the left, is a dead man. While alive, he was well known and – though this might well have nothing to do with anything – strikingly attractive in a stubbly, cowboy-without-a-hat kind of way. If I were to include his name in this account, I think most people would have heard of him. Some of you might shudder and say, 'Oh, not that vile bigot!' or, more light-heartedly, 'Not that ridiculous attention-seeker!' Others would think, 'Oh, I *love* him – he says all the things I'm too scared to say.' Our dead body is (was) somebody who inspired strong feelings, you see. So strong that he got himself murdered.

How was he killed? Well, this is the interesting part. The murder process comprised several stages. First, he was immobilised. His arms were pulled behind the back of his chair and taped together at the wrists. The same was done to his ankles, which were taped together round the pole of the chair's base, beneath the seat. Then his murderer stood behind him and brought a heavy object down on his head, rendering him unconscious. The police found this object on the floor beside the dead man's desk: it was a metal kitchen-knife sharpener. It didn't kill our well-known man (the pathologist told the police after examining the body), though it would have made an excellent murder-by-bludgeoning weapon, being more than heavy enough to do the job. However, it seems that although the killer was happy to use the knife sharpener to knock his victim out, he did not wish to use it to murder him.

There was a knife in the room too, but it had not been used to stab the dead man. Instead, it was stuck to his face with parcel tape. Specifically, it was stuck to his closed mouth, completely covering it. The tape – of which there was plenty – also completely covered the lower part of the murder victim's face, including his nose, causing him to suffocate to death. The knife's blade, flat against the dead man's mouth, was sharp. Forensics found evidence that it had been sharpened in the room, and detectives suspect that this happened after the victim was bound to the chair and unconscious.

Above the fireplace, on the wall between two bookshelf-filled alcoves, someone had written in big red capital letters, 'HE IS NO LESS DEAD.' I imagine that the first police to arrive at the scene took one look at that and leaped to a mistaken conclusion: that the red words had been written in the victim's blood. Then, seconds later, they might have noticed a tin of paint and a red-tipped brush on the floor and made a more informed guess that turned out to be correct: the words on the wall were written in paint. Dulux's Ruby Fountain 2, for anyone who is interested in the details and doesn't already know them.

Detectives examined the dead man's laptop, I assume. They would have found this surprisingly easy because the killer had red-painted, 'Riddy111111,' on a blank sheet of white A4 paper that was lying on the desk. This was the well-known man's password and would have led police straight to his email inbox. There they'd have found a new, unopened message from a correspondent by the name of No Less Dead, with an email address to match. There were no words in the message, only a photograph of someone standing in the room beside the unconscious, not-yet-deceased victim, wearing what looked like a protective suit from a Hollywood film about biological outbreaks – the sort that covers the head and body of the person wearing it. The killer's eyes would presumably have been visible if he or she hadn't taken care to turn away from the camera; as it was, the picture showed a completely unidentifiable person with one outstretched arm (for the taking of the photo), holding aloft a knife in his or her other hand, above the unconscious man's chest, in a way designed to suggest that a stabbing was imminent. The knife in the photograph was the same one (or identical to the one) that ended up taped to the murder victim's face, suffocating him rather than spilling his blood.

And now the question is coming up, so pay attention, ladies! (Actually, it's questions, plural.)

The murderer planned the crime in advance. It was about as premeditated as a killing can be. It involved bringing to the crime scene a knife, a knife sharpener, parcel tape, red paint, a paint-brush and a bio-hazard suit. The killer obviously knew the deceased's computer password. How? There was no evidence of a break-in. Did her victim let her in? (I'm saying 'her' because that's my hunch: that it was a woman. Maybe it was you?) Did the well-known man say to her, 'Go on, then: bind me to my chair, knock me out and kill me'? That seems unlikely. Maybe the killer pretended it was some sort of erotic game, or maybe I'm only speculating along these lines because Intimate Links is the perfect place to do so – the online home of sexual game-players of all kinds.

The most puzzling question is this: why arrive at the victim's house with a knife and a knife sharpener when you have no intention of stabbing him? Why sharpen that knife at the crime scene if all you're going to do is tape it, flat, against his face? For that purpose, the knife would work just as effectively if its blade were blunt.

Or, looking at it another way . . . if you've got a newly sharpened knife, and you've covered your clothing to protect it from blood splashes, and if, coincidentally, you also want to write a strange message in big red letters on the wall, why *not* stab the guy and use his blood to write with? Because you particularly want to suffocate him? Then why not do it more straightforwardly, with, say, a plastic bag over his head, taped round his neck to make it airtight? Why use a knife at all?

For some reason, you wanted to kill this man with a sharp knife, but you didn't want to stab him. Why not? And the photograph you emailed – what's that about? What are you trying to communicate? Is it 'Look, I could so easily have stabbed him, but I didn't'?

I realise I've slipped into using 'you' when I talk about the murderer, rather than 'she', or 'he or she'. I'm sorry. I'm not accusing you of killing anybody. Maybe you're not the murderer of the well-known man. You might be someone who wishes he were still alive, someone who loves him, or once did – a lover, a close friend. I'm really not sure. All I know is that you're reading this and you know the answers to the questions I'm asking. You desperately want to tell someone what you know.

I'm the person to trust with the information. I've taken a huge risk in sharing so many secrets, in the hope of eliciting a reply from you.

So, please, contact me. I'm waiting, and I promise I won't judge you. Whatever you've done, you had your reasons. I am ready to listen and understand.

Looking forward to hearing from you soon.

C (for Confidant) x

- Location: Wherever You Are
- It's NOT OK to contact this poster with services or other commercial interests

Posted: 2013-07-04, 16:17PM GMT

I

Monday 1 July 2013

It can't be him. All policemen wear high-visibility jackets these days. Lots must have sand-coloured hair that's a little bit wavy. In a minute he'll turn round and I'll see his face and laugh at myself for panicking.

Don't turn round, unless you're someone else. Be someone else. Please.

I sit perfectly still, try not to notice the far-reaching reverberations of every heartbeat. There is too much distance trapped in me. Miles. I can't reach myself. A weird illusion grips me: that I am my heart and my car is my chest, and I'm shaking inside it.

Seconds must be passing. Not quickly enough. Time is stuck. I stare at the clock on my dashboard and wait for the minute to change. At last, 10:52 becomes 10:53 and I'm relieved, as if it could have gone either way.

Crazy.

He's still standing with his back to me. So many details are the same: his hair, his height, his build, the yellow jacket with 'POLICE' printed on it . . .

If it's him, that means I must be doing something wrong, and I'm not. I'm definitely not. There's no reason for him to reappear in my life; it wouldn't be fair, when I'm trying so hard. Out of everyone sitting in their cars in this queue of traffic, I must be among the most blameless, if I'm being judged on today's behaviour alone: a mother driving to school to deliver her son's forgotten sports kit. I could have said, 'Oh well, he'll just have to miss games, or wear his school uniform,' but I didn't. I knew Ethan would hate those two options equally, so I cancelled my hair appointment and set off back to school, less than an hour after I'd got home from dropping the children off there. Willingly, because I care about my son's happiness.

Which means this has to be a different policeman up ahead. It can't be him. It was my guilt that drew him to me last time. Today, I'm innocent. I've been innocent for more than three weeks.

Drew him to you?

All right, I'm guilty of superstitious idiocy, but nothing else. If it's him, he's here on Elmhirst Road by chance – pure co-incidence, just as it was last time we met. He's a police officer who works in Spilling; Elmhirst Road is in Spilling: his presence here, for reasons that have nothing to do with me, is entirely plausible.

Rationally, the argument stands up, but I'm not convinced.

Because you're a superstitious fool.

If it's him, that means I'm still guilty, deep down. If he sees me . . .

I can't let that happen. His eyes on me, even for a second, would act as a magnet, dragging the badness inside me up to the surface of my skin, making it spill out into the open; it would propel me back to where I was when he first found me: the land of the endangered.

I don't deserve that. I have been good for three weeks and four days. Even in the privacy of my mind, where any transgressions would be unprovable, I haven't slipped up. Once or twice my thoughts have almost broken free of my control, but I've been disciplined about slamming down the barriers.

Turn round, quick, before he does.

Can I risk it?

A minute ago, there were at least fifteen cars between mine and where he's standing on the pavement, a few hundred metres ahead. There are still about ten, at a rough guess. If one of the drivers in front of me would do a U-turn and go back the way they came, I'd do the same, but he's more likely to notice me if I'm the first to do it. He might recognise my car, remember the make and model – maybe even the number plate. Not that he's turned round yet, but he could be about to. *Any second now . . .*

He'd wonder why I was doubling back on myself. The traffic isn't at a standstill. True, we're crawling along, but it's unlikely to take me more than ten minutes to get past whatever's causing the delay. All I can see from my car is a female police officer in the road, standing up straight, then bobbing down out of sight; standing up again, bobbing down again. I think she must be saying something to the driver of each car that passes. There's another male officer too, on the pavement, talking to . . .

Not him. Talking to a man who, please God, isn't him.

Inhale. Long and deep.

I can't do it. The presence of the right words in my mind is not enough to drive away the panic, not when I'm breathing jagged and fast like this.

I wish I could work out what's going on up there. It's probably something dull and bureaucratic. Once before, I was stopped by fluorescent-jacketed police – three of them, like today – who were holding up traffic on the Rawndesley Road as part of a survey about driver behaviour. I've forgotten what questions they asked me. They were boring, and felt pointless at the time. I remember thinking, My answers will be of no benefit to anyone, and answering politely anyway.

The car in front of mine moves forward at the exact same moment that the policeman with his back to me turns his head. I see him in profile, only for a second, but it's enough. I make a choking noise that no one hears but me. I'm embarrassed anyway.

It's him.

No choice, then. Driving past him is unthinkable – no way of avoiding being seen by him if his colleague stops my car to speak to me – so I'll have to turn round. I edge forward and swerve to the right, waiting for a gap in the oncoming traffic on the other side of the road so that I can escape. *Please.* I'll feel OK as soon as I'm travelling away from him and not towards him.

I edge out further. Too far, over the white line, where there's no room for me. A blue Toyota beeps its horn as it flies past, the driver's open mouth an angry blur. The noise is long and drawn out: the sound of a long grudge, not a fleeting annoyance, though I'm not sure if I'm still hearing its echo or only remembering it. Shock drums a rhythmic beat through my body, rising up from my chest into my throat and neck, pulsing down to my stomach. It pounds in my ears, in the skin of my face; I can even feel it in my hair.

There's no way a noise like that car horn isn't going to make a policeman – any policeman – turn round and see what's going on.

It's OK. It's fine. Nothing to worry about. How likely is it that he'd remember my car registration? He'll see a silver Audi and think nothing of it. He must see them all the time.

I keep my head facing away from him, my eyes fixed on the other side of the road, willing a gap to appear. One second, two seconds, three . . .

Don't look. He'll be looking by now. No eye contact, that's what matters. As long as you don't see him seeing you . . .

At last, there's space for me to move out. I spin the car round and drive back along Elmhirst Road towards Spilling town centre, seeing all the same things that I saw a few minutes ago, except in reverse order: the garden centre, the Arts Barn, the house with the mint-green camper van parked outside it that looks like a Smeg fridge turned on its side, with wheels attached. These familiar objects and buildings seemed ordinary and unthreatening when I drove past them a few minutes ago. Now there's something unreal about them. They look staged. Complicit, as if they're playing a sinister game with me, one they know I'll lose.

Feeling hot and dizzy, I turn left into the library car park and take the first space I see: what Adam and I have always called 'a golfer's space' because the symbol painted in white on the concrete looks more like a set of golf clubs than the pram it's supposed to be.

I open the car door with numb fingers that feel as if they're only partly attached to my body and find myself gasping for air. I'm burning hot, dripping with sweat, and it has nothing to do with the weather.

Why do I still feel like this? I should have been able to leave the panic behind, on Elmhirst Road. With him.

Get a grip. Nothing bad has actually happened. Nothing at all has happened.

'You're not parking there, are you? I hope you're going to move.'

I look up. A young woman with auburn hair and the shortest fringe I've ever seen is staring at me. I assume the question came from her, since there's no one else around. Explaining my situation to her is more than I can manage at the moment. I can form the words in my mind, but not in my mouth. *I'm not exactly parking. I just need to sit here for a while, until I'm safe to drive again. Then I'll go.*

I'm so caught up in the traumatic nothing that happened to me on Elmhirst Road that I only realise she's still there when she says, 'That space is for mums and babies. You've not got a baby with you. Park somewhere else!'

'Sorry. I . . . I will. I'll move in a minute. Thanks.'

I smile at her, grateful for the distraction, for a reminder that this is my world and I'm still in it: the world of real, niggly problems that have to be dealt with in the present.

'What's wrong with right now?' she says.

'I just . . . I'm not feeling . . .'

'You're in a space for mothers with babies! Are you too stupid to read signs?' Her aggression is excessive – mysteriously so. 'Move! There's at least fifty other free spaces.'

'And at least twenty-five of those are mother-and-child spaces,'

I say, looking at all the straight yellow lines on the concrete running parallel to my car, with nothing between them. 'I'm not going to deprive anyone of a space if I sit here for another three minutes. I'm sorry, but I'm not feeling great.'

'You don't know who's going to turn up in a minute,' says my persecutor. 'The spaces might all fill up.' She pushes at her toothbrush-bristle fringe with her fingers. She seems to want to flick it to one side and hasn't worked out that it's too short to go anywhere; all it can do is lie flat on her head.

'Do you work at the library?' I ask her. I've never seen a Spilling librarian wearing stiletto-heeled crocodile-skin ankle boots before, but I suppose it's possible.

'No, but I'll go and get someone who does if you don't move.'

What is she, then? A recreational protester whose chosen cause is the safeguarding of mother-and-child parking spaces for those who deserve them? She has no children with her, or any books, or a bag big enough to contain books. What's she doing here in the library car park?

Get the bitch, says the voice in my head that I mustn't listen to. *Bring her down.*

'Two questions for you,' I say coolly. 'Who the hell do you think you are, and who the hell are you?'

'It doesn't matter! What matters is, you're in the wrong space!'

'Read the sign,' I tell her. To save her the trouble of turning round, I read it aloud to her, '"These spaces are reserved for people with children." That includes me. I have two children. I can show you photos. Or my C-section scar, if you'd prefer?'

'It *means* for people who've got children with them *in the car*, as you well know! Shall I go and get the library manager?'

'Fine by me.' I'm starting to feel better, thanks to this woman. I'm enjoying myself. 'She can tell us what she thinks the sign means, and I'll tell her what it says, and explain the difference. "People with children" means "parents". Those with offspring, progeny, descendants: the non-childless. There's nothing in the wording of that sign that specifies where the children need to be, geographically, at this precise moment. If it said, "This space is reserved for people who have their kids with them *right here and now in this library car park*", I could see a justification for moving. Since it doesn't . . .' I shrug.

'Right,' Short Fringe snaps at me. 'You wait there!'

'What, in the parking space you're so keen for me to vacate?' I call after her as she stomps towards the library. 'You want me to stay in it now?'

She makes an obscene finger gesture over her shoulder.

I'd like to wait and argue with the librarian – all the librarians, if possible – but the return of my normal everyday self has brought with it the memory of why I left the house: to deliver Ethan's sports bag to school. I should get on with it; I know he'll worry until he has it in his hands.

Reluctantly, I slam my car door shut, pull out of the library car park and head for the Silsford Road. I can get to the school via Upper Heckencott, I think. It's a ridiculously long-winded way of getting there, involving skinny, winding lanes that you have to reverse back along for about a mile if you meet a car coming in the opposite direction, but you generally don't. And it's the only route I can think of that doesn't involve driving down Elmhirst Road.

I check my watch: 11.10 a.m. I pull my phone out of my bag, ring school, ask them to tell Ethan not to worry and that I'm on my way. All of this I do while driving, knowing I shouldn't, hoping I'll get away with it. I wonder if it's possible, simultaneously, to be a good mother and a bad person: someone who enjoys picking fights with strangers in car parks, who lies, who gets into trouble with the police and nearly ruins her life and the life of her family, who thinks, Fuck you, every time anyone points out what the rules are and that she's breaking them.

I blow a long sigh out of the open window, as if I'm blowing out smoke. Ethan deserves a mother with no secrets, a mother who can drive to school without needing to hide from anyone. Instead, he has me. Soon he'll have his sports kit too.

It could be worse for him. I'm determined to make it better, to make myself better.

Three weeks and four days. A verbal scrap with a self-righteous idiot doesn't count as a lapse, I decide, at the same time as telling myself that I mustn't let it happen again – that I must be more humble in future, even if provoked. Less combative, more . . . ordinary. Like the other school mums. Though less dull than them, I hope. Never the sort of person who would say, 'A home isn't a home without a dog,' or, 'I don't know why I bother going to the gym – forty minutes on the treadmill and what do I do as soon as I get home? Raid the biscuit tin!'

As safe and honourable as those women, but more exciting. Is that possible?

I like to have it both ways; that's my whole problem, in a nutshell.

~

As soon as I arrive at school, I am presented with an opportunity to put my new non-confrontational manner to the test. 'We discourage parents from going into classrooms,' a receptionist I've never seen before tells me, standing in front of me to block my way.

Since when? I've been into both Sophie's and Ethan's classrooms many times. No one's ever complained.

'It's emotionally disruptive for the children if a parent suddenly pops up during lesson time,' she explains. 'Some of them think, Oh look, Mum or Dad's here – they can take me home, and get very upset when Mum or Dad disappears again, leaving them behind.'

'I promise you Ethan won't be upset.' I smile hopefully at her. 'He'll just be pleased and relieved to have his sports kit.' *And, obviously, since he wants it for games this afternoon, he won't, on having it handed to him, expect to leave school immediately and miss the PE lesson that he needs it for, you stupid cow.* 'There's really no downside to letting me take it to him myself, honestly,' I add in what I hope is a wholly positive tone of voice. 'It'll save you a job too.'

'Nicki!' a high-pitched female voice calls out, one that would be better suited to a cheerleader than a head teacher. *Correction: headmistress.*

I sag with relief, knowing that everything is about to be all right. Kate Zilber is here: five foot short, petite as a ten-year-old, the most indiscreet person in professional employment that I've ever met. Kate refuses to be referred to as 'principal' or 'head'; 'headmistress' is her title, prominently engraved on the sign on her office door, and she insists that people use it. She once described herself to me as a megalomaniac; I soon discovered that she wasn't exaggerating.

'Is that Ethan's PE kit?' she says. 'It's OK, Izzie, we can bend the rules on this occasion. Actually, I can bend them whenever it suits me, since I run the place – perk of the job. We don't want Nicki worrying about whether the kit was safely delivered, do we?'

Izzie shrugs ungraciously and returns to her desk.

Kate pulls me out of the office and into an empty corridor. Once we're alone, she says, 'And the chances of it being safely delivered by Izzie are slim. She's a lobotomy on legs.'

'Really?' I must stop questioning everything she says. I keep assuming she's joking, but she never is. I'm not used to people who work in primary schools speaking their minds in the way Kate Zilber does. Still, Freeth Lane is well known to be the best independent school in the Culver Valley, and Kate's the person responsible for that. She could probably pelt the parents and governors with rotten eggs and get away with it.

'Quick pep talk for you.' She gives me a stern look. 'If you want to take Ethan his sports kit because you trust no one else to do the job properly, fine. But if there's an element of wanting to get a quick glimpse of him to reassure yourself that he's OK . . . not so fine.'

'Why not?' I ask.

'If you indulge your own anxiety, you'll make Ethan's worse. He needs his sports kit; you've brought it in – problem solved.' She squeezes my arm. 'There's no need for you to see him, Nicki. You'll only read unhappiness into his expression, whether it's there or not, and work yourself up into a state. If he smiles at you, you'll worry he's putting on a brave face in front of his new friends. If he doesn't smile, you'll imagine he's in the grip of a powerful inner torment. Am I right?'

I sigh. 'Probably.'

'How about I take him his sports kit instead?' she suggests. 'I'm the most reliable person on the planet. You know that, right? I'm even more efficient than you.'

'All right.' I smile and hand her the bag. For some reason, this tiny, shrewd, girly-voiced woman I barely know has a talent for very quickly making me feel ten times better. Every time she does, I can't help thinking of Melissa, who has the opposite effect and is my closest friend.

'Thank you.' Kate turns to walk away, then turns back. 'Ethan really will be fine, you know. He'll be as happy here as Sophie – you wait and see. Some children take longer than others to form emotional attachments and adapt to a new environment, that's all. The other kids are really rallying round, looking after him – this term even more than last. It's sweet. He's made so many new friends.'

'Ethan's always been more sensitive than Sophie,' I say. 'He doesn't handle change well.' *And his mother, knowing this, took him away from the school where he was happy. Two terms later, he still tells me at least once a week that he'll never love this school as much as his old one – that however many friends he makes, Oliver-who-he-left-behind-in-London will always be his true best friend, even if he never sees him again.*

'Nicki.' Another stern look. 'Ethan's *fine*. He occasionally gets anxious about things. Lots of kids do. It's really nothing serious. Your anxiety, on the other hand . . . You should take yourself to a head doctor, lady,' she concludes affectionately.

'Kate, I—' I break off. What am I thinking? I can't tell her anything. I can't tell anyone, ever.

'What?'

'Nothing.'

'Bugger "nothing". You can't start and not finish. Tell me or I'll expel your children.'

'I've . . . been under a lot of pressure recently, that's all. I'm not normally so twitchy.'

Kate raises a plucked eyebrow. 'Don't fob me off, Nicki. That wasn't what you were going to say.'

The urge to tell her – something, anything – is overwhelming.

'I lied to you.'

'Ooh! This sounds promising.' She moves closer, rubbing her hands together. No one else I know would react so enthusiastically to hearing they'd been deceived. *If only they would.* 'Lied to me about what?'

'First time I came in to look round,' I say, 'you asked me why we wanted to leave London and move to Spilling.'

'And you said what so many London offcomers say: better schools, bigger garden, cleaner air, perfect rural childhood, yada yada. Whenever parents tell me that, I think, Ha, just wait till your fourteen-year-old's roaming those big green fields you prize so highly, off his tits on illegal substances because there's no Tube to take him anywhere worth going, and sod all to do in his local idyll.'

I laugh. 'Are you this frank with all the parents?'

Kate considers my question, then says, 'I tone it down a bit for the squeamish ones. So, come on – the lie?'

'My real reason for moving here was entirely selfish, nothing to do with fresher air and bigger gardens. I wasn't thinking about my children, or my husband. Only myself.'

'Well . . . good,' says Kate.

'Good?'

'Absolutely. It's when we imagine we know how others feel and presume to know what's best for them that mistakes are made. Whereas no one knows our own needs better than us.' She glances at her watch. 'Looking after number one's not as daft a policy as it sounds: make the only person happy that you can, let everyone else do the same and take care of themselves. So why did *you* want to move to Spilling?'

I shake my head, look away. 'It doesn't matter. It stopped being relevant shortly after we got here anyway. Sod's Law. I just wanted you to know: that's the reason I get anxious about Ethan.'

'I get it,' says Kate. 'His suffering is your punishment. You don't believe you can avoid retribution for being as selfish as you've been, therefore Ethan must be suffering horribly?'

'Something like that,' I mutter.

'I wouldn't think that way if I were you. Women need to be ruthlessly selfish. You know why? Because men are, and so are children. Both will turn you into their skivvy unless you give back as good as you get on the selfish front.' I find myself looking at her left hand to see if she's wearing a wedding band; I've never noticed, and her name gives nothing away: she's Dr Zilber, not Miss or Mrs.

She is wearing a wedding ring. A thin one – either white gold or platinum. The skin around it is pink, chapped and flaky, as if she's allergic to it.

'Listen, Nicki – much as I'd love to pry further into your secret reason for moving here, I'd better get on. There are people still on my staff who belong in the dole queue.' She nods towards Izzie. 'I can't rest until that's rectified. But first stop: Ethan's kit.'

I thank her, and return to my car feeling more optimistic than I have for a while.

Maybe nothing all that terrible has happened to me. Maybe I'm not the guiltiest woman in the world. If I told Kate, she might laugh and say, 'God, what a story!' in an appreciative way. I'm so used to Melissa's harsh glare and pursed lips and, more recently, her refusal to listen, but she is only one person. *The wrong person to try and share a secret with, if the secret's anything more controversial than 'This is what I've bought so-and-so for their birthday – don't tell them.'*

The conclusion I've been strenuously trying to avoid reaching glows in neon in my brain: I need to give up on Melissa and find myself a new best friend. I can't get away from her – she's managed to tie us together forever, even if that wasn't her intention – but I can demote her in my mind to 'acquaintance'; she'll never know I've done it, if I'm still friendly on the surface.

Is there a website, I wonder: newbestfriend.com? If there is, it's probably full of people trying to turn it non-platonic, looking for 'fuck buddies' or 'friends with benefits'.

Kate Zilber wouldn't have let a run-in with a policeman stop her from doing what she wanted and needed to do. She wouldn't have been doing it in the first place unless she'd decided it was OK, and she wouldn't have been terrified and ashamed if caught. I doubt she'd have disappeared from Gavin's life with no word or explanation, as I did.

The fairest thing to do, for his sake and my family's – that's what I told myself.

Liar. Coward.

I owe him an explanation. For whatever reason, however stupid and crazy it was, he was significant to me for a while. He mattered. I think I mattered to him too.

I drive along the Silsford Road with the window open, thinking about the possibility of contacting him now. Could I extend my definition of being good to include emailing him just once more, to tell him that my disappearance wasn't his fault, that he did nothing wrong?

No. It wouldn't be only once. He'd hook you again.

Cutting off from Gavin took all my willpower; I might not have the strength to do it a second time.

I decide to allow myself the luxury of not deciding immediately. I want to cling to the possibility – not of going back to how it was, but of one last communication, to end things in a proper way. I know better than anyone that sometimes a possibility is enough to keep a person going, even if it never becomes a reality.

Will Gavin still be checking, three weeks and four days after he last heard from me, or will he have given up by now? If it had been the other way round and he'd suddenly stopped emailing me, how soon would I have stopped looking to see if he'd written?

The phone's ringing as I pull up outside my house. I grab my bag, lock the car door and fumble with the front-door key, knowing the call will be about Ethan. Something's happened: he's sobbing, locked in a toilet cubicle. Or there's a problem with his sports kit – part of it's missing. How sure am I that I put all the right things in?

Let him be OK and I swear I won't email Gavin, or even think about it any more.

I run into the lounge and grab the phone, wondering why I persist in offering God these phony deals. If He exists, He must be reasonably intelligent – maybe not the academic four-A*s-at-A-level kind of clever, but powerfully intuitive, and with a deep understanding of people. He must have spotted the pattern by now: I never stick to my side of the bargains I make with Him. Time and time again, He goes easy on me and I think, Phew, and forget about what I promised I'd do in return, or invent a loophole to let myself off the hook.

I pick up the phone. 'Hello?'

'Is that Mrs Clements?'

'Yes, speaking.'

'It's Izzie here, from Freeth Lane. We just met, when you came in before?'

'Is Ethan OK?' I resent the time it takes me to ask: endless stretched-out seconds of not knowing.

'Oh.' Izzie sounds surprised. 'I don't know.'

'What do you mean, you don't know?' I snap.

'I assume he's all right. I haven't heard that he isn't.'

'So you're not phoning about Ethan?'

'No.'

I exhale slowly as I fall into a chair. 'Right. So what can I do for you?'

'It's Sophie.'

Sophie, who's never problematic in any way, who I don't need to worry about. I take her well-being for granted. I feel as if my heart has been lobbed at the wall of my gut, feel it sliding slowly downwards, flattened by dread.

The children of guilty mothers, hostages to karma, always in imaginary peril that feels so real, so asked for . . .

'She's been sick,' says Izzie. 'She seems fine now, and she says she wants to stay for the rest of the day, but it's policy to let parents know.'

'I'm coming in now to see her,' I say. 'Tell her I'm on my way.' I'm not taking the word of Lobotomy Izzie when it comes to the health of my daughter; I want to check for myself if Sophie's well enough to stay at school. Which means driving the round trip, yet again. And then again at home-time, either to pick up both children or, if I bring Sophie back with me early, to pick up Ethan. Fleetingly, I consider collecting them both now to save me having to drive back to school later for the fourth time in one day, but then I realise I can't make Ethan miss games, not after I've taken in his kit; he'll be looking forward to playing football or cricket or whatever it is, expecting the rest of his day to unfold predictably and without incident.

I decide that I'll be brave and try the Elmhirst Road route again. Getting to Sophie as quickly as possible matters more than my fear. If the sand-haired policeman is still there, I'll stay calm and pretend not to recognise him. Or maybe I'll wink at him. I can imagine Kate Zilber doing that. Winking isn't illegal. He wouldn't be able to warn me or threaten me. A wink proves nothing, and in any case, there has been nothing to prove since I turned good.

~

The routine when Sophie and Ethan get in from school at the end of the day is always the same. Panting and groaning, they shrug and wriggle their way out of their coats and shoes in the hall, as if divesting themselves of chains that have bound them for decades, before making a dash for the lounge and slamming the door. They have an urgent appointment with the television that nothing would induce them to miss.

I am left to pick up the discards from the hall floor and throw them, in a big pile glued together by wet mud from the soles of football boots, into the coat cupboard; it's mess relocation rather than tidying up. Adam is patient and always waits until the cupboard's interior is indistinguishable from a compost heap before he complains. When he does, I either say, 'I know. Sorry – I'll sort it out tomorrow,' or I snap, 'If you don't like it, do something about it,' depending on my mood.

The CBBC channel starts to chatter mid-sentence. That's my cue to pour the juice and make the toast. Once they're on the kitchen table, I call out, 'Snack's ready!'

'Bring it in here!' Sophie yells. She is more vocally militant than her brother, who is happy to be represented by her in all parent-child disputes.

'No!' I shout back.

'Yes! Remember, I was sick! I feel a bit weak!'

'You *were* sick – you're not now!' Nor was she when I arrived at school to check on her; she looked at me as if I were crazy, told me she had no intention of coming home with me and turned back to her friends. I left empty-handed, a person-with-children temporarily without her children, just as I was this morning in the library car park. It was only on my fourth and final trip to school that I came away with what I wanted: Sophie and Ethan in the back seat, and an overwhelming feeling of relief. I can't fully relax unless they're under the same roof as me; that's been true since we moved here from London.

Kate Zilber's right: I should probably get some therapy. I'm too anxious. Once, waiting to collect the children at the end of the day, I started to have palpitations because a man looked at me in a way that made me feel uncomfortable: a long-drawn-out superior smirk. He's one of the school's most pleased-with-himself Flash Dads. I often see him leaning against his expensive-looking blue BMW in the part of the playground where the showiest parents always wait. His hair is subtly streaked. It looks deliberate, which I know I shouldn't disapprove of, but I do. There are some things men just shouldn't do, and streaked hair is right up there alongside cosmetic pubic-hair removal. Though I've never seen his child or children, I enjoy imagining them as rebellious teenagers, covered with tattoos and piercings that spell out, 'My dad's an utter cock.'

'Please, Mum!' Sophie yells from the lounge.

I could refuse again, but what's the point? I'll give in eventually; I always do. I don't know why I bother going through the daily ritual of putting the plates and glasses down on the table in front of two chairs. I think it's because I like the idea of my children coming into the kitchen and chatting to me, so I create the conditions that will make it possible. Seeing the toast and juice neatly laid out on the table makes me feel like a proper mother.

We don't have many rules in our house. The few we do have – like no eating in the lounge – are broken every day. Adam thinks it's stupid and inconsistent to ban things we disapprove of and then allow them to happen anyway. I'm torn. I admire people who don't allow themselves to be constrained by rules, and cheer inwardly every time my kids demonstrate that they have no intention of obeying me.

If I believed myself to be a fine, upstanding pillar of the community with a strong moral code, I might feel differently. Who am I to tell anyone how they ought to behave?

I take the toast and juice into the lounge. Sophie tells me to 'Shh' before I've said a word. Her eyes are glued to the television screen, as are Ethan's. I say, 'Thank you, darling mother,' loudly before leaving the room.

'Yeah, thanks, Mum,' says Ethan. Three whole words. Amazing. He and Sophie tend to lose the ability to speak for about an hour and a half after they get home from school. They find their voices again at supper-time, after which we usually can't shut them up until bedtime.

Having delivered the snack, I pull the lounge door closed behind me and hover in the hall, not sure what I'm going to do next. I have a strong suspicion, but that's not the same as being sure.

I should get to work in the kitchen. The dishwasher needs unloading and reloading before I can start cooking.

I shouldn't, definitely mustn't, email Gavin.

But you will. You're about to.

Breaking other people's rules might be commendably independent-minded, but breaking your own, which you made willingly, to protect yourself and your family? What kind of fool does that?

I want to continue to believe in the fantasy that I have a choice, but it doesn't feel true. The decision has been made, in the shadowy part of me that logic never reaches, where a force far greater than my willpower is in charge.

I look at my watch. Adam will be home in about half an hour. If I don't do it now, I won't have another chance until tomorrow.

Too long to wait.

As I run upstairs to our box room, which houses the family computer, I wonder how I've managed to resist doing this for so long. Three weeks and four days. Until I saw that policeman again today, I was finding it easy to be good. The shock of my first meeting with him was all the motivation I needed. I don't understand why a second almost-encounter with him has driven me in the opposite direction.

You can still do the right thing. Sending one quick explanatory email for politeness's sake isn't the same as starting it up again.

It's what I should have done all along, instead of my cowardly vanishing act.

I close the box-room door behind me, making sure I've shut it properly and not just pushed it to, and sit down at the desk. This will be the first time I've opened my secret Hushmail account since my first run-in with the policeman. I've been scared of discovering that Gavin's emailed me, scared I wouldn't have the strength to delete his message without reading it.

I type in my password, my heart beating like the wings of a trapped bird in my ears and throat, and prepare to confront my greatest fear: an empty inbox. What if he hasn't been in touch for the whole three weeks and four days that I haven't contacted him? That would mean that he was never as keen as I thought he was.

Good. It's good if he's not keen. It's good because we're over.

Though we never agreed it in so many words, we operated a strict 'turns' system throughout our correspondence, both of us always waiting for a reply before emailing again. No exceptions. Did Gavin stick to the pattern and take my lack of response to his last message as a sign that I was no longer interested? Would he give up on me so easily? Surely he'd have wondered, after I didn't reply for a whole day – and then another and another – whether his last email went astray. I would have, in his position.

My finger hovers above the 'return' key. If I press it, I'll know within seconds.

I can't do it.

I push my chair back from the desk, afraid that I'll press 'return' by mistake, before I'm sure I want to.

You don't have to look. Ever. Turn off the computer, go downstairs. Forget about him.

No. I won't take the coward's way out, not this time. I've done that already today, more than once. Despite vowing that I wouldn't, I avoided Elmhirst Road when I went back to school to check on Sophie; I went via Upper Heckencott again, there and back. I did the same both ways when I went to collect Ethan and Sophie at the end of the day, though on each of the four journeys I lied to myself right up until the second before I chickened out.

I slide the wheels of my chair closer to the computer. The eleven asterisks that represent the hidden letters of my password are still sitting there, in the box. My password is '11asterisks'. I'm still proud of myself for thinking of that: the password that in attempting to conceal itself does the opposite – reveals itself so brazenly that no one would ever guess.

Wincing, I press the 'return' key before I can change my mind.

I gasp when I see my inbox. There are seven unread emails from Gavin. Seven.

Thank you, thank you.

No point pretending this surge of excitement is anything else. Even a talented self-deceiver like me wouldn't swallow that one.

I'd have given up before I wrote the seventh email, however distraught I was. Gavin didn't.

This is it: why I lie, and keep secrets, and take crazy risks – for this feeling. No chemical could give me the same buzz: the thrill of being so wanted, so sought after.

I start to open the messages, one by one. They were all sent within four days of my decision to break off contact with Gavin: four on the first day of my silence and then one on each consecutive day after that.

Hi Nicki, I'm writing to check that my last email to you didn't go astray. Let me know. G.

It's pathetic, isn't it, me worrying because you haven't emailed me for a few hours? Don't want you to think I can't last a day or even several without hearing from you, but you know what it's like – once a pattern's been established, any disruption to said pattern causes concern. And did you realise that we've emailed each other **at least** twenty times a day since we started? G.

PS – in case you've forgotten when our exchange started, it was 24 February. You made a reference once to deleting all your emails from me, for security. I deliberately kept shtum (not wanting you to think I'm careless about security, which I'm not) and I don't know if you assumed that I delete all your emails after reading too, but I don't. I keep them. I reread them. They mean a lot to me. I hope that's OK with you. That's why I wasn't upset by the idea of you deleting your side of our conversation, because I'm keeping it safe at my end. Don't worry. I promise you no one but me will ever see it. G.

PPS – feelings, eh? They complicate things, don't they? I hope I haven't freaked you out by writing about what can only be described as non-carnal matters. I won't make a habit of it, I promise. Let me know you're OK and aren't sick of me yet, and I'll go back to talking mainly about your nipples, I promise. (Well, I might cover a few other parts of your body, to be fair. In my emails and, in due course, with my own body – I hope.) G.

No, no, no. This is wrong.

I feel dizzy, disorientated. I want and need words from Gavin, but not these words. This doesn't sound like him. This sounds too much like a real person, someone I might know or be friends with. Gavin has always sounded like . . .

What?

Like something automated. Short toneless sentences, short paragraphs. Like an android giving erotic instructions. The kind of written voice that disembodied words on a screen might have if they had a voice.

And that was exactly what you wanted, wasn't it? What does that say about you?

In due course with his own body? Did he really mean that? Do I want him to mean it?

Gavin and I arranged to meet once, in May, after agreeing we were ready to take things to the next level. Then he had to cancel; he didn't say why. After that, neither of us mentioned rearranging. I didn't mind. Secretly, I was relieved. If we didn't meet, that meant that what I was doing wasn't as bad. If I thought of him as unreal, one-dimensional, a computer program generating words designed to elicit a specific physical response, then I could almost persuade myself that I didn't really have another man in my life, one who wasn't my husband.

Still wrong.

Not as grievously wrong as a physical affair, though. Maybe. And the emails were enough. God, they were so much more than enough: endless, detailed, graphically descriptive orders from a man I'd never met, whose face I'd never seen, not even in a photograph. None of my real-life lovers has ever been so uninhibited in the words he used or the things he asked and expected me to do – and nor was I ever so . . . pornographic, for want of a better word, with any of them. Gavin swept away all my inhibitions by ignoring them completely, refusing to acknowledge they existed and simply repeating his demands. Eventually, I stopped bothering to mention that I was too shy and simply did as I was told.

And loved it. Craved more and more of it.

All I know about Gavin is that he's English, in his mid-forties, married with no children and works from home. That's what he's told me, anyway. I suppose any or all of it might not be true. I didn't and don't really care. All I cared about was the way he made me feel. On two occasions, his insistent explicit words alone were enough to push me over the edge – just the words and my imagination, and not even a brush of a fingertip. No other man has ever had that effect on me.

Not even King Edward.

Whom I swore I wouldn't allow into my mind again. That's why Gavin: to block out King Edward. Amazing, really, how well it worked.

Until now.

I am gasping for breath, though I've done nothing physically strenuous. I grip the desk to steady myself.

Think about Gavin. Not . . . anybody else. Gavin.

The blank tonelessness of his words was an important part of the attraction. So different. And yet three of the four new messages from him that I've just read – all but the first one – don't sound like him at all. Did my abandonment panic him so much that his online persona slipped?

I promise you no one but me will ever see it . . .

I won't make a habit of it, I promise . . .

I'll go back to talking mainly about your nipples, I promise . . .

Feelings, eh?

A shudder rocks my body. I don't want Gavin's feelings or his promises. King Edward gave me feelings and promises, and they counted for nothing in the end. And I don't want amusing banter and wordplay from Gavin either. Adam jokes around. So did King Edward. I love witty men, normally. I mean, I used to.

You still do love Adam. Never forget that.

Gavin has never been funny, warm or affectionate before. It's the reason I felt safe in my dealings with him. I wanted and needed him to be avid but not caring, never emotional. I can't stand to think of him as a vulnerable man whose heart I might have broken.

I don't want to think about him any more today – it's already too much – but I can't log out, not without reading everything.

I open message number five:

Nicki, seriously, are you OK? I'm starting to indulge in paranoid worst-case-scenario delusions here. Has your husband found out about us? Have you found out something about me? Are you in hospital, with no access to email? G.

Nicki? Where are you? G.

Do you want to hear my latest theory? You always sign your emails 'N x'. I always sign mine 'G'. You've decided I'm a cold,

emotionless husk because I won't sign off with a kiss. That's why
you've gone missing from my cyber-life. Right? For your information, I've never signed emails with an 'x' and I don't think I ever
would, however I felt about someone. It's fine when women do it,
but from a man it would look somewhat effeminate, I think. Also, I
can't believe this would bother you suddenly when it never has
before? Or maybe it has, and you've been waiting and hoping
. . . ? Look, I'm a big boy. I can handle honesty. Will you tell me
what I've done wrong? G x (just this once, for strategic effect,
because . . . well, because I'm rather fond of you, Nicki. Perhaps
I should have said so before.)

No. No. This is unbearable.
Kind, sincere, affectionate words. Of all the things to become
phobic about. *Fuck you, King Edward. You're to blame for this.*
I'm glad there's no mirror in this room. I would hate to see
what I look like.
*A disaster area. There's not a person on the planet who
wouldn't be better off without you in their lives, not even your
children.*
Instead of shutting the computer down and running away, I
force myself to read all seven of Gavin's emails again – not once
but several times. By the time I've finished, the words seem less
threatening and my hands have stopped shaking.
How can he care about me this much? He barely knows me.
Correction: he doesn't know me at all.
And yet, not knowing him either, I care about him too. The
way he rescued me from the brink . . .
Far from objecting to it, I like the little dot he always puts
after his initial. I like his vulgar email address, mr_jugs@hush-
mail.com, and his habit of putting two asterisks on either side
of a word or group of words to convey insistence.
Have you found out something about me? What did he mean
by that?
What should I do?

No one to ask, or answer, apart from myself. At one time, I'd have told Melissa. I told her everything, before she resigned from her position as my confidante.

There is no one I can think of – not one single person in my life – who would be interested in discussing the changeable writing style of a man who goes by the name of 'Mr Jugs' in order to seek anonymous physical gratification online.

If I ever did muster the courage to tell anybody, I would get no useful analysis, and plenty of soul-destroying condemnation: from my female friends, my brother, my parents; from Adam, assuming he'd speak to me ever again if he knew the truth, and not simply throw me out on the street in horror. And – though I hate to think about it – I would get shock and disgust from Sophie and Ethan too. They might only be ten and eight, but they understand what betrayal is even if they wouldn't use the word.

My children. Who are downstairs. Who believe I'm looking after them because all three of us are in the house at the same time and I'm the adult.

Tears fill my eyes as a violent internal current sweeps my breath away. This used to happen a lot before I stopped emailing Gavin, often when I was sitting here, in front of the computer screen: a sudden flood of realisation that something terrible is happening – something precious is being irrevocably destroyed – and, though it's my fault, I can't stop it. I have no control.

Four or five seconds later, my eyes are dry, and I can breathe easily. I couldn't recreate the doomed feeling if I tried; it's as if it never happened.

I press my eyes shut so that I can't see the computer in front of me, and wish that the Internet had never been invented. I tell myself that I absolutely mustn't – *must not* – email Gavin, for the sake of my family, but instead of hearing my own voice saying the words, I hear Melissa's, which blend with the sand-haired policeman's, though neither of them has ever said those words to me.

Their judgement, though I've conjured it out of nowhere, is too heavy a burden to bear. I can only escape if I defy it outright.

I should reread Gavin's messages once more before writing to him – allow their significance to sink in. There might be something I've missed . . .

No. No time. Adam will be home any minute. And Gavin has waited long enough to hear from me. I might still matter to him as much as I did when he sent those emails; by tomorrow, he might have stopped caring. I don't want to leave it too late.

I open his most recent message and press 'reply'. My fingers are numb, unreliable. It takes me three attempts to manage 'Hi Gavin' without typos. Then I delete it and write, 'Dear Gavin,' instead. 'Hi' is too casual.

I'm so sorry I haven't replied before now. Until today, I haven't opened my Hushmail account for more than three weeks. I decided I couldn't do what we were doing any more. It was nothing you did wrong, so please don't worry about that. I don't want to go into detail, but I had a minor skirmish with the police that was kind of linked to my involvement with you. It shook me up and I lost what little courage I had. I decided we had to stop before something irreversible happened. In an ideal world, I would love for us to be in touch again. You saved my sanity and brought unexpected pleasure into the darkest patch of my life. But it's just not possible. Once again, I'm so sorry. I wish you all the very best. N x

I press 'send', wiping away my tears with my other hand. There. I've done the right thing for once. I'm glad the urge to behave honourably doesn't seize me more often if this is how it feels: like hollowing out my heart and stuffing it full of greyness.

The darkest patch of my life. Was that an over-the-top way to put it?

In February, thanks to King Edward – King Edward VII, to give him his full alias – I considered taking my own life. For a few days I wasn't sure that even the thought of Sophie and

Ethan, motherless, would be enough to persuade me to stay in this world.

I'm about to sign out of Hushmail when a new message appears in the inbox.

Gavin. Oh God. Christ, God. Of course it's him: no one else knows I have this email address. I used to email King Edward from a Gmail account. I didn't know Hushmail existed until I answered Gavin's advertisement and he wrote back from a Hushmail account.

How has he managed to reply so quickly? Has he been sitting in front of his computer for three weeks and four days, waiting?

I hope he hasn't. Almost as much as I hope he has.

I try to grasp the mouse, aim wrong and knock it off the table. Having restored it to its place on the mat, I take a deep breath and click to open the message.

It's one line long:

More detail about your encounter with the police, please. G.

I type an equally short response:

No. It was horrendous. I want to forget it ever happened.

I don't sign off with my usual 'N x'. I hope this is a tactful way of demonstrating that we are no longer an item, insofar as we ever were. My replying doesn't mean I've entered back into a correspondence with him, and this exchange has nothing to do with sex. He's just being nosey; as soon as he sees that it won't work, he'll give up.

Another new email appears in my inbox. I open it.

All right, so you had a brush with the police and decided you couldn't write to me any more – fair enough (or I'm sure it would be, if I understood why). So what changed today? Did they only just let you out of jail? G.

I smile in spite of myself.

So, Gavin turns out to have a sense of humour. Is that so bad? Not all charming, funny men are evil. Adam, for example.

My fingers hover over the keyboard. I want to answer, but how can I justify responding a second time if I really want to break this off?

Does Gavin think that if he puts nothing sexual in his messages, I'll decide it's OK to write to him?

If we're not going to do the cyber-sex thing, what's in it for him? Or for me?

I don't want him as a platonic friend. That would be awful. If I have to choose between types of loss – and it appears that I do – I'd rather have the sudden dizzying kind, not a long-drawn-out diminishment.

I type:

No jail. I saw the same policeman again today. It reminded me that it was because of him that I'd stopped writing to you. I decided I owed you an explanation. That's all. Please stop emailing me. I don't want to be your pen pal. All or nothing for me, and it has to be nothing. Again, I'm so sorry. N x

I press 'send'.

All done.

Log out, Nicki. Why are you still sitting here, staring at your inbox? How devastated will you be if he doesn't write back immediately?

Then why did you order him not to?

His reply arrives within seconds.

I agree: you owe me an explanation. What happened with the policeman? First time and second time, please. All or nothing is a sound principle – and since you've already given me some of the story, you must now supply all of it. G.

This sounds more like the Gavin I'm familiar with: wooden. Giving me orders. Desire stirs inside me. I shift in my chair.

Should I tell him? If I don't, he'll never understand, not really. Can I bring myself to write what happened in an email? The prospect makes my skin prickle.

I click on 'reply'. Downstairs, a door bangs shut, making me jump.

'Kids!' I call out. 'Don't slam the door!'

'Not kids. Me. Sorry.'

Adam. *Shit.*

Terror floods my body, freezing me in place. It's a few seconds before I can move again. I grab the mouse. 'I'll be down in a sec,' I shout. *Please don't come upstairs.*

What will Adam do? I listen for clues, with the cursor hovering over 'Sign Out' in the top right-hand corner of the screen. *Please go into the kitchen, Adam. I need a few more seconds . . .*

I hear the creak of a door – the lounge, I'm guessing – followed by Adam trying unsuccessfully to talk to the children. He gives up after a minute or so. I hold my breath, listening for footsteps on the stairs.

Nothing. He must have gone into the kitchen, or to the loo. *You don't know that. Sign out. Don't risk it.*

I type:

Need to go now. Might explain later. No promises, though. Bye. N x

I press 'send', then sign out. Then I go to 'History', click on 'Show All History' and delete all the Hushmail entries. I'm so grateful that I can do this. It's the online equivalent of saying a few Hail Marys and being absolved of all your sins. *Thank you, technology.*

What next? I can't think straight. Oh yes, I know: Yahoo Mail, my respectable email account.

Adam pushes open the box-room door as I'm opening a message from my mum. 'Hi, hon,' he says. 'OK day?'

'Brilliant, thanks,' I tell him. 'You?'

'Why brilliant?'

'Well, actually . . . not *that* brilliant.' *Come on, Brain, start working, for fuck's sake.* I have nothing to be excited about, not officially. I must keep this in mind – for the rest of my life, ideally.

It's a good sign that, after only three weeks and four days of being good, I am already much worse at lying.

I'm not going to start lying to Adam again. I can't.

'I had to go to school and back four times,' I say. The email from my mother about when we're next all going to get together is still up on the screen. Not at all secret from my husband, but still . . . I ought to feel more guilty about this ongoing corre-spondence than I do about the one with Gavin.

If I'm making a list of people to cut off contact with, my parents have surely earned their place at the top.

You're not cutting anyone off, though, are you? You never will.

How did I not hear Adam on the stairs? He could so easily have caught me.

But he didn't.

Being bad and getting away with it: there's no feeling like it.

Who's a Bad Sport, Keiran?

Damon Blundy, 6 September 2011, *Daily Herald Online*

In *The Times* yesterday, Keiran Holland <u>explained</u> why he believes that disgraced sprinter Bryn Gilligan doesn't deserve a second chance, now or ever. Having read Holland's sermon and found it unpalatable, both conceptually and digestively, I would like to offer Holland one of the greatest gifts one human being can offer another. By coincidence, it's the very thing he seeks to deny Gilligan: the gift of a second chance. Keiran, you must be embarrassed about what you wrote, so why don't I take a week off to reread my Jeeves and Woosters, and you take my next column, with my blessing. Use it wisely. By which I mean, use it to lament the ethical cataracts that prevented you from seeing clearly in the bad old days (<u>yesterday</u>, <u>this morning</u>) when you were a hapless churner-out of received opinion.

My regular readers know all about Bryn Gilligan, since I've <u>written</u> about him <u>more than once</u>. Gilligan was found guilty of doping and, having first <u>protested his innocence</u>, eventually made a <u>full confession</u> and apologised. Later, he apologised <u>more satisfactorily</u>, for all the good it did him. Yesterday, his appeal to overturn his lifetime Olympic ban was rejected by the Court of Arbitration for Sport. Keiran Holland believes Gilligan's life sentence must remain in place because '<u>His contrition is plainly not genuine</u>.' 'If that sounds harsh, it isn't,' Holland assures us. 'Bryn Gilligan is a liar and a cheat, and has admitted as much himself.'

There's a problem with this argument that I hope all proud owners of more than half a brain cell will be able to spot instantly. It was the lying and cheating Gilligan did that created the occasion for his apology. People who say sorry tend, on the whole, to be those who have made mistakes, often serious ones. If the fact of their having done something wrong dictates that we mustn't accept their apologies, doesn't that mean there's no point in anybody apologising for anything ever again? Should contrition be banned outright?

Keiran Holland doesn't think so. If he did, I might have more respect for him. Personally, I'm a fan of the centuries-old tradition of acknowledging one has cocked up and resolving to do better in future, but I respect a man who can hold a consistent line on an issue, however outlandish. Keiran Holland is not that man. As usual, he simply hasn't thought it through. Indeed, what he claims to have wanted from Gilligan was a *better* apology, one that was less 'weaselly'. Holland wanted the pure, special stuff: contrition of the highest grade.

Would he have forgiven Gilligan and lobbied for the lifting of his ban if he'd got the abject grovel-fest he was after? No – as evidenced by <u>his response</u> to Gilligan's subsequent more fulsome apology, which can be summarised as 'He's only grovelling now because he saw that his original rubbish apology wasn't cutting any ice, therefore we must continue to haul him over the coals forever.' Forgetting that Inspector Javert is nobody's favourite character in *Les Misérables*, Holland omits to explain why a perfectly worded apology that follows cheating at sport plus a flawed apology is unacceptable, while arguing that the very same perfect apology after *only* cheating at sport would have been ideal. Logically, it doesn't stack up.

While I agree that Gilligan's use of the word 'oversight' in his initial statement and in relation to deliberately pumping himself full of banned substances before each race was an evasion at best – indeed, I said so <u>here</u> – what I find remarkable is that Holland seems to have no idea why Gilligan's first reaction to being exposed as a sinner might have been so inadequate. The apologies of disgraced celebrities tend to be, don't they? 'I'm sorry, but . . .' when there is no possible 'but'; 'I'm sorry for the part I played' when no one else played any role at all; 'I'm sorry if certain people were offended' when only those under general anaesthetic could fail to take offence, so unquestionably vile was the transgression. I hope I'm not the only person who has noticed that deficient apologies seem to be perennially in vogue. There's an obvious reason for this – so obvious that I'm not going to waste time explaining.

I'm keen to know why Holland is so lacking in compassion where Bryn Gilligan is concerned. What is it about the combination of drug-taking and cheating that he so objects to, when he has no problem with either one in isolation? He <u>cheated on his wife</u> for at least six months with <u>Paula Riddiough</u>, former Labour MP and <u>saboteur of her only son's education</u> (though to be fair, any red-blooded male would be tempted by the luscious Paula), so it can't be Gilligan's prolonged dishonesty that bothers Holland. A cheat himself, one might hope he would show a bit of leniency towards his underhand compadres. I've had the misfortune to be <u>married twice</u> – to <u>Princess Doormat</u> and <u>Dr Despot</u> – and I cheated on them both with gay abandon of the hetero-sexual kind. It's a sad fact that however beautiful the woman you marry, you will always meet one who is more or equally beautiful, eager to wrap her limbs around you and possessed of the additional appeal of being not-your-wife. So . . . having said all that, am I shocked to the core that Bryn Gilligan broke the rules in order to win races? No. How could I be, as a rule-breaker myself? To paraphrase the well-known adage, I read news stories about the repugnant behaviour of famous people to know that I am not alone.

Is it the drugs, then, that Keiran Holland can't forgive? No, I can prove it's not that. Holland was one of the judges, in the Supernatural/ Horror category, of <u>this year's Books Enhance Lives Awards</u>. The <u>unanimously chosen winner</u> in that category was <u>Reuben Tasker</u> for his novel *Craving and Aversion*, which begins with the line 'Every translucent love contains particles of rot-green hate.' Only if you're paranormally stoned, I'm afraid, Reuben.

Tasker's enduring devotion to cannabis is an open secret in the literary world, as is his belief that the drug expands his imagination. He's on record as saying he doesn't think he'd be able to write a book worth anyone's time without it. Assuming some or all of this year's other Supernatural/Horror contenders are tediously abstemious on the narcotics front, doesn't that mean that Tasker's drug-taking might have given him an unfair edge over the competition? Shouldn't he have to give back his prize money, arrange a head-hung-in-shame photo-shoot and sob within dampening distance of Piers Morgan?

Did this dilemma cross Keiran Holland's mind even for a fleeting instant? Did it occur to him retrospectively, as condemnations of Bryn Gilligan poured forth from his keyboard, that he was one of a panel of judges that awarded a prestigious prize to a law-breaking substance abuser?

Before everyone jumps down my throat: yes, of course I can see that the two cases are different – cannabis is not as unambiguously performance-enhancing as whatever it was that Gilligan took. One writer's prose might be boosted by illegal drugs, another's by instant Nescafé or the sugar rush from a packet of Minstrels. My own reaction to cannabis is to fall asleep within ten seconds of ingesting it, so it wouldn't do anything for my writing style, whereas a strong cup of brick-coloured tea is all I need in order to be able to produce the seamless brilliance you're reading now.

So, yes, it's different. But is it different in a way that matters, assuming one doesn't believe rules should be adhered to simply because they're there? I don't think it is. I think it's crazy that sports-people are subject to such different constraints from writers and artists when it comes to professional competitions. How can the discrepancy be justified? More interestingly, how can Keiran Holland's hypocrisy be justified?

'He's a liar and a cheat.' Yes, Keiran – you are, aren't you?

2

Monday 1 July 2013

'Than,' said DC Simon Waterhouse. He turned away from the red letters on the wall of Damon Blundy's study. He was sick of looking at them, must have read the words more than a hundred times since arriving at 27 Elmhirst Road earlier in the day: 'HE IS NO LESS DEAD.'

'Than?' DS Sam Kombothekra repeated.

'Yeah. It's the most important word. The silent "than". You can't see it.'

'You mean . . .' Sam approached the wall to inspect it more closely. 'Can *you* see it?'

'No.' Simon smiled at his skipper's confusion. 'Because it's not there.'

Neither was Damon Blundy's body, not any more. It had been photographed, examined and removed. Yet the chair beside the desk didn't feel empty; it still contained the solid idea of a dead man. It was the perfect illustration of murder, Simon thought: someone once present who was now absent. A space where a person ought to be, a perceptible negative. Simon could see the deceased Blundy in his mind as clearly as if he'd still been slumped there. *Parcel tape on his face, the knife taped tight against his mouth* . . . The picture was as vivid to Simon as the missing 'than' on the wall.

As always, he was more interested in what he could imagine than in what he could see. The props still present in the room – the knife sharpener, the tin of red paint, the brush – no longer held his interest. Even the photograph that the killer had sent to Damon Blundy, the password painted on A4 paper and left beside Blundy's laptop to ensure the police would find the email containing the photograph . . . Simon could happily have spent days pondering the meaning of these two things in combination, but he felt no need to look at either one again. Why waste his time? Sam and the rest of the team could scour all that was clearly visible while he looked behind and beyond, trying to coax hidden motives and grudges out of the shadows.

'I see what you mean. A "less" implies a "than".' Sam sounded relieved to have finally worked it out.

'He is no less dead than what, though?' said Simon. 'Whoever painted those words knows the answer, and chose to be cryptic instead of letting us in on the secret. Which means either he wants us to work it out or he wants us to fail. If we fail, he gets away with it, proves he's cleverer than us.'

'And if we succeed?'

'Then he's going down for murder.'

'Maybe,' Sam said. 'All these . . . weird features might be clues to something – to motive, perhaps, or something about Damon Blundy – but not necessarily to the killer's identity.'

'Joking, aren't you? Crime scene like this –' Simon gestured around the room '– motive's going to be as unique as a fingerprint. Soon as we know why, we'll know who.' *How soon?* Simon could feel his impatience overheating already, and this was only day one.

Not knowing the answer always put him in a foul mood, especially in the hours immediately following a murder. The disappointment of arriving at the scene and not being able to work it out straight away, the feeling of failure, the fear that he'd never get to the truth if it didn't leap out at him in the first five minutes . . . He clung to the hope that it would happen to him one day, the ideal scenario he always prayed for: a revelation in those first few precious moments, before all the major and minor players started chucking their lies at him.

He walked over to one of Damon Blundy's overcrowded bookshelves, half pulled out a pale-blue-spined paperback – P. G.

Wodehouse – then pushed it back in again. The sight of so many books made Simon think about authorship. 'This killer's invested a lot of time and effort, planning and execution,' he said. 'He's proud of his handiwork. Wouldn't want us to work out why in isolation, without knowing who – that'd feel like Mr Nobody getting the credit.'

'So he wants to be caught?'

'I wouldn't put it that strongly.' It bothered Simon that Sam was treating his ill-thought-out ramblings as statements of fact. He was too proud to say, 'I've no idea if I'm right – this is pure speculation,' so said instead, 'He doesn't *want* to be caught, no, but he's prepared to be. He wouldn't bother with the cryptic clues if he didn't want to give us a chance of working it out, however unlikely he thinks it is that we will. No fun for him to outwit us if it's a foregone conclusion.'

'Couldn't he outwit us more easily if he didn't leave us any clues at all?' Sam asked.

Simon nodded. It was a good point. 'But he also wants acknowledgement – of his grievance as well as his cleverness. So maybe he *does* want to be caught – maybe I got it the wrong way round and getting away with murder would be the consolation prize. Or he might be equally happy with either outcome: win-win for him. Either we're too stupid to interpret his clues and he gets away with it – massive ego boost – or he has the consolation of police and media attention for his cause, whatever it is – political or personal.'

'Political?' Sam sounded surprised.

'Could easily be,' said Simon. 'I've been working my way through Damon Blundy's columns from the *Herald*. His vocation was pissing off as many people as possible: women, Jews, Muslims, atheists, pro-choice-ists, left-wingers, right-wingers, journalists, dog-owners – you name it. Someone's going to have to read every word he's ever published, and all the comments threads online. We'll probably find at least five hundred people who've threatened to kill him at one time or another.'

'I've been assuming this is personal,' said Sam. 'The strange quirks of the murder scene . . .' He ran his gloved hand over the jukebox in front of him. It was impressive. Simon had never seen one close up before. If Sellers were here, he'd suggest they took turns to choose songs.

'What if all the cryptic stuff's a smokescreen?' Sam said. 'Designed to look as if it means something when it means nothing at all?'

The idea turned Simon's stomach: deliberately staged false significance. It was a possibility he couldn't bear to consider, let alone discuss, but since Sam had raised it, he had to conquer his phobia and answer. 'No. If the killer wanted to send us on a wild-goose chase, he might have left us one cryptic mislead – the words on the wall, or the photograph . . . One. Not this many. The paint, the brush, the knife sharpener . . . It's too much to be fake. And we know one thing the killer left us was genuine: the password for the laptop. It got us into Blundy's email. He wants us to know he knew Blundy well enough to know his password.'

'Or he forced the password out of him at knife-point, once he'd taped him to the chair,' said Sam.

'Possible. Unlikely, though. This killer's demonstrating that he's the expert: on Blundy, his computer password, why he deserved to die. He's boasting. Look around you: this whole room's a display of self-congratulation in crime-scene form. He knows everything; we know nothing. Or she.'

'You think it's a woman?'

'Did I say that? Still, Blundy's wife's more likely to know his password than anyone else, isn't she?'

'Is she?' Sam asked. 'If you password-protect a laptop that lives in your house, aren't you mainly protecting your privacy from the person or people you live with?'

'How long before I can talk to her?' Simon asked.

Sam looked towards the open door of the study. 'There's no point in either of us trying until she's capable of stringing a sentence together.'

Hannah Blundy was two floors below, in her converted basement kitchen-cum-dining room with a family liaison officer. She'd found her husband's dead body at ten thirty this morning when she'd brought him up a mug of tea that never made it into the room. Hannah hadn't yet calmed down sufficiently to tell anyone anything useful, but judging by the mess on the landing, it seemed likely that she'd got to the top of the stairs, seen Damon framed in the doorway of his study, murdered and bound by tape to his desk chair, and dropped the mug where she stood.

Shock. Or designed to look like shock by the same person who had so carefully orchestrated the rest of the murder scene. Simon wanted to know which.

'If Hannah Blundy calmly and methodically murdered her husband and then staged the distraught meltdown we witnessed when we arrived—' Sam broke off, shook his head. 'She'd almost deserve to get away with it if she can act that well. I don't really mean that,' he qualified quickly.

'Anyone can weep and collapse on the floor,' said Simon, though in fact he couldn't imagine ever managing to be so emotionally unrestrained in public, however distressed he was. 'Especially a murderer surrounded by police, terrified they'll see through her act.'

'I don't think so,' said Sam. 'I can't see Hannah Blundy as a killer.'

'I can. If I had to lay a bet now, my money'd be on her.'

'For any other reason than that she's his wife?'

'I haven't met any other suspects yet, have I?'

Sam's face reddened.

Simon took pity on him. He was too easy to wind up. 'Actually, it's not that. Or that she's his wife.'

'Then what?'

'She's a psychotherapist. Her website says she specialises in relationship and familial issues.' Seeing that Sam was about to object, Simon said, 'I know – it doesn't mean anything. Except

45

. . . she's chosen to devote her life to helping people who hate the people they're supposed to love. Maybe she did too – hated her husband, wanted him dead.'

'I think that's . . . a stretch, simply from her choice of profession,' Sam said after a few seconds.

'Well, I'm not wrong about the missing word,' said Simon, keen to return to safer ground. 'What might come after the "than"?'

Sam shrugged helplessly. 'There must be infinite possibilities. How can we narrow it down?'

'A person's name,' said Simon. '"He is no less dead than . . . Fred." Let's say it's that, for the sake of argument. What would that mean? That he's *more* dead than Fred? Or the same amount dead? There's no such thing as more dead,' he answered himself.

'If it's a name – Fred or Mary or whatever – that could suggest other victims,' said Sam. 'Each one no less dead than the one before.'

'Yeah.' Simon nodded slowly. 'I like that.' A bit. Not a lot, not enough to stick with it. 'Or how about another meaning: "He is no less dead than he was while alive"? No, that'd make better sense if it was "no *more* dead".'

'Simon, it could be anything.'

'I know that, and I know your shall-we-just-give-up? voice.'

'No, I wasn't—'

'We need to think of every single thing it might be, anything and everything that could conceivably come after "than".' Simon walked over to the desk, nearly tripping over the knife sharpener on his way. It was black, heavy and could have doubled as a doorstop. 'Too much and too many to be meaningless,' he muttered, 'but maybe only *one* meaning . . . Yeah. One.'

'Explain?' said Sam.

'All the things the killer's left us are different routes to the same information – different prompts. Whatever that shit on the wall means, whatever it means that he could easily have stabbed Blundy with the knife in the photo but chose instead to suffocate him with a knife and some tape . . . he's given us lots of clues, but it's not like a crossword, where each one's designed to give you a different answer. Imagine a crossword with numbers one to twenty across and numbers one to twenty down and in all forty cases it's the same nine-letter word we're trying to guess.'

'Why nine letters?' Sam asked.

'Random,' said Simon impatiently. 'Call it eight or ten if you like. Point is, the crossword creator *really* wants us to guess the answer – this ten- or nine- or eight-letter word's important to him. He thinks we need to know it, but he also thinks we're stupid – unlikely to twig unless he gives us lots and lots of clues.'

'So . . . ?'

'So this is our way into the "than",' said Simon, feeling positive for the first time since arriving at 27 Elmhirst Road. '"He is no less dead *than* . . ." Whatever comes afterwards, the meaning has to be the same as the meaning of the paint, the brush, the photo, the knife . . . They're all problems with the same solution.'

'What about the laptop password?' said Sam. He walked over to Damon Blundy's desk, picked up the red-painted page and held it in the air. 'Riddy111111. Does that also mean the same thing?'

'If it's a new password, thought up by the killer, then yes,' said Simon. 'If it was Blundy's choice of password and nothing to do with the killer, then no. Even so – it has to mean something. Riddy one-eleven one-eleven. Riddy triple one triple one.'

'Damon always claimed it meant nothing,' said a woman's voice from the landing. 'It's been his password for a long time – at least a year.'

Simon turned. Hannah Blundy was standing at the top of the stairs, holding on to the bannister with one hand. She was still crying, but more passively now; the tears seemed to be doing their thing without her involvement or attention.

She was an odd-looking woman: broad-shouldered, square and stocky from the waist up, with long skinny legs. Her round face, if it were all that you saw of her, would make you think she must be fat, but she wasn't. Looking at her made Simon realise how well designed and coordinated most people's bodies and faces were. He didn't think he'd ever seen anyone before whose top half clashed so markedly with their bottom half, and both halves with their face.

Having said all that, Hannah Blundy wasn't ugly. Her features were inoffensive, and her shiny dark brown shoulder-length hair was attractive. It looked like hair Simon had seen on TV advertisements and rarely in real life.

'I never believed him,' she said. 'Whatever "Riddy one-eleven one-eleven" means, or even if it means nothing, he must have got it from somewhere, otherwise why those letters? Why those numbers?'

'So you knew it was his password?' asked Sam.

Hannah nodded. 'I made him tell me what it was. I told him mine. If he had no secrets from me, why would he mind me looking on his laptop? He said it was just random, Riddy111111. It was a lie, but I can't prove it. I . . . Please, if you find out . . .' She bit her lip and looked down at the floor, as if she'd lost confidence in the rest of her sentence.

Simon took a step towards her. 'Find out what?'

'About the password. What it means. I want to know.'

'More than you want to know who murdered your husband?'

'Simon . . .' Sam murmured.

'No, I want to know that too,' said Hannah. She looked surprised. 'Of course I want you to find out who killed Damon. That's part of it, I'm sure, and the password is part of it. I never imagined the police might one day help me solve the mystery. This is my chance.' She sniffed, wiped her face with the back of her right hand.

Since she didn't seem stupid, Simon assumed she would have known as soon as she discovered his dead body that the unlawful suffocation of her husband would attract serious and immediate help from detectives. And her 'one day' suggested something that had been bothering her for a long time, not a crime that had been committed between half past eight and half past ten this morning. Therefore . . . the mystery Hannah Blundy was referring to couldn't be Damon's murder. That, in her eyes, was the chance to solve the puzzle; it wasn't the puzzle itself. *Interesting.*

'What do you mean, Hannah?' Sam asked. 'This is your chance for what?'

'To find out the truth that my husband was so determined to keep from me,' she said, staring down at her feet. 'Whatever it is, I hope it's what got him killed. If it wasn't – if that was something completely different and unrelated – then whatever you find out about the murder won't help me. I'd given up hope of ever knowing, but now . . .' She stopped with a ragged gasp, wide-eyed. 'Promise me you'll tell me the truth if you find out.'

'The truth about what?' Simon asked.

'Why Damon pretended to love me,' said Hannah.

~

'Charlie, have you got a minute?'

Sergeant Charlie Zailer was on her way to the canteen for a cup of tea and a cake, if there were any left that had icing and didn't look too dry and stale. She turned round and saw DC Chris Gibbs in the corridor behind her. He was smiling a better man's smile: gracious and innocent. It bore no resemblance to anything Charlie was used to seeing on his face. Instantly, she was on her guard. He wanted something, and, without knowing what, Charlie wasn't inclined to give it to him.

'Not really,' she said. 'I've got an early evening meeting.' Which would be fine if there was going to be wine there, but there wasn't. The provision of refreshments was not the Culver Valley Cultural Awareness Action Group's strong point. 'Why?'

'It's the Damon Blundy murder. Something's cropped up on the CCTV. Simon and Sam are still at the house.' Gibbs shrugged and managed to look almost shy. 'I'd like to know what you think.'

'Why? I don't work for CID any more.' Charlie said this whenever she could, to anyone who would listen, in the hope that she would one day be able to say it without it causing her pain.

Gibbs grinned. 'Except when you do, unofficially.'

Now Charlie was really suspicious. 'When I do unofficially, it's because Simon drags me in – something you've never done or tried to do. So why now?'

'Spur-of-the-moment impulse? Maybe I miss my old skipper.'

'Gibbs, what's going on? Why are you being nice to me? If Liv's dumped you and you're looking for a new bit on the side with similar DNA, forget it. I'm a married woman – not the Liv kind. The boring sort that only shags her husband.' God, that sounded priggish. Charlie felt almost ashamed as she remembered the promiscuous risk-taker she used to be. She distrusted moral-majority attitudes on principle, and was only faithful to Simon because she was in love with him and the thought of being with another man turned her stomach. In the abstract, she had no problem with sexual infidelity as long as the individuals involved weren't her exasperating younger sister and her surly former DC.

She'd often wished she loved Simon less, so that she could enjoy a secret sex life he knew nothing about. Involving someone Olivia worked closely with, ideally – give her a taste of her own medicine, see how she liked her sister trespassing on her territory.

Gibbs and Liv had been having an affair for several years. It had started on the night of Charlie and Simon's wedding and, despite Charlie's hopes that it would end disastrously and early, it had proved irritatingly durable. So far it had survived Gibbs becoming the father of twin girls and Liv's marriage to another man – a wedding Gibbs had attended. He and Liv had gazed at each other longingly over the heads and between the torsos of the other guests, seeing nobody in the room apart from one another, while Dominic Lund, Liv's husband, had done his best to talk to all the people Liv was busy ignoring. No doubt he'd imagined, incorrectly, that he was the romantic hero of his own wedding. It was one of the strangest social occasions Charlie had ever attended.

'Bit on the side?' Gibbs frowned. 'Is that what you think Liv is to me?'

'Do you prefer "mistress"?'

'How would you feel if I mocked your relationship with Simon?'

'You mean how *did* I feel, on the many occasions that it happened?' As soon as she'd said it, she regretted it. Charlie hated thinking about that part of her past: getting engaged to Simon with everyone knowing they hadn't yet slept together, all the mockery they'd had to endure, the speculation at the nick about the cause of Simon's abstinence, heavily weighted in favour of it being somehow Charlie's fault . . .

'I haven't mocked you and Simon, separately or together, for a long time,' Gibbs said.

It was true. As always, the reality of being mean to someone was proving less enjoyable than the idea of doing so. 'Fair enough,' Charlie said. 'Look, what's this about? Why are you hovering? Spit it out. Are you leaving Debbie? Is Liv leaving Dom?' *I'm at work, for fuck's sake. I don't want to be talking about my sister.* Charlie doubted she'd ever get over her profound regret that her family had found its way into her professional life without her permission, and vice versa.

'Nothing like that.' Gibbs was smiling weirdly again, a nervous-about-meeting-the-Queen kind of smile.

'Then what? Tell me!'

'Nothing. I just thought you'd be interested in the latest on the Blundy case. But you're busy, so . . . forget it.' Gibbs turned and started to walk away.

'I've got about quarter of an hour.' Charlie looked at her watch to check that it was true.

Sort of. Not really. It wouldn't matter if she missed the first ten minutes of cultural awareness – not to her, anyway. 'Show me some grainy black and white film,' she said. 'I'll pretend I'm watching a tedious art-house picture with no plot or mass-market appeal – the kind Liv used to *love* before she fell for you and decided she preferred *Mission Impossible II* to Eric Rohmer.'

'If you're sure?'

'I'm sure, polite boy.'

Charlie followed Gibbs to the viewing room on the first floor. DC Colin Sellers was already in there – had been for some time, by the look of it. His tie was draped over the back of his chair, and he'd undone the top two buttons of his shirt. The lower buttons looked as if they might be next to give way, under pressure from Sellers's sizeable beer-and-kebab belly. 'What are you doing here?' he asked Charlie.

'Charming. Lovely to see you too, Colin.'

Sellers shrugged, scratched one of his sideburns and turned back to the screen in front of him. He was normally jollier than Gibbs. Charlie hadn't often seen him looking as glum as this. She couldn't think of anything she'd done that might have upset him, and concluded that he must once again have been disappointed in lust. That women existed who were between the ages of twenty and sixty and didn't want to have sex with him was an unending source of misery to Sellers. He notched up more rejections in a week than most men do in a lifetime on account of his determination to proposition every female who crossed his path when he wasn't with his wife, Stacey – in pubs, takeaways, shops, on the street – and practised infidelity on a scale that made Gibbs and Liv's affair look as quaint and wholesome as a chaste Victorian courtship. Luckily for him, Sellers's policy of indiscriminate approach netted him as many yeses as nos; it was easy, he'd told Charlie a few months ago, once you'd worked out how to identify desperation in strangers.

Nice.

'Show her,' said Gibbs.

Sellers picked up the remote control. Charlie leaned against the wall at the back of the room. 'What am I looking at?' she asked. 'I mean, traffic, obviously, but . . .'

'See the silver Audi?' said Gibbs. 'This is from the camera on the corner of Elmhirst Road and Lupton Road. Here's our silver Audi travelling north on Lupton . . . and turning into Elmhirst at ten fifty-five this morning.'

'And here . . .' Sellers pressed the fast-forward button, held it down for a few seconds. 'Same silver Audi coming back less than five minutes later. Looks like a woman behind the wheel – so why did she change her mind and double back on herself?'

'Maybe she didn't,' said Charlie. 'Maybe she stuck a birthday card through a letterbox at the Lupton Road end of Elmhirst Road, then did a U-ey and headed back home. Or, if she was planning to drive all the way along Elmhirst and subsequently changed her mind . . . well, there could be any number of reasons.'

'If it was a one-off, I'd agree,' Sellers said. He stood up, took the tape out, slotted another one in. While he fiddled with the remote control, Gibbs filled Charlie in on the background. 'Damon Blundy's house is on Elmhirst Road. He was found dead by his wife at ten thirty a.m. She called it in at ten thirty-five. Uniforms were there within minutes, stopping drivers on the Blundy-house side of the road for on-the-spot interviews.'

'Quick work,' said Charlie.

'Simon's idea,' Gibbs told her. 'I'm guessing you've heard about the, er, unusual crime scene.'

'Yeah, I spoke to Simon at lunchtime. It sounds . . . weirder than usual. Even than usual-for-you-lot.'

'Simon reckoned the killer might want to try and observe police response at close range, having taken such care over his gruesome death installation,' said Gibbs. 'For the benefit of an audience, presumably – so he wouldn't want to miss out on seeing how that audience reacted.'

'Makes sense,' said Charlie.

'Anyway, at ten fifty-five, the Audi driver would have found herself crawling forward in slow-moving traffic, delayed by police in the road ahead – police she'd have been able to see stopping and talking to other drivers – but she'd also have been able to see that the delay wasn't severe. Wherever she wanted to go beyond Elmhirst Road, she'd have been quicker waiting than doubling back and taking a different route. And no one else waiting in the queue did a U-turn. Not one single other driver.'

'I refer you once again to my birthday-card-delivery scenario,' said Charlie.

'Except look at this,' said Sellers. 'Same camera fifty minutes later. The same silver Audi drives along Lupton Road coming from the Silsford direction, heading south this time. It doesn't turn into Elmhirst, but look . . . see how it slows almost to a standstill as it passes the junction?'

It was undeniable.

'The driver wanted to see if the police were still there,' said Gibbs. 'Why else would she have slowed down as she approached the junction? And why does she care what the police are up to?'

'Nosiness?' Charlie suggested. 'Most people like to have a gawp if they think something excitingly horrible's going on. We're all ghouls at heart.'

'Would most people be nosey enough, and have the spare time, to come back to the same place twice in one day to gawp?' Gibbs asked. 'Also, if she wanted to know what was going on, why didn't she stay in the slow-moving traffic, let the police stop her when it was her turn and just ask them what was happening?'

'OK, so we fast-forward again . . .' said Sellers, 'to . . . here.' He pointed the remote control at the screen and pressed 'play'. 'Forty minutes later, she's back, other side of the road, going north again. This time, she comes to a complete stop on Lupton Road at the exact point that'd give her the best view up Elmhirst, holding up the cars behind her.'

'O . . . K,' said Charlie. 'So she's very, *very* nosey.'

'And then we fast-forward again and find . . .'

'She comes back *again*?'

'An hour and five minutes later, yeah,' said Gibbs.

He, Charlie and Sellers watched in silence as the Audi on the screen drove southbound along Lupton Road and started to brake as it neared the junction with Elmhirst.

'Again, she stops and sits at the end of Lupton, blocking the traffic,' said Sellers. 'For even longer this time. Look at the queue behind her – can't you just hear the beeping of all those angry horns? Still, she stays put for a full minute.'

'So, something's fishy there, chances are,' said Charlie. 'I'm assuming you know who owns the Audi, since you know it's silver and our drama premiere's in black and white.' She nodded at the screen.

'Car belongs to a Mrs Nichola Clements,' said Sellers. '19 Bartholomew Gardens, Spilling.'

'So why aren't you round there talking to her now?' Charlie asked.

'It's definitely worth doing that, isn't it?' said Gibbs.

Charlie laughed. 'Are you kidding me? Have you got so many other promising leads that you can afford to ignore this one?'

'No, I mean . . . *I* think it's worth it, but I wanted your take on it. It could be perfectly innocent, just a local busybody, as you say.'

'Course we have to talk to her,' said Sellers.

Charlie exhaled slowly. 'What's this about, Gibbs? You're trying to flatter me by making out my opinion really matters to you – I get that, though I've no idea why – but couldn't you have found something more interesting to ask me, something a bit less obvious? Anyone with a brain, seeing what you've just shown me, would say you should speak to Nichola Clements as soon as you can.'

'I've been saying it,' said Sellers.

'Anyone with a brain, and Sellers as well, would say interview Nichola Clements,' Charlie teased.

Sellers attempted a smile, but it didn't take. 'What the fuck's wrong with you?' Gibbs asked him.

A good moment to leave them to it, Charlie decided. Even stone-cold-sober cultural awareness was preferable to this.

~

'I can't prove that Damon never loved me, so if it's evidence you're after, you'll be disappointed. As I have been.' Hannah Blundy faced Simon and Sam across the large oval-shaped wooden table in her kitchen. The family liaison officer, a young woman called Uzma who seemed incapable of performing any action quietly, was making them all tea, if the available visual evidence was reliable and if you considered it in isolation; the sound effects suggested a train crash at close range. Irritating though it was, Simon welcomed the background noise; it helped to add a veneer of normality to one of the most unlikely conversations he'd ever had, and he'd had a fair few.

'I understand,' said Sam. 'You mean there was nothing concrete, only a . . . feeling you had?'

'No, if I'd allowed myself to be guided by feelings alone, I could have been blissfully happy in my marriage,' said Hannah. 'Damon told me he loved me all the time. He behaved as if he loved me. Our physical relationship was great – very passionate.' As she spoke, she seemed to be conducting a kind of inner audit: *Is that statement true? Yes. And is this statement also true? Yes. Am I sure? Yes.*

'But . . . you didn't *feel* loved?' Sam tried again.

'Well, no, I did,' said Hannah. 'It was hard not to. Damon lavished attention on me – physically, emotionally. In every way. I've never known anyone give another person such care and consideration. You could put Damon's treatment of me in a Hollywood romance and it wouldn't be out of place.'

Simon and Sam exchanged a look: *where to go from here?*

'He complimented me constantly. He had great respect for my intelligence. Took all my needs and wants seriously. There's nothing he wouldn't have done for me, as he demonstrated over and over again.' Hannah spread her hands and stared down at her palms. Simon couldn't help but look at them too: white and dry like creased paper gloves.

'I'd ask the impossible of him sometimes, to test him. More often than not, he'd prove it was possible. He really didn't put a foot wrong, never once let the mask slip. That was the problem: his deception was so seamless that I *did* feel loved.' Hannah let out a jagged sigh. 'At the same time, I knew that euphoric feeling he gave me was based on a lie, so I tried not to allow myself to trust it.' She laughed abrasively. 'Easier said than done. My emotions were responding to Damon's . . . rolling programme of false stimuli. I was being manipulated. Brilliantly, to give him his due, but . . . I didn't want to feel loved if I wasn't. I wanted to know the truth. And from the day we met until he died this morning, he would never tell me. He denied there was anything to tell.'

'When did the two of you meet?' Simon asked. He was going easy on himself, starting with questions likely to yield answers he'd understand. Getting to grips with dates and times was easier than trying to make sense of Hannah's bizarre account of her husband's spotlessly plausible hoax love. 'How long were you and Damon together, and how long married?'

'We met on 29 November 2011 and married in March 2012,' said Hannah. 'On 18 March.'

'And . . . no children?'

'No. I'm not too old – I'm only thirty-nine – but Damon wasn't keen. He said he loved me too much to be willing to share – another lie. He wasn't keen on children at all. Used to say they were boring and pointless. I could probably have persuaded him, though. He'd have given in if I'd framed it in the right way – "Prove you love me by giving me a baby" – but I didn't want children either, not with him. Not until I'd found out what he wanted from me.'

'How long after you married Damon did you, er, start to suspect that his love for you wasn't genuine?' Sam asked.

'I didn't suspect; I *knew*,' Hannah said. She was a clarifier, Simon noted: pedantically obsessed with the accuracy of her own words as well as everyone else's. It was a personality type he didn't often encounter, but he recognised it when he did. Clarifiers made good witnesses normally. Except when they were telling you stories that made no sense at all.

'Long before I married Damon, I knew,' Hannah went on. 'The first time he said he loved me, I thought, "No, you don't. You can't. It's not possible." If you're wondering why I stayed with him . . . ?'

'Go on,' said Sam.

'Several reasons at first: I'd been single for a long time and was afraid I'd never meet anyone. Then I met Damon, or rather he met me. I was minding my own business, looking at cheap wool blankets in the National Trust shop on Blantyre Walk – folding and unfolding them, frowning and muttering complaints under my breath because none was quite right. I doubt I could have looked more frumpy spinster-ish and less sexually enticing if I'd tried. Damon . . .'

'Are you OK, Hannah?' Sam asked when she stopped. 'We can take a break if you—'

'No. Thank you. Let me carry on.' Having said this, she pressed her lips shut as if she'd resolved never to speak again.

Simon and Sam waited.

Eventually, she said, 'I didn't notice Damon until he accosted me and started talking to me as if we'd been friends for years. I was flattered that such a good-looking man would even glance in my direction. I found him compelling to listen to, and, later, to talk to – conversations with Damon were like verbal firework displays. And I was intrigued. Intellectually curious. I wanted to work out what he was up to. That was what I thought at first: that I'd stay with him only until I'd figured out what he wanted so badly from me that he was willing to lie so ruthlessly and convincingly. Thanks, Uzma.'

Three cups of tea were slammed down on the table like heavy

auction hammers. Uzma retreated and started to load the dish-washer; if he'd closed his eyes, Simon could have convinced himself that he was listening to a dangerously out-of-hand bottle fight.

Hannah had produced a tissue from the pocket of her jeans and was dabbing at the corners of her eyes. 'Sorry,' she said. 'You'd think I wouldn't be too fussed about him being dead, in the circumstances.'

Right. You're only his wife. Proximity to Widow Weirdo was making Simon's flesh itch. He knew he was being unfair, but the fact that Hannah was so suspicious of her late husband, and not in the least ashamed of being so, made him suspicious of her.

'Of course you're upset about Damon's death,' Sam said gently. 'You . . . loved him?'

'Yes, I did. Very much. I got hooked on the fake stuff, that was the problem. I responded with the real thing.'

'Fake . . . love?' Sam asked.

Hannah nodded. 'No man had shown an interest in me for some time, so I succumbed to the pull of the phony. My love for Damon was as real as his for me was a sham, but the sham nourished my spirits more than an absence of authentic love would have. I was happy for long spells sometimes. Then it would hit me again: he's acting. I tried telling my heart it had been tricked and mustn't fall for it, but it didn't listen to me any more than any heart ever does to wise advice.' She looked doubtful suddenly. 'I don't know, maybe it wasn't so wise. Fake love's better than no love. It must be, or else why do the majority of my patients stay in non-nurturing romantic relationships?'

'In your work as a psychotherapist, have you ever come across a situation like yours with Damon?' Sam asked her. 'People claiming their partners don't love them but are just . . . convincingly pretending?'

'No, never,' said Hannah. 'Don't worry – the irony isn't lost on me. I'm excellent at my job – sorry, I don't do false modesty.

I've never failed to get to the bottom of a patient's relationship issue. Never. Sometimes it takes a while, but the moment always comes when things slot into place and I think, "Aha, that's what's going on here." With Damon, I never got there, never found my answer. Maybe I was too close to see it.'

Simon's impatience had started to tick inside him. It was time to confront her. 'Hannah, sorry if I'm being slow, but . . . if Damon's act was so flawless, how can you be sure he didn't really love you?'

'Because he said it too quickly. On our second date. He was – he *pretended* to be – too besotted too soon. So I suppose what I said before wasn't strictly true: there *was* a flaw in his act, at the beginning. If he'd seemed to like me only a bit at first, to find me interesting enough to want to see me again . . . If he'd gone for a more gradual build-up and let me see his enthusiasm growing as he got to know me better, that I might have believed in. If he'd waited a few months before telling me he loved me for the first time—'

'So it was the speed of his love that you didn't trust?' Simon interrupted her.

Hannah gave him a pointed look to let him know she'd noticed. 'At that stage, yes. Later on, there were other things. He never got angry or irritable with me, never missed an opportunity to be kind to me, never pretended to listen to me while secretly tuning out, the way *all* husbands do. With Damon, it was as if he was . . . I don't know, trying to commit every word I said to memory. Like people are at the very beginning, when they want to drink in as much information and detail of a new partner as they can. Damon was like that permanently, from the moment I met him. It's so hard to explain to anyone who hasn't experienced it. It was as if he was sucking up to me the whole time, but not pathetically, not off-puttingly.'

'I'd kill for one like that,' Uzma chipped in undiplomatically from across the room. Hannah didn't seem to notice.

'Hannah, just to play devil's advocate for a moment,' Sam

began hesitantly. 'Isn't it possible that . . . well, that it *was* love at first sight for Damon?'

No. Not this woman. Simon felt guilty for thinking it and was pleased no one but him would ever know he had.

Sam was persisting with his romantic fantasy. 'I can imagine that if you're swept off your feet and if that feeling lasts . . .' he said to Hannah. 'I mean, maybe that explains why Damon thought you could do no wrong, and why he listened to you properly. Everything you've described, it sounds to me as if it could be . . . well, love. Not a fake.'

Hannah smiled at him. 'That's sweet, if a little naïve,' she said. 'Do you listen to every word your wife says?'

'Maybe not every word, but—'

'Do you believe in love at first sight?'

'I do, yes,' said Sam.

'You?' She turned to Simon.

He shook his head. 'Something that feels like it, maybe,' was the most he could manage. *A lust-fuelled delusion, a form of insanity.* He'd experienced it only once and hoped never to again, preferring the kind of love he had for Charlie, the slow-to-start sort that you added to gradually, that ended up being worth so much more; love that was more like a savings account than a spending spree.

Alice Fancourt. Simon would never forget that name. It passed through his mind at least once a day.

'You mean the frenzied obsessive attraction that sweeps through people like forest fire?' said Hannah. 'That I-must-devour-you urge that we call love because it's the most powerful word we have?'

Simon made a non-committal noise.

'No, that's not what I meant when I said Damon lied about loving me on our second date. I'm not saying he was infatuated or in a pre-love state that he mistook for love. I'm saying he felt nothing for me beyond a desire to use me for his own ends, whatever they might have been.'

'How can you know that for sure?' Sam asked.

Hannah glared at him. 'It should be obvious to you,' she said. 'There are some people who inspire passionate love-at-first-sight feelings and some who never have and never will – women like me.'

'What do you mean?' said Sam. Simon knew exactly what she meant.

'Look at me, Sergeant Kombothekra.' Hannah pushed back her chair and stood up so that he could see more of her. 'What man would take one look at this face and this body – or even two looks, or three – and decide he had to have me or he'd go mad? This isn't self-pity talking. I'm not secretly hoping you'll both tell me how gorgeous I am. I know I'm not physically attractive. A long way from hideous, yes, but not actively good-looking, and not even ordinary. I look odd. My face is asymmetrical; my body's out of proportion—'

'Hannah, you're being way too hard on yourself,' Sam interrupted gallantly. Simon said nothing. Having listened to her assessment of her own appearance, he was inclined to take her tales of Damon Blundy's phony love more seriously.

'I'm being hon-est.' Hannah elongated the last word as if she thought Sam might not have heard it before. 'Realistic. I know lots of men love women who aren't pretty, but at first sight? When you look like me, and when it's a man as handsome as Damon, who could have anyone he wanted, assuming they didn't loathe him from reading his column? No. I don't buy it.' She fell heavily into her chair, as if the effort of standing had drained all her energy. 'I'm not saying I'm unlovable. I think lots of men might love me if they had the chance to get to know me – intelligent men who care about more than looks – but that sudden at-first-sight kind of love? No. That's rooted in the superficial. We see an object that, physically, fits some kind of pre-existing fantasy archetype that we harbour, and we start to project onto it – inappropriately strong feelings that have nothing to do with the person within.'

'And you think that, physically, you couldn't have been Damon's ideal fantasy type?' Simon asked.

'Exactly.' Hannah sounded satisfied.

'Why not? You said it yourself: you're odd-looking.'

'Simon . . .' Sam muttered.

'It's OK,' said Hannah. 'Let him speak.'

'Your appearance is unusual,' said Simon. 'Lots of men, maybe even most, would prefer a supermodel type, but not everyone's the same. You must know that from your patients – aren't some of their problems unique? And Damon . . . from a quick look at some of his writing, he doesn't strike me as having been an average man.'

'He wasn't,' said Hannah. 'And thank you for not saying what everyone else I've ever discussed this with has said: that I'm beautiful in my own way, that men are just as likely to fall in love with me as they are with a stunning model. Of course they aren't!'

'Stunning models often don't look as if they'd be very interesting if you got to know them,' said Sam.

Hannah ignored him and addressed Simon instead. 'You mentioned my patients. You're right. Most psychological problems and relationship issues are as common as physical attraction to pretty faces and hourglass figures, but every now and then someone turns up with a completely new one, and I think, "Wow. I really ought to write a paper about this case and publish it in a journal." I had a patient recently who had a pathological terror of train and bus drivers, taxi drivers, aeroplane pilots. She was neurotically convinced that all the people who might conceivably drive her anywhere were in league against her, conspiring to take her to some unspeakably frightening destination that she couldn't even imagine. She really believed that if they succeeded in getting her there, she'd be destroyed. I mean, she knew logically that it couldn't be true, but she couldn't get over her phobia.'

'I feel that way every time I get the number forty-five bus from Rawndesley to Spilling in the morning,' Uzma called out from the other side of the room. 'The speed of some of those drivers, tearing round corners.'

Hannah looked sharply at Sam as if to say, *Isn't it bad enough that my husband's been murdered? Did you have to send me this idiot as well?*

'So maybe Damon had outlandish taste in women,' said Simon, enjoying Sam's discomfort at his frankness. 'Maybe odd-looking was his thing.'

'No,' said Hannah. 'There might be a rare man somewhere on this earth whose perfect fantasy woman looks as if she's been assembled from odd parts found at a car boot sale, but not Damon. You'd know that if you'd read his columns. He wrote in one that he could never love an ugly woman. When I asked him about it, he said, "You're not ugly, darling," as I knew he would. His two ex-wives are both beautiful: Princess Doormat and Dr Despot.'

'Pardon?' said Sam.

'That's what Damon called them, in his column.'

'We'll need to talk to them. What are their real names?'

'Verity Hewson, doormat, and Abigail Meredith, despot.'

'Why "Princess Doormat"?' Simon asked.

'Damon thought she was spoiled by her father – that's who she was a doormat for, not Damon. She always tried to persuade him to do whatever her father thought they should do: buy the house he wanted them to buy, tone down his column so as not to embarrass Daddy at the golf club. That's if you believe Damon,' Hannah added. 'I did, actually, about that. I don't think he lied to me much about anything else – only about loving me.'

'Were Verity and Abigail still on decent terms with Damon?' Sam asked.

'No, terms of pure hatred, in both cases,' said Hannah. 'He was vile to both of them, during and after the marriages. There you go: concrete proof that he's not a man who's nice to his wives – so why was he to me? What was he hoping to achieve?'

Simon didn't know, but he wanted to. He reminded himself that Hannah might be lying. That struck him as more likely than her being honest but wrong.

Why dream up such a bizarre lie?

'Do you think Verity or Abigail might have hated Damon enough to kill him?' asked Sam.

'Either, yes, easily,' said Hannah. 'But that applies to dozens of people. Every time Damon published a column, he made between three and ten new enemies.'

'A list of names would be helpful,' Simon said. 'The ones you know.'

'It'd make more sense to give you a list of people who didn't hate him,' said Hannah. 'Me. There, that was quick. He should have pretended to be kind and caring with more people the way he did with me. He might still be alive.'

'Going back to this morning . . .' said Sam. 'You said Damon went up to his study at eight thirty?'

'Yes, after breakfast. I didn't see or hear from him until ten thirty when I took him up a cup of tea and found him.' Hannah stiffened in her chair at the memory. 'What does "He is no less dead" mean?' she asked suddenly, as if the strangeness of the words had only just struck her. 'Why would someone put that on the wall?'

'We don't know,' said Sam. 'You can't think of anything it might mean?'

'No. It makes no sense to me.'

'Between eight thirty and ten thirty, did you hear the doorbell?' Simon asked.

'No, and I would have. It's loud down here. No one rang the bell.'

'I'm wondering, in that case, how the killer got into the house without breaking in.'

'I don't know,' said Hannah.

'And you didn't hear Damon talking to anyone, any footsteps, laughter?' Sam asked.

'No, nothing. But I had the radio on, so nothing that wasn't really loud would have filtered through. Only the doorbell would have.'

'The phone?' Sam asked. 'The landline, I mean.'

Hannah shook her head.

Simon wanted to ask her which radio station she'd been listening to, and what programmes she'd heard, but now wasn't the moment.

She loved her husband. But she didn't trust him. So she also hated him.

She killed him because she'd got nowhere trying to solve the mystery of his secret on her own. If she wanted police help, a murder was the way to get it . . .

No. Far-fetched.

'Did you have any contact with Damon between eight thirty this morning and when you found his body at ten thirty?' Sam asked.

'No. None. He went upstairs after breakfast. I switched the radio on . . . That was it.'

'Before you found his body this morning, when was the last time you'd been in his study?' asked Simon.

'Yesterday evening – I went in to put some books back on his shelves. He leaves them lying around all over the house.'

'And when you went in there yesterday, the room looked normal? Nothing there that shouldn't have been, nothing out of place?'

Hannah shook her head. 'Nothing. Just Damon's study, the way it always looked until . . . today.'

'Hannah, can I clarify something?' Sam cut in. 'Between eight thirty and ten thirty this morning, you didn't go upstairs *at all*? Didn't catch sight of Damon, didn't get any text messages or emails from him?'

'No,' said Hannah. 'Nothing. Damon writes in the mornings and resurfaces at lunchtime. I steer clear so as not to interrupt his chain of venom. That's what he calls it.'

'But this morning you didn't steer clear,' Simon pointed out. 'You went up with a cup of tea for him at ten thirty, you say.'

'Yes.' Hannah's mouth twitched. 'Sometimes in moments of weakness, I'd do that: try and catch him in the act.' She said this as if it were perfectly normal.

'Catch him doing what?'

'How can I answer that when I don't know why he pretended to love me? It wasn't a carefully thought-out strategy; it was just something I did from time to time. If someone's keeping something from you and you want to find out what it is, it's worth walking in on them every now and again when they least expect it. Who knows what you might find?'

'And?' Sam asked.

Hannah shook her head. 'Nothing. Whenever I surprised Damon, he was writing his column. Thinking about it now, maybe he anticipated that I'd turn up in his study unannounced from time to time. Maybe he was extra vigilant during those times. Oh, who knows, who cares! I want to stop caring! I need to *stop*.' She pulled at her hair with both hands. 'But I can't, even now he's dead, because he didn't just have a heart attack or a fatal car crash – he was *murdered*. That means people more powerful and effective than me suddenly need to know all his secrets as much as I do. Which means new hope for me, and new dread, because now I might find out the truth. It's horrible. You being here means I can't let myself give up. It prolongs the torture. Can you understand that?'

'You think Damon's murder was directly linked to his . . . pretending to love you, or to whatever made him feel he had to do that?' Sam asked.

'I don't know,' said Hannah. 'Maybe I'm imagining a pattern or shape that isn't there, but when someone lives a lie – makes a lie of their *entire life* the way Damon did – aren't they tempting fate in a very specific way?'

'How do you mean?' asked Simon.

'They're issuing a challenge, to death and to the truth: "Come and get me." Well, one of them turned up this morning,' Hannah said matter-of-factly, as if she were talking about an actual visitor rather than an abstract concept. 'I think they both did,' she added quietly after a few seconds. 'I think they arrived together.'

From: Nicki <nickibeingnaughty@hushmail.com>
Date: Tue, 2 July 2013 09:19:13
To: <mr_jugs@hushmail.com>
Subject: Distress signal

Hi Gavin,
Something strange and upsetting has happened. Why am I telling
you this, when I'm not supposed to be writing to you at all? I
don't know. There's no one else I can/want to tell. Have you
heard of the journalist/columnist Damon Blundy?
N x

From: Mr Jugs <mr_jugs@hushmail.com>
Date: Tue, 2 July 2013 09:23:08
To: <nickibeingnaughty@hushmail.com>
Subject: Re: Distress signal

Hasn't everyone? Not a particularly nice man.
G.

From: Nicki <nickibeingnaughty@hushmail.com>
Date: Tue, 2 July 2013 09:30:26
To: <mr_jugs@hushmail.com>
Subject: Re: Distress signal

Why do you say that?
N x

From: Mr Jugs <mr_jugs@hushmail.com>
Date: Tue, 2 July 2013 09:32:10
To: <nickibeingnaughty@hushmail.com>
Subject: Re: Distress signal

Are you kidding me?? I only know him from his little-boy-seeking-attention columns, but based on those, he's always struck me as pathetic – someone who gets off on needlessly hurting people. Why? What's the weird, upsetting thing that happened? And why aren't you telling me about either of your encounters with this policeman? I still want to know about those.
G.

From: Nicki <nickibeingnaughty@hushmail.com>
Date: Tue, 2 July 2013 09:40:21
To: <mr_jugs@hushmail.com>
Subject: Re: Distress signal

I can't get over the change in your 'voice'. You sound just like an ordinary, real person. Is it the same you?

I've just found out that Damon Blundy was found dead yesterday in his home. It was on the radio a minute ago. He lived on Elmhirst Road in Spilling, ten minutes from where I live.

My second encounter with the policeman, the one that made me decide to contact you again, was yesterday on Elmhirst Road. I was driving to my kids' school and the traffic was really slow. I saw police up ahead, including this particular one who I'd met before. They were stopping drivers, talking to them. I'm now thinking the reason they were there had to be Damon Blundy's death. Apparently it's being treated as suspicious.

I'm very upset. Please don't ask me why.
N x

Sophie Hannah

From: Mr Jugs <mr_jugs@hushmail.com>
Date: Tue, 2 July 2013 09:45:05
To: <nickibeingnaughty@hushmail.com>
Subject: Re: Distress signal

Why are you very upset that a contrarian newspaper columnist who happened to live near you has died?

Yes, this is the same me. If I were to order you to lie face down on the carpet and remove your underwear **very** slowly, would that help to reassure you? Somebody could have hacked into my account, I suppose, but . . . they haven't. It's me.

So someone murdered Damon Blundy? Really?? What took them so long? ☺ (An uncharacteristic emoticon – it's **still** me.)

Seriously, if you want to worry about the suffering of strangers, I'd pick someone more deserving than Damon Blundy.
G.

From: Nicki <nickibeingnaughty@hushmail.com>
Date: Tue, 2 July 2013 09:49:34
To: <mr_jugs@hushmail.com>
Subject: Re: Distress signal

Er, seriously (to quote you)? I'd be sorry to hear that anyone had been murdered unless they were out-and-out evil. Damon Blundy wasn't evil.

Sorry, have to go – someone at door!
N x

From: Mr Jugs <mr_jugs@hushmail.com>
Date: Tue, 2 July 2013 10:15:22
To: <nickibeingnaughty@hushmail.com>
Subject: Re: Distress signal

And you know that Damon Blundy wasn't evil how? He might
have been. Some people are.
G.

From: Nicki <nickibeingnaughty@hushmail.com>
Date: Tue, 2 July 2013 10:34:02
To: <mr_jugs@hushmail.com>
Subject: Re: Distress signal

Gavin, a detective is here. He wants me to go with him to the
police station. It's about Damon Blundy.

Fuck. Scared.
N x

Sent from my BlackBerry 10 smartphone

3

Tuesday 2 July 2013

'It means nothing,' I blurt out, breaking the silence that's closing in on me. 'What is it, some kind of riddle?'

No answer, only a half-smile from the detective sitting across the table from me, Sam something or other. His surname is multi-syllabic and weird; I forgot it as soon as he'd said it. I try to look only at him and not at his thick-set, heavy-jawed, hulking colleague who is hovering in the corner by the barred window and hasn't smiled once.

'It's nonsense,' I say. 'There's no such thing as less dead, or more dead. There aren't . . . levels of deadness! You're either dead or you're not.'

This can't be happening. I can't be in a too-small, too-hot interview room in a police station, answering questions in connection with the murder of Damon Blundy.

I clutch the tissue Detective Sergeant Sam gave me. It's already soaked and shredded, falling apart. *Taken from my home, bundled into a car by police without being told why, driven to a police station to be interrogated . . .* It's my worst nightmare.

I daren't ask for another tissue, which means I have to stop crying. And shaking. I'm terrified of how guilty I must look, even though I've killed nobody and know nothing about any murder.

The police are trained to sniff out guilt, but not to distinguish one variety from another.

'Those words mean something to whoever killed Damon Blundy,' says DC Simon Waterhouse, the unfriendly one. 'But you're saying that's not you, right?'

It's the third time he's asked me. 'Look at me!' I sob, seeing myself as they must see me: a cowering wreck in a flower-print dress, tiny compared to the two of them.

And to Damon Blundy. I saw him on TV once. He looked tall and sturdy. The idea that I could overpower a man of his size is laughable. 'Do I look as if I'd have the mental or physical strength to kill anyone?' I ask tearfully, praying that Waterhouse will see sense. 'I didn't know Damon Blundy! I've never met him! I only know what he looks like from seeing him on TV and in newspapers. I couldn't have known him any less if I'd tried.'

The word 'less' vibrates in my mind.

He is no less dead.

What is that? It reminds me of something, but I can't think what; there's a familiarity about it, an association in my mind: the faint, far-off tickling of a memory.

It's gone before I can grasp it. If I've heard those words before – and I'm fairly certain I haven't – then I've no idea where or when.

How are they linked to Damon Blundy's death?

I mustn't ask. It's none of my business. I'm not a detective, not a murderer; uninvolved and uninformed is what I am, and I have to make sure I stay that way, which means conquering my curiosity, asking no questions.

'There are ways of killing that rely less on physical strength and more on psychological manipulation,' Waterhouse says woodenly. 'How good are you at that?'

'Not as good as you! You're trying to bully me into confessing to something I didn't do.'

Do they know about my encounter with the sand-haired policeman? Has he told them? That must be why I'm here; he must have seen me do a U-turn on Elmhirst Road, recognised my car . . .

'If you had nothing to do with Blundy's death—' Waterhouse begins.

'I didn't!'

'Then why are you so upset? Why are you refusing a lawyer?'

'Because . . . no one can know I'm here. Not a lawyer, not my husband, not my children – nobody! It's bad enough that *I* know I'm here!' I don't want this to be real. A lawyer would mean it was serious, and it's not. It's a misunderstanding. Soon they'll be telling me I can go. Before I have to set off to pick up Sophie and Ethan from school, definitely. Long before.

'My husband can't know about this,' I say. 'Can you give me a guarantee that he won't find out?' The idea of Adam getting involved makes me shake again. This can't be allowed to spill over and touch him and the kids. How can I explain that I'm not really a whole person, however much I might resemble one? I'm split down the middle: two Nickis, two lives that must never meet. The Nicki that's married to Adam would never get herself noticed by the police.

'What are you so worried about?' Waterhouse asks. 'If you're innocent and you know nothing about Damon Blundy's murder, then we've brought you in for no good reason. We're the ones who've messed up, not you. Wouldn't it be an interesting story to tell your husband over dinner – how you got dragged into a murder investigation through no fault of your own?'

'No!' Bile rises in my throat. I press my hand over my mouth.

'We'll do our very best to respect your privacy, Nicki,' says Sergeant Sam. 'If you tell us the unedited truth, that will make it easier – for us and for you.' He looks puzzled, as if he doesn't understand why I'm so distraught. Does that mean the Elmhirst Road policeman hasn't told him about the first time he met me? If Sam and Waterhouse knew, they would understand my fear, my desperation to get the hell out of here. Would they confront me, or test my commitment to honesty by waiting to see if I volunteered my sordid little secret?

It doesn't feel little any more. It feels as if it's taking over the safe, respectable part of my life. This wasn't supposed to happen. I remember being certain it never would.

Stupid. Recklessly, inexcusably stupid.

'I don't think she wants to tell the unedited truth,' Waterhouse says to Sam. He's spot on. My commitment to honesty? I don't have one. I'm committed to only one thing: making my life as happy and fulfilling as possible, and protecting the people I care about, making and keeping them happy too, all of them: Adam, the children; Gavin, until recently; King Edward before him . . .

I can do both. When I'm feeling strong, it doesn't feel like too much to cope with; I'm confident that I can manage everything and keep everybody in their different compartments. All I need is to get the police off my back; then I'll be fine. I'll be able to persuade myself that I'm a fearless optimist, not a negligent idiot.

'You don't want to confide in us, do you, Nicki?' Waterhouse says. He pulls out a chair and sits down at the table, next to Sergeant Sam. 'You're hiding something, and since it doesn't involve Damon Blundy or his death, you think it's got nothing to do with us. If it's so bad that you can't bear the thought of telling your husband, why would you be any more willing to tell two strangers? I understand that – so let me give you an incentive. Sergeant Kombothekra and I don't care what you've done if it has nothing to do with our investigation. It's probably none of our business, but we need to know what it is so that we can satisfy ourselves that it's unrelated. So . . . what's the story? What are you withholding?'

Panic rises in my throat. I hear an undignified yelping sound and realise it came from me. How much more self-control am I going to lose before I can leave this room? Thinking about this frightens me more than being suspected of murder. Is the truth going to spill out of me whether I want it to or not, like my endless tears? Waterhouse looks confident. As if he knows he can make me talk. I'm not sure I can hold out when everything about him suggests he knows already, but I have to try.

How can he know? It's impossible; if PC Sand-hair had told him, he'd have mentioned it by now.

'Try to stay calm, Nicki,' says Sergeant Sam. 'Let me ask you a few simple questions, give you a chance to compose yourself. We need to get some basic details from you.'

Why? I want to scream. *We're not going to be keeping in touch. I'm going to be leaving here very soon, pretending this never happened, and you're going to forget you ever met me or knew my name.*

'How old are you?'

If I had a lawyer here, he or she would know if I had the right to refuse to answer. 'Forty-two.'

'Full name?'

'Nicki Clements.'

'No middle name?'

'Yes, one that I hate, which is why I don't mention it. Do you really need to know my middle name?'

'We always take full names,' Sam says. 'Sorry.'

'Jasmine.' It's a big clue to the kind of daughter my parents wanted: uncomplicated, sweet, compliant. I hate flower names. I might label a packet of potpourri 'Poppy' or 'Daisy', but never a person.

'Just Nicki?' Waterhouse asks. 'Not short for anything?'

Bastard. 'Nichola.' Which would be OK if my father's name weren't Nicholas.

'Are you employed?' asks Sam.

'No. Not since I had my two children.'

Damon Blundy, murdered. I can't believe it. *Gone. Irreplaceable.* I never met him, but I know he was unique – somebody the world couldn't afford to lose. No one else will ever think what Damon thought, or write what he wrote. Why can't it be some boring average person who died instead? Someone like me.

'Names and ages?' Sam asks.

'I . . . Pardon?' *Get it together, Nicki.*

'Your children.'

'Sophie and Ethan. Ten and eight.'

'And before you had them, what did you do?'

'I was an NHS manager. I supervised a team of midwives and health visitors in North London. We only moved to Spilling very recently.'

'How recently?' Sam asks. 'And from where?'

'Just over six months ago, from London. Highgate. On 20 December last year.'

I'm surprised to find that answering these questions is doing me some good. Listing facts about myself makes me feel as if I have a solid presence in the world that couldn't easily be erased.

'And your husband? What's his name, and what does he do?'

He doesn't erase me. None of this is his fault. I love him.

The only person threatening the Nicki Clements that Sam and Waterhouse are looking at now, the only person likely to want or need to erase her, is the other Nicki, the secret one.

If the only danger I'm facing comes from within me, there ought to be something I can do to stop it. So why do I feel as if I can't?

'Nicki? Your husband?' Sam prompts.

'Adam. Clements – same surname as me. He works in IT support. For the army.'

'Did the army transfer him from London to the Culver Valley?'

'He got a transfer to the Rawndesley army careers office when we moved, yes.'

'Thank you.' Sergeant Sam smiles, my reward for good behaviour. 'And your address?'

'Nineteen Bartholomew Gardens, Spilling.'

The urge to pull my phone out of my bag and check my Hushmail account is overwhelmingly strong. Has Gavin emailed me since I last looked?

Who cares? How dare he call Damon Blundy evil? If that's what he really thinks, then he doesn't know the meaning of the word.

He might have emailed to say sorry.

Maybe I could subtly slide my phone out and . . . No. *Crazy.* I clench my fists in my lap.

Waterhouse says, 'If you're wondering why you're here, it was your car that gave you away. We were trawling CCTV for anything unusual around Elmhirst Road. Do you want to have a stab at telling us what we saw?'

All right, Nicki. This is the bit you've prepared, your chance to come across as honest. This should be easy.

'I don't know where your CCTV cameras are positioned, so I don't know what you saw, but I'll tell you what I did,' I say. 'I set off mid-morning in the car to go to my children's school. My son had left his sports kit behind and he needed it for the afternoon. My normal route takes me down Elmhirst Road, but there was a delay on my side of the road. The traffic was slow, and I could see police officers further up, stopping drivers. I realised that if I carried on up Elmhirst, they'd get a good look at me and my car, and I couldn't let that happen.' I swallow. All true, so far.

'Because?' Waterhouse asks. He shuffles his chair closer to the table.

Calm. Focused. You can do this.

'For the past week or so, my car has been missing its wing mirror on the passenger side. If I'd carried on along Elmhirst Road and they'd stopped me, there's no way they wouldn't have seen it – seen that it was gone, I mean.' I sigh. 'I know I should have taken it straight to the garage. I know I shouldn't have been driving without a side mirror, but I'm so busy all the time . . . I thought I could get away with it, just for a few days. Obviously I would have got the car fixed eventually. I mean, soon. I would have done it later this week, probably.'

It's not exactly a lie; it's an old true story, chronologically enhanced for present-day purposes and with my current car replacing my old Renault Laguna in the lead role. I *was* too busy to go to the garage immediately, even though I didn't have children then. And I drove far more carefully for those six weeks than I ever have before or since, to compensate for my car's deficiency.

In a last-minute burst of defiance, I add, 'It is actually perfectly possible to drive safely without one wing mirror.'

'Spare us your theories about road safety,' Waterhouse says. 'You didn't want to get too close to the police in your non-roadworthy car, so what did you do?'

'Turned round and went back the way I came. I drove to school via the Heckencotts—'

'Which school?' Sam asks. 'Sorry to interrupt.'

'Freeth Lane.'

'Thanks. Carry on.'

'I dropped off my son's sports kit, drove home again, same detour. I passed the end of Elmhirst Road on my way back, so I had a nosey – I was curious to see if the police were still there, and they were. Then I hadn't been home more than five minutes when I got another phone call saying that my daughter had been sick. I wanted to get to school quickly to check she was OK, so I stopped *again* at the junction of Elmhirst Road and Lupton Road to have a look. I thought maybe the police would be still there but not stopping people. I might have risked it if I'd seen drivers sailing past, but no such luck. They were still stopping every car and saying something to whoever was inside it – I figured there was no way they wouldn't notice my missing mirror, so I took the long, inconvenient detour again. And on the way back, and on my way to collect the kids from school at the end of the day, and on the way back. I drove to school and back four times yesterday – eight journeys in total. If you're thinking that's a ridiculous way for an intelligent woman to spend her day, I agree with you.' As soon as I've said this, I feel horribly guilty; I would drive any distance, repeat any journey a hundred times, if my children needed me to.

Then later you'd attend to your own needs by emailing a man your family knows nothing about.

A few flattering, greedy words on a screen from a stranger who wants me without having met me – why do I need that so badly? Why can't I give it up?

'Your story matches our CCTV,' Sam tells me. He looks pleased: as if he was hoping I'd turn out not to be a liar.

Sorry, Sergeant. Thanks for being fooled, and don't worry – I'll hate myself on your behalf.

Why does everybody prize honesty so highly? Does anyone ever stop to ask themselves why lying is wrong, or do they just assume it is? What are we supposed to do when the world requires us to be a particular way and we can't manage it?

Someone should invent a new word that means the same thing as lying except with positive connotations. Deceit needs a fresher, more upbeat image.

Waterhouse and Sam are staring at me. I realise I've neglected a crucial aspect of my deception. I need to demonstrate that I'm worried about wing-mirror repercussions, as no doubt I would be if that were all I had to fear. 'Listen, the last thing I need right now is to be done for a driving offence,' I say solemnly. 'Is there any way you could let me off if I promise not to drive the car again until it's fixed?'

'How did you lose the mirror?' Waterhouse asks.

'A teenage boy racer drove too close to me and smashed it off. He was so desperate to get ahead of me he overtook me on the wrong side, on the left.'

'Did you report it?'

'No. He didn't stop; I didn't get his registration – he got away too quickly, just . . . whizzed off into the sunset.'

'When did this happen, exactly?'

'Why does it matter? It's got nothing to do with—'

'When was the accident?'

'Not last Wednesday but the one before.'

'Is there anyone who can verify that you've not had a passenger-side wing mirror since a week last Wednesday?' asks Waterhouse. 'Your husband, maybe?'

'No. *Please* leave him out of this.'

'Anyone else, then?'

'No!' I clutch the disintegrating tissue in my right hand. 'Look, my husband doesn't know, OK? I park my car in the garage. He parks his in the drive, and he's always out before me in the mornings and back later than me at the end of the day. He hasn't seen my car since the mirror's been missing.'

'You didn't mention it to him?' Sergeant Sam asks.

'No, I didn't! You know why? Because he'd have made a big holier-than-thou thing of it – insisted I get it fixed before I drove the car again, and that just wasn't . . . practical! I didn't want him to give me a hard time, so I kept quiet about it.'

Sorry, Adam. It's kind of true, though.

'Did your children notice your car had lost a mirror?' Waterhouse asks.

I shake my head. 'Not the kind of thing they'd spot.'

'So you can't prove that what you're saying's true?'

'Yes, I can!' I hate this man. More than I would if I had nothing to hide. I hate him for seeing through me. The only person allowed to know how flawed and desperate I am is me. 'Come to my house anytime you want – right now, if you like, and I'll show you my car!'

What the fuck are you doing, Nicki? What if he says, 'All right, let's go'? What's the plan then?

'So you've not driven anyone anywhere for a week and a half? No one's sat in your passenger seat and noticed a gap where a mirror should be? A friend, maybe? A family member?'

My heart starts to pound like the hooves of a frightened horse.

A friend and a family member. Melissa, the Sunday before last.

How can he know? He does, though, I'm sure of it. What other CCTV footage has he looked at, apart from today's? His eyes are drilling into mine, challenging me.

I'm going to have to tell the truth and worry about Mel later.

I clear my throat. 'My sister-in-law, Melissa. Last Sunday – not this one just gone, the one before. She . . .' I can't finish the sentence.

'She was in your car?' Sergeant Sam helps me out. 'She noticed the mirror wasn't there?'

Shit. Shit. What do I say?

'Yes. I drove to her house to pick her up so that we could go to an auction together. She likes auctions,' I add pointlessly. *And I don't.* I go to keep Melissa happy, and I never buy anything because I hate the principle: see something, love it, bid for it, possibly go home empty-handed. No, thanks. 'Then, afterwards, I gave her a lift home.'

'Where does Melissa live?' asks Waterhouse.

'What's that got to do with anything, for God's sake?' I snap.

'If we check out your story and it holds water, that counts towards credibility,' Sergeant Sam explains.

'She lives in Highgate,' I tell him rather than Waterhouse, rooting around in my handbag. I pull out a crumpled leaflet and hand it over. 'There you go. Proof that an auction took place in Grantham a week last Sunday. Satisfied?'

'Grantham,' says Waterhouse, as if it's a bad word. 'That's, what, half an hour's drive from Spilling?'

'Yes. Why don't you email the auction people? I'm sure they'll happily add you to their mailing list. I picked up a fantastic grandfather clock once – it was an absolute *steal*.'

'Sister-in-law's name and phone number?' Waterhouse is ready to write it down.

'Melissa Redgate.' I recite a number that is almost hers, but with the six and the four in the wrong order. That should give me time to get to Melissa before the police do. I'll have to throw myself on her dubious mercy.

Waterhouse doesn't bother to thank me. One of the advantages of deliberately misleading people: when they turn out to be rude and ungrateful, you're pleased you didn't make the mistake of treating them well. Retribution in advance.

'Where were you between eight thirty a.m. and ten thirty a.m. yesterday?' Sergeant Sam asks me.

'At home. I think I set off round about ten thirty to take Ethan's sports kit to school. Before then I was in my kitchen, ringing or being rung by the school secretary, about five hundred times.'

'Why so many times?'

'First, Ethan thought he'd be OK without his kit; then he got upset; then they thought they'd found him a spare; then it didn't fit properly; then he thought he could manage; then he changed his mind . . .'

'These calls were on your landline or your mobile?' asks Waterhouse.

'Landline.'

'And what about at eight minutes past eleven a.m.? Where were you then?'

'Eight minutes past eleven? That's very specific.' Is that when Damon Blundy was murdered? The idea makes me shudder. No, it can't be: no time-of-death estimate could be that specific. 'I would have been . . . Oh, I know!' This is amazing; I know exactly where I was at eight minutes past eleven. 'I was in the car park at Spilling Library, arguing with a woman who appeared out of nowhere and gave me a hard time for parking in a mother-and-child space.'

Sam and Waterhouse exchange a look that I can't read.

'What did she look like, this woman?' Waterhouse asks eventually.

Oh shit. *Shit, shit, shit.* Are they going to try and track her down, ask her if she noticed my missing wing mirror?

I can't believe they'd go to such absurd lengths, but I can't take the risk. 'She was about sixty,' I lie. 'Fat, frumpily dressed. Grey curly hair. Kind of like a . . . strict-grandma type.'

'What were you doing parked outside Spilling Library?' Sam asks. 'Weren't you on your way to your son's school?'

'I pulled into the library car park to look at my *A–Z*, plan an alternative route.'

Waterhouse stands. 'I'll give you a lift home,' he says. 'Have a look at your car.'

No. No, no, fuck, no.

'I'm not going home straight away,' I say as calmly as I can. 'Since you've dragged me into town, I'm going to do some shopping. I'd say go and help yourself to a look, but the car's in the garage, which is locked. Can you come round later?'

'No. Do your shopping, come back here and I'll take you home then. I can wait.'

Somehow, I manage to assert myself. 'Look, I've done nothing wrong. I haven't murdered anyone. I'm not being bundled into a police car like a criminal. Once was bad enough. If you really care that much, drive to my house now and wait for me there. I'll be back in an hour or so – that ought to be good enough for you.'

'It's fine,' says Sam. 'We'll pop round later. When would be good for you?'

I don't know. Can't think straight any more. 'Between two and three,' I say eventually.

'It's not that we don't believe you, Nicki. We have to check, that's all.' He smiles.

Waterhouse turns away. He doesn't believe me. He's the cleverer of the two.

~

It takes me forty minutes to get home, running most of the way. By the time I arrive, dripping sweat and panting, it's one o'clock. For the first time since we moved here, I'm grateful for the wooden bench Adam bought for our small front garden – to make it more than simply a patch of grass between the house and the road, he said when I asked what the point was. I couldn't imagine ever wanting to spend time sitting in front of my house when I had a lovely back garden to sit in that was completely private.

I'd like some privacy now, but not as much as I'd like to put an end to the pain in my aching legs. I stagger towards the bench, unable to stay on my feet for the last three or four metres to my front door.

What kind of idiot am I, thinking I can lie to the police and get away with it? They could turn up any second, and my car still has two wing mirrors.

I land in an awkward position on the bench and have no energy to improve upon it. Several of my neighbours will be watching me, for sure – standing well back from their windows to remain out of sight. They'll wonder why I'm wearing a smart summer dress and strappy sandals if I've been for a run, and why I took a large handbag with me.

Fortunately, I'll never have to explain because no one will ask. That's the kind of place Bartholomew Gardens is. Its inhabitants see everything, but pretend to see nothing.

I look around at the still, silent cul-de-sac, shaped like a perfect question mark: sixteen square, beige-brick detached houses, all with shiny black front doors and double garages built on. It still doesn't feel like home: the street, the house, Spilling, the Culver Valley. I'm starting to think it can't and never will: part of my punishment.

I wish we'd never come here. I wish we could move back to London, but I daren't suggest it to Adam. What reason would I give? He'd have to ask work for another transfer – a return trip – or look for a new job . . .

No.

Other people, when they realise things they want are impossible, stop yearning for them. Why can't I be like them? Why can't I ever give up on anything?

Hearing a car, I stiffen, but the noise soon dies away. Whoever's driving, their destination is not my house; their mission is not to catch me out.

OK. The police aren't here yet. This means I have a chance to make my lie true. I need to sort that out before I check my Hushmail. There's a clear order of priorities that even I'm not stupid enough to ignore.

I unzip my handbag, reach for my phone. Look, I can see it in my bag – touch it, even – and still put it down. I have will-power when it matters.

My eyes fill with tears. I badly want to check my secret email account.

No. Not enough time.

Gavin will have apologised by now, surely. He'll have realised that what he said about Damon Blundy was out of order.

What do you care if he hates Damon Blundy? You never knew him. He's nothing to you.

I told Sergeant Sam to come between two and three. That gives me an hour.

I haul myself up off the bench, hobble to the front door and let myself in. Dropping my bag in the hall, I run to the kitchen and drink as much water as I can, refilling the pint glass three times. Then I take my car keys from the hook in the utility room and head for the garage.

I have no idea if I'm a skilled enough driver to precision-crash my car. I'll have to scrape the wing mirror against something hard enough to break it off – a wall, the corner of a house – but I'll need to take care to do no damage apart from that. I can't overdo it and cave the passenger door in, or scrape off half of the paintwork. At the police station, I mentioned no damage to my car apart from a missing mirror.

A hard, vertical surface in a deserted place: that's what I need. The corner of a building, a lamp post . . . As I start the engine and press the button to open the garage door, I wonder if there might be an easier way: instead of driving off in search of something to crash into, I could stay at home and hunt for something heavy that I could slam down on the wing mirror from above and smash it off that way.

No. The police might have a way of spotting that. If they sent my car away for forensic tests, or whatever the equivalent of a post-mortem is for vehicles . . .

They're not going to do that. Get real.

I can't take the risk. As closely as I can, I have to try and replicate what I told Waterhouse and Sergeant Sam: an impact from the side, at speed.

I turn left out of Bartholomew Gardens onto Neather Street because if I turned right, that would take me in the direction of Lupton Road, which is the way to Elmhirst Road and Damon Blundy's house. If I was keen to avoid the murder scene yesterday morning, when I didn't know it was a murder scene, I am even keener now. The thought of being there, near his house, makes my throat close up.

He is no less dead.

I still can't make out what those words are pointing to in my mind. I should stop worrying away at it; maybe then the answer will come to me.

It's a relief to be out of the dark garage, away from Bartholomew Gardens. I drive in the direction of Rawndesley with no clear idea of what I'm looking for but hoping to know it when I see it. I drive past walls, fences, postboxes: all hard enough to take a wing mirror off a car. Nothing looks quite right, or there are too many pedestrians around. And there's a blue car behind me, too close.

Please. Please, something, be round the next bend in the road. The hour between one and two that felt so long ten minutes ago is shrinking all the time.

Finally, when I'm starting to despair, I turn a corner and see a children's playground ahead, separated from the pavement by tall, chunky metal railings with sharp points at the top. There's no one around apart from a mother pushing her daughter on a swing. *A woman pushing a little girl on a swing*, I correct myself. I of all people should know that it's impossible to identify a relationship from the outside.

Sometimes it's equally hard from the inside.

The woman and the girl are both facing away from me. This will do.

The kerb is high here, all the way along, and I'm going to have to mount it to get close enough to the railings. I try to work out if this is better approached at speed in a high gear or slowly, in first. I'm not the world's greatest driver.

Maybe I could find somewhere more suitable.

Or maybe not.

It takes me several attempts, but finally I manage to get my car up over the kerb. The exhaust makes a metallic crunching noise as it scrapes against the pavement. The woman and little girl turn and stare at me. I stop and wait, unwilling to do any more with them watching. A few seconds later, they get bored of gawping and look away.

I reverse, adjusting the car's position as I go so that it's parallel with the beginning of the railings. Then I drive forwards, accelerating fast, veering to the left until the passenger-side mirror hits against one metal railing after another. The noise is unbearable. I clench my teeth and wince. I can't stand to look at the damage I'm doing; knowing it's happening is bad enough.

It must be gone by now.

I keep accelerating all the way to the end of the railings, then brake and look.

My car no longer has a passenger-side wing mirror. *Thank God.*

My relief doesn't last long. The woman in the playground has left the little girl on the swing and is hurrying towards me with a concern-creased forehead and a 'We need to have a serious talk' expression. Why, for fuck's sake? The railings are fine. I haven't hurt anyone, only an object – one that belongs to me and is none of her business.

Slamming down my foot on the gas, I screech round the corner and disappear before she can get to me, powered by my desperation to escape as much as by an engine. I've thought this before, in February, the month I try not to remember, driving to and from the Chancery Hotel every day for a week: fear is potent psychic fuel that, in exceptional circumstances, can be transmitted through the ether from person to car and increase speed. I should write to Jeremy Clarkson, suggest this as a theme for an episode of *Top Gear.*

She can't have seen my number plate. I drove away too quickly. I'm safe.

It'll be easier to pretend to myself that I haven't just done what I've done once I've put some distance between me and the scene. Fifteen minutes from now, I'll be at home, with a car that's missing one wing mirror; the story I told the police will be truer. True, in fact.

I don't understand how I can do this: deceive myself and believe it, while knowing I'm lying.

The word 'lying' gives me a jolt. I look up at the rear-view mirror. There's a car immediately behind me – blue again, and too close, like before. Is it . . . could it be the same car? No, that's paranoia. I accelerate so that I can see the make: BMW. Like Flash Dad's from school. I dismiss the stupid idea that Flash Dad might be following me and sigh with relief when the car takes a left turn and disappears from view.

I spend the rest of the drive home checking my mirror every two seconds. Nothing.

Back in my house, with my newly wrecked car safely stowed in the garage, I avoid looking at my BlackBerry while I make the cup of coffee that's essential to my survival for even another ten seconds, then ring Adam at work and tell him I need him to come home straight away. 'Melissa's summoned me,' I say. 'I have to go to London.'

I used to call her Mel, when she was only my best friend, before she met my brother, Lee, and decided to double up as my sister-in-law. I called her Mel when they moved in together, and when they got married. I switched to Melissa a few months after their wedding, when she explained her new policy to me – how everything was going to be different between us from now on. Including her name in that 'everything' made sense to me: an effective way of signalling the change in the way I felt about her. I'm sure she's noticed, though she's never commented.

'What? That sounds inconvenient for me,' Adam says cheerfully. 'Though not impossible, I suppose. What's wrong with Melissa?'

'I don't know.'

'But . . . she's not ill or—'

'No, she said it's nothing like that. Could be a her-and-Lee issue. She refused to talk about it on the phone. I think it's something private. She made me promise not to mention it to anyone, including you.' Every time I lie to Adam, I feel a spurt of fear that I have to struggle to overcome. I'm terrified of what I'm doing to our relationship: polluting it with deceit, pushing him further away with each manipulation. I've been living with this dread for too long: maybe one day I'll push him so far that I won't be able to retrieve him when I'm ready to be close to him again.

I can't let that happen. I have to save us.

It's only when this panic floods my system that I realise I couldn't bear to lose Adam, and feel the stab of horror that ought to stop me from endangering what we have. If only I could feel it all the time . . . but he's too embedded in my world for that to be possible. Sometimes I can barely distinguish him from myself and the children; at others his presence in my life strikes me as absurdly jarring, as if I've woken up to find I'm living with someone I once met at a bus-stop and have exchanged no more than a few friendly words with.

Like when you're emailing Gavin, you mean? That's how you feel about your husband – that he's an intruder – while you're secretly writing to a man whose presence in your life looks sometimes like a BlackBerry and sometimes like a laptop computer? A man whom you don't know, let alone love, and shouldn't need?

I don't want this kind of marriage. Don't want to live in a state of permanent threat.

Yet you've created the threat, and prolonged it. For the sake of what? Excitement? Adventure?

I'm finding it harder every day to pinpoint where pleasurable anticipation ends and fear begins.

'So you want me to leave work early and go and pick up the kids?' Adam asks.

'Yes, but I need you to come home first – now – and drive me to Rawndesley Station.'

'What's wrong with your car?'

'It's missing a wing mirror. Long story,' I say briskly. 'I'm going to leave it in the garage with the door unlocked and slightly open – the police are coming round later to have a look at it.'

'Nicki, what's going on?' Adam sounds worried. 'Have you had a crash?'

It would make sense to tell him as much of the truth as I can afford to, but I can't bring myself to mention Damon Blundy, the CCTV footage, being taken to the police station by two detectives. I'll have to think of another story, but not now. I need to get to Melissa before the police work out that I gave them the wrong number for her and track down the correct one.

'I'll tell you on the way to the station, but . . . please, can you set off now?'

He agrees, as I knew he would.

It will take him at least half an hour to get here.

BlackBerry or computer? I prefer to be sitting at a desk, for Gavin. It helps me to think more clearly. Our box room has become my cyber-adultery office.

I run upstairs to the computer.

From: Mr Jugs <mr_jugs@hushmail.com>
Date: Tue, 2 July 2013 10:39:24
To: <nickibeingnaughty@hushmail.com>
Subject: Re: Distress signal

The police? At your front door? Are you serious? Why would the police come to your house?
G.

Sophie Hannah

From: Mr Jugs <mr_jugs@hushmail.com>
Date: Tue, 2 July 2013 10:50:02
To: <nickibeingnaughty@hushmail.com>
Subject: Re: Distress signal

Nicki, are you there/OK? I am concerned. I don't want to have to
ring your local nick and ask if they've got you in custody!
G.

From: Nicki <nickibeingnaughty@hushmail.com>
Date: Tue, 2 July 2013 13:43:15
To: <mr_jugs@hushmail.com>
Subject: Re: Distress signal

Yes, the police really did come to my house and take me back to
the police station with them. It was about Damon Blundy – my
car was seen near his house so they wanted to talk to me. I am
now back at home and fine.

I hate to be argumentative, but . . . what you said before about
Damon Blundy was silly. Yes, some people are evil, but that in
no way proves that Damon Blundy was, so don't say it in a
way that makes out it does. That's as stupid as saying I don't
know that Barack Obama isn't a vegan, since, after all, some
people are vegans. It's possibly the weakest argument I've ever
heard.
N x

From: Mr Jugs <mr_jugs@hushmail.com>
Date: Tue, 2 July 2013 13:46:05
To: <nickibeingnaughty@hushmail.com>
Subject: Re: Distress signal

Why so defensive on behalf of Damon Blundy? Is it compulsory
for me to like him?
G.

From: Nicki <nickibeingnaughty@hushmail.com>
Date: Tue, 2 July 2013 13:50:33
To: <mr_jugs@hushmail.com>
Subject: Re: Distress signal

Did I say it was compulsory for you to like him? No, I said that to
point out that some people are evil in a way designed to suggest
this proves something about DB is a dishonest, and daft, way to
argue. Which it is. And so is accusing me of saying something I
never said.

Do you have trouble reading and interpreting words? If not, I
suggest you reread Damon Blundy's columns. He almost
always argued for truth or goodness of some sort. My take
on him (which you will probably do your best to misunderstand)
is that he was embarrassed by his desire to make the world
a better place and so did his best to hide it under surface
outrageousness.

Sorry if I'm sounding harsh. I'm probably being unfair to you, and
if I am, I'm sorry. The police-station thing wasn't fun. I'm not in
the calmest frame of mind.
N x

From: Mr Jugs <mr_jugs@hushmail.com>
Date: Tue, 2 July 2013 13:56:07
To: <nickibeingnaughty@hushmail.com>
Subject: Re: Distress signal

What exactly happened at the police station?

You're not being harsh. Or rather, if you are, I assume I must deserve it. And I do love your bizarre analogies.

I admire your fierceness. When the war starts, can I be in your unit?
G.

From: Nicki <nickibeingnaughty@hushmail.com>
Date: Tue, 2 July 2013 13:59:04
To: <mr_jugs@hushmail.com>
Subject: Re: Distress signal

Bizarre analogies? What do you mean? Please tell me exactly why you said that.
N

From: Mr Jugs <mr_jugs@hushmail.com>
Date: Tue, 2 July 2013 14:02:35
To: <nickibeingnaughty@hushmail.com>
Subject: Re: Distress signal

Just 'N', no 'x'? What have I done wrong now?
Bizarre analogies? Barack Obama being a vegan!
G.

From: Nicki <nickibeingnaughty@hushmail.com>
Date: Tue, 2 July 2013 14:07:23
To: <mr_jugs@hushmail.com>
Subject: Re: Distress signal

Barack Obama being a vegan is only one analogy. You said, 'And I do love your bizarre analogies,' plural, as if a) I have come up with quite a few, and b) you've been fond of and familiar with this tendency of mine for a while. What other analogies have I ever put in my emails to you?
N

From: Mr Jugs <mr_jugs@hushmail.com>
Date: Tue, 2 July 2013 14:09:07
To: <nickibeingnaughty@hushmail.com>
Subject: Re: Distress signal

Nicki, what are you getting so steamed up about? I don't get it.
G.

From: Nicki <nickibeingnaughty@hushmail.com>
Date: Tue, 2 July 2013 14:10:04
To: <mr_jugs@hushmail.com>
Subject: Re: Distress signal

Husband back – have to go to London.
N

From: Mr Jugs <mr_jugs@hushmail.com>
Date: Tue, 2 July 2013 14:23:19
To: <nickibeingnaughty@hushmail.com>
Subject: Re: Distress signal

Are you on the train? Email me, please.
G.

From: Nicki <nickibeingnaughty@hushmail.com>
Date: Tue, 2 July 2013 14:56:04
To: <mr_jugs@hushmail.com>
Subject: Re: Distress signal

No, I'm in the Avis Rent-a-Car office in Rawndesley. The trains are
buggered today.
I don't know why I'm answering you.
N

From: Mr Jugs <mr_jugs@hushmail.com>
Date: Tue, 2 July 2013 15:02:08
To: <nickibeingnaughty@hushmail.com>
Subject: Re: Distress signal

What have I done to piss you off? Please tell me.
G.

From: Nicki <nickibeingnaughty@hushmail.com>
Date: Tue, 2 July 2013 15:15:31
To: <mr_jugs@hushmail.com>
Subject: Re: Distress signal

'When the war starts, can I be in your unit?' Ring any bells?
N

Sent from my BlackBerry 10 smartphone

~

'Nicki. It's you.' Melissa's voice is swallowed by the roar of traffic behind us. She and Lee live on a main road in Highgate, in a modern brown three-bedroom maisonette that looks like a chocolate bar with windows. Adam and the kids and I used to live five minutes' walk from here, in a shabby, gardenless Victorian terrace that we couldn't afford to renovate.

81 Enfys Road. Home.

Standing on Melissa's doorstep, I feel like someone returning from the dead. I miss this noise. I need to move back to London, as soon as I can. That would cancel everything out, as if none of it ever happened. It would bring me back to life, if anything could.

I try not to think about what has happened most recently, about what I believe I've proved to myself beyond all reasonable doubt. *Gavin . . .*

Stop. You can't fall apart now. Don't think about Gavin, King Edward, any of it.

It doesn't work. I tried all the way here, in my rented car. Push the thoughts away and the numb horror is still there. Worrying away at it intellectually is probably better for me: questioning, trying to recall as many details as I can. At least it feels like doing something. But not now, not here. I have to force myself to stop.

Focus. You're here to sort out the wing-mirror problem.

'It's me, in Adele mode,' I say to Melissa, blinking back tears.

'Hate to turn up out of the blue, uninvited, but . . . I need to talk to you. Can I come in?'

'What's Adele mode?'

'"I hate to turn up out of the blue, uninvited" – Adele's most famous lyric. You do know who Adele is? The singer?' Melissa probably doesn't listen to pop music any more. Lee doesn't much like any kind of music – he never has. Noise of any sort agitates him.

When we were teenagers living on the same street in Wimbledon, Melissa and I used to call round at each other's houses unannounced all the time. Since she's lived with my brother, she prefers to see me by arrangement only. I've become something she likes to be warned of in advance.

As she stands aside to let me in, her eyes are full of something more complicated than 'hello and welcome'. It's the same mix of emotions that I see in Lee's eyes when he greets me, and in my parents': vigilance, nervousness and, the dominant note, hope: that everything will be all right even though Nicki is here and Nicki is trouble.

Melissa is so much more a member of the Redgate family than I am; she's the anxious, obedient daughter my parents should have had.

'Lee back yet?' I ask.

'No.'

'Good. I need to talk to you alone.'

Melissa rolls her eyes. 'Oh, not this again, Nicki. If you're going to beg me not to tell Lee—'

'Lee's the last thing on my mind at the moment.' Beg? Is that how she sees me: permanently on my knees in her saintly presence? 'It's the police I need you not to tell. I wouldn't ask, but it's kind of an emergency.'

She stops. If she's having second thoughts about letting me get as far as the kitchen, it wouldn't be the first time. She holds up her hands, flat, fingers stiff and extended. As if she's trying to push something away. 'The police? Again?'

I flinch. 'Forget last time. The only thing I hoped you'd do then was listen. I needed to talk to someone and you wouldn't let me tell you—'

'Oh, so you *are* dragging this up again?' Melissa says angrily. 'Can't you let it go? It's my choice. You should respect it.'

I wish she'd at least offer me a comfy chair before starting with the shoulds and shouldn'ts. We're still in the hall, which is as perfectly smooth and rectangular as every other space in Melissa and Lee's house. There's not a curve in sight – not a cornice or alcove anywhere to disrupt the lines. Each storey is a rectangle made up of rectangles, and so is the building as a whole. So are the four identical houses attached to it; together, the five form an uber-rectangle that looks as if it's serious about subjugating, if not flat out annihilating, all the circles, squares, ovals and triangles in the Greater London area.

Adam said to me once, 'Nicki, *all* houses are made up of straight lines. Don't you think you might be . . . projecting slightly?'

'I don't want to get into our usual argument again,' I say to Melissa. 'I've got a favour to ask you. You can say no if you want, but at least make me a cup of tea and let me ask.' I gesture towards the kitchen.

Melissa stays where she is. 'And I can tell Lee?'

Her question makes me gasp. I must look like what I am – someone whose life has been blasted apart, again, after an email correspondence with a man I don't know, again – and all Melissa cares about is whether she has my permission to report back to my brother about me.

'Tell Lee twenty times if you want to,' I say. 'Have you got a Dictaphone? Record my request and your refusal so that you can play it back to him later.'

Melissa nods. I have said the right thing, albeit snidely, and am now allowed access to the second stage of conditional welcome: refreshments – in theory, at least. I'd be foolish to take anything for granted until I've got a mug of PG Tips in my hand. I've got through to kitchen level on a couple of previous occasions and then been ordered to leave before the kettle's boiled.

I follow Melissa down the hall, clamping my arms against my sides as I pass the shelf of meticulously aligned ornaments: a clear glass heart-shaped paperweight, a white ceramic angel and a wooden boat. They're precisely spaced so that the one in the middle is equidistant from the other two. Whenever I'm within touching distance, I imagine sweeping them off the shelf with my elbow and sending them crashing to the ground. One day, the fantasy might not be enough for me.

Not safe yet. Just outside the kitchen door, there's a framed studio photograph of Lee and Melissa beaming joyously, like people who have never met either Lee or Melissa, with their heads touching in a way that suggests they'd ideally like to be conjoined twins.

These are the kind of horrible thoughts I can't help having when I'm inside the rectangle of rectangles. Hard edges, straight lines and sharp corners – in this house, that's how you blend in, how you survive. Even when you stare down at the varnished wooden floor because you can't bear to look anywhere else, the floorboards remind you: *straight edges, hard lines . . .*

I manage to walk past the conjoined-twins photograph without pulling it off its hook and stamping on it, but I can't help tormenting myself by looking at it for longer than I need to.

The gleam of teeth from matching smiles . . .

I've never believed it when people say that married couples start to resemble one another physically, but since Melissa and Lee got together, she has taken on several aspects of his style. She's still as dark and olive-skinned as he is blond and pale, but her once-unruly long hair is now short and tidy, and she wears only plain, solid colours, never patterns any more.

I can remember Lee becoming hysterical, aged five, when Mum tried to put a stripy cardigan on him. 'It's messy!' he screamed. 'There are things on it! Take it off!' Mum did, straight

away. Everything that frightened Lee as a toddler was immediately removed by our parents: patterned clothes, bananas, books
with scary pictures in them, the cuddly penguin in his bedroom
that apparently shrieked at him at night while everyone else was
asleep, the bicycle he fell off and couldn't forgive.

Mum and Dad would have performed a similar life-improving
service for me if they'd been able to, except in my case it was
trickier. I didn't mind what I wore or ate, and wasn't scared of
any of my toys or books. I wasn't a fussy, high-maintenance
child like Lee. Nothing made me unhappy apart from the other
members of my family, and Mum and Dad could hardly remove
themselves from my orbit. They didn't realise they needed to;
they thought I was the problem.

Perhaps they were right.

I sit down at the glass-topped table in Melissa's kitchen, my
least favourite room in her house. It looks as I imagine a morgue
would look if morgues had yellow jars labelled 'Tea', 'Coffee'
and 'Sugar' on their windowsills: white tiles on the floor and
on the walls; stainless-steel appliances, sink and taps; chairs
with thin metal legs that make me think of insects from science-
fiction films and scrape horribly against the floor if you shift in
your seat even slightly. There's a clock on the wall that's past
its best; its tick sounds louder and more intrusive every time I
visit, like the string of an instrument being plucked hard and
then left to settle.

I always sit facing away from the clock so that I can see out
of the window. Still I can't escape the geriatric ticking, and
always half expect Melissa to place an exam paper down on
the table in front of me. I would fail, of course.

Being here makes me long for my own kitchen. For both my
kitchens: the one in Enfys Road that I left behind, and the one
in Bartholomew Gardens where Adam is now, preparing his and
the children's supper. I can see him clearly, even though I can't
see him at all. He's taken off his jacket and shirt and put on a
T-shirt, probably his Rolling Stones one. He'll have the radio

on, and he'll keep muttering about how boring each station's offering is and changing the channel at the same time as holding an uncooked meatball, which he'll squash accidentally and blame on whichever pompous presenter or inane DJ has annoyed him most recently. This will lead to not-entirely-serious grumbling about the BBC having no right to be government-funded when it's so blatantly sub-standard.

If I were with Adam now – and I long to be – I would bury my face in his dark wavy hair and he'd put his arms round me without thinking, still moaning about the radio, and I would know that I don't need any other man in my life apart from him.

I don't. Not after today's shocks. I just want to feel safe, whether or not I deserve to.

You know exactly what you deserve. And you keep getting it, don't you? From King Edward, from Gavin . . .

He is no less dead . . .

My breath catches in my throat. I freeze. What was it, the thought that flashed in my mind before disappearing? It was there, and felt huge, but it's gone now. For a fraction of a second, I knew something . . . and then I didn't. Something about Gavin and the words 'He is no less dead'? Did I have the answer and lose it, or is my mind playing tricks on me?

There.

Gone.

Melissa fills the kettle. 'Well?' she says. 'What's this request you think I'm going to refuse?'

Her voice cuts through me like iced wire. For a split second, I see everything clearly. I think, *It's you. You're the danger to my family, you and Lee. I wouldn't be in the mess I'm in now if it weren't for you two.* A moment later, though the words linger as vividly in my mind as letters inscribed by burning sparklers on a black night, I have no idea what they meant to me when I was so sure they were the truth.

I make an effort to compose myself. 'It's about the Sunday we went to the auction,' I say. 'There's a chance a detective from

Spilling Police might get in touch with you and ask you if my car was missing a mirror that day. A wing mirror.'

Listening to my rehearsed introduction, I have a better idea than the one I arrived with. I was planning to ask Melissa to lie for me and tell the police that my mirror was missing when it wasn't. *Stupid*. I ought to know from depressing experience that she cares more about her principles than about me. Why be kind when you can be right? – that's her motto. Which means I must be more devious.

'If you're asked, can you *please, please* tell the police my car had both its mirrors when I drove you to and from the auction?' I say. *Now* I'm begging: a little treat for Melissa's ego. I hope she enjoys it, since it's unlikely to happen again. 'I know it was irresponsible of me to drive to London, then Grantham, then back to London with a missing wing mirror. It's not something I make a habit of doing, and, honestly, I'll never do it again if you'll help me get the cops off my back just this once.' I put on my best desperate-sinner-praying-for-mercy face. It's probably indistinguishable from my normal everyday expression, come to think of it.

'No. No.' Melissa's shaking her head as she pours milk into a mug for me. She looks scared, as if she thinks I might be able to force her to agree. 'I'm not lying to the police for you, Nicki. No way. It might only be a minor driving offence, but—'

'Actually, it's a bit more complicated than that. Have you heard about Damon Blundy?' A name I haven't mentioned in Melissa's presence for a while . . .

She drops the teaspoon she's holding. It lands with a bang on the white granite work surface. 'What about him?'

'He's dead. He lived on Elmhirst Road in Spilling. Near me.'

'Yes, I knew that.'

'Really?' This strikes me as unlikely, yet I can't see why she'd lie about it.

'Not the road name, but I knew he lived in Spilling. I read his column about how he had to leave London because there were too many ugly people in it. Of all the places he'd ever visited, the Culver Valley contained the most attractive women, so he was moving there.' Melissa spins round to face me. 'And that's why you moved there, isn't it?' she asks with a tremor in her voice.

'So that I could meet attractive women? No.' I laugh to disguise my discomfort.

'What's Damon Blundy got to do with your wing mirror?' Melissa asks as she puts my mug of tea down on the corner of the table furthest away from me. I have to stand to reach it.

'He's been murdered. Elmhirst Road, where he lived, is on my route to the kids' school. It was full of police yesterday. They spotted my car, asked me how long I'd been driving without a side mirror. I told them it had only just been snapped off that morning.' Who'd have guessed it was possible to come up with so many variations on the same lie? 'I thought that'd be it, but they got all serious on me, wanting to know if anyone could back up my story, asking who'd been in my car and how recently—'

'And you mentioned me? Thanks a lot.'

'I didn't want to mention anyone, but I panicked! I didn't feel comfortable lying once I realised I'd brushed up against a murder investigation. Don't . . .' I raise a hand to stop Melissa from stating the obvious. 'I knew I'd lied already, about the mirror. That's why I didn't want to make it worse. I wish I'd told them the truth from the start.'

'Then why don't you? You still could.'

'Or I could stick to my story and you could back me up?' I offer her what I hope is a winning smile with lowlights of appropriate humility. 'If the police believe I genuinely lost my mirror only a few minutes before they saw my car on Elmhirst Road, I'm pretty sure they'll let me off. I told them I was going to take the car to the garage as soon as I'd dropped off Ethan's sports kit at school, and look.' I pull the keys to my rental car out of my handbag and wave them in the air. 'I hired a car to drive here, like a good responsible citizen.'

'How can you live like this, Nicki?' Melissa squints at me, as if I'm forcing her to look at something gruesome she'd like to turn away from.

Me. I'm that thing.

Fuck you, best friend. I haven't killed anyone. I haven't even driven without a wing mirror – not recently, anyway. And nothing bad happened to any living thing – human, plant or animal – when I did. I'm not going to feel guilty about a so-called sin I committed that harmed no one.

'Scheming all the time, covering up, calculating . . . How can you bear it?'

'It's called life on the planet earth,' I snap. 'For those of us who aren't perfect, that is.'

I shouldn't let her rile me. I ought to be savouring my success. Plan B worked. She hasn't said, 'But, Nicki, your wing mirror *wasn't* missing when we went to the auction in Grantham. What are you talking about?'

What Melissa isn't saying is ideal. Couldn't be better. It's what she *is* saying that's hard to take.

'I'm worried about you, Nicki. You're going to come a cropper one of these days.'

'You hope. You'll have been painstakingly good all these years for nothing, won't you, if I get away with the heinous crime of being me?'

She's taken a mug from the cupboard to the left of the window and is shaking decaffeinated instant-coffee granules into it straight from the jar. 'My answer's no,' she says quietly. 'I'm not prepared to lie to the police for you. People can end up in prison for that kind of thing.' She brings her mug of coffee over to the table and sits down opposite me. 'And when I tell Lee about this conversation, he'll probably ring the police.' She sighs.

Nice of him.

'You know how he feels about honesty.'

I nod. 'So . . . you're not going to tell him?'

'I don't know.' Melissa's mouth twists. 'I'd rather not be put in the position of having to make these horrible choices!'

'Again . . . life on the planet earth. Sorry.' I don't sound it, because I don't feel it. 'You don't like the idea of Lee landing me in it, but you're not prepared to lie for me if the police contact you? Interesting ethical distinction. Might there be some cowardice and hypocrisy involved?'

'Nicki, stop.' A tear rolls down Melissa's cheek. The sight of it makes me stiffen. The last time I cried in front of her – three weeks and five days ago, after my first encounter with the sand-haired policeman – she told me that whatever I was upset about was bound to be my own fault, and declared herself unwilling to hear any of the details.

I'm equally incapable of comforting her now. I like to think I'm open-minded, but it's hard to sympathise when I'm me, and having me as a friend is the cause of all her pain. Even I don't think I'm that bad.

'Are you trying to arrange it so that I won't be able to speak to you at *all*, Nicki?' Melissa blurts out. 'Is that what you want? Maybe you'd like me to be so frightened of what you might say that I don't open the door to you any more, or take your calls.'

'Frightened? What's the worst I'm going to do, Melissa? Oh, wait, I'm not going to –' I mimic a prissy voice '– *put you in a difficult position*, am I? No, as it happens, *I'm* not. You put yourself in that difficult position when you decided to shack up with my brother!'

Even if I live to be a hundred, I doubt I'll ever forget the way Melissa chose to tell me. I remember the date too: 24 May 2010. She rang me up and, without saying hello, asked, 'How would you feel if Lee and I . . . you know, sort of got together?'

'Lee? My brother Lee?' He and Mel had recently met for the first time in many years at my birthday party a few months earlier. As far as I was aware, they hadn't seen each other since that night. Realising that there must have been subsequent secret contact between them didn't especially bother me; unlike my mother, father and brother, I don't feel I have an automatic right to know everything about those close to me. I'm not against secrecy; it's hypocrisy I can't stand – people who preach honesty and straight-forwardness, then keep you in the dark when it suits them.

People like Lee and Melissa.

'Yes, your brother,' Mel said nervously. 'Sorry if this comes as a bit of a shock.'

I knew it must have taken all her courage to ask for my opinion and so her feelings for Lee must be serious. In normal circumstances, Mel would have preferred to disappear off the face of the earth, leaving no trace, than instigate something that might be contentious.

Don't do it. Avoid him. He's not normal. He'll destroy you. These were the first things that flashed through my mind, but I didn't say any of them. I decided I was being unnecessarily melo-dramatic, and I loved and love my brother, in spite of everything. I didn't want to tell Mel the horror story I could have told her; it wouldn't have been fair to Lee if I had. We all make mistakes, I thought. We all deserve a second chance. Lee was a child when all the bad stuff happened; he couldn't be blamed, could he?

I realised Mel was waiting for my response. I could feel her growing anxiety pulsing out of my phone. 'It's not really up to me, is it?' I said diplomatically. 'I mean, if you and Lee want to start seeing each other, it's none of my business. I'd be unrea-sonable if I tried to stop you.'

'Yes, but I still want to know how you'd feel about it,' Mel said. 'I'd hate to do anything that'd upset you, or change things between us.'

'I wouldn't feel great about it,' I admitted. 'You're my best friend. He's my brother. If you and he get together and stay together, suddenly the loyalties start to shift. You know stuff about me that I don't want him ever to find out.'

'Nicki, I would never tell Lee anything you've told me in confidence,' Mel said solemnly.

I felt better when I heard those words. I thought, *Good. I'm covered.* Little did I know that, six months later, Mel would summon me for an important chat and explain that, from now on, I wasn't allowed to tell her anything that she couldn't share with Lee. She would continue to keep any secrets of mine that had got in before the deadline, but this was the cut-off point: I was forbidden from confiding in her in future, unless it was something I didn't mind Lee knowing about too.

'The thing is, we kind of . . . *are* already seeing each other,' she went on hurriedly, keen to get it over with now that she'd finally taken the plunge. 'Lee's asked me to move in with him and . . . I've said yes.'

'Oh. Well . . . congratulations.'

'Are you sure you don't mind?' Mel asked.

I hadn't said I didn't mind. I had said, as tactfully as possible, that I did. Or I thought I had. I minded the manipulation: the fiction that they cared how I felt about it, and that their relationship was no more than a vague notion at this stage, awaiting my approval. I later found out that before she'd rung me, Melissa had confirmed her booking of the removal van that would transport her possessions to Lee's flat the following Friday.

Do what you have to do, and indeed have already done, I should have said, *and if I want to tell you how I feel about it, that's up to me.*

'It's fine,' I reassured Mel instead. 'I hope you'll be very happy together.' This is the thing about deception that some people forget: its practitioners don't do it solely for their own sakes. Often they do it to make others happy. It's embedded in the training programme we liars go through: we see that when we tell the truth, our instructors scowl, raise their voices, turn red in the face. Anyone who cares more about pleasing other people than about their own happiness – anyone who believes, deep down, that everyone else matters more than they do – learns fluent dishonesty at a young age.

I swallow the last of the tea in my mug. Something inside me cracks and gives way. I can't keep up my brittle act any longer. 'What's happened to us, Mel?' I say.

Her eyes widen at my use of the old nickname.

'Does it really have to be this way?' *I will not cry. Will not.* 'Look, we can't change the facts – I'm a reprehensible slut, and you're a self-righteous prig who imagines she has to tell her husband everything, even things about his sister that are none of his business – but can't we accept each other's shortcomings and get beyond them? I'm sorry for asking you to lie to the police. Don't do it if you don't want to.'

'It *is* Lee's business if his wife and his sister conspire to keep things from him,' Melissa insists. 'He'd hate it. You know he would.'

'And he'd have no right to,' I say flatly. *Please see sense, Mel. Please tell me I can tell you anything and you'll keep my secrets. You never minded before. You knew I lied – we used to laugh together about the scrapes I'd get myself into. I need so badly to tell you about Gavin.*

His name is like an icy hand closing around my heart. I shudder.

'What's Lee told you about our childhood?'

Melissa looks uncomfortable. After half a minute or so of silence, she mutters, 'I know about the . . . lunatic asylum.'

I force out a laugh, while my heart freezes over.

Did he tell her it turned out to be a hospice? That it was all my fault, that I brought it on myself? I'd ask, but I'm slick with sweat suddenly, and desperate to change the subject. Bardolph House: a name I'd like to forget but never will.

Tell her about Lee. Tell her the full story. They deserve it, both of them.

I can't. If it would turn her against him, then I can't do it. And if it wouldn't turn her against him, I'd want to die even more than I do already.

I've gone over and over the dilemma in my mind and always arrive at the same conclusion: it wouldn't be fair to tell her. She loves Lee, and so do I. To me, he will always be my sweet little brother, wailing about a stripy cardigan and a cuddly penguin. I still want to protect that small, fragile boy who doesn't exist any more. I try not to let myself think about this; it makes me cry whenever I do.

'Nicki? Are you OK?'

'No. No, I'm not OK.' Maybe I should throw myself under a train – do everyone a favour. That's how I'd do it. I decided in February, though I'm not sure 'decided' is the right word. The knowledge was already there, in my head. If I did it, I would do it by jumping under a fast-moving train.

'I can't . . . collude with you, not now that I'm married to Lee,' Melissa says. 'Please try to understand. If you want to do things you shouldn't be doing, fine, I can't stop you, but you can't expect to come round and have a good gossip about what you've been up to and have me go along with it as if it's not wrong!'

'Collude? Anyone would think I was . . .'

'A murderer?' Melissa says sharply.

I stare at her and notice that she is shaking. Does she think I killed Damon Blundy?

When I told her he'd been murdered, she didn't express shock or regret. Not even surprise.

I wait for her to avert her eyes, but she stares back at me. A cold feeling spreads upwards from the pit of my stomach. *Hard to breathe.* I have to get out of here.

I grab my bag and make for the front door – walking, not running, though I'd like to. No one has ever said so, but I assume running would be forbidden in my brother's house.

I wait for Melissa to call me back.

Nothing.

Pulling open the front door and breathing in the loud exhaust-fume air feels like being saved. It's a good feeling.

I don't want to die.

I'm halfway to my car when a familiar face stops me: the

man from the school playground, with the streaked hair and the blue BMW. Smoking a cigarette and leaning against his car, which is parked opposite mine – directly across the road from Melissa's house.

Flash Dad from Freeth Lane School in Spilling. In Highgate, North London. What the hell is he doing here? Did he . . . ? He can't have followed me. Why would he?

I can't think of any other explanation for his presence.

That's when I notice his car registration . . . It's the same BMW I saw behind me, too close behind, when I was driving home after crashing the wing mirror off my car. That was him.

He's getting into his car. In a hurry, cigarette dropped, half smoked, on the pavement.

I don't think he expected me to reappear so soon.

Seeing him move quickly jolts me out of my shocked stillness. I start to run towards him. I might have changed my mind about throwing myself under a train, but I'd risk putting myself in front of his wheels if it'd give me the chance to ask him what the hell he thinks he's doing.

I'm not fast enough. He's gone in a screech of tyres before I'm halfway across the street.

~

From: Mr Jugs <mr_jugs@hushmail.com>
Date: Tue, 2 July 2013 15:47:08
To: <nickibeingnaughty@hushmail.com>
Subject: Re: Distress signal

Nicki,

Forgive me. I don't know if you understand, or misunderstand, the full extent of what I'm asking you to forgive me for, but . . . forgive me.

I would forgive you anything.

I will even forgive Damon Blundy for being a bad man, if you ask me to. Evil is a strong word, but I do believe he was toxic. I assume it's all right for us to disagree about this?

The only person I know whom I can never forgive is my wife. I've never told anybody this, but shortly after we got married, I found out something about her that I couldn't get past. (No, it wasn't that she'd cheated on me. She's never done that.) I pretended to forgive her, but I never truly could, and in my heart I knew things were irreparable between us from that moment on.

If she righted the wrong of her own accord, without prompting by me, then maybe . . . but I know she never will.

In spite of this, I couldn't, and can't, leave her because I know how much she loves and needs me. I couldn't do that to her. You see, she's done nothing wrong. Nothing at all. What is a grave wrong in my mind and heart is not, in her eyes and in the eyes of the rest of the world, wrong at all.

It was my inability to forgive her that drove me to the Intimate Links website.

G.

'I'm No Cheat,' says Man Who Admitted to Cheating – a Lateral Thinking Puzzle

Damon Blundy, 20 September 2011, *Daily Herald Online*

When I spoke up for <u>disgraced sprinter Bryn Gilligan</u> in my <u>column</u> two weeks ago, I expected to be set upon first by *The Times*'s Keiran Holland, Inspector Javert to Gilligan's Jean Valjean, and then by <u>all the Usual Cesspits</u>. I couldn't have been more wrong. The attack, when it came – the preposterous threat of legal action, no less – hailed from an unexpected quarter: Bryn Gilligan. Yes, that's right: the same Bryn Gilligan I'd risked the opprobrium of decent folk like you in order to defend. Bryn Gilligan <u>condemned me</u> for expressing my support for Bryn Gilligan. (Warning: the rest of this story is the logical equivalent of a painting by Escher. I hope some of you can get your heads round it, because I can't.)

Why is <u>Gilligan so angry</u> with his solitary supporter? Well, apparently because I <u>called him a cheat</u> and besmirched his good name, even though he no longer has one. In a <u>letter to this newspaper</u> that has to be read to be believed, he accuses me of trashing his character and claims that he is not and has never been a cheat – not even while he was cheating, apparently. On the contrary, he says, he is a principled man to whom professional propriety was, is and evermore shall be of the utmost importance. With specific reference to his '<u>mistake</u>' (and to clarify, he is here referring to his ingestion of prohibited performance-enhancing drugs over a period of at least five years) he asks us to believe that he was in some kind of fugue state each time he cocked up by guzzling the 'roids and illegally winning a race. In his own <u>words</u>, 'I had become detached from myself. My actions no longer had any connection with the honourable man I know myself to be.'

You see how it works? Gilligan cheated, but he wasn't a cheat when he cheated. He was a non-cheat from whom some uncharacteristically devious behaviour had emanated. He had great respect for the rules even while the detached unscrupulous bit of him was breaking them.

If you say so, Bryn. In fact, it was Keiran Holland, not me, who described Gilligan as a cheat and a liar, as I'm certain my column made clear. I don't intend to withdraw my support simply because Gilligan is no admirer of mine. To remix Groucho Marx, I'd hate to speak up for any cause that would have me as an advocate. I still believe Gilligan has learned his lesson and that his ban should be revoked, however unconventionally he might express his regret. Who could fail to learn, and learn hard, from the experience of being a newsworthy pariah for an extended period of time?

Keiran Holland has of course seized on Gilligan's latest public state-ment, holding it up as evidence of the sprinter's dishonesty, and proof of what Holland knew all along: that none of Gilligan's apologies have been genuine. Once again, I'm afraid, Holland has missed the point as desperately as a man confined to a Siberian gulag must miss the comforts of home.

Gilligan cheated and he knows it. I assume he has no desire to be ridiculous as well as reviled, so why is he objecting to the use of the word? Could it be because idiots like Holland keep forgetting the crucial distinction between sin and sinner, and trying to persuade anyone who'll listen that Gilligan is not merely someone who has cheated, but 'a cheat' – innately and irreversibly, as if it's in his DNA and he can never change? If we create a climate in which anyone who does something wrong must be branded a scumbag forever, can we really blame those who lie and cheat – which, by the way, is all of us from time to time – for pretending that they haven't, even after admitting that they have?

Think about how hard, not to mention ineffective, it would be to stand up in public and say, 'I did something unforgiveable that only a scoundrel would do, yet I'm not a scoundrel and you must forgive me.' It sounds like a paradox, doesn't it? Well, it's one we must embrace if we are to make any progress as a species, because we all do the bad things that only bad people would do, as well as the good things that only good people would do, which is why we mustn't hold anything against one another. If we want better apologies, we need to be more forgiving – it's as simple as that.

If Keiran Holland wants to hear Bryn Gilligan say, 'Yes, I cheated and I'm truly sorry,' he ought to think about what he himself needs to say first. I suggest something along the following lines: 'I'm not going to condemn you, Bryn. You cheated, but we all do – especially me, on my wife, with former Labour MP Paula Riddiough – and so I'm not going to write you off and call you "a worm with minimal integrity", because you're probably a decent guy, or else you have the potential to be one, and I believe in you. You're a talented sprinter who must have been under a lot of pressure when you made the mistakes you made, and I think you deserve a second chance.'

Speaking of second chances, I wonder if the delectable Paula Privilege is on the verge of deciding to award one to Holland. Does she regret ending their affair, and is she hoping that by attacking me, she might win him back? In a blog post two days ago, she described me as a 'vile, shameless hack'. My crime? Making 'needlessly personal and hurtful comments about the journalist Keiran Holland'. Notice her distancing use of 'the journalist' rather than, say, 'my ex-lover, who cast aside his wife for me, only to be ditched and left stranded'. Perhaps she would care to explain why it is 'indefensible' that I should sneer at Holland in my column while it's perfectly all right for her to discard him like a pus-stained plaster when the better option of a fling with an American movie director presents itself.

Paula, shall we ask Keiran Holland to tell us which of us has hurt him more? I see a pattern emerging here, old bean. Have you forgotten the time you lashed out at me for 'maligning' your son's 'educational experience', obliging me to point out that while I, a stranger, might have maligned it, you, the boy's very own mother, had been actively sabotaging it over a period of years?

I don't like to hurt people unnecessarily, but I do like the truth, apart from when it might get me into trouble. And I hate hypocrisy, always. Sometimes the truth stings. Horror writer Reuben Tasker took to his website last week to express his anger and sadness at my casual dismissal of his novel *Craving and Aversion*, winner of a Books Enhance Lives Award. Tasker made a fair point: I ought not to imply that his book is rubbish without having read it. I apologised in the comments beneath his blog post and promised to make up for my sloppiness by buying a copy. I have now read it. It's rubbish: badly structured, pretentious and violent in the way that only a perverted author's sexual fantasies tend to be. One central character has her 'waist-hugging ropes of flaxen hair' cut off and stuffed into her vagina, for example, before the end of Chapter One. 'Waist-hugging'? Does this woman's hair grow downward from her scalp like traditional hair or horizontally from her stomach? It makes no sense that this novel won a prize, until we consider that one of the judges was Keiran Holland. How tragic that a man as judgemental as Holland should possess such poor judgement.

4

Wednesday 3 July 2013

Did most men have female gatekeepers? Simon wondered. So far this morning on the Damon Blundy case, he'd interviewed a rabbi and a plastic surgeon, both of whom had been protected by a woman-barrier who would only let him through after a thorough interrogation – a wife in the rabbi's case and a PA for the surgeon.

Bryn Gilligan's gatekeeper was his mother, Jennifer: a tough-looking woman with muscly arms and three small diamond earrings in each ear, who lived in a strange kind of bungaloid mansion: very flat – only one storey – but covering roughly the same square acreage as a large hospital might.

Simon was struck by the contrast with his own mother, her house, her behaviour. Kathleen Waterhouse, throughout Simon's childhood, had refused to open the front door of their three-bedroom red-brick semi at all, let alone block it with her body to protect her son. Not that anyone had ever come to the house who posed a threat to Simon; apart from the parish priest, no one had come to the house at all.

Jennifer Gilligan's aim in barring the entrance to her ultra-modern concrete-and-glass detached bungalow was not simply protective. She wanted to brief Simon before he came into contact with Bryn. 'I don't think he should be interacting with these people all day long,' she said urgently, in a whisper. 'Most of the time he's in front of his laptop, and when he has to be away from it, he's got his iPhone. Fine, if he were using them to communicate with friends, but he's not! He's spending all this time with people calling him names and telling him they hope he dies. It's not doing him any good.'

'No,' Simon agreed. 'It sounds . . . unhelpful.'

'He doesn't just read them, which'd be bad enough – he insists on answering every damn single one of them! He thinks if he engages with them, they'll see he's got a good heart, but the worst ones aren't capable of seeing, because they haven't got hearts at all! They want to carry on hating – it's their hobby. Avoiding them, ignoring them, disconnecting – that's what he needs to do. I've said all this till I'm blue in the face, and he nods and says I'm right, but nothing changes.'

Simon hoped she was just letting off steam, but feared it was more than that. As Jennifer's forehead creased, and she opened her mouth to speak again, he knew what was coming. 'You couldn't . . . ? I mean, I know you need to ask him about Damon Blundy . . . who he didn't touch, by the way. I know my son. He wouldn't harm any living creature, believe me. I've seen him run along the hall with a spider to throw it out the front door instead of killing it. But . . . if there's any way you could talk to him about this horrible Internet obsession, I'd be very grateful. He might listen to you.'

Sam Komobothekra, in Simon's place, would agree without question. As Sam himself had admitted, he was better suited to hand-holding than to police work. Charlie would say, 'If I see him doing it while I'm talking to him, I'll mention it – how does that sound?'

Simon found himself unable to respond directly to the question. Helping people to live happier lives wasn't his job; solving murders was. He wanted to say, 'No,' but that would have sounded too harsh.

'Can I come in?' he said instead.

Jennifer nodded and moved aside so that he could pass. She pointed down the hall. Simon looked and saw the two of them reflected in the largest mirror he'd ever seen. It took up a whole wall. 'Bryn's in the kitchen. Straight down to the end, turn right, then left, straight along again – it's at the far end of the house. Do you want me there or not?'

'I'd rather talk to him alone if that's all right,' said Simon.

'Fine. If he forgets to offer you a cup of tea, ask for one. He'll probably forget. Oh, one thing.'

'What?'

'If he asks you what you think about what he did, what's happened to him, whether he should be banned from sprinting for life, what's your answer going to be?'

'I'll say I'm not here to discuss that.' Simon saw that this wasn't enough for her. 'Or I'll tell him the truth – I know nothing about competitive sport and what the rules should or shouldn't be. I don't have a view. I've never thought about it.'

'If he tells you he's changed and that he wouldn't do it again, what'll you say to that?'

'I'll say . . . that's good – I'm pleased to hear it?'

Jennifer seemed to relax. 'Thank you,' she said. 'Maybe a positive response in real life'll count for more than all the haters online. I hope so.'

The huge mirror, it turned out, was part of a collection. Simon passed at least twenty more, on his way to the kitchen. It was the Hall of Mirrors – not in Versailles but in Norwich.

Bryn Gilligan didn't look up as Simon walked into the room. He was hunched in front of a laptop computer, tapping away at the keyboard. His pale ginger hair was wet, and he was wearing a grey towelling bathrobe. 'Sorry,' he said, looking up. 'I meant to get dressed before you arrived, but . . .' He nodded at the screen in front of him. 'Are you on Twitter?'

'No,' said Simon, thinking that Bryn Gilligan was one of those rare people who looked much younger than he was. He would probably always have the face of a teenager.

'Very sensible. I'd stay well away from it if I were you.'

Not much point giving him the warning he's just given me, Simon thought. Bryn evidently knew his mother was right, but had difficulty putting the theory into practice.

'So, you're here to ask me if I murdered Damon Blundy,' said Bryn, his voice taking on a hard edge. 'Yes, I probably did.'

'Pardon?' Without asking permission, Simon pulled out one of the chairs from under the kitchen table and sat down.

'I probably killed him. Let's see: I'm an evil cheat and liar with no integrity; I don't care about the rules, don't care about anyone but myself. I took Blundy to task for misrepresenting me once, even though he was trying to stick up for me – September 2011. I was in crazy defensive mode, lashing out at anyone who mentioned my name. One of those people was Blundy, and I attacked him for defending me. It was a stupid thing to do, nearly as stupid as doping for years and thinking I wouldn't get caught. Whoever killed Blundy did a stupid thing too – they'll probably get caught.' Bryn smiled. 'It's sounding more and more like me, isn't it? The killer has my psychological profile. *And* I was here in the house on my own on Monday morning, so I've got no alibi – therefore, yes, I probably did murder Damon Blundy.'

'Did you tweet or email anyone from that computer between eight thirty and ten thirty on Monday?' Simon asked. 'If you did, we can prove where those communications came from. If it's a server in Norwich, two hours from Spilling, then you're in the clear.' Was it a server he meant or a router? No – definitely not a router.

Simon's IT knowledge was limited. The other day, Charlie had laughed at him for not understanding what 'the Cloud' was. He glanced down at his watch. It was eleven. He was meeting Charlie for lunch at one. He needed to set off now, ideally. This morning he'd been up at four to fit in the rabbi and the surgeon. He'd left tired behind hours ago and was now approaching shattered.

Bryn was shaking his head. 'I'm not in the clear. You might be able to prove that someone using my Twitter ID was tweeting all morning from this computer, this kitchen, this house, but how can you prove it was me? It could have been anyone who knew my password and felt inclined to defend me for a few hours. My password is "cheating1", in case you're wondering.'

'Did you kill Damon Blundy?' Simon asked, reeling a little.

The density of Bryn's self-loathing was making it difficult to breathe. Simon wished Sam were with him.

'No, I didn't. But as Twitter'll tell you from dawn to dusk three hundred and sixty-five days a year, my word's not worth shit. So . . . when you don't immediately find your killer, you'll think about me, and how I was here on my own the day Blundy was killed, and you'll come back and arrest me. So why not do it now? I'd rather get it over with.'

'I don't believe you killed anyone, so I'm not arresting you,' Simon told him.

'You're not arresting me *yet*,' Bryn said knowingly. 'And yet, I'm so arrestable – I don't know how you can resist. You'll be back, I'm sure.'

'He is no less dead,' Simon said, making sure to speak clearly.

Bryn frowned. 'No less dead than what? What do you mean?'

Well, that was one test passed with flying colours.

He's lied before, though, about his drug use . . . repeatedly, convincingly.

'Who do you think might have killed Damon Blundy?' Simon asked.

'Keiran Holland,' Bryn said without hesitation. He took a sip of what looked like cloudy apple juice from the glass beside his laptop.

'You sound certain about that.'

'No. I've no idea. You asked me who I thought *might* have done it. Keiran Holland's a man without a shred of compassion in his soul. For all I know, he's got a rock-solid alibi, but if he hasn't . . . Lack of compassion, plus known hatred of Damon Blundy . . .' Bryn shrugged. 'If I were you, I'd have Holland somewhere very near the top of my suspect list.'

~

'No Waterhouse?' Detective Inspector Giles Proust looked disappointed. He pushed in between Gibbs and Sellers on his way to his desk as if they were inconveniently positioned items of furniture. Gibbs was familiar with the manoeuvre. Debbie often swept past him in a similar way, without looking at him.

'Simon's still with Bryn Gilligan,' said Sam Kombothekra. 'He wants to know if any kind of appointment diary for Damon Blundy's been found from 2011.'

'Not at the house,' said Sellers. 'There might be something on his computer, which is with the Tech guys. I'm going there from here, so I'll ask. Why? Why 2011?'

'I don't know,' said Sam. 'Simon didn't explain, just said he's keen to see Blundy's diary from that year if it's around.'

'He'll have a good reason,' said Gibbs.

Sam smiled. 'One we won't be able to work out, however hard we try,' he said.

'Have I interrupted the omnibus edition of a Simon Waterhouse tribute programme?' Proust said icily, earning his 'Snowman' nickname, as he did reliably at least once a day. 'Any chance the talking heads could talk about the investigation? What have we got from the scene? The killer took Blundy's phone, we think, but did he leave anything? Any large helpful flakes of DNA?'

Sam shook his head. 'It's not looking promising, sir. The protective suit he was wearing has scuppered us, I think. The good news is, we're better off when it comes to possible suspects.'

'A lot of people loathed Damon Blundy,' said Gibbs. 'Many are household names: Bryn Gilligan, Jacob Fedder—'

'Super-Rabbi Jacob Fedder?' Proust asked. 'Hasn't he got better things to do?'

'One of the many bees in Blundy's bonnet was the circumcision of baby boys,' Gibbs told him. 'You know, like Jews and Muslims do. Blundy thought it was child abuse and should be illegal. Bad as female genital mutilation, he said in several of his columns. He didn't say it tactfully.'

Proust snorted. 'Some people like to make life difficult for themselves, don't they? If I had a bonnet, I'd go to considerable lengths to avoid having that particular bee in it. So the rabbi was incensed, was he?'

'Yep. So were lots of other Jewish and Muslim leaders – Fedder was the most vocal, but there were loads. They petitioned the *Daily Herald*, demanded that Blundy be fired. This was after he referred to "neurotic blade-wielding maniacs suffering from a collective obsessive-compulsive disorder, trying to appease an imaginary tyrant in the sky by lopping random body parts off their so-called loved ones".'

'I spoke to the *Herald* this morning,' said Sam. 'Off the record, I was told they were on the point of letting Blundy go when some equally determined free-speech enthusiasts started their own petition to save his column, even though many of them apparently despised Blundy as much as his detractors did. In the end, the free-speech lot won the day.' Sam shrugged. 'Despite being unpleasant and offensive, Blundy was one of the *Herald*'s main attractions. He shifted papers. Goodness knows why.'

'No, Sergeant, goodness – as personified by you – has no idea why. Goodness of the unimaginative bog-standard variety looks at a man like Damon Blundy and can't see the point of him at all.'

'You liked his columns, sir?'

'They weren't written to be *liked*, Sergeant. Let's get back to the Muslims and the Jews. We're interviewing them, yes? All the . . . the main ones?'

'Not yet,' said Sam. 'Once we've got our reinforcement personnel from Silsford, which should be within the hour, we'll be interviewing everyone who's ever publicly expressed antipathy towards Damon Blundy. It's going to take a while. That same circumcision column that Gibbs quoted from ended with Blundy asking how readers would feel if he hacked off the earlobe of the little girl who lived next door to him and justified it by claiming it was a sacrifice to a goblin living on a cloud that only Blundy could see. The girl's mother took exception and sold a hatchet-job-from-next-door-neighbour's-point-of-view on Blundy to the *Mail*, accusing him of leading a promiscuous and debauched lifestyle, which he happily admitted to

– this was after ex-wife number two and before he married Hannah.'

'So stick the little girl's mother on the list,' said Proust. 'Who else? Any family? I'm not pinning my hopes on Rabbi Fedder or Bryn Gilligan. Both strike me as bland and ineffectual from what I've seen of them on TV. Damon Blundy's murderer might be insane but certainly isn't bland.'

'Blundy's parents and three sisters all live in South Africa and were all in Johannesburg when Blundy was killed, going about their normal business.' Sellers answered the question Proust had forgotten he'd asked. 'Relations were strained. Blundy's parents had all but disowned him, by the sound of it.'

'Why?' Gibbs asked.

'No dramatic reason,' said Sellers. 'They just didn't like him, and he didn't like them.'

'Simon said something interesting about the killer's character,' said Sam.

'Has the commercial break finished, Sergeant? Is this Part Two of the tribute programme?'

'Sir, I think it's worth repeating. I can't remember Simon's exact words, but—'

'And you're willing to risk paraphrasing? Won't all the magic be lost in translation?'

'Most murder scenes reveal either cold, pre-planned detachment or spontaneous chaotic passion,' Sam persisted. 'This one's a mixture of the two – lots of planning involved, enough detachment to think about logistics and . . . image management, for want of a better term, but also, without a doubt, strong feelings. Whoever killed Blundy was passionate about him.'

'According to Waterhouse,' Proust added the qualifier Sam had omitted.

'And to me,' Sam said with uncharacteristic firmness. 'It makes sense. Simon thinks whoever did it has difficulty openly expressing his or her emotions. So, feels things deeply, but is also a control freak with years of experience of preventing unmanageable feelings from spilling out. A bottler-up. Someone who wouldn't let passion emerge unchecked, but would craft it into something safe, structured and anonymous. He both wants us to know how he feels and doesn't, so he conveys his message cryptically, half hoping we'll guess, half hoping we won't.'

'That sounds consistent with the Damon Blundy murder scene to me,' Gibbs said.

'It sounds consistent with DC Waterhouse,' said Proust impatiently. 'Am I the only one who notices that all his quack profiles are thinly veiled descriptions of himself? Is it his secret ambition to get himself arrested for every murder we investigate?'

'Simon thinks that room, that . . . display, with the knife taped to his face and everything – it's an invitation to misunderstand,' Sam said. 'The killer's saying, "Go on, prove to me that you can work me out – no one else has ever managed to." When we fail, he wins, because he's outwitted us, and loses because all his worst fears are confirmed: no one gets him; no one cares enough to make the effort. That murder scene is likely to be the first public expression of his feelings for some time – maybe his whole life.'

'"*When* we fail", Sergeant? Could you brainstorm titles for your autobiography some other time? I'd like you to pretend your motto is "When we succeed", at least until you retire.'

'Sir, I meant from the killer's point of—'

'Shall we stop playing Simon Reckons and return to work?' the Snowman cut Sam off. 'Who else hated Damon Blundy, apart from Bryn Gilligan, Rabbi Jacob Fedder, other Jews, some Muslims and a neighbour keen to protect her daughter's earlobe?'

'Paula Riddiough, ex Labour MP for Culver Valley East,' said Sam.

For whom Sellers had voted for reasons that had nothing to do with politics and everything to do with his pornographic fantasies about her, Gibbs remembered with a grin.

'Blundy laid into her in one of his columns for sending her

son to a state school and the two of them quickly became well-known enemies,' Sam said.

Gibbs waited for Sellers to make a joke about laying Paula Riddiough, who was indisputably hot, and not only for an MP.

Nothing. Sellers hadn't been himself for a while and seemed not to want to talk about it. 'Just *insist* that he tells you,' Liv had said on the phone last night.

'You mean private school?' Proust asked Sam. 'Blundy laid into Riddiough for sending her son to a *private* school?'

'No, she sent him to a state school,' said Sam.

'Isn't that what good Labour MPs who believe in state education are supposed to do?'

'You can read the column if you want, sir – we've got the collected works of Damon Blundy next door. Riddiough comes from pots of money and went to Cheltenham Ladies' College. Blundy accused her of culpable negligence with regard to her child's future prospects, said she was one of the worst mothers in the UK. He called for social services to take her son into care.'

'On what grounds?' Proust sounded curious rather than shocked.

'On the grounds that all good parents, even flawed ones, want better for their children than whatever they had themselves,' said Sam. 'Blundy said Riddiough could have afforded the very best for her son, but she'd actively sought to ensure that he had an education that was vastly inferior to her own, in an uglier building with fewer resources, dragged down by the stress and hopelessness common to all teachers in what Blundy called "perkless institutions", and surrounded by gangster-chavs-in-the-making rather than the intellectually curious children of scientific innovators and visiting diplomats – or something like that. He accused Riddiough of doing it purely to annoy her rich, Tory parents while hypocritically pretending it was some sort of left-wing principle.'

'They're proper aristos, the Riddiough family,' Gibbs chipped in. 'Seat in the House of Lords until recently.'

'Until all the hereditaries were replaced by inarticulate cockneys from reality-TV programmes, you mean?' Proust got angry suddenly. 'Paula Riddiough didn't kill Damon Blundy! I mean, if we're going by Waterhouse's nonsense theory about the inability of our killer to express himself openly in public – Paula Riddiough expresses herself in every perishing newspaper supplement I ever see, even now that she's no longer an MP. Wasn't it her oversharing that prompted the calls for her resignation?'

'Yes, sir,' said Sam. 'And it seems that the more Blundy attacked her, the more she overshared.'

'She and Blundy are two of a kind,' said Gibbs. 'Shock jocks. I agree, it's unlikely she killed him, but I wonder—'

'All right, talk to her,' Proust cut him off. 'You have to, don't you? I wish Blundy had considered the inconvenience to us in the event of his murder. It's going to take us until next year to interview everyone who might have wanted him dead, by the sound of it. Who else?'

'Two ex-wives, Verity Hewson and Abigail Meredith,' said Sam. 'Referred to by Blundy in his columns as Princess Doormat and Dr Despot.'

'Going back to Paula Riddiough . . .' Gibbs decided to risk airing his thoughts. 'What about Blundy's computer password, Riddy111111? "Riddy" could be short for "Riddiough". It was the first thing I thought when I heard her name.'

'When you speak to her, ask her if anyone calls her Riddy,' said Proust. 'Continue with the list of enemies, Sergeant.'

'A writer of horror novels, Reuben Tasker, and the journalist Keiran Holland. Both hated Blundy.'

'Keiran Holland?' Proust looked surprised. 'The Britain-must-join-the-euro guy?'

'I don't think he does so much economic journalism these days, but—'

'Talk to them both,' the Snowman cut Sam off. 'What about Hannah, the grieving widow? What do we think about her claim that Blundy can't really have loved her?'

'Simon and I both thought she believed what she was saying, but . . . I think that's probably paranoia on her part. Low self-esteem.'

'Not as ugly as she thinks she is?' Sellers asked.

'She's not most people's idea of attractive, and as she pointed out herself, Blundy was forever harping on about how he loved gorgeous women and hated plain ones, but . . . I don't know.' Sam shook his head. 'To be honest, she sounded . . . well, a bit mad. She had no evidence – no sign that he'd ever had an affair, nothing she'd seen or overheard to back up her belief. And Blundy was a loving, devoted husband to her for the whole of their marriage. Could he really have faked it for so long? Why would he?'

'Don't ask me,' said Proust. 'Most married men have the opposite problem: they love their wives but find it hard not to behave as if they can't stand them. Sergeant, please don't look at me with the eyes of a rabbit dying of myxomatosis while Mr Garfunkel sings "Bright Eyes" in the background! It's not sexism, it's the truth! Gibbs and Sellers know what I mean.'

'Since he was so keen on shocking people, Blundy could easily have written a column saying he could never love an ugly woman just to be provocative,' Sam said, red in the face from the rabbit comparison.

'Or he could have been using his love life as yet another rebellion opportunity, in addition to his column in the *Herald*,' said Gibbs. 'He was famous, well-off – he could have had anyone. Well, not anyone, but—'

'Anyone who didn't mind cruelty,' muttered Sam.

'Maybe he thought it'd shock people if he had an unattractive wife,' Gibbs said. 'If you want to shock and keep shocking, you can't be predictable. So if you've written about your fondness for fit women—'

'So then Hannah's right,' said Sellers. 'He didn't love her. He married her for her freak-show value.'

'Hannah's not a freak,' Sam said emphatically. 'I could be wrong, but I don't find it plausible that anyone, however much they enjoyed shocking or rebelling, would deliberately choose a partner they weren't attracted to just to create a certain reaction. Being plain, like Hannah, or even downright ugly, doesn't mean no one would fall in love with you at first sight.'

'Are you sure about that, Sergeant? I'm not. I think Hannah Blundy might have a point.'

'Sir, it's not as if people always agree about these things. Maybe Damon Blundy thought Hannah was beautiful.'

'You've seen her and I haven't,' said Proust. 'Could any man think she was beautiful? Is it within the bounds of possibility?'

Sam looked confused. 'It *has* to be,' he said eventually. 'These things are so subjective. Anyone could look beautiful to at least one person. Couldn't they?'

'No, Sergeant. Think of Superintendent Barrow. His head looks like a goitre, disfiguring a neck from an unusually elevated position.'

'You should send your CV in to the *Daily Herald*, sir,' Gibbs suggested. 'Now that Blundy's dead, they'll be looking to fill their offensive-columnist gap.'

Proust looked irritated. Then he grinned. 'That's not a bad idea,' he said. 'I wonder if I could notch up as many enemies as Blundy.'

'More, I reckon,' said Gibbs.

The Snowman's smile remained in place. He turned to Sam. 'I assume you'll be looking at the comments beneath Blundy's columns, the digital versions?'

'We've already started, sir. Any names that come up regularly are being noted, anyone who seems suspiciously keen or regular, anyone veering towards obsessive – whether they're pro- or anti-Blundy. There's stacks about him. And we'll be doing more house-to-house as soon as—'

'Put the Silsford team on that,' Proust barked. 'Waste of time! No one saw anything, end of story. No one looks at the world outside any more. We're all glued to our tiny screens. Did you speak to Karen Sanderson?'

An audible shudder filled the Snowman's small glass-sided room. Every police officer in Spilling knew the name. A thirty-five-year-old chartered surveyor with a day-trader husband and no children, Sanderson was a good citizen of the obsessive kind who, for no reason that anyone could fathom, had taken it upon herself several years ago to crack down, personally, on drivers who parked unethically in disabled and mother-and-baby spaces. She'd been cracking down ever since and regularly turned up at the nick to harangue the police about their apparent willingness to leave it all to her.

'Sanderson corroborates Nicki Clements's story,' said Gibbs, who'd had the misfortune of interviewing her that morning. 'At eight minutes past eleven, when the email containing the killer's photo was sent, Sanderson was yelling at Nicki in the library car park for parking in the wrong place. She's sure about the times – she noted it down in her little black book of sinful parking. For the duration of her row with Sanderson, Nicki didn't touch her phone – Sanderson's certain.'

'So whoever emailed Damon Blundy a photograph of his killer encased in a protective suit, brandishing a knife as if to stab him imminently . . . it wasn't Nicki Clements,' said Proust.

'No,' Gibbs agreed.

'Yet Clements describes the woman she fought with in the library car park as an old-granny type. Did you ask Sanderson if she was in granny fancy dress at the time?'

'She told me she looked the same as she always does,' said Gibbs. 'Trendy haircut, tarty crocodile boots. Nor was she helped to fight the good fight by any passing grannies. It was just her and Nicki Clements.'

'I think that's what they call "a telling error", Detective. Nicki Clements was right about every detail of her car-park row apart from the description of her adversary. Why?'

'She's lying,' said Gibbs.

'Our best guess is that she started to tell the truth, told a bit of it, then panicked,' Sam said. 'She was afraid we might try and track down this strange woman who shouted at her in a car park. She wouldn't have known we'd recognise Karen Sanderson instantly from her description of their exchange. There was a risk that Sanderson would tell us Nicki's car had both its wing mirrors when she saw it, and Nicki had just lied to us about having lost one more than a week ago. I think she gave us the granny description of Sanderson to make it less likely that we'd find her.'

'The lie about the missing mirror wasn't thought through at all,' said Gibbs. 'In the CCTV footage, which Nicki *knew* was what led us to her because Simon and Sam told her, there's clearly something sticking out of the passenger side of her car where the wing mirror ought to be. Of all the stories she could have told, she picked one that was ridiculously easy to prove untrue.'

'She was in a complete state,' said Sam. 'I'm surprised she was able to produce any kind of story, though she did calm down once she started to talk about the mirror, funnily enough. It was almost as if the process of creating her lie . . . I don't know, kind of soothed her.' He turned to Gibbs. 'Though I suppose it's just about possible the mirror thing wasn't a lie? What if the car prang she described knocked the mirror out of its casing, or container, or whatever – the sticky-out bit that's there in the CCTV footage? No.' Sam disagreed with himself before anyone else could. 'When Simon and I arrived at her house on Tuesday afternoon, the whole of the passenger-side wing-mirror attachment was gone. She'd left the garage door wide open so that we could see it. Obviously she'd done something to break it off between getting picked up on CCTV and us seeing her car. I also think . . . when we got to the house, we bumped into her husband, Adam, who was on his way to pick up the kids. He said Nicki had gone to London – she'd hired a car to get there. Adam was in a tearing rush to get off to school because he'd had to drive her to the car-hire office once she'd found out the trains were messed up . . .' Sam broke off. 'Lots of alarm bells were ringing at that point. I'd like to know what was so important to Nicki, immediately after we'd questioned her, that required a hired car and a trip to London, and dragging her husband home early from work.'

'Lying was so important to her,' said Proust. 'She's a compulsive liar.'

'I think that conclusion's unavoidable,' Sam agreed. 'She refused a lift home on the grounds that she had chores to do in town. Simon followed her out of the building once the interview was finished – she didn't head for town. She ran – literally ran – out of town, in the direction of Bartholomew Gardens, where she lives. She couldn't risk us turning up at her house at the same time as her. That wouldn't have given her the chance to smash off her wing mirror before we arrived to check.'

'You can stop,' said Proust. 'You had me at "compulsive liar". Bring Nicki Clements in again. Put the fear of me into her. Find the connection between her and Blundy, and find out why she took a suspicious interest in Elmhirst Road on the day of his murder.'

'*You* said "compulsive liar", sir,' Gibbs pointed out.

'I have to praise Sergeant Kombothekra for something, Gibbs. No one can work effectively without positive reinforcement, or so I'm told.'

~

Charlie was watching Simon watching his phone. It lay on the red tablecloth between them, next to the breadbasket, and had yet to earn the attention it had been getting since the beginning of lunch. They were in the Little Lamp, a new and mostly underground café-cum-second-hand-bookshop on Spilling's Market Square that Charlie had wanted to try for ages. Simon normally insisted on going to the Pocket and Pound, a dismal pub that he either loved for no good reason or pretended to love because he was a contrary sod and no one else liked it at all. Today, he'd been too preoccupied by the Blundy case to argue and Charlie had got her way.

Now, with scraps of other customers' conversations echoing around her head, she wished she'd picked somewhere less eccentric that offered more privacy. It was an odd place, the Little Lamp. For a bookshop, it didn't contain enough books. Charlie estimated that there were fewer than fifty. She'd seen two already that she thought she might want to buy – one a psychology book that she'd have to hide from Simon – but still, forty-six books was a long holiday for two people, surely, not a commercial proposition.

The not-enough theme wasn't confined to the books. There were only six tables in a space that could have taken twelve, and only three main courses on the menu, which would have been fine if it were a menu of the day, but this one had a stiff, laminated permanence about it. On the floor beside Charlie and Simon's table was a small lamp with a square pottery base, a plain green fabric shade and a long white lead that was grubby grey in places. From a lighting point of view, there was no need for the lamp, and indeed it wasn't switched on. Charlie suspected it was there so that customers could see it and think, Aha! I get it: a little lamp! Everything about this place suggested that the owners were indulging in a fantasy of running a business rather than actually running one. Charlie gave the café less than six months.

Simon had eaten no more than a mouthful of his lasagne, and his appetite for conversation appeared to be equally absent. Several times Charlie had asked him whose call he was hoping to extract from his phone using the sheer force of his glare, and the same number of times she had been ignored as if she hadn't spoken. There probably wasn't much point in bringing it up again. Except if she adopted that attitude consistently, to all aspects of her life with Simon, there might be nothing but silence and inactivity between them forevermore. When he sunk into moods like this – his walled-in phases, as she privately thought of them – Charlie found it hard to believe that he was ever otherwise; her memories of good conversations they'd had, times when he'd included her in his thoughts, no longer seemed trust-worthy.

'Simon?'

'Hmm?'

'Who are you hoping will ring?'

'Paula Riddiough's personal assistant.'

'Paula Riddiough our MP?' So he didn't mind her knowing, then; he mustn't have been listening when she asked before.

'Ex-MP. She resigned in January last year. She wasn't ours, anyway. She was Culver Valley East.'

'Yes, I've always suspected she resigned mainly because she couldn't bear to slum it in Combingham any more with the proles. No offence, but why would anyone associated with Paula Privilege, the UK's most glamorous champagne socialist, ring the likes of you?'

Simon dragged his eyes away from his phone, looked up. 'You know her as Paula Privilege?'

'I don't know her at all, but that's her nickname, or it was. Lots of politicians have nicknames, usually snide ones: Red Ed, Tony Bliar . . .'

'Do you know where the name Paula Privilege came from?'

'I can guess. I've heard her plummy voice often enough.'

'Damon Blundy.' Simon sounded satisfied. He loved knowing things that other people didn't. 'Paula Privilege was an abbrevia-tion. In the first column he wrote about her, he called her Saint Paula of Privilege. He cut it down later, made it snappier. It stuck.'

'Right.' Charlie tried not to sound too grateful that he'd finally tossed her a few scraps of information. 'So you're waiting for Paula Priv to ring in connection with the Blundy case? That's my even-more-abbreviated abbreviation.'

'Already,' Simon said.

'What do you mean?'

'Hmm?'

'You said, "Already."'

'No, I didn't,' said Simon.

Deep breaths, Charlie. In, out. In, out.

'You—'

'I said, "Or Riddy." Someone with the surname Riddiough might be nicknamed Riddy, mightn't they?'

'They might,' Charlie said doubtfully. 'Why?'

Simon waved her question aside to make way for another of his own. 'Could you fall in love with someone you'd only met once or twice?' he asked. 'Even if they weren't good-looking at all?'

Charlie considered it. She'd felt a strong attraction towards Simon the first time they'd been introduced. He'd looked at her with eyes full of warning: *You won't talk to me for longer than necessary if you know what's good for you.* He wasn't conventionally handsome, despite being big, broad-shouldered and strong-jawed, but for Charlie, it had never been about his looks. He radiated a force that she found irresistible. Love, though? Not that soon. But certainly the recognisable beginning of something that could – and did – turn into love, and a feeling, as soon as she saw him, that she knew him already and always had.

She felt no closer to him at this moment, and no more distant from him, than she had then.

'I probably could,' she said after a few seconds. 'If the person in question gave off the right aura or . . . vibe. Why?'

'Damon Blundy,' Simon muttered.

Charlie sighed. 'You mean, "It's something to do with the Blundy case, but I don't want to share it with you at the moment"?'

Simon's phone buzzed. He grabbed it, grimaced when he saw the screen. 'Text from Liv, for you,' he said. 'Where's your phone?'

'In my bag. I thought I'd have lunch with my husband, not my phone.'

'Look at your messages, she says.'

Nothing annoyed Charlie more than remote-control ordering-around by her younger sister. She'd have liked to ignore the demand, but knew she couldn't afford to. A text from Liv could be anything from 'You MUST read Book X by Writer Y – it is SO good, you will love me FOREVER' to 'Gibbs and I are running away together tomorrow and joining a travelling circus.'

What an apt metaphor, Charlie thought as she reached into her handbag for her phone; Liv and Gibbs had been walking the precarious tightrope of secret infidelity for several years now. How long before they fell off and got found out by one or other of their spouses? Perhaps this was the 'Oh my God, we've been rumbled' text that Charlie was always, on some level, expecting to arrive.

Thankfully, it wasn't. The message said, 'Can't make drinks later, sorry! Can we rearrange? I'll send other dates! xxx!'

Fine. Good, in fact. Though rather odd – Liv had almost insisted on meeting this evening, so why the sudden blasé cancellation? Charlie couldn't summon the energy to send a reply. The crisis that Liv would one day inflict on her had been staved off for the time being, but the pattern of breath-holding followed by post-ponement was growing ever more draining. Charlie resented the small bursts of relief she felt every time a message arrived from Liv that wasn't notification of a state of emergency; she hated the idea that her sister could at any moment become a disaster area that she would have to drop everything in order to attend to.

Like when she had life-threatening cancer. Except that hadn't been Liv's fault. Falling in love with Chris Gibbs was.

'Has Gibbs been different with you lately?' Charlie asked Simon. 'Ingratiating himself more than usual?'

That caught Simon's attention. 'Now you mention it . . . yes. He's put himself out for me a few times recently when there was no need.'

'He's been sucking up to me too. Then yesterday Liv rang and said she wanted to take me out for cocktails, her treat – that's what she's just cancelled. They're up to something. Whatever it is, they need us buttered up and onside. They want something from us.'

'If Liv's cancelled, though . . .' Simon shrugged. 'Maybe they've decided they don't want it, whatever it is.'

'Liv never decides she doesn't want something,' said Charlie. 'She always decides she wants even more.'

'Six ones.'

'Pardon?'

'Six ones, in a row,' Simon said. 'What does that mean to you?'

'Nothing.'

'Anything.'

'One hundred and eleven thousand, one hundred and eleven?' Charlie suggested. It was bound to be the wrong answer: too obvious.

'Riddy one hundred and eleven thousand, one hundred and eleven.'

'What's—'

'Here's the important question,' Simon talked over her. 'Did the killer turn up at Blundy's house intending to stab him, sharpen the knife and then change his mind for some reason, or was there never going to be a stabbing? Was it never part of the plan?'

At last, a question Charlie understood. Simon had described the murder scene to her within minutes of seeing it himself, which made it all the more frustrating that he was now keeping things back. 'If he changed his mind, why did he?' she asked. 'And if he didn't, if he was never going to stab Blundy . . .'

'Go on,' Simon urged. 'What you're about to say could be important. I'm thinking the same thing, but I need to hear someone else put it into words.'

'That's what I'm struggling to do, because it's so . . . odd,' Charlie said. 'If he never intended to stab Blundy, then he must have brought a knife and knife sharpener to the scene for some *other* reason. What could that reason be?'

'Go on.'

Charlie doubted she'd get a favourable response if she said, 'Er . . . that's it.'

'Also, he could have murdered Blundy in any number of ways, if he'd decided against stabbing,' she said. 'Once he'd taped him into his chair, he could have strangled him, or clocked him over the head several times with the knife sharpener. If he'd wanted to suffocate him, he could have just taped over his mouth and nose – with tape! Why tape a sharp knife against his mouth and suffocate him in an unnecessarily convoluted way? It's the weirdest thing I've ever heard.'

Simon was nodding. 'At a rough guess, it would have been maybe five times quicker to shatter Blundy's skull with the knife sharpener. Hannah, Blundy's wife, was two floors down in the basement kitchen. She could have come up at any time. Killing Blundy as quickly and efficiently as possible would have increased the killer's chances of getting in and out without being seen. Instead, he did the opposite.'

'You're assuming the wife didn't do it?'

Simon looked caught out. 'You're right.' He sighed heavily. 'I shouldn't assume that.'

'I wouldn't,' said Charlie. 'If she didn't kill him, that means someone else gained access to the house without either breaking in or ringing the doorbell, created a theatre set of a murder scene at his leisure, offed Blundy, then escaped undetected. How likely is that? Though I suppose if we apply Occam's Beard . . .'

These last two words made Simon wince whenever he heard them, including now. Occam's Beard was Charlie's pet name for the law that seemed to apply to nearly all of his cases: the simplest explanation is never the correct one. It was the opposite of Occam's Razor. Charlie thought it was one of her greatest inventions, and was secretly hurt that Simon refused to recognise it or mention it by name.

'I don't think Hannah Blundy did it,' he said. 'Having said that, I reckon I've never been more likely to be wrong. She's very . . . intense.'

Charlie smiled. 'So are you. That's why she makes you feel

uneasy. You prefer people who are nothing like you – and you trust them more.'

'Even if Hannah did it, that doesn't answer the main question,' said Simon. 'Why do it in such an elaborate, counterintuitive way? Everyone knows knives are for stabbing, not for suffocating.'

'Shh,' said Charlie, paranoid that the other lunchers in the café had abandoned their own conversations in order to listen to a more interesting one. 'I don't know. I can't see the logic behind it.'

'Unless?' Simon prompted.

'Unless it was symbolic. Making some kind of point.' Charlie cut another small piece off her spinach and goat's cheese tart. She was too full to eat any more, but it was there. What she really wanted to do was squash it with the back of her fork and make green and white gunge ooze through the tines. She reminded herself that she was a grown-up and resisted the urge.

'So your scrote didn't want to stab Damon Blundy, but he *did* want to kill him with a knife,' she said. 'He also wanted to write big red words on the wall – and because he didn't stab Blundy, he couldn't use his blood. He had to inconvenience himself by bringing paint and a brush. The whole murder scene's screaming, "I could so easily have stabbed him, I prepared for a stabbing, a stabbing would have created all the conditions I wanted, but I *didn't* stab. I killed him with a knife, but not in the obvious way." Ow!' Charlie yelped as Simon grabbed her hand with both of his.

'That's it,' he said, his eyes shining as if someone had turned up a brightness dial inside his head. 'He didn't stab, but Blundy's *no less dead* than if he had.'

'Yes, but it's more than that,' said Charlie, wanting to check Simon hadn't missed what she thought was her best point. 'It's not only "I didn't stab him, but he's no less dead than if I had." It's "I didn't use the knife in the way knives are meant to be used, but the end result is the same." It's about knife use specifically – a knife not being used in the way that it normally is. I'd say the killer wants you to focus on two questions: why was he so keen to use a knife to kill Blundy, and why was he determined to use it so . . . unconventionally?'

Simon's phone had started to vibrate on the table, but he was busy mouthing something to himself silently and didn't notice. Charlie picked it up with her free hand. 'Hello?'

'Oh.' A surprised-sounding woman's voice. 'I was hoping to speak to DC Simon Waterhouse.'

'I'll pass you over. Who's calling?'

'Gemma Dobson. I'm Paula Riddiough's PA.'

'Hold on a second.'

Charlie waved the phone in front of Simon's face. He swatted it away as if it were an insect, then did a double take and grabbed it. 'Hello? Hello? . . . Yes. Thanks for getting back to me.'

Gemma Dobson's voice was loud enough to be audible across the table, but only as a noise – no identifiable words, which was frustrating. 'Pen,' Simon mouthed. Charlie fished in her handbag, pulled out a biro and handed it to him, then went back in for a scrap of paper. She knew there were lots in there, but they'd all gone into hiding; everything Charlie's fingers touched was hard and three-dimensional. She couldn't imagine what all these objects were that she carried around with her every day, and when she peered in, she could make out very little. This was the worst bag she'd ever owned. It was far too big – like a network of pitch-black subterranean caves with a smart leather exterior and a shoulder strap. By the time she'd found a suitable receipt for Simon to scribble on, it was too late: he'd already started to make notes on his non-disposable cloth napkin.

He'd written, '26 October 2011, 10.30 a.m., Rose Lounge, Sofitel St James Hotel, London.' Then, underneath, '11 November 2011.' Charlie watched, waiting for him to write down a time to go with the second date, but the pen hovered in mid-air.

'Really?' he asked Gemma Dobson. 'You're sure? Not eleven or eleven thirty? . . . Right . . . No, I'm not doubting you.

Thank you. You've been helpful.' Simon tried to stuff his phone into his inside jacket pocket and missed. It fell to the floor. He bent to pick it up. 'I knew it,' he said to Charlie. 'Six ones. Not one hundred and eleven thousand one hundred and eleven, but 11 November 2011. Paula Riddiough and Damon Blundy met twice, according to her assistant. The second time was on eleven eleven eleven. So that's Blundy's computer password explained: Riddy111111.'

'I see,' said Charlie. 'Must have been a significant meeting for him, are you thinking? If he used it as his password?'

'Yeah, and Blundy knew it was going to be significant.'

'You mean he picked that as his password before 11 November 2011 – when the date was arranged but before it had happened?'

Simon smiled. 'No. I don't know how long it's been his password.'

'Then—'

'How do I know Blundy knew his three-elevens appointment with Riddiough was going to matter to him before it had happened?'

Charlie waited. Tried not to mind being toyed with.

'Guess what time they arranged to meet?' said Simon.

Not eleven or eleven thirty? he'd said to Gemma Dobson. There was only one way in which the time could possibly be significant . . . 'If you're asking me to pull something else out of thin air that's probably going to be wrong . . . my guess is eleven minutes past eleven,' said Charlie.

'Spot on. What does that tell you?'

'Obvious, isn't it? It must have occurred to Blundy, or Paula Priv, or both of them, that they were meeting on the eleventh day of the eleventh month of 2011. What could be more fitting than to meet at eleven minutes past eleven? They probably thought it was funny: five elevens instead of three. Except . . .'

It was Simon's turn to wait. Impatiently. 'Go on,' he said.

'Well, why are they arranging to meet in an in-joke kind of way when they're supposed to be enemies?' said Charlie. 'He's a demolition-job columnist who's invented a nasty nickname for her—'

'And called her the UK's worst mother more than once.'

Charlie shook her head. 'Doesn't make sense,' she said. 'If you were meeting an enemy on 11 November 2011, you'd meet them at half ten, or eleven. You wouldn't say, "Tee hee, let's meet at eleven minutes past eleven." It's too . . . cosy.'

'Let's say you were meeting Liv,' said Simon.

'No. No, let's not, please.'

'All right, Stacey Sellers or Debbie Gibbs.'

'Thanks for giving me such a sparkling fantasy social life,' Charlie said sarcastically.

'If it was 11 November 2011 that you were planning to meet, would you suggest meeting at eleven minutes past eleven?' Simon asked.

'No.'

'And if they suggested it?'

'I'd think it was weird. Unless it was . . .' Charlie stopped. 'It's flirty, isn't it? In a purely platonic relationship, you wouldn't suggest it. Would you?'

'I don't think so. I agree.' Simon looked pleased. 'Also, you wouldn't choose the date you met a purely platonic friend as the password for your laptop.'

'So he was cheating on his wife, having an affair with a hot MP,' said Charlie. 'I guess that explains why he moved to Spilling. He used to live in London, didn't he? I remember reading his column about moving – he said he'd had a dream about moving to the Culver Valley and being set upon by sexy women, and he had to try and make it come true. Sounds like his wife's got an ample motive for murder,' Charlie summed up.

'He wasn't married to her when he wrote that,' said Simon. 'He and Hannah met on 29 November 2011 and got hitched in March 2012.'

'So . . . eighteen days after his second meeting with Paula

Priv, the one that was so important to him that he made it his password, he met the woman he went on to marry?' Charlie frowned. 'That's all very . . . quick. Perhaps his fling with Paula only lasted two weeks. Things can move fast in relationships, I suppose. Not ours, obviously, but I've heard of speedy romantic developments happening to other people.'

'I need to talk to Paula Riddiough.' Simon stood up. 'She lied to me. When I spoke to her on the phone earlier, she said she'd met Blundy twice but couldn't remember the exact dates, but you wouldn't forget agreeing to meet on 11 November 2011 at eleven minutes past eleven, would you?'

'I don't think so, no.'

'When she pointed me in the direction of her assistant, she knew what I was going to find out. I reckon she was throwing me a hint deliberately. Toying with me. She wants me to come after her for the real story. She must do.'

'Of course she does.' Charlie laughed. 'If there's one thing about Paula Privilege that's beyond doubt, it's that she loves being pursued by men. You need to be prepared to suspect her in a different way from what you're used to.'

'How do you mean?'

'She might act like someone with a guilty secret just to reel you in and keep you focused on her. Course, I don't know her personally, but . . .'

'You really think she'd act like a possible murderer in order to get a bit more attention? Most people—'

'Paula Privilege and most people are light years apart,' said Charlie. 'And if that's not apparent the second you meet her, then it's not the real her that you've met.'

'The person you're describing sounds like a potential killer,' said Simon.

Charlie thought about it. 'Yes,' she said eventually. 'I wouldn't rule that out either.'

~

'She asked me if I wanted to go back to her place,' said Sellers. 'That was all she said: her place. We were in a bar – I assumed her place was a house, a flat . . . somewhere normal.' He sighed and shook his head.

'You don't have to tell me if you don't want to,' said Gibbs, keen to hear what was coming next. Being with Liv had made him more curious about other people than he used to be.

He and Sellers were in the Brown Cow, which was busier than usual. Gibbs had noticed that it tended to be packed and noisy whenever he needed to concentrate on an important conversation, and silent and empty whenever he was keen to avoid one. Place should change its name to the Sod's Law, he thought.

'I'll tell you, and you can tell Liv – and then can you get her off my back?' said Sellers. 'She's emailed me twice on my work email, asking me how I am and if I've got any news. I barely know her!'

Gibbs smiled. He found it hard to be angry with Liv, even when he knew he probably ought to be. 'She thinks you should talk to someone about it, whatever it is,' he said. 'And thanks to her, you are.'

'Just ask her to leave me alone, all right?'

Gibbs nodded. 'So . . . this woman invited you back to her place, and . . . ?'

Sellers took a long sip of his pint, then mumbled something inaudible.

'What?'

'It was a refuge, all right? Her "place" turned out to be a fucking . . . refuge for battered women.'

'"All right, love, wipe yourself . . ."'

'Will you shut the fuck up? It's not funny. It wasn't then and it isn't now.'

'So . . . what happened?' Gibbs asked.

Sellers looked away.

'Don't tell me you went in there and did her anyway?' Of

course he had. Sellers, on the promise of a shag, would stop at nothing. 'I hope she had her own room at least.'

'Yeah. Own room.' Sellers sighed. 'I thought it was OK, you know? She seemed to like me; she'd invited me there – I hadn't pushed it at all. And at first it *was* all right. The sex was decent. It was a bit odd being in a refuge, but a place is just a place, right?'

'Something went wrong?' Gibbs guessed.

'You could say that. Afterwards, when I tried to leave . . . she had a major freak-out. Suddenly, I was a shit who'd used her, just like all the others. I don't know what she expected, how long she wanted me to stay, but I had to get home. I'd told her I was married, hadn't promised her anything. I thought it was just a bit of fun. She started hitting me, punching me in the face and in the stomach. I had to hold her wrists to stop her. It was a nightmare.'

'You were in a battered women's refuge, mate. What did you expect?'

'Yeah, a *battered* women's refuge!' Sellers said indignantly. 'I didn't expect to get battered in there, *by* a woman!'

'You didn't tell her your name, did you? Or your job?'

'I'm not that stupid. I was just Colin, no surname, electrician.'

'So you *did* tell her your name.' Sellers was a giver by nature; that was his problem: too generous-spirited, too talkative. 'What happened? Did you manage to calm her down?'

'Yeah. She wasn't happy about me leaving, but she agreed to let me go without trying to kill me. I couldn't talk her out of thinking I was a shit, though.' Sellers turned to Gibbs. 'I'm not a shit, am I?'

'No.'

They drank their pints in silence.

'That wasn't the end of it,' Sellers said once he'd finished his drink.

Gibbs groaned. 'Don't tell me you went back for more?'

'No. Wouldn't go back there if you paid me. But . . . it was horrible. Leaves a bad taste, having something like that happen. It's never happened to me before. I didn't want to go home feeling like crap, so I . . . well, I tried again. Not with the same woman.'

Gibbs shook his head in despair. 'Let me guess: you went back to the bar, picked up another woman who turned out to be even more psycho?'

'I didn't go back to the bar,' Sellers corrected him. 'I wish I had. As I was leaving the refuge, I bumped into someone. A young woman, really pretty. One of the other residents. She was in the kitchen. I walked past. We got chatting.'

'You don't learn, do you?' said Gibbs. Then he thought about his own situation. 'Don't s'pose any of us do,' he said.

'I thought she liked me, and I just . . . I wanted to end the night on a high note. So I started flirting with her. Nothing too direct – I didn't proposition her or anything, I was just seeing how far she'd let the flirty banter go, but . . . suddenly she turned really cold. Said if I didn't fuck off, she'd "press the alarm". I tried to explain that I didn't mean any harm and she started yelling in my face. Told me to go fuck a hornets' nest and die.'

'That's . . . extreme.' Gibbs stored the insult away for future use. It was a good one.

'All in all, one of the worst nights of my life.'

'When was this?'

'Weekend before last. I know I should forget it, get on with my life, but it's shaken me up. I don't feel the way I used to. Couple of nights ago, I was at the supermarket and I saw this gorgeous woman, on her own. I was on my own . . . I didn't go anywhere near her. Couldn't do it. Anyway . . . enough about me and my sad life. Have you taken the plunge yet?'

Gibbs raised his eyebrows as his heart started to beat faster. 'You mean . . . ?'

'Not the *plunge* plunge, not the big one. I meant have you told Simon and Charlie?'

'Not yet. Liv was going to meet Charlie for a drink later and tell her, but then I had a message from her saying she'd changed her mind. So now we've moved to Plan B.'

'Which is?' Sellers asked.

'A relief,' said Gibbs. 'Let's face it, Charlie and Simon were always going to hate Plan A, weren't they? I always thought telling them was a crazy idea.'

'So what's Plan B?'

Gibbs was prevented from answering by the sudden appearance of PC Robbie Meakin, looking irritatingly cheerful as always.

'All right, Robbie,' said Sellers. 'How goes it? Get us a round in, will you?'

'Yeah, all right, then. What you having?'

'Pint of Landlord.'

'Same,' said Gibbs.

Instead of heading for the bar, Meakin answered the first question Sellers had asked him. 'I'm knackered, but I think that's a permanent state once you've got kids, isn't it? How are you doing on the Blundy case? The man that every citizen of the UK expressed a desire to kill at one time or another.'

'It's going OK.' Sellers looked at the bar.

'Good. Glad to hear it.' Meakin seemed to be waiting for something. Did he want money to buy the drinks? Gibbs wondered. *Cheap bastard.*

'That silver Audi you mentioned – the one that turned round and sped away?' said Sellers. 'Turns out the driver took a suspicious interest in Elmhirst Road, not just once but lots of times throughout the day. It's all on CCTV, the incident you described and several others: driving past Elmhirst Road multiple times, slowing down to have a look. The driver denies having a particular interest in Damon Blundy, but we don't believe her, so we've got something to work on there.'

'Right. That's . . . great.'

Gibbs was puzzled by the anxiety in Meakin's voice. 'You OK, Rob?' he asked.

'Yeah, fine. When you say several times . . . I only saw that car once. Definitely just once.'

'Driver's a mother of two, had to go back and forth to her kids' school a few times that day,' Sellers told him. 'Elmhirst Road's her direct route. After the U-turn you saw, she didn't risk getting so close again, but she had to drive past the bottom of Elmhirst to get to the school even going the long way. Each time, she slowed down and had a nosey in the direction of the Blundy house.'

'It might not have been the house; it might have been . . .' Meakin stopped and shook his head. His pale freckled skin had turned red. 'Forget it,' he said. 'Two pints of Landlord, yeah?'

'Hang on,' said Gibbs. 'If there's something you've not told us, spit it out. This is a murder case. You were first at the scene. You saw what some sick fuck did to Blundy. Just because the victim was Damon Blundy doesn't mean—'

'Course it doesn't.' Meakin's eyes widened. 'That's what I've been saying since it happened. I had to have a word with a few smart-arses in the canteen this morning. They were saying Blundy had been asking for it for years. First time I've heard that said about a white, middle-class, famous male murder victim. I'm all for equality, but . . . let's be equal by condemning all murderers, not all victims.'

'Right,' said Gibbs.

Meakin sat down again. 'Tell you the truth, I liked Blundy's columns. Don't tell anyone I said that, especially not my wife. She reckons he was a bastard who hated women, but . . . well, he said things I'd never dare say, and that's always good to read, isn't it? He wasn't scared of anything or anyone.'

'That didn't work out so well for him, did it?' said Sellers.

'What's the deal with the silver Audi?' Gibbs asked Meakin.

'All right, look, I'm absolutely sure this has got *nothing* to do with Blundy's murder,' said Meakin, his face still red. 'I'm going to feel horrible for telling you, and I still think I should probably keep it to myself, but . . . like you say, it's a murder case. The driver of the Audi that turned round, Nicki Clements—'

'How do you know her name?' Sellers asked.

'I've met her before.'

'Shagged her?'

'No. Definitely not.' Meakin looked alarmed.

'In a battered women's refuge,' Gibbs murmured so that only Sellers would hear.

'Have you interviewed her?' Meakin asked. 'What did she say about why she did a U-turn?'

Sellers relayed the story of the missing wing mirror. 'We think it's a lie,' he said. 'It's true she had to go to her kids' school and back several times that day – we've verified that, and it's the only part of her story that's genuine. Elmhirst Road's the only sensible route to the school. By bypassing it, she added half an hour to each of her journeys. We don't believe for a second that her desire to avoid driving past Damon Blundy's house had anything to do with a mirror.'

'No, it didn't,' said Meakin. 'But it also had nothing to do with a murder. Her detours weren't about Blundy.' He sighed. 'I suppose at least once you know, you'll be able to rule her out as a murder suspect. That's some consolation.'

'Robbie, you're not making sense,' said Sellers. 'Do you have some reason for caring what happens to Nicki Clements?'

'I gave her my word I wouldn't tell anyone. I don't want to let her down, that's all. I felt sorry for her in the end.'

'Robbie, you're making no sense,' said Sellers. 'The end of what?'

'What were her detours about if not avoiding a murder scene?' Gibbs asked.

'Me,' said Meakin. 'She wanted to avoid me on Elmhirst Road on Monday. Nearly as much as I wanted to avoid her.'

IntimateLinks > uk > all personals
Reply: 21398733@indiv.intimatelinksUK.org
Posted: 2010-06-03, 23:10PM GMT

I Want a Secret

LOCATION: LONDON

I don't know why I'm doing this, or if anyone will read it. Nor do I know what I want specifically. So, that's helpful, isn't it?

Let me try to do better.

I'm new to this website. The first thing I did was look at the 'Men Seeking Women' section. I saw 'BBC 4 Lovers' in the subject heading of one man's advert and naïvely thought, 'Oh good, a cultured man. This isn't going to be nearly as sleazy as I imagined.' Then I opened the ad and was embarrassed and – yes, I'll admit it – a little shocked to discover that 'BBC 4' referred to a sexual organ of Afro-Caribbean origin being offered generously to any and all interested parties, and NOT to the TV channel that I like to watch. So – that tells you a bit about what kind of person I am, I hope!

I'm also married, with children, about to turn forty. I want something exciting in my life that no one else knows about. Not necessarily something sexual, not necessarily an affair, but definitely something I will need to keep secret from everyone in my life. Maybe even something a little bit dangerous.

I would love to hear from anyone who thinks he might like to be my secret. A man who, once he becomes my secret, won't allow me to keep any secrets from him. I want someone who would leave no stone unturned in his determination to find out every single secret thing there is to know about me. I promise I will reciprocate.

If you're the man I'm looking for, then I want to hear from you. And . . . if you also happen to like BBC4, the television channel, that would be great too! Maybe one day we could watch it together – in secret, of course!

- Location: London
- It's NOT OK to contact this poster with services or other commercial interests

Posted: 2010-06-03, 23:10PM GMT

5

Wednesday 3 July 2013

'I got *nothing*,' says Ethan bitterly. '*No* marks. Even though I definitely got four of the five questions right! I should have got eight out of ten. The last question wasn't even a question!'

'Yes, tragedy, tragedy,' Sophie drawls. 'Can you bloody well shut up about it now? I can't hear the TV.'

'Mum, Sophie just—'

'Yes, I heard her, Ethan. I'm standing right next to her chair. Sophie, don't say "bloody". It's a swear word.' I manage to recite my parental line of dialogue without fluffing it or sinking to the floor in a sobbing heap. I need Ethan and Sophie to be as easy and unobtrusive as possible for as long as there's a strange man following me and police officers suspect me of murder. Unfortunately, I can't explain this to them. I don't want to; I want to have as much energy as their petty little dramas and fights require of me, not to be so consumed by my own ongoing crisis that there's nothing left of me.

And so you're going to do . . . what? Just hate yourself as usual and continue to behave like a self-destructive idiot?

'You're wrong, Mum,' says Sophie. '"Bloody" is not a swear word. Neither is "Oh God". Alexis in my class, her mum won't let her say "Oh God". If she says it and her mum hears, she loses her computer privileges for a week.'

'I'm not bothered about "Oh God", but "bloody" *is* a swear word.'

'What about "damn"?' Ethan asks.

Oh God. 'Can we not debate rude words? Ethan, this test – if you got four out of five questions right, you'd have got some marks. If you got no marks, you can't have got any right.'

'I *did*,' he squeaks indignantly. 'One of them was, "What's your name?" I put, "Ethan Daniel Clements."'

'That *is* his name,' says Sophie, yawning.

'OK, there's some mistake or misunderstanding involved,' I say, relieved. 'After supper, you can show me the test and we'll sort it out. All right?' Ethan nods. I tick it off in my head: unhappy son, happier. Toast and juice delivered to lounge – already ticked off, eaten, drunk, sticky plastic tumblers and plates bearing crusts and crumbs on the floor. *Nearly free.* If I have to wait much longer to ring Kate Zilber, I'll explode. She was away all yesterday and today on some kind of training course for head teachers. I managed to persuade Izzie to pass on a message, and was told grudgingly at home-time this afternoon that I could ring Kate on her mobile anytime after 4.45 p.m.

I glance at my watch. Dead on a quarter to five. I don't care if I look too eager: I want to know the name of the man who's been following me. I haven't seen him in the playground since Monday, which is perhaps not surprising. Until I've spoken to Kate and heard whatever she can tell me about him, I won't know if I want to tell Adam or the police.

I pull the door closed as I leave the lounge and head for the phone furthest away from Sophie and Ethan's ears, the one in the box room. My right hand seems to start to sweat the moment I pull the scrap of paper with Kate's number on it out of my trouser pocket.

Two doors between me and the children now: one pulled to and one firmly closed. This is how habitual liars measure their safety: by the number of closed doors between them and their loved ones. 'Answer, answer,' I hiss as I listen to the rings, feeling helpless. I can't imagine that Kate Zilber has ever been as keen for someone to answer their phone as I am now.

'Hello?'

'Hi, Kate. It's Nicki Clements.'

'Hi, Nicki – Izzie said you'd probably ring. Is there a problem?'

'I don't know. Well, actually I do know.' I laugh awkwardly. 'Don't worry too much – I mean, nothing's happened yet, but . . . one of the dads from school has been following me. On Tuesday, he followed me all the way to London, where I used to live. Which means he must have followed me from my house to the train station and then on to a car-hire—'

'Whoa, whoa,' Kate silences me. 'Which dad? Most of them wouldn't have the gumption or the energy to follow the mother of another child. I'm almost impressed. Tell me everything, from the beginning.'

I do my best, aware of the inadequacy of my story. Until two days ago, I simply didn't notice him apart from in the school car park. He might have been following me for months, or he might have only started on Tuesday.

The day after Damon Blundy was murdered.

I describe him as accurately as I can: the kind of clothes he wears, his car, the streaks in his hair. 'I've always thought of him as Flash Dad,' I tell Kate.

'Can you describe his child or children?' she says quietly, after a short pause. 'Let me answer that question for you: you can't, can you? You've never seen him with his children.'

'No. Not that I've noticed. How did you know that?'

A longer pause. 'You say you've noticed this guy in the car park at morning drop-off and home-time a lot – going back a few months?'

'Yes. I can't remember when I first noticed him, but . . . yes, certainly a month or two.'

'Have you ever seen him talking to any of the other parents?'

'No, but that's not unusual for a school-gate dad,' I say. 'It's the mums that want to talk, generally. Lots of the dads keep their heads down and pray no one'll put them out by forcing them to have a conversation. Look, just tell me who he is,' I blurt out.

'I've no idea who he is,' Kate says.

'Then how did you know I'd never seen his kids? Why do you sound so worried, as if you've worked something out and you're wondering whether you should tell me or not? You should. This man *followed me to London*, to my brother's house!'

'OK, don't freak out. You will, but don't. The guy you described isn't a parent at Freeth Lane. I know every parent – more's the pity – and there's no dad with streaked hair and a blue Beemer. And before you ask, no, there are no mothers' boyfriends, male nannies . . . There's no one I can think of who fits that description, Nicki. No one associated with Freeth Lane.' Kate sighs. 'Which means . . . well, I'm sure I don't have to tell you.'

I want to protest – to say it's impossible, he must be a parent – but I'm interrupted by the door of the box room opening. Ethan walks in holding a piece of paper. 'My test,' he says. I press my finger against my lips to shush him. He mouths, 'Zero marks out of ten,' just in case I'd forgotten. I give him my best solemn nod, then steer him out onto the landing and close the door again. Sophie would never let me get away with ushering her out of the room so frantically. She'd have narrowed her eyes and said, 'All right, what's going on? And don't lie!'

'Nicki? You still there?'

All those days and weeks, leaning against his shiny blue car, looking like a bored dad, waiting. 'It was the perfect way to follow me, wasn't it?' I say. 'Pretend to be a parent, blend in with all the other parents. Hang around the school in full view, in a way that no one would unless they had a child there, or unless they were some . . . psychopath, so practised at following people that they know how to do it without arousing suspicion.'

'I'd have said professional, not psychopath, but . . . yeah. That's my conclusion too.'

'Professional?'

'A private detective of some kind,' says Kate. 'What's going on with you, Nicki? I've always thought you seemed far more interesting than any other school parent who's ever crossed my path. You must have an exciting life if someone's paying to have you followed! If I invite you round and bribe you with cocktails, will you tell me the full story?'

It's so tempting. The full story, though? Maybe not quite. But Kate doesn't need to know that. Thinking about it, I don't know the whole story myself. Assuming I decide I want to trust her with it, should I tell her only what I know for certain, or what I suspect as well? What do I know for sure? I can't think straight – haven't really been able to since I opened my front door to the police on Tuesday.

Analogies. Gavin said he loved my bizarre analogies, plural, but in my entire correspondence with him I only produced one: the vegan Barack Obama. I read all my emails to Gavin again last night to check.

King Edward, with whom I carried on a proper correspondence for more than two years, heard many of my analogies. The one he seemed to find most entertaining was the one about private tutors and bikes. I mentioned a parent at Sophie and Ethan's old school who'd hired a private tutor, and he said, 'What's the point in paying to send your kids to private school and then having to pay for a tutor on top of that?' I asked him if he thought it was all right for state-school children to have private tutors and he said yes, that made more sense: if he had children at a state school, he might hire them a tutor if they needed one, but not if they went to a private school. 'That's ridiculous,' I said. 'That's like saying if you have a car that was given to you as a present, it's OK to buy a bike, but if you've paid for your own car, then you mustn't buy a bike.'

A bizarre analogy, King Edward said. He used those same words. 'It's hilarious, and I'm not criticising you,' he said, 'but why not stick to the relevant subject?' I told him I find it hard to think clearly about certain situations unless I compare them to other similar things. Analogies help me to get my bearings. I said, 'If someone smacked me over the head with a hammer, I'd probably say, "How would you feel if I hit you in the stomach with a brick? Because that's just as bad and, in fact, exactly equivalent to what you've just done to me!"'

Just as bad . . . What? What alarm bell did those words just ring? Something I know so well that won't announce its presence in my mind, though I know it's there, waiting.

He is no less dead . . . A white-cold spark of terror jolts me. Then I go limp, as whatever fear it was that gripped me passes. For a fraction of a second, I knew what those words meant.

I didn't want to know. I pushed them out of sight. That was the jolt I experienced: my memory trying to toss the evidence away, like a . . .

I stop myself before I come up with another pointless analogy. I use them too often. Gavin – the man who calls himself Gavin – was right to use the plural.

When King Edward finally backed down and admitted I was right about the private-tutor thing, he said, 'I surrender. You win. When the war starts, can I be in your unit?' Gavin said the same thing to me in our latest exchange.

The horror is still sinking in, though I've known since Tuesday: Gavin is King Edward. There's no room for doubt. I have not had two cyber affairs with two different men; King Edward and Gavin are the same man. King Edward knew precisely what I'd be looking for after what he put me through – I was moronic enough to spell it out for him. He created the Gavin identity to attract me, and I fell into his trap. Until Tuesday, it didn't once cross my mind that, in Gavin, I had found King Edward under a different alias.

How could he do that to me? After nearly destroying me once . . .

Those horrible words – *He is no less dead* – are connected to King Edward somehow, I'm certain of it. My sudden pulse of terror that passed so quickly brought his name with it – his false name. The knowledge is there, like something dark swelling inside me. I can feel the answer tapping at the back of my brain, trying to get in.

Did King Edward murder Damon Blundy? I know he was aware of him, perhaps even obsessed by him . . .

'Nicki?' Kate Zilber's insistent voice drags me out of my morbid thoughts. 'Have you gone into a tunnel? Have *I* gone into a tunnel?'

'Sorry,' I say, trying to pull myself together. 'Yes, I . . . I could do with talking to someone,' I say. 'When are you free?'

'How about tomorrow night?'

'That should be OK . . . Kate, I'm going to have to go. That beeping noise means I've got another call.'

'OK, let's confirm at school tomorrow. Meantime, if I see Streaky Boy, I'll rugby-tackle him to the ground.'

I almost smile as I press the 'line 2' button. Kate's not worried, not any more. Though she sounded all portentous at first.

Because she thought Flash Dad was a Freeth Lane parent and therefore her problem? No, that's unfair. She was probably just trying to make me feel better by treating it all as entertainment and nothing to be scared of. She succeeded. I didn't see Flash Not-Dad today. Maybe I've scared him away.

'Hello?' I say, on line 2, shivering.

No response. Silence. Then a breath.

'King Edward?' I whisper.

~

If Melissa and Lee hadn't decided to fall in love, if Melissa hadn't told me she didn't want me to tell her my secrets any more, I would never have looked at the Intimate Links website. I looked – there, and on Craigslist, and Forbidden Fruit, and several other similar websites – because I felt as if something important had been ripped out of my life. I wanted a replacement for the person who'd been my best friend since the first day of secondary school – someone I could confide in no matter what stupid thing I'd done. I'd never heard of any New Best Friend websites, but I knew there were sites for those seeking new lovers, and I soon found plenty of them. I chose Intimate

Links because, aesthetically, it was my favourite. It had a better look than the other sites.

I called my advert 'I Want a Secret'. I wrote it quickly, off the cuff, and posted it not really expecting any decent replies. Indecent ones flooded in, from people who couldn't spell and seemed incapable of writing more than a line or two. I deleted them all. Then, after about four days, I got a reply that sparked my interest, from a man calling himself King Edward VII. We began a correspondence, and within a week I was completely hooked on him. By email we discussed all kinds of things: our mutual love of secrecy – we talked about that a lot, and the possible reasons for it. We listed our favourite everything: books, films, songs, animals, cities, countries, wine, colour, words, food. Then we moved on to our least favourite.

Once, we spent days going back and forth on the subject of Clark Kent and Superman. King Edward asked me, out of the blue, whether Superman was always still Clark Kent on some level, even while in Superman mode, or whether he completely ceased to be Clark Kent when he became Superman. I was firmly of the view that he never entirely lost his Clark Kent identity, even with his magic cape on, and King Edward drew all sorts of far-fetched conclusions about my character from this one opinion.

Conversations with him, on any topic, glimmered with unpredictability. He was more interested in the contents of my mind than anyone has ever been, before or since – totally absorbed in me. He wanted to know absolutely every detail about everything and everyone I mentioned. He had fascinating, unpredictable views on whatever topic came up, and he wrote really well: long, thoughtful emails. I had the impression that he was devoting all his attention to me, to the point of neglecting the rest of his life. After a while, he said he was curious to know more about me, and to know what I looked like, so I told him as much as I could without revealing my identity. He said he was falling in love with me – more strongly than he'd ever fallen for anyone before. I sent him a head-and-shoulders photo of myself. He replied saying he wouldn't have minded whatever I looked like but that he was glad I was as beautiful as my emails. I loved that – the idea that my emails were attractive.

At that point, our correspondence became overtly romantic. We started to write to each other more erotically – nothing too graphic, but we talked a lot about love. And even when we tried to talk about other things, it always came back to love. He'd become my significant other: the only person in the world that I wanted to share anything with. I'd never experienced such an intense connection before. I was living with Adam, Sophie and Ethan, but there was no doubt that King Edward had taken over as my 'significant other'. I couldn't wait to get away from my family, any chance I got, so that I could read his latest email and reply to it.

We discussed the possibility of meeting, but by the time we got round to discussing it, I was terrified of putting it into practice. He admitted he was too. What we had seemed so perfect; we both feared we'd endanger it if we subjected it to the reality test. So we continued with the emailing – which was passionate and amazing and didn't really feel like 'not enough' in any way – for several more months.

I became discontented before King Edward did. In July 2011, after I'd known him just over a year and with only his emails and my fantasies to represent his presence in my life, I started to crave real-world physical contact with him, and I told him so. I was scared things might start to become a little less urgent and exciting between us if we didn't take them to the next level soon. King Edward said he felt the same, but that, having seen a photo of me and knowing how stunning I was, he'd be too scared of rejection to meet me in person. He said he wasn't anywhere near as good-looking for a man as I was for a woman. I told him, truthfully, that I honestly couldn't care less what he looked like. I've never fancied men for their looks – it's always their attitudes, and personalities, and I knew I loved King

Edward's. To me, the idea of me rejecting him in person was unthinkable, to the point where I couldn't quite understand why he was so worried about it.

I asked if we could maybe speak on the phone. He said no; he didn't want me to hear his voice. He didn't like his voice, he said.

One day, an anonymous parcel arrived for me. It was a copy of what he'd told me was his favourite book – *Naked Lunch* by William S. Burroughs. In it he'd written, 'For Nicki – we must have naked lunch together one day. KE7 x'. I was touched but scared. I told him not to send anything to the house again. He never did.

The lack of real-world physical contact wasn't the only thing that bothered me; I was starting to feel that a weird inequality was undermining our closeness. King Edward knew almost everything about me, past and present, but he didn't seem nearly so willing to discuss himself and his life or past. He would write at length about his feelings and his ideas – so it wasn't as if he was ungenerously refusing to share himself with me – but I started to have this sense of him as a soul that was kind of detached from any sort of reality. He revealed the bare-minimum details about his life, whereas he knew almost as much about mine as I did.

I tried to explain to him that I felt there was an imbalance between us. He was horrified to think he might have done anything to offend me, and I did my best to make it clear that I wasn't offended, but that I felt he was keeping secrets from me, rather than with me. I asked him if he'd send me a photo, or tell me his first name at least, since he'd known my full name for a while, as well as the names of my husband and children. He said I had every right to ask, and apologised for his fears and his caginess. He kept saying, 'Just give me a bit longer to get my head round it. I just need another few days. It's a big step.'

I tried to be patient. I was in no doubt that he loved me

– that helped. Adam loved me too, but he wasn't obsessed in the way King Edward quite clearly was. Adam has never been obsessed with me in that way. He's more of a stable, low-key kind of person, not one to go over the top emotionally about anything. King Edward was the opposite. He wrote more than once that he would die for me without a second thought. I know I should have been firmer with him and insisted on seeing a photo and knowing his name, but I was bowled over by him in every way. His obvious hunger for me – limited though it was – had obliterated all my defences.

Of course, he could have sent me any photo, couldn't he? He could have told me any name. And, eventually, he did.

I was thrilled and relieved when, in October 2011, he finally said he'd decided he wanted to be more open with me. He'd hidden his identity, he told me, because he was famous. He was someone I would know of, someone I might not have entirely positive feelings about. It was this, he confessed, rather than any worries about his looks, that had made him reluctant to allow me any closer. I teased him, saying things like 'Are you a famous mass murderer?' and 'Are you George Osborne?' No, he said, he was none of those, but he was as unpopular in certain quarters 'as George Osborne at a Socialist Worker Party rally'. After a bit more cat-and-mouse teasing of this sort, he finally told me: he was Damon Blundy, *Daily Herald* columnist – loudmouth, rabble-rouser, troublemaker.

I'd read one or two of Damon Blundy's columns in the past, and I certainly didn't hate him. I didn't have any opinion about him. I'd always assumed that most newspaper columnists say any old thing that comes into their heads to provoke a bit of controversy, whether they really believe it or not.

As soon as King Edward revealed that he was Damon Blundy, I did my homework, and very soon it was Damon I was in love with. Or rather, it was both Damon Blundy *and* King Edward, except in my mind I'd joined them up to make one person: a man I now knew was absolutely gorgeous, apart from anything else. This new knowledge re-energised my correspondence with King Edward. Since he'd told me who he was, I saw no reason why we shouldn't meet. So I asked him. And he refused.

Looking back, it's clear why he had to say no. King Edward wasn't Damon Blundy, and if we met, I would notice that he wasn't. Of course, he couldn't admit that was the reason, having lied about his identity, so he came up with some nonsense about not being able to live with himself if he cheated on his partner. I Googled him and could find nothing about any partner anywhere. He said they hadn't gone public yet. All this time, we were emailing constantly, with him telling me in great detail what I meant to him and how much he loved me. He'd become my whole world – I barely noticed Adam and the children when they passed me in the house. My real offline life was like a shadow around me that I couldn't see clearly. Deep down, I knew I ought to be worried about this, but I was too much in love with King Edward to care.

Then, in early December 2011, Damon Blundy wrote a column in which he mentioned getting engaged to a psychotherapist called Hannah. He'd never said explicitly, but I'd assumed he was already married, like me, and was gallantly not mentioning his wife in the way that I tried not to mention too often that I had a husband, even though he knew I did. I thought it was a courtesy thing – an unspoken agreement between us. I was shocked to the point of physical sickness to discover he was unmarried and at the beginning of an exciting new relationship with this Hannah person. I emailed him – King Edward – and demanded to know how he could have failed to mention to me that he was about to get married. He said he hadn't told me because he didn't want to upset me. I was already married to Adam, he said, so what was the big deal? I asked if he was really so naïve as to imagine that I wasn't an avid reader of his column. I'd started to make my own little contributions, in the comments sections. He claimed he never read the comments and therefore hadn't noticed.

Unbelievably, we managed to get past all this. I'd have forgiven him anything, I think, because he was so amazing in so many ways. He seemed to understand everything I said and felt in a way that no one else ever had. He was certainly more interested in me than anyone ever had been before. Every single issue or topic, he wanted to know what I thought about it, in detail. But he still wouldn't agree to meet.

And then one day he confessed to me that, crazy though he knew it was, he believed cheating in the flesh was much worse than cheating only via emails. He said he wasn't sure his moral code would allow him to go to the obvious next stage.

I laughed when I read that, before the anger took over. I just couldn't see it. We were spending all our days and evenings, pretty much, obsessively writing to one another. I'm amazed Adam didn't notice. A less secure, more needy husband would have done, I'm sure, but Adam was happy to spend most evenings watching TV in the lounge while I emailed King Edward from the computer upstairs, pretending to be on Facebook.

King Edward – Damon, as I thought at the time – admitted that his 'line in the sand' as he called it, was spurious and hypocritical, but he said he couldn't help the way he felt. Right or wrong, that was his 'code'. I couldn't reconcile the Damon I knew from our emails with the Damon Blundy I encountered in the *Daily Herald* – the one who said outrageous things on *Question Time*, like 'A high-speed rail link between Manchester and London would completely ruin the North-South Divide', and laughed when people booed him. Damon Blundy the famous columnist seemed to have no problem with adultery, and a huge problem with moral hypocrisy. He wasn't scared of anything, whereas the Damon I was emailing seemed to shrink nervously away every time I brashly suggested making our cyber affair a real-world affair.

I challenged King Edward about his apparently split personality. He said that Damon the columnist wasn't the real him, though he contained aspects of the real him. But mainly, Famous

Damon was a fictional character, designed to provoke and entertain. I believed this. It confirmed my assumptions about newspaper columnists.

King Edward's reluctance to meet went on and on. I went through several phases of reaction. I thought about ending it, breaking off email contact. I thought about turning up at his house unannounced to see how he'd react. Irate people he'd offended occasionally posted his address on Twitter and encouraged other people to join them in a vigilante mob on his doorstep, so I knew exactly where he lived, and considered doorstepping him – a lovesick vigilante mob of one.

Neither ending it nor gatecrashing Damon Blundy's life felt like a genuine possibility. I couldn't bear the thought of losing him. By email he was still being so loving and attentive, and, crude though it sounds, his words were still providing me with more sexual satisfaction than any man's physical touch ever had. He was the person I wanted to share everything with – stupid funny things that happened, annoying things.

Eventually, I resigned myself to never having a real physical relationship with him. I told myself I must think of it the same way I would if he were paralysed from the neck down, or in a high-security prison. I knew that it wasn't lack of enthusiasm that was preventing him from meeting me, and I did my best to make allowances.

Then, in August 2012, he wrote to me to say that his wife was going away for a week in February 2013, abroad, and that during this phase while she was away he might feel it was safe enough for us to meet. It would have to be somewhere nowhere near his home, he said. The whole email had a reverential urgency about it that made me love him even more. He suggested a hotel: the Chancery Hotel in Bloomsbury. Would I agree to spend that week with him there in February next year?

A whole week together . . .

I experienced almost superhuman levels of bliss. And the sudden burst of unexpected joy into my life inspired me to do something crazy: relocate my family from London to Spilling. Even if King Edward and I could only meet in person every couple of years, I wanted to be closer to him all the time. I asked him about it before suggesting it to Adam, and he agreed it was the best idea ever: he would feel so much happier also, he said, knowing I was close by.

He said this while pretending to be Damon Blundy.

I moved to Spilling in December last year on a cloud of euphoria, thinking that in February King Edward and I – Damon and I – would finally consummate our relationship. I'll never forget his email in response to mine saying, 'Hooray – we're in! I now live just a short drive away from you!' He wrote back immediately, saying he could feel my presence, and how it was going to enhance his life so much just knowing I was nearby, that Spilling had a new magic ingredient added to it now that I was there.

All lies. It wasn't Damon Blundy who wrote those words. I don't know where King Edward lives because I don't know who he is, but it's unlikely that he lives in Spilling, I think.

Our correspondence fizzed with new passion and energy for the rest of December and the first half of January, in anticipation of our prearranged week in February. And then, in late January, I got a two-line email from King Edward – the shortest one he'd ever sent me – saying, 'Nicki, I have to ask you something. If we do meet at the Chancery Hotel in February, will you be very disappointed if I can't make love to you?' I felt dizzy with horror when I read those words. Why was he saying 'if' when our week together was a firm arrangement we'd made, one that had been in the diary for months? I wrote back and asked what the hell he meant. He replied saying he might not be able to 'go too far' with me. *Go too far?* I thought. This was a grown man, for Christ's sake! What was wrong with him?

I should have told him to get lost and stop messing me around. I should have spotted that something was very much amiss. Nothing I was reading in King Edward's emails sounded anything like the confident, promiscuous Damon Blundy I was reading in the *Daily Herald* every week. I told myself the confident womaniser tone was a front, needed precisely because the real Damon was sexually timid and insecure.

I'd cure him of his shyness and his doubts, I told myself.

The day before we were due to meet at the Chancery, he emailed me and said, 'Nicki, I'm so sorry. I don't think I can go through with it.' I thought he was cancelling on me and I lost my cool. Not that I have much in the way of cool, in any situation ever; it's not my strong suit. I sent King Edward an outpouring of horrified hysteria by way of reply. He wrote back and said, 'Go to the Chancery as planned. Take your phone or a laptop so that we can keep in touch. I will do my very best to get myself there.'

I told Adam I was going on holiday with some old school friends – a reunion – and I went to London. Adam had to take the week off work. He didn't mind, but I felt sick with guilt every time I thought about him and the kids at home together, keeping each other company and being a normal happy family while I did what I was doing at the other end of the normality spectrum.

I sat in a characterless hotel room in Bloomsbury, containing a bed, a chair, a desk and a built-in wardrobe, and I waited. The first day and night, the second day and night, King Edward didn't come. We emailed each other constantly – him saying how guilty he felt knowing he was letting me down, what a useless coward he was; me saying he mustn't be too hard on himself, and please come, and if he doesn't want to be unfaithful to his wife, we can just talk. No, he said – he couldn't bear to be in the room with me and not touch me. Crazily, I suggested he book the room next door to mine, so that we wouldn't even need to see each other. We could talk on the phone, maybe, instead. I would have settled for anything – any tiny morsel that would have allowed me to feel that we were moving forward. I'd have settled for knowing that the man I loved was on the other side of a wall in the Chancery Hotel.

Yes, I do hate myself rather a lot – thanks for asking.

Halfway through my third day of sitting alone in an uninspiring red and grey hotel room, crying and never quite managing to muster sufficient dignity to draw a line under this ghastly experience and go home early, an email arrived from King Edward with the subject heading 'A possible plan'. My heart leaped sky-high. Everything might be OK, I thought; everything might be saved.

King Edward's plan was an odd one – one no sane woman would agree to, I'm sure. Luckily, he suggested it to the only deluded fool on the planet who was deranged enough to say yes. Which I did.

He said he'd thought of a way that would make it possible for him to come and meet me. We would agree a time in advance for the following day. I would, in the meantime, get hold of a blindfold. I would leave a key for him at reception, with instructions for the receptionist to give it to him when he arrived. At the agreed time, I would make sure I was in bed, wearing nothing but the blindfold. He would then let himself into the room. Neither of us would utter a single word throughout: no voices – this was very important to him. He would do what he wanted with me. (I was more surprised by this than by anything else, I think, because up until this point he had seemed so solicitous and caring about what I wanted.) With no words spoken, he would communicate his orders, using touch and movement only. I would obey those orders. I wasn't to remove the blindfold at any point. We would make love, and then he would let himself out of the room and leave, without my having seen him at all.

I agreed to all of it. Yes, it was strange, but I told myself it might be fun too. Erotic. I tried to think of it as a fun, kinky thing, not alarming craziness.

The arrangements were made.

I had no idea where to get a blindfold, so I went to Accessorize at King's Cross Station and bought a long black silky scarf that I could wind twice round my head.

The next day was the day we'd agreed to meet. He didn't let me down – not then, anyway. He arrived at the agreed time. I couldn't see anything because of the blindfold, and I desperately wished that I could see him, but not being able to was exciting too, in its own way. Maybe even more exciting. All my other senses were on overdrive. I breathed in the smell of him when he lay down next to me. Touching him, tasting him, feeling his bare skin against mine – I've never experienced anything like it, before or since. Which is what makes it so much worse, given what happened next: that he was my best ever.

I can't let myself think too much about that, or I start to go a bit crazy, and I'm crazy enough already.

He used his mouth and his fingers to give me so much pleasure, but I was aching to feel him inside me, and after several hours, I started to wonder when that would happen. I assumed he was working up to it – deliberately withholding what he knew I wanted for as long as possible, saving it up . . .

And then, without warning, it was all over. His skin was no longer touching mine. At all – not anywhere on my body. I heard the rustle of clothing, the metallic jingle of a belt buckle. I opened my mouth to speak and he clapped his hand over it, enforcing his no-talking rule. And then he left, slamming the door behind him.

Within fifteen minutes I was emailing him: 'What the hell happened then? Why did you run off?'

No reply.

I emailed over and over again, all evening, all night. Nothing.

The next morning, I wrote several more times. My emails became progressively more hysterical. In the *Daily Herald* that day, Damon Blundy pulverised supporters of abortion rights for women who were against the death penalty, and supporters of the death penalty who were anti-abortion – 'It's either acceptable to end a life for a truly excellent reason or it isn't' – but King Edward remained silent. In desperation, I nearly posted a comment in response to Damon's abortion/death-penalty rant, saying, 'Why the fuck are you ignoring me?' Thank God I didn't, since he wouldn't have had a clue who I was or what I was talking about.

I stayed in the Chancery Hotel for the full week, checking my Hushmail inbox every three seconds. King Edward didn't get in touch. I wept a lot. Then, when my time alone ran out, I went home and tried to pretend I was OK, though I was far from it. So many times I nearly collapsed in a sobbing heap on the floor. I told Adam I was feeling sick and that I was probably coming down with a bug. He believed me and was sympathetic. I felt like a repulsive zombie who had somehow infiltrated a lovely, respectable middle-class family.

Three days after I returned home, I got an email from King Edward – Damon, as I still believed he was, since by now he had been signing his emails 'Damon' for more than six months. He apologised for his silence. It was unforgiveable, he knew. The reason for it was guilt. I wrote him back a long email explaining why he mustn't feel guilty – true love was true love and should never be denied, all that kind of rubbish.

His response came straight away. 'You don't understand,' he'd written. 'The man you were with at the Chancery Hotel, the one who drove you wild for hours and then disappeared without warning – it wasn't me, or anyone you know. He was a stranger.'

~

'Nicki, it's Mum. Who's King Edward?'

Involuntarily, my hands clench. Did I really pick up the phone and whisper his name out loud? *Get a fucking grip, Nicki.* 'Oh, I'm just looking at Ethan's history homework,' I say, glancing down at the failed test on the table in front of me. I must make time to read it, take it in, take it seriously. Soon. 'Mum, I'll have to ring you later,' I say. 'I'm bursting for the loo.'

'Ring me straight back, please,' she says. 'It's important.'

'Is something wrong? You sound . . .' She sounds the way Kate

Zilber sounded when I first told her I was being followed, the way I don't want anyone ever to sound when they speak to me. Nothing horrifies me more than that *Please sit down because I have some very bad news* tone. *Please follow me to that room over there in which something deeply unpleasant will happen.* It's never as bad once you find out what the thing is. I'd far rather someone screamed, 'A nuclear war's just started!' in my face, without warning. Why add a layer of pre-suffering suffering?

'Do you want to have the discussion now, or do you want to ring me back?' asks my mother.

'I'll call you in five minutes,' I say. As soon as I'm off the phone, I run to Adam's and my bedroom and get my three tiny glass angels out of my bedroom drawer. It's an embarrassing superstition that I have, one I can't seem to shake off: if I'm going to be speaking to or seeing either or both of my parents, I need to have the angels with me – in a pocket, in my sock, somewhere. They're my lucky charm. No one knows about them, not even Adam or Melissa.

Once they're safely in my trouser pocket, I go back to the box room and ring Mum, feeling adequately armed. That doesn't mean she won't wound me, but it will prevent the wound from being fatal.

'What's so urgent?' I ask her.

'Did you kill this Damon Blundy man?' she asks without preamble. 'Were you having an affair with him?'

I feel like a fisherman who, after an agonisingly long wait, has caught a large, rare fish. There's something satisfying about getting proof – yet more proof – that I'm right not to trust my mother, right to believe she doesn't and never has had my best interests at heart. Ideally, she would indicate that she thinks I'm bound to have murdered someone every time I spoke to her; that would save me the hassle of wondering, periodically, if she might not be quite as monstrous as my father.

'I definitely didn't kill Damon Blundy, but thanks for thinking of me,' I say. 'As for an affair, that's none of your business.'

'It's the police's business, since he's been killed,' Mum says. 'And . . . Dad and Lee say, and they're right, that it needs to be Adam's business too. You're the mother of his children, with them every day, their main carer. Adam needs to know the truth about you. We're not happy about any of this, but you've left us with no choice. You've gone too far this time, Nicki.'

She thinks I did it. She really thinks I killed him. I didn't, but I feel a cold, hard pride all the same.

'No, you've gone too far,' I correct her unemotionally. It's not an act. In the presence of my parents and Lee, my feelings do a runner. I couldn't cry or get angry now if I tried. I'm an android, specialising in sarcastic put-downs. 'By the way, the gone-too-far-this-time line would have had more impact if you hadn't been saying it to me since I was a toddler.'

'Put Adam on the phone. Or do you want me to drive round there?'

I manage to force out a laugh. 'So, wait, let's see if I've got this right: Dad and Lee have decided to bring me to justice, appointed you as the messenger, and the message is that you've all snitched on me to the police? And you're going to share your inventive theory with Adam too?'

'There's no point lying any longer, Nicki. Melissa's told us everything.'

'Everything and more, by the sound of it, since me killing Damon Blundy isn't part of everything. Nor is me having an affair with him. And feel free to tell Adam whatever you want, but there's nothing about me he doesn't know, as of yesterday. After my interview with the police . . . I assume Melissa told you all about that?'

'She did, yes. She's worried about you. We all are.'

'Thanks. I'm touched.'

'Melissa, as your best friend—'

'Best friend?' I laugh. 'Yes, a best friend containing a Trojan horse containing a worst enemy – that kind of best friend. It was talking to her yesterday that made me decide to tell Adam everything. I had a feeling that some unwarranted suspicion of murder and a huge betrayal might be just round the corner. I didn't want anyone holding me to ransom, so I told him all my secrets. Which, I'm afraid, means I've spoiled your fun. You can always tell him anyway if you want? I can ask him to pretend he doesn't already know.'

I'm going to have to tell Adam, now that I've called Mum's bluff. Confess all my sins. I will worry about that once I get her off the phone.

Some of my sins. I don't have to tell Adam everything.

Thankfully, Melissa knows nothing about King Edward and the Chancery Hotel.

'I even told Adam whether I did or didn't kill Damon Blundy,' I say childishly.

'You just told me you didn't kill him,' says Mum. 'Are you admitting you did now?'

'No. I'm saying I told Adam the truth about whether I did or didn't.'

'And you told me a lie?'

'No. I told you the truth too.'

'This isn't a game, Nicki.'

But everything must be a game, mustn't it? Or else it's all too much to bear. Everything is a game and I have to win.

'Have you and Dad hired a man with streaked hair to follow me?' I ask. 'Or has Lee?'

'What man with streaked hair?'

'I've no idea. That's why I'm asking you. A man's been following me.'

'You'll probably end up in bed with him,' says Mum. It's the first flare-up of anger I've heard in her voice since the beginning of the conversation.

'No, he runs away when I turn round,' I say. 'Perhaps it's a weird kind of sexual "What's-the-Time-Mister-Wolf?" role-play game?'

'What did Adam say when you told him about your various

one-night stands and your long-running affair with Damon Blundy?' Mum asks.

'He said, "I'll forgive you all your sins, but only if you take me on a no-expense-spared snowboarding holiday in the French Alps." No, he didn't really. I'm kidding. And I had no long-running or indeed short-running affair with Damon Blundy. I thought you believed in honesty – doesn't it bother you to make up a pack of lies about me and keep putting it forward as the truth?'

'What did Adam say, Nicki? When you told him about your many infidelities?'

Many? Melissa only knows about two since I got together with Adam. Add to those my fictional affair with Damon Blundy: three. Hardly 'many'. Mum needs to get out more. Actually, given that she lives with Dad, she needs to get out permanently. If she'd been braver as a young woman and allowed herself to see him for what he is and act on it, there might have been some hope for her.

'It's none of your fucking business what Adam said. Generally, I tend not to discuss my private life with people who inform on me to the police when I'm innocent.'

I hang up and sit still in my chair, waiting for my feelings to catch up with what's just happened. It will take a while. I must make the most of this numb time to get as much done as possible. *Preparations.*

Will Adam ask for a divorce? Is this the true beginning of my life falling apart?

I must do whatever it takes to extricate myself from being suspected of murder. If that means telling the police my real reason for making a quick getaway on Elmhirst Road on Monday, so be it. I'm not a coward like my mother. I'll do what I have to do.

I pick up the phone and ring Adam at work. When he answers, I say, 'I need you to come home.'

~

An hour later, Adam and I are in our bedroom with the door closed. Downstairs, the TV reassures our children by producing its usual comforting early evening burble of voices. Sophie and Ethan have no idea that they might soon need more comforting than usual. Hopefully, if I handle this right, they will never find out how close they came to having their world shattered.

'So . . . what is this?' Adam asks. 'Don't tell me you've dragged me home from work to show me three coloured glass angels?'

I've laid them out in a neat row on the bed. The duvet's plain white and they stand out nicely. 'I need to tell you something you're not going to like at all,' I say to Adam. 'But first I want to tell you a story about when I was a child, and I want you to tell me what you think about that story.' Without waiting for his agreement, I start to tell him.

I stole the three angels from my playgroup when I was four years old. One is pink, one green and one yellow.

Aged four, I didn't realise I'd stolen them. I simply saw them in the toy tin at playgroup, loved the way they looked and decided to take them home with me. When I showed them to Mum, excited about my haul, she didn't say a word, but she looked at them as if they were capsules containing ricin. She went to get Dad, who bellowed at me until long after it got dark – about serious crimes and punishment and bad people getting their hands chopped off.

The next day, Mum stood over me at playgroup while I recited the apology she and Dad had made me learn by heart and practise in front of them several times over breakfast. It contained none of my own words. Neither of them had smiled at me even once since my semi-accidental confession the day before; both were still as angry as they'd been at the moment of discovery.

I returned the angels to the tin, and did an excellent job of pretending I didn't care. Inside, I was screaming, *But I need them!* By this point, I'd decided that I preferred the three angels to my parents. The woman who ran the playgroup kept telling my mum that it wasn't important, and Mum kept contradicting her and saying that it was. After Mum had gone home, the nice playgroup owner said I could have the angels as a present, since I liked them so much. I remember thanking her, and thinking, You've no idea, have you? There's no way I could ever take them home and let my parents see them, no matter what story I tell them – not even if they're accompanied by a letter from you insisting that you want me to have them and that it was your initiative, not mine.

Being four, I didn't phrase it to myself quite like that, but I understood the impossibility of taking the three beautiful angels home. I also understood that the kind playgroup woman didn't understand, which was even more distressing.

On the other hand, I had to have the angels. I had to risk it, even if something unimaginably terrible happened to me as a result. My liking for them had turned to deep love. I would have risked anything. So I said thank you and put them in my shoe. From that day until the day I left home, the day after my eighteenth birthday, I kept those angels safe in my parents' house. Mum and Dad never found out I had them. They still don't know. I often wonder if they'd recognise them if I pulled them out of a jacket pocket one day and said, 'Look.'

I tell Adam that I can't face seeing or speaking to my parents without having the angels hidden somewhere in my clothes. 'I've never told you before because I was scared you'd think I was crazy.'

Adam frowns. 'It *is* a bit weird, Nicki, you've got to admit. I bet there's no one else – I mean, not even one other person on the planet – who can only speak to their parents with secret angels concealed about their person.'

'I'm sure you're right,' I say. 'Any other comments on the story?'

'Um . . .' He looks caught out. 'Maybe you should try and find a way to *not* need the angels when you see your folks? Stupid superstitions like that – why keep them going? Why not choose to behave rationally instead?' Seeing my face, Adam changes tack and says, 'Though I suppose it's a harmless enough ritual, and if it makes you feel better . . . I'm not quite sure what you want me to say.' He frowns. 'Lovely of the kindergarten lady to let you keep them – very shrewd of her.'

'Why shrewd?' I ask.

'Well, she obviously twigged that your mum was guilt-tripping you above and beyond what the situation required. She felt sorry for you and probably thought being allowed to keep the angels would cheer you up.'

I can't be bothered to ask him any more questions. 'I've been unfaithful to you,' I say quickly, to have it over and done with. 'I need to tell you about it because it's connected to a murder investigation. I wouldn't have told you otherwise. I did it because there's something in me . . . I mean, it's nothing to do with you or our relationship. I'd have been unfaithful to anyone I was married to. I love you just as much as I always—' I stop with a gasp.

Just as much as . . .

He is no less dead. He is just as dead. The meanings are interchangeable.

I know what it means. Exactly what those words mean. And, though I still don't know who killed him, I know that Damon Blundy's death is my fault.

Mine and King Edward's.

Spontaneous Media Combustion

Damon Blundy, 1 November 2011, *Daily Herald Online*

What can I say? I was wrong. It happens sometimes, and when it does, I admit it. In an <u>exclusive interview</u> with the *Sunday Times*, Saint Paula of Privilege has finally revealed her true reason for sending her son Toby to a failing state school when she could easily have afforded to send him to an excellent private one. (Toby is mentioned by name in the feature, incidentally, and his photograph also appears; let's hope the boy has no yen for privacy.)

It seems that Paula wasn't, as I <u>once suggested</u>, motivated by the desire to score political points for a rotten cause at the expense of her only child's welfare and future. Nor was her decision, as I later <u>play-fully posited</u>, a passive aggressive one-in-the-eye for her aristocratic Tory parents who sent her, our very own Paula of the Proles, to an exclusive all-girls boarding school where she suffered the torment of receiving a world-class education. No, gentlest reader, none of the above. Our Paula sent young Toby to Gorse Edge School because she was having an illicit affair with its deputy head, Harry Bowers.

I'm sure Bowers and his wife, Julie, would rather you and I didn't know this, but, thanks to Saint Paula's obsessive desire to prove me wrong, we do. We and all the other *Sunday Times* readers, and all their friends and families, have the <u>full story</u>, in Paula Privilege's own words. I particularly like the parts that refer to me specifically. I get no fewer than four mentions, which proves that I am currently the person upper-most in Saint Paula's mind. I pity poor Mr Privilege. How's he coping with all this media attention? By 'poor', I of course mean unfortunate; last time I looked, Richard Crumlish was just about managing to scrape by on his heir-to-colossal-diamond-fortune private income.

Still, a vast fortune is no substitute for a faithful wife, one could argue, and this <u>isn't the first time</u> that Saint Paula's adulterous exploits have spilled over into the public sphere. Remember Keiran Holland? I try not to, but sometimes it's unavoidable. Remember the mediocre American movie director whose name I have forgotten? Both Crumlish and Labour let those two indiscretions pass, and no doubt for the same reason: hotties like Paula are few and far between. Will Crumlish stand by his woman again, now that she has cheated on him a third time and freely shared the full details of her betrayal with a national newspaper? It's early days, and, while we remain glued to every facet of their unfolding marital misfortune, we can only speculate: will it be stick or carats for Saint Paula?

Whatever happens to her marriage, her political career is over, or very soon will be. Charitable as it is in allowing the likes of Eds Miliband and Balls onto its front benches, the Labour Party's goodwill cannot possibly stretch as far as retaining an MP who announces to the country without a hint of regret that she chose a school for her son with a view to sneaking into the stationery cupboard with her tastiest constituent seconds after she'd dropped off little Toby at his classroom door.

Just in case Labour are feeling especially lenient about both infidelity and exhibitionism at the moment (you never know – they might have heard that the Tories are making moves in that direction and be keen to follow suit), Saint Paula made sure to add another choice revelation to her spontaneous media combustion:

'If Damon Blundy wants to add lustre to his sad little life by trashing me week after week in his column, can I suggest that he judges me for the shoplifting problem I had as a teenager that lasted into my early twenties? Oh, sorry, I forgot – Blundy doesn't know about that because I never got caught. Perhaps he'd like to admit that he has no idea what kind of person I am – good, bad or indifferent – just as I have no idea what kind of person he is, though I do know, as we all do, that he chooses to behave for much of the time like a vile bigot. But we mustn't let his bigotry, disgusting though it is, blind us to his foolishness. It is tempting to assume that those who offend and upset us are telling hard truths that we can't stand to hear, but sometimes, as in the case of Blundy, they are as wrong as they are unpleasant. Only a fool would imagine that my decision to send my son to a state school was in any way controversial or a matter of public interest. Thanks to my relationship with Harry, I was in the fortunate position of knowing enough about Gorse Edge and its staff to trust it completely, but even if that hadn't been the case, I would have sent Toby to his local state primary school because I believe in state education.'

I choose to behave like a vile bigot? Oh, Paula, that's not fair. No one chooses how to behave – not you and not me. Free will is the greatest lie we've ever been sold as a species. If humans have free will, why would Bryn Gilligan spend <u>all day and night on Twitter</u>, engaging at length with creep after creep on the subject of whether or not he ought to end his life? Why would Reuben Tasker imagine there's any point in his <u>forbidding me to read any more of his books</u> since I evidently don't appreciate them? Why would Keiran Holland <u>attack me</u> for lobbying to strip Tasker of his <u>Books Enhance Lives Award</u>? Having done no such thing, I'm a little baffled. I thought I'd been arguing to give Bryn Gilligan back his Olympic medals, and merely using Reuben Tasker as a convenient analogy. I'm equally baffled as to why Holland should feel the need to explain to me in <u>such detail</u> the difference between Olympic sprinting and a horror novel. In case any of you have been waiting for clarification on this point, here's a small extract from his lengthy treatise on the subject:

A novel is the product of a process; it is not the process itself. Reuben Tasker's artistic creation is his novel, not his ability to write a novel, whereas Bryn Gilligan's product is his ability to run fast and nothing more than that. In competitive sprinting, product – the sprint sprinted – and process are interchangeable. A race does not last through the decades or the centuries, and so is inseparable from the ability to run, which is why that ability mustn't be chemically enhanced. In the case of a novel, we do not and should not care how it came into being, only about what it is.

I can think of other differences that Holland omits to mention. Sprinting requires a pair of trainers and a can of Lucozade. Horror novels can manage without both. Sprinting involves moving fast. A book doesn't necessarily have to move fast (read Reuben Tasker's if you want proof). On the other hand, horror novels and Olympic sprinting have some features in common: both can make you sweaty, whether from fear or exertion. Both have a competitive aspect – there are sprinting prizes and book prizes. If illegal drugs are a bar to winning in one, why not in the other? After all, the cash prize goes to the law-breaking drug-taking writer, not to the book itself. Books do not have bank accounts. Keiran Holland has yet to offer a persuasive reason why Bryn Gilligan should be deprived of his medals while supernaturally stoned Reuben Tasker should get to hang on to his.

6

Thursday 4 July 2013

'Nicki Clements is a liar,' Melissa Redgate told Gibbs. 'She always has been.' *Unlike me, you and all decent people* was the clear implication.

Speak for yourself, thought Gibbs. Though, of course, Melissa hadn't spoken the words out loud. Gibbs couldn't prove – yet – that she was a self-satisfied moral majority type. It was just a sense he had. He wasn't enjoying being in a small interview room with her. What kind of person contacts detectives, unsolicited, and says, 'You might want to suspect my best friend of murder, even though I have no proof'?

Nicki Clements hadn't murdered Damon Blundy, unless she was far cleverer than she appeared to be. The secretary of Freeth Lane Primary School had endorsed her alibi: Nicki had been on the phone to the school, on her landline, on and off all morning. She wouldn't have had time to drive to Elmhirst Road, kill a man and drive back home between phone calls.

Having heard Robbie Meakin's account of his meeting with Nicki, Gibbs couldn't help but pity the woman. She sounded more like a desperate idiot than an evil genius.

Melissa handed Gibbs a blue box file that she'd brought in with her. 'There's a printout of an advertisement in there that Nicki posted on a casual-sex website called Intimate Links. I'm fairly sure Damon Blundy answered and the two of them started having an affair.'

Gibbs flicked through the pages in the box. 'There's a lot more here than one advert. Are these . . . ?'

'A selection of Damon Blundy's newspaper columns, plus

comments sections. I printed them out to save you having to look them up on the Internet. And there are plenty more, if you're interested. Those are just a random sample. Between October 2011 and February this year, Nicki commented on nearly all of Blundy's columns – always sticking up for his point of view, however craven it was, and attacking other commenters for attacking him. Why would she do that if they weren't having an affair? As far as I know, she's never gone in for online commenting, before or since.'

Gibbs reread the Intimate Links advert. He held it up. 'The date on this is June 2010. You say Blundy replied and they started an affair – why wouldn't Nicki start commenting on his columns immediately? Why wait till October the following year?'

'Again, I'm not sure, but . . . my guess is that for quite a long time, she didn't know who he was. I think they emailed back and forth and, at first, didn't know much about each other. You'd have to build up trust, wouldn't you? Especially someone in the public eye like Damon Blundy.'

That made sense. 'And she stopped commenting on his columns in February this year?' Gibbs asked.

Melissa nodded. 'I suspect that's when they broke up. She stopped mentioning him then too – until Tuesday, when she came round to tell me he'd been murdered, and asked me to lie for her.'

'Hang on, rewind a bit,' said Gibbs. 'You say she mentioned him . . . Did she tell you they were having an affair, then?'

'No, never. Nor did she ever tell me she'd posted an advert on Intimate Links.' Melissa looked caught out. Guilty, even. 'Nicki and I have been best friends since school. She used to tell me everything – all her secrets, all her lies. Then, a few years ago, I started going out with her brother. He and I are now married. I didn't realise how bad an effect Nicki's lying had had on him, his childhood, their family life . . . So I asked Nicki to stop telling me anything that I'd have to keep from Lee. He hates lying – absolutely hates it. Honesty's more important to him than anything.'

She seemed to be waiting for Gibbs to say, 'Quite right too.'

'So . . . Nicki didn't tell you she was having an affair with Blundy because she wouldn't have wanted her brother to know?'

'Right,' said Melissa. 'And I'd have refused to keep it from him. She knew that. But . . . she can be a bitch, Nicki. She hated me being with her brother – I think she regarded it as some sort of betrayal of our friendship. And she hated not being able to tell me things any more, so she found a way round it: she told me without telling me. One day she told me, out of the blue, about this website, Intimate Links. I'd never heard of it before. I asked her why she was bringing it up. She said, "Oh, no reason," in an exaggeratedly innocent tone that told me everything I needed to know. "People advertise on it, for lovers," she said. "Most of the ads are appallingly badly written. You should have a look – one or two are quite entertaining." I knew exactly what she was telling me, and *she* knew I'd look and find her advert – it was obviously her: she's always saying BBC4's the only telly channel worth watching – and she knew I wouldn't say anything to Lee because she hadn't actually told me anything, and she could easily deny it if asked, and would have, most definitely!'

The anger in Melissa's voice was unmistakeable. 'Then, a few months later, she started to mention Damon Blundy, and how interesting and clever his writing was. Again, the mock-innocent tone: "I hope you don't mind me mentioning Damon Blundy so often?" she'd ask, all wide-eyed. "It's just that he's my new favourite columnist. It's so important to have a favourite columnist, isn't it?" I read his columns, and there was Nicki in the comments thread every time, sticking up for him. I'd asked her not to tell me about what she was getting up to – this was her way of saying, "Sod you, I'll do what I like, as always." I snapped one day and said, "I get it, Nicki – you're sleeping with Damon Blundy. Bully for you." She pretended to be shocked: "What? Where have you got that from? I'm not, and even if I were, I wouldn't tell you, would

I? You've asked not to be told." Trust me, she was having an affair with him. Why else would she suddenly leave London and move to Spilling? She's not an escape-to-the-country sort of person. She loves London. But Damon Blundy moved from London to Spilling, so she had to follow. She made Adam ask for a transfer at work so that she could be nearer to Blundy.'

'Did you tell Lee what you suspected?' Gibbs asked.

'No. Not until Tuesday, after Nicki asked me to lie to the police. That brought home to me how serious it was. Before that . . . no. Lee'd have told his mum and dad, and they'd have told Nicki's husband, Adam – everything that happened when I told him on Monday would have happened a lot sooner. I don't actually want Nicki's life to fall apart, or Adam's, and since I didn't know for sure—'

'Hold on,' Gibbs stopped her. 'On Tuesday, you told your husband that you suspected his sister had been involved with Damon Blundy and . . . he told their parents?' *Why would he do that? Anyone sensible would want to keep the parents out of it, surely.* 'And they told Nicki's husband?' *Nice family.*

'They told Nicki they were going to. She said there was no need – she'd already told him. I don't know if that's true or not. If I know Nicki . . . I think she might have told Adam something, knowing her parents would otherwise, but not the whole truth. No way.'

Gibbs leaned back in his chair and folded his arms. 'All right, so let's say Nicki was having an affair with Damon Blundy. Does that mean she killed him?'

Melissa looked confused. 'No, of course not. But . . . it means she might have done, doesn't it? Lee thinks so, and he's her brother. If she's got nothing to hide, why's she asking me to lie to the police for her?'

'Where's Lee today? Why didn't the two of you come in together?'

'He's at work. He asked me if I'd be OK on my own and I said I would.'

'What does he do for work?' Gibbs asked.

'He's a speech writer. For the Home Office.'

And for his wife: a speech called 'Why You Should Convict My Husband's Sister of Murder'.

'And you? What's your job?'

'I work from home,' said Melissa. 'I do the admin for a mail-order company that sells herbal remedies and health supplements. I'm also doing a part-time law degree. Why do you want to know all this?'

'I just do,' said Gibbs. It came out more aggressively than he'd intended it to.

'Look, I sincerely hope Nicki didn't kill Damon Blundy,' Melissa said, no doubt sensing his antipathy towards her. 'I'm not saying she did it, but it'd be irresponsible of me not to come to you with my concerns, especially knowing that she's a . . . well, she's basically a pathological liar!'

Gibbs said nothing. He sensed that Melissa hadn't finished.

'She doesn't only lie to get herself out of trouble, like most people. She lies for fun. It's her hobby. She commits crimes for fun too. Once, she stole a pair of shoes, kids' shoes, at a soft-play centre. They belonged to a toddler who'd been mean to Ethan. Nicki stole his shoes, as revenge, and threw them in a bin on the way home. Once, she contacted the local paper – this was while she still lived in London – and slagged off Sophie and Ethan's primary school. When a critical article appeared, instead of telling the head, "Yes, I was unhappy with the school so I dished the dirt to a newspaper," she pretended . . .' Melissa stopped. She looked embarrassed. 'It's so flagrantly implausible it's almost funny. She denied flat out that she'd gone to the press. She told the head she'd been discussing it with a friend, privately and responsibly, and the deputy editor of the local paper had happened to be standing behind them at the time – in the super-market, she said – and he'd then gone off and used it as a story without her permission or knowledge, the *bastard*.' Melissa shook her head. 'I heard her on the phone to the head. She actually called the guy a bastard, then burst out laughing as soon as she'd put the phone down. "Did that sound OK, in a so-implausible-it-must-be-true kind of way?" she asked me.'

And I bet you laughed along with her, didn't you? I bet you were more fun before you hooked up with Lee.

'There are probably stories like that about most people,' said Gibbs.

'Not me,' said Melissa. 'I've never stolen anything. I don't lie habitually like Nicki does. I'm sure you don't either.'

Gibbs's confidence in her judgement shrank to less than zero. 'Tell me about Tuesday,' he said. 'Nicki asked you to lie to the police?'

'She didn't have her car with her. She turned up, uninvited, and that was the first thing I noticed: a set of car keys in her hand that didn't belong to her. She said her car was missing a mirror and the trains were knackered, so she'd hired a car. Then she told me Damon Blundy had been murdered, without sounding particularly shocked or upset about it. She sounded as if that were a minor detail and not what she'd really come to talk to me about. Then she asked me to lie.'

'About?'

'Two Sundays ago, she and I went to an auction together in Grantham. She said detectives investigating Damon Blundy's murder might contact me, and she asked me not to tell them that her passenger-side wing mirror was missing that day.'

'She asked you *not* to tell the police that the mirror was missing?' Gibbs straightened up in his chair. Nicki had told Sam and Simon it had been missing when she and Melissa had gone to Grantham, and that Melissa would verify this.

'Nicki thought she was being clever. She wanted the exact opposite of what she asked me for. I was supposed to object to the proposed dishonesty and insist that, if questioned by the police, I'd tell the truth. Only one problem: it *wasn't* the truth. Her wing mirror *wasn't* missing that day. It was definitely there. It was a warm day and I had my window down most of the way to Grantham. I looked at my reflection in the wing mirror, several times.'

'You're sure?' Gibbs asked.

'A hundred per cent. The car was a tip, as always, and so full of crumbs you could have stuffed a cushion with them, but all the mirrors that should have been there were there.'

As Gibbs was writing down this new information, Melissa said in an aggrieved voice, 'Damon Blundy wasn't the first time Nicki had cheated on Adam, and Tuesday wasn't her first encounter with the police.'

'What do you mean?' asked Gibbs. 'About the police,' he clarified. 'I don't care if Nicki's slept with four men or forty.' He was still annoyed about Melissa's casual categorising of him as someone who wouldn't habitually lie, when he lied to his wife, Debbie, every single day of his life.

'A few weeks ago, Nicki turned up at my house – again, unannounced – and said something terrible had happened; this was the worst day of her life; it was something to do with the police—'

'When?' Gibbs interrupted. 'Do you know the date?'

'Yes. I looked at my diary yesterday and worked it out. It was Wednesday 5 June, about two o'clock. The bell rang; I answered the door. Nicki barged in and said she had to talk to me, it was an emergency, and I wasn't allowed to tell anyone, not even Lee. She was pretty hysterical. I think she thought it was big enough and serious enough to sweep aside my reservations about hiding things from my husband.'

'Did it?'

'No. The opposite. If it was something important, I was even more determined not to have to lie to Lee about it. I explained to Nicki that she'd have to find someone else to confide in and discuss her . . . problem with. I tried to be as sensitive as I could, but . . . she didn't take it well. Things got a bit out of hand.'

'Did she become violent?' Gibbs asked.

'No, nothing like that. Just . . . nasty.'

'In what way?'

Melissa sighed. 'She said that when I lost my heart to Lee, I really did lose my heart – altogether. I'm heartless, apparently, because I'm not willing to be drawn into her lies. Then . . . I don't know, just a load of rambling stuff designed to mess with my head and manipulate me. She said she didn't know who she was any more, or if she could bear to be that person for much longer, but at least there was no danger, thank God, that she'd ever end up like me, and how overwhelmingly grateful she was for that . . . that kind of thing. I asked her to leave. She had one more go at persuading me: I was the only person who really knew her; I'd known her for years; only I could help her . . .' Melissa shuddered. 'I just wanted her out of my house. I didn't mention it to Lee because I couldn't bear to think about it, once it was over.'

It's called feeling guilty. With good reason.

Melissa frowned. 'Lee's right: I should have told him straight away. He knows everything now. I've told him everything I know.'

'It sounds as if Nicki might have wanted your help with a problem she was having,' said Gibbs neutrally.

'I'm sure she did,' Melissa said with feeling, her face colouring. 'I'm equally sure it was a problem entirely of her own making.'

'And you think she might have made herself a new problem on Monday, by killing Damon Blundy?'

'Lee thinks so. And I . . . Well, let's just say with Nicki anything's possible.'

'Where were you and Lee on Monday morning between eight thirty and ten thirty?' Gibbs asked her.

~

'I hope you enjoy reading horror.' Damon Blundy's first wife handed Sam Kombothekra a copy of her memoir, *A Hole in the Stone*. Sam barely noticed the title, or the subtitle: *How I Survived the Marriage From Hell*. He stared instead at the name on the jacket: Verity Hewson.

Verity Hewson, Abigail Meredith, he recited silently in his head. *Verity Hewson, Abigail Meredith*. Not, as they had quickly come to be known by CID, Doormat and Despot. If he could get through this interview without slipping up and calling either of Damon Blundy's ex-wives a 'D' word, Sam would be a happy man.

The inconvenience of Verity living in Lothersdale, a small village in North Yorkshire, was mitigated by her having Abigail Meredith as a houseguest. Sam would have preferred it if they'd arranged it the other way round, since Abigail lived in Oakham, which was nearer to the Culver Valley, but you couldn't have everything. And although it was a four-and-a-half-hour drive from Spilling to Lothersdale, Sam was enjoying being back in Yorkshire, where he'd lived and worked for eleven years. As he'd driven through the unspoiled greenery on his way to Verity Hewson's converted barn, he had finally been able to confirm something he'd long suspected about Yorkshire: parts of it were visually stunning, yes, but it didn't have a kind heart in the way that, say, Devon did. The fields and trees of Yorkshire were not welcoming Sam home today, much as they had failed to greet him warmly when he'd first moved to Bingley, near Bradford, from London. If Lothersdale had been a person, it might have said to him, 'Well, then. Let's hear what you've got to say for yourself. I doubt we'll be impressed by it, whatever it is.'

'You're wasting your time on us, unless you're just here to get background,' Abigail Meredith said. She was sitting sideways in a low-backed chair with her legs draped over its arm. 'Vet was busy being a birth partner for a friend of hers on Monday morning – she got to cut the cord and everything. I was more boringly at work all day, surrounded by colleagues. I'd much rather have been murdering Damon.'

'Abby,' said Verity authoritatively.

'Sorry. It's all just so horrible.' Abigail swung her legs round so that she was sitting straight in her chair. 'I can't stand the endless *gloom* of death. I mean, even after the death's happened, the gloom just goes on and on! You know who'd agree with me? Damon! He'd laugh if he could hear me joking about murdering him.'

'If I'd known he was going to be killed . . .' Verity's lower lip shook. 'I feel as if I've spoken ill of the dead, even though he wasn't when I wrote the book.'

A good reason never to speak, or publish, ill of anyone, Sam thought.

'Why? It's all true,' said Abigail. 'Was then and is now. Damon said exactly what he wanted, when he wanted, and he approved of others doing the same. You should write another memoir, about losing him. I'll co-write it with you.'

Losing him? Was Abigail referring to Damon's murder? Hadn't both women lost him when their respective marriages to him had ended?

'So . . . you two are good friends, obviously,' Sam said.

'Yes,' said Verity. 'I couldn't have got through these last few days without Abby. She's held me together.'

'We *are* friends, but that's a by-product,' Abigail amended. 'We started out as a very exclusive victim support group. We're the only two victims of marriage to and divorce from Damon Blundy – the only two in the world. We always hoped Hannah might join and swell our ranks, but she can't now. She's Catherine Parr to our Anne Boleyn and Anne of Cleves.' Abigail made a violent neck-slicing gesture with her index finger, then shrieked with laughter.

Both women looked and sounded less like victims than almost anybody Sam had ever met. They had the loud, expansive voices of people who took for granted that others would listen; they were both stylishly dressed and startlingly attractive in their different ways. Abigail had masses of blonde curly hair, soft features, full lips and a flawless complexion. When she wasn't laughing about beheadings or flinging her legs over pieces of furniture in a way that flashed rather a lot of bare leg, she looked angelic. Verity was tall and slim with short, glossy dark brown hair, large green eyes and what Sam's wife, Kate, would call 'film-star cheekbones'. And someone had evidently interior-designed the living daylights out of her immaculate home. Bland person-height wooden sculptures of wavy rectangles, like sheets of paper bent by the wind, were strategically positioned in the large open-plan living-cum-dining room.

Appearances could be deceptive, Sam knew. Perhaps beneath the shiny exteriors of these two women lurked spirits that had been crushed by Damon Blundy, but he doubted it.

Doormat. Despot.

'How long have you been staying here, Abigail?'

'Since Tuesday night. Vet and I both had the same reaction to the news – we wanted to be together. We understand each other's feelings in a way that no one else can.'

'I don't mean to pry, and I hope it's not an insensitive question, but . . . how *do* you both feel?' Sam asked. 'I mean, neither of you was married to Damon any more . . .' He didn't know how to finish, so he left the question dangling.

'We're devastated,' said Abigail. 'Not straightforwardly-sad devastated – in some ways, that would be much easier. It's so hard to describe if you haven't been through it. I don't suppose you've ever had a murdered former husband?'

'I haven't,' Sam confirmed.

'You can't grieve in a normal, healthy way if it's someone you loved and then hated. The love you once felt springs back to life when they die.' Abigail frowned. 'It's as if death has cancelled out the real Damon Blundy, the one I despised and would have done anything to be rid of, and who's left to fill the space? Fantasy Damon, the one I first fell in love with – the charming, gorgeous, witty, entertaining, charismatic, intelligent . . . perfect love-object. Now that the real Damon's gone, the superior version that made such a powerful impression on my imagination all those years ago is somehow . . . resurrected.'

'That's exactly it,' Verity agreed.

'I know why it is!' Abigail announced triumphantly. 'When someone dies – especially violently or tragically – you can't help feeling sorry for them. What's happened to them is . . . well, it's just the worst thing *ever*, so much worse than whatever bad things they've done, and so you pity them, and once you pity someone, you have to forgive them – that's the cunning trick death plays. I'm sure you know the story of Thomas Hardy and his first wife.'

Sam tried to look as if he too was sure he did.

'He'd come to loathe her, but then when she died, he fell in love with her all over again: "Woman much missed, how you call to me, call to me/Saying that now you are not as you were/When you had changed from the one who was all to me . . ."'

'"But as at first, when our day was fair,"' Verity completed the verse.

'So . . . Damon wasn't all bad, then?' Sam asked. Damn, that sounded crass. Though not as crass as *Please stop quoting poetry and going on about Thomas Hardy's first marriage.*

'Damon was an amazing man,' said Verity. 'That was the trouble. When he channelled his amazingness into making you feel good . . . wow. You'd do anything to have that experience again. But when the opposite happened, when you found your-self out of favour . . .' She broke off, shook her head. 'I'm amazed Hannah was able to stand it for as long as she did.'

'Damon and Hannah were married for less than two years,' said Sam, puzzled.

Verity half smiled. Abigail laughed. A private joke. Sam waited to be included.

'Two years would be hardly any time in normal circum-stances,' said Abigail eventually. 'In marriage-to-Damon terms . . . Guess how long I was able to stick it out? Four months. Vet did a bit better – seven months. Neither of us could believe it when Hannah got past the one-year mark.'

Oddly shaped, unattractive Hannah Blundy. And yet, by her own account, Damon had never channelled his amazingness into making her feel bad, not even once. She had remained permanently in favour. Why? How?

'Can I ask you both a strange question?' Sam said. 'Could you imagine Damon ever being a consistently kind, loving husband? Could you see him marrying someone – the right person for him – and treating them well all the time?'

'*Fuck*, no,' said Abigail. 'Apart from anything else, Damon was volatile. He loved drama, so one minute everything would be fantastic, the next he'd be ranting and fuming. He wouldn't be able to live with anyone for longer than a week without them getting a glimpse of his vicious streak.'

'It's hard to explain the power of his personality to someone who didn't know him,' said Verity. 'His hostility pushed you so far away . . .' She shuddered. 'He was never physically violent, but he didn't need to be. Why do you think I ended up here and Abby moved to Oakham? We both used to live in London.'

'You moved because of Damon?' Sam asked.

'Divorcing him and moving to a different part of London didn't feel safe enough,' said Verity. 'For either of us. We both felt so . . . destroyed by him, we had to get further away. London felt as if it belonged to him.'

'And then he moved to the Culver Valley!' Abigail said bitterly. 'I nearly moved again at that point – to Inverness or Aberdeen or somewhere. But then I thought, No, why should I? So I forced myself to stay put. I wasn't prepared to let him win.'

'It's not that we hated him,' Verity explained. 'We did in a way, or we told ourselves we did, but . . . at the same time, we both feared he'd decide he wanted us again, drag us back into his life. He couldn't be without a woman, Damon.' She looked at Abigail. 'I couldn't have held out. I'd have gone back if he'd pursued me hard enough. Let him destroy me all over again.'

'Oh, me too,' said Abigail, as if Verity had said, *I fancy a cup of tea*. 'We were saved by the fact that *he* no longer wanted *us*. And that's not because we were deficient; it's because Damon was a fanatic – a perfectionist of the most neurotic kind. No one could ever have been good enough for him.'

'When we'd been married for just over a month, I found out he'd slept with another woman,' said Verity. 'It took me three weeks to pluck up the courage to confront him about it. He was in a being-nice-to-me phase and I didn't want to ruin it, but it was eating away at me. Daddy persuaded me that I had to say something, and thank goodness he did. If he hadn't, I might have kept quiet. I might never have found out the truth about my own marriage. Damon . . .' She broke off, pinching her lower lip between her thumb and forefinger.

Sam steeled himself. One of the less pleasant parts of his job was having to listen calmly to details of inhumane behaviour. Every time he was told a new horror story, he had to resist the temptation to say, 'Not really?' or, 'You're joking?' After everything he'd seen and heard in his years as a detective, he still couldn't believe that his fellow human beings were capable of such depravity.

'Damon said nothing at first,' Verity went on. 'I thought he might deny it. I had proof, and was psyching myself up to produce it if necessary. Then, after a long silence, he shrugged and said, "Of *course* I screw other women. What do you expect? You can't let me down in the way you have and expect me not to retaliate. You're lucky I didn't duck out of the wedding."' Verity repeated her ex-husband's words without emphasis or tone. Sam guessed they'd been delivered to her rather more forcefully.

'I had no idea what he was talking about – not a clue. As far as I knew, I'd done nothing wrong. Damon had certainly never complained . . .'

Sam waited.

'It turned out he'd been trying to protect me from the devastating truth, but since I'd forced the issue, he decided I deserved to suffer. I wasn't perfect. That was my crime: having imperfections. Hundreds of them. He started to list them, counting them off on his fingers as he went along: I was lax about shaving my legs and plucking my eyebrows; I kept clothes that were past their best and should have been binned long ago; I folded back corners of book pages instead of using a bookmark; I squeezed the toothpaste tube in the wrong place; I'd talked too much on this occasion, too little at that party. And those were the mild ones. It got worse: I drooled sometimes when I was asleep and made a mark on the pillowcase; the bathroom stank after I'd used it – not in the way that it would after anyone had used it, but . . . in an even worse way.'

Verity walked over to the window, turned her back on the room. 'He also said I had a funny smell about me when we had sex, that it put him off. Horrible, horrible things, interspersed with the stupid stuff, as if there were no difference: the time I threw away the recycling in the wrong bin, after he'd carefully rinsed out jars and bottles. It took him nearly two hours to get me up to speed with everything about me that fell short of his ideals, and the really chilling thing was, he didn't have any of it written down. That would have been frightening in a different way, but . . . it was all there in his head, stored away. He came out with it so effortlessly.'

'It's all in Vet's memoir,' Abigail told Sam. 'Which, thanks to Damon, became a bestseller. He plugged it incessantly – told his readers it was definitely the best book of the year because it was the only one about him. Even though it portrayed him as a total shit. He could be . . . surprising like that.'

'The man you're describing sounds like a monster,' Sam said, feeling queasy. 'You said before that you'd have gone back to him. Both of you said it. Is it really true?'

'I hope not. I fear yes.' Abigail gave Sam a *c'est-la-vie* look. Verity nodded in confirmation.

'Why?'

'If he'd wanted us back – either of us – he'd have produced such a dazzling display of fresh-start, new-leaf high romance that we'd have ended up believing we'd never see his cruel streak again,' said Abigail. 'Damon at his best was irresistible.'

'Did he do the same to you?' Sam asked her. 'Keep a list of everything you did that he disapproved of?'

'I'm sure he did, but he never said so. Yes, I'm certain he did, thinking about it. I don't think he could help himself. On the eve of our wedding, he told me that I was "verging on hefty" – those were his exact words – even though I'm actually not at all overweight and nor was I then. And he couldn't bear it if my nail varnish was chipped.' Abigail waved her hands in the air. No chips in the pink that Sam could detect.

'There was a morning on our honeymoon when I woke up and found him sitting beside me in bed, crying,' she said. 'I was frantic, as you might imagine. He wouldn't talk, wouldn't explain what was wrong, however much I begged him to. He left the room without a word and disappeared for most of the day. I thought I must have talked in my sleep, declared undying love for one of my exes or something. When Damon finally turned up again, he told me that if I ever snored again the way I had the night before, he would leave me and never come back.'

'Snored?' Sam could hardly believe what he was hearing.

Abigail nodded. 'Snoring – the antithesis of femininity, according to Damon. I'm a quick learner. I didn't snore again, though I didn't sleep properly either. Half of my brain had to stay awake, on the lookout. And I made sure my nail polish was always immaculate, but . . . once Vet and I became friends and she told me about the list of criticisms he threw at her, I realised that all my efforts were in vain. For every flaw of mine that Damon upbraided me for, there would have been at least another forty he silently resented.'

'You've both described a man who couldn't tolerate any kind of deviation from unrealistic perfection,' said Sam.

'That's true, but only of the women he fell in love with and put on pedestals,' said Abigail. 'He liked his male friends to be as flawed as possible – outrageously so, ideally. Damon's fantasy dinner party would consist of sociopathic, objectionable men and perfect, beautiful women.'

'So what was he playing at with wife number three?' Verity said bitterly. She looked at Sam. 'You've met the latest Mrs Damon Blundy, I take it?'

Sam nodded.

'It's out of the question that Damon would have loved a woman like that,' said Abigail. 'What did he want with her? Why did he keep her so long?'

'You asked before if we could imagine Damon being a consistently kind, loving husband,' said Verity. 'Is that how Hannah described him?'

Sam saw no reason why he shouldn't answer honestly. 'Yes, it was.'

'Well, then either she's lying or . . .' Verity broke off.

'Or what?' Sam asked.

'Or Damon was planning something,' said Abigail. 'If I were you, I'd be wondering pretty hard about what that something was, and who might have found out about it and decided to stop him.'

~

'It sounds whiny to say, "Why me?" but I have wondered why me, many times,' Keiran Holland told Sellers. 'I'd never written a word against Damon, never even mentioned him. Yes, I'd expressed opinions he disagreed with, and I know bullies like him need targets, and anyone will do, but he did seem to have a special antipathy towards me in particular.'

They were in a room Holland had described without cracking a smile as 'the drawing room' in the journalist's home in Wandsworth. Holland's wife, Iona Dennis, sat in a wing-backed armchair in the corner, apparently happy to let her husband do all the talking. She hadn't spoken yet, and had greeted Sellers, when Holland had introduced him, with a silent smile. She had a book on her knee with her own name on the spine. Sellers assumed it was either by her or about her. The former seemed more likely.

'And Paula Riddiough,' he said. 'Damon Blundy attacked her as often as he attacked you.' Seconds after mentioning Riddiough's name, he regretted it. Holland looked stricken, and Iona turned her face away, as if the former MP's name were a rock Sellers had lobbed at her.

This is what cheating does to people. This is the reality. Say the wrong name in the wrong house and the whole house falls down.

Sellers banished the disturbing thought from his mind.

'Oh no he didn't,' said Holland, once he'd recovered. 'He didn't savage her nearly as often – I've actually compiled the statistics: I can prove it to you. And even when he did go for Paula, it wasn't with quite the same loathing that he reserved only for me. With most of Damon's attacks on people, there was a sort of affection about them that you could just about detect around the edges of his hostility, but not with me. He unequivocally hated me – and, as I say, I have no idea why. I mean, it can't have been snobbery – yes, I grew up on a northern council estate and my parents were a drain on the state, but . . .'

Sellers waited for him to say, '. . . but I now have a drawing room.' Holland didn't sound as if he grew up on a northern council estate. Sellers came from exactly that background himself and had the accent to match, even after twenty years in the Culver Valley.

'No, I don't think it was that,' Holland went on. 'Damon was extremely right wing, but he wasn't a social-class snob. He didn't care where anyone came from. And, all right I've got a column in *The Times* and he's stuck at the *Herald*, but he'd certainly have regarded that as a win for *him*, not me. He'd have cited the *Herald*'s huge readership in comparison with the *Times*'s, as if that were what mattered.'

Sellers kept his mouth shut, sipped his tea and wondered what did matter about a newspaper if not how many people read it. Perhaps that it should be read by the right people – was that what Holland was implying?

Listening to Holland eliminate reason after reason why Damon Blundy chose to persecute him, Sellers started to feel irritated. The focus of this conversation so far was all wrong. An alien beamed down from a spaceship into this room and told only that a policeman was here to investigate a terrible crime could be forgiven for thinking that Keiran Holland was the victim and Damon Blundy the perpetrator.

Rather than the other way round?

'Mr Holland,' Sellers cut into the ongoing monologue, 'I need to ask you some questions about Monday morning. That's when Damon was killed. You're not under any suspicion, and this is just a routine question, but . . .'

'Where was I? Walking. Thinking. I often go for long walks when I've got a piece to write. It clears my mind.'

'Where did you walk?'

Holland's forehead creased as he considered the question. 'Um . . . I can't say I remember exactly. Around and about. On the common, round the streets. I tend to just amble about.'

'Where were you, Mrs Holland?'

'Ms Dennis,' Iona corrected him. 'I was at my publisher's offices. I'll give you my editor's email, if you like.'

'That would be helpful.'

'I'm sure there are wives who'd murder anyone who said a bad word about their husbands, but I'm not one of them,' Iona added with a smile.

'Though you've been very supportive whenever Damon's attacked me,' said Holland, speaking to his wife but looking at Sellers to make sure he got the point. 'No, as I say, I've no idea why he zeroed in on me and set about proving I was the worst human being who's ever lived. The first time he devoted a column to attacking me was late April 2011, during the AV debate – you know, the alternative voting system? Remember that?'

Sellers nodded and tried not to groan. Were they back to this again? He thought he'd successfully changed the subject.

'Damon was against AV – called it the most nonsensical voting system ever to be created – and I was passionately in favour. That was when we first locked horns, but then he dug up other columns I'd written, some from years ago. He attacked me retrospectively for my stance on the euro, for having supported the Iraq War – I still say there was a case for removing Saddam—'

'Mr Holland, if we could get back to Monday morning,' Sellers spoke over him. 'While you were out walking, did you see anyone you knew?'

Holland laughed. 'Are you serious? I need an alibi? You think I killed Damon?'

'Not at all. I'm sure you can appreciate, Damon Blundy being who he was, that we're asking a lot of people where they were on Monday morning.'

'No, I didn't see anyone I knew,' Holland said impatiently. 'I sometimes do, and I sometimes don't. Maybe you should put up a poster on Wandsworth Common with my mugshot: "Did anyone see this man here on Monday morning, or is this the face of a murderer?" Ridiculous.'

'DC Sellers has to ask,' said Iona. 'Even though it's you.'

'What the hell's that supposed to mean?' Holland snapped at her.

She seemed to find his anger amusing. 'It means, *darling*, that even though you know and I know you didn't kill Damon Blundy, DC Sellers doesn't. I assume you don't want a police force that takes everybody's word for everything?'

'You're right,' said Holland after a few seconds. 'I apologise, DC Sellers. But I'm afraid I can't help you. I went for a walk. I didn't go to . . . wherever it is and stab Damon Blundy.'

'Why do you say "stab"?' asked Sellers.

Holland frowned. 'No reason. I mean . . . well, he was killed in his house, wasn't he? I assumed . . .' He broke off and laughed. 'All right, I'm going to sound like an idiot when I admit this, but no doubt I deserve the attendant embarrassment: in my mind, shootings happen outside and stabbings happen inside. Daft, illogical, but there we are.'

'What about stranglings, poisonings?' Sellers asked him. 'Couldn't they happen inside too?'

'Of course, but . . . aren't they more rare?' Holland lost interest in his question before it was answered. 'Look, if you're trying to suggest that I knew Damon was stabbed because I stabbed him, you're way off the mark. I just said it without thinking.'

'Damon Blundy wasn't stabbed,' Sellers told him.

'What?' Holland looked confused. 'But then why . . . ?'

'Why what?'

'If he wasn't stabbed, what on earth does it matter that I assumed he was? It's not relevant to anything.'

'Perhaps not,' Sellers said, thinking, We'll see. His kids hated it when he said, 'We'll see,' in response to their various requests. 'Just say no if you're going to say no!' they often snarled at him.

'They say people hate anyone who's too similar to them, don't they?' Holland mused. 'I'm nothing like Damon Blundy, thank God. I've wondered if it was almost the opposite syndrome, though. Damon was obsessed with what I thought about every issue, and with attacking my opinion. Maybe he couldn't cope with the idea of my thoughts because they were the opposite of his, almost always. I mean, it must be a somewhat disconcerting experience, coming up against someone who's undeniably intelligent but cancels you out on every point, when you believe yourself to be intelligent. A bit like seeing your own mind in a mirror – it would make you wonder what your mind *really* looks like, wouldn't it?'

'I think DC Sellers might like another cup of tea,' said Iona, swallowing a yawn. 'I would, anyway.'

'That would be great, thanks,' Sellers said.

Iona didn't move.

Holland stood up. 'Right, I'll go and put the kettle on,' he said.

When he'd left the room, Iona said, 'My husband is many

things, but he's not a murderer. And I'm not just saying that because I'm his wife.'

'If you could encourage him to try and remember if he saw *anyone* he knew, anyone at all—'

'No,' said Iona. 'Sorry. You encourage him if you want to.' She smiled.

Strange woman. *My husband is many things . . .*

'I've spent years encouraging him to see the stark staring obvious about why Damon Blundy kept targeting him in a way that he targeted no one else. Keiran's right about that, Blundy did do that. I try to tell him why and he doesn't hear me. It goes in one ear and out the other. He speculates endlessly – cancelling out, mind in a mirror – it's all crap! Overblown crap.'

'Then what was it?' Sellers asked. *Jealousy, because Holland had slept with Paula Riddiough and Damon wanted to?*

'Damon loved to argue and scrap,' Iona said. 'There are many people one can argue with about individual issues, but . . .' She stopped talking as Keiran reappeared.

'Sorry to interrupt,' he said. 'Milk and sugar?'

Sellers opened his mouth to answer, but Iona spoke too quickly. 'There are very few people who are wrong about *every*-thing,' she told Sellers, as if her husband weren't there. 'That was Keiran's unique appeal from Damon Blundy's point of view: that he was wrong about absolutely everything.'

~

'It's on her ignorant head, and no amount of denying's going to change that,' the schoolgirl with the stubby blonde plaits shouted at her two friends, who looked as if they were ready to agree with her whatever she said. Gibbs guessed they were around sixteen – sixth-formers, maybe. Did sixth-formers wear uniform? At Gibbs's school they hadn't, but perhaps different rules applied in King's Lynn, a town Gibbs had never visited before.

The girl who had spoken had obviously been crying; she'd

also removed her tie and fastened it round her leg like a garter, with the ends trailing. Her shirt was unbuttoned, revealing the top of a red lacy bra. 'She might not have meant it to happen, whatever, I don't care! It's still on her head. Like a big fucking fat . . . *hat*, man. I swear to God!' Much giggling from all three girls followed this conclusion.

They swept past Gibbs in exactly the way that, a few moments earlier, they'd swept past the square black dustbin embedded in the pavement. Anything that wasn't part of their all-consuming drama was invisible to them; Gibbs could remember girls in his class like that; they'd never looked in his direction either. He found himself wishing he'd known Liv as a teenager, that she'd been in his class at school. *Stupid*. What was the point of wishing that?

After the three girls came a few more clumps of uniformed bodies, all traipsing along unenthusiastically in the direction of the open gates to Gibbs's left; their lunch hour was over and they had no choice but to return to their prison.

Keen to get away from the pupil procession, Gibbs crossed the wide main road again and tried Reuben Tasker's doorbell for the fourth time. Still no answer. Gibbs had been certain someone was in – he could have sworn he'd heard movement from inside the first time he'd rung the bell – but he was starting to wonder if he'd imagined it. It seemed plausible that a man who had no landline or mobile phone, was addicted to cannabis and had failed to respond to six emails marked 'urgent' might ignore his own doorbell, but that didn't make it impossible that Tasker was out. Weedheads who worked from home needed to visit their dealers, after all.

Gibbs looked up at the tall red-brick three-storey house. He was too close to see into the windows on the top two levels. A white ceramic sign screwed to the brickwork beside the front door told him that this was 76 Gaywood Road. The numbers and letters were fussy and old-fashioned. Chosen by a woman, thought Gibbs.

On the phone this morning, Tasker's literary agent had used words like 'dedicated' and 'committed' to describe Jane Tasker. He'd made Reuben Tasker sound more like a good cause than a man.

Gibbs turned round to see what was happening on the other side of Gaywood Road. It was nowhere near as busy. That was where he needed to be, to get a better view of the top part of the house. He decided to give it a couple more minutes, then cross over again once the last of the uniformed stragglers had slouched through the school gates to be penned up for the afternoon. If Tasker was in and not opening the door, he wouldn't be able to resist looking out of a window eventually to see if all was clear, and he was more likely to pick one on a higher floor to avoid a face-to-face encounter.

Gibbs walked round his car, which was parked on the paved area that would once have been number 76's front garden, and waited for a gap in the traffic. There wasn't one, so he crossed anyway, raising his middle finger at a driver who used his horn to protest. Seconds later, he regretted his overreaction. He ought to buy a punchbag – set it up in the spare room at home. Maybe it would help to sort his head out if he could spend an hour a day beating the crap out of something he couldn't hurt.

On the pavement opposite Reuben Tasker's house, he looked up and made an involuntary noise as he saw a face framed in the single dormer window at the top. It was Tasker: gaunt, black-haired, bare-chested. Gibbs recognised him from the photograph on his website, and waited for him to pull back from the window, fearing he'd been spotted. Tasker stayed where he was. Staring.

So he'd been in all along. And wanted it known that he could have come to the door but had chosen not to.

Tasker's gaze was neutral rather than actively defiant, but Gibbs felt the defiance all the same. There was something chillingly arrogant – no, something *more* chilling than arrogance – about looking at someone so expressionlessly, as if nothing they could do or say could have any effect on you, positive or negative. Tasker was watching the world in the way that a ghost separated from the living would watch.

He did it. He killed Damon Blundy. And he thinks he can get away with it.

Gibbs shook his head and swore under his breath. Who did he think he was, Simon Waterhouse? Most people's hunches were worthless, and Gibbs was realistic enough to include his own in that category. Tasker was a weirdo, but that didn't make him a killer. 'Not the easiest man in the world to deal with,' the literary agent had said. Neither was Gibbs, so the two of them were well matched.

Gibbs pointed in the direction of Tasker's front door and mouthed, 'Come down and let me in?' He pulled his ID out of his pocket and held it up.

Tasker disappeared from the window. Gibbs wove his way through the heavy traffic of Gaywood Road again. *Why did the detective cross the road? To talk to a weed-addicted horror writer.* It wasn't much of a punchline.

He didn't see the point of ringing the bell again, so he waited, listening for the sound of feet on the stairs.

Nothing. Once he was certain he'd waited long enough, he knocked loudly on the door, then opened the letterbox and shouted, 'Mr Tasker! DC Chris Gibbs, Culver Valley CID. I've sent you several emails. Can you open up? I'd like to talk to you.'

The bastard wasn't coming to the door. Gibbs pressed his finger down on the doorbell and kept it there for a good minute and a half. Then, too angry to stay where he was, he marched back out into the traffic, attracting multiple horn beeps. This time he managed to resist making any obscene gestures.

He's going to be back in the window again, staring blankly out as if nothing's happened.

On the pavement opposite, Gibbs looked up and got a shock. Tasker had reappeared, but only partially. His hairless bare chest was visible, and the bottom of his neck, but not his face. Tasker had stuck a large square of black paper to the window – with Blu-Tack by the look of it; Gibbs could see four pale dots, one at each corner – and was standing behind it.

'What the fuck . . . ?' Gibbs murmured.

He watched as Tasker did the same with a second square of black, fixing it beneath the first so that the edges lined up. Now hardly any of him was visible – only his right arm.

'Detective Gibbs?' A woman who looked somewhere between thirty and forty was standing beside him.

'Detective Constable. DC Gibbs.'

'I'm Jane Tasker, Reuben's wife.' She was holding the handle of a black, waist-high shopping trolley on wheels. A loaf of bread and a packet of raspberry-flavoured ice lollies poked out of the top. Didn't she drive? Or use the Internet? She seemed to have been to the supermarket on foot with what was effectively an open-topped suitcase to wheel her groceries home in. *Bizarre.*

Her face, free of make-up, had a raw, pink, peeled look – as if it had been scrubbed vigorously over and over again. She was wearing jeans that bunched at the bottom, around the tops of her scuffed black ankle boots, and a bulky red padded anorak in spite of the warm weather.

'Your husband doesn't seem to want to talk to me,' Gibbs told her.

'No, he does. He rang me as soon as you arrived. That's why I hurried back, to let you in. He doesn't like having people in the house unless I'm there too, and he hates to have to interrupt his writing to come downstairs. Shall we . . . ?' She made a gesture that suggested crossing the road.

Gibbs shook his head in disbelief. He was about to follow her when it occurred to him that her husband had probably been watching their exchange. He looked up.

It was impossible to tell if Reuben Tasker was there or not. If he was, he was no longer able to watch the street as he had been a few minutes ago. While Gibbs had been talking to his wife, Tasker had covered the whole window – top to bottom, side to side – with black paper.

~

Charlie's bag started to vibrate against her hip as she walked briskly along the corridor. She would have ignored it, except it might be Simon and it might be important. Even if it wasn't, he would think it was. He could, of course, wait, but he wouldn't think that he could. Charlie sighed, jammed the files she was holding under her left arm and rummaged in her bag for her phone. She pulled it out and looked at the screen.

Simon. Waiting. He was the only person in her life who could communicate impatience telepathically. Other emotions, not so much. 'Make it quick,' she told him by way of greeting.

'Why?'

'I'm on my way to interview Nicki Clements. She's here with her husband, which is . . . interesting. Let's see if she tells the same story Robbie Meakin tells about their . . . um, meeting. She said she'd only talk to a woman, so I think it's looking promising.'

'Why you?' Simon asked.

'What, you think Gaynor from the canteen would do a better job? The Snowman asked me extra nicely. His exact words were, "You're Waterhouse's X chromosome – you do it." Where are you, by the way?'

'Walking,' said Simon. 'Thinking. I need you to find out something for me, and not mention it to anyone else.'

'Sorry,' said Charlie. 'Interviewing Nicki Clements is the only favour I'm doing for you today. I haven't got time to—'

'Melissa Redgate. Find out if she drives. Find out if she *can* drive, but also if she does, and how she feels about it – does she have any issues about driving? Is she one of those women who won't drive on a motorway, or at night, or in the snow, or on a route she's not familiar with?'

'No,' said Charlie. '*You* find out all those things.' She tried to smile at Sergeant Jack Zlosnik as he passed her, walking in the opposite direction. It was hard to snap at one person while simultaneously smiling at another.

'Will she only drive if her husband's in the car, maybe?' Simon went on. 'Also, find out if she's got a car – not one she shares with her husband that she doesn't have access to all the time, but her own car that she can drive whenever she wants. Has she ever been in a crash? Has she lost relatives in car crashes?'

'Why do you want to know all this?' Charlie asked.

'I'll tell you when you get me the answers to those questions, and any others you can think of that I haven't. Anything to do with Melissa Redgate, cars or driving – I want to know about it.'

'Like, is her car tidy or messy?'

'No, that's irrelevant.'

'Ah. OK. As the asker of these questions, aren't I more likely to be able to work out what's relevant if you . . . Simon? You still there?'

Unbelievable. He'd cut her off mid-sentence.

7

Thursday 4 July 2013

Adam is driving. I am thinking how much I wish we were driving to a police station because I'm kind of a suspect in a murder case, but one who has no other terrible problems. Not one who has just confessed to cyber infidelity, and been told she's forgiven, and doesn't believe it for a second.

'You can't forgive me,' I say. 'I don't believe you have. Not so soon.'

Adam sighs. 'Well, I have. I'm not sure what you expect me to do to convince you. I've not shouted, or refused to talk about it. I'm not being off with you, am I?'

He sounds anxious to please me. I sense he's turned to look at me. I wish he'd be more careful while he's driving. Keeping my eyes on the road, I say, 'You're being exactly the same as you always are. How is that possible? Don't you care?'

I want him to care. Two days into my correspondence with him, King Edward asked me how I'd feel about us pledging to be exclusive to one another, though he made clear that this vow of exclusivity couldn't include spouses. I said yes. I stuck to it too. It's the only time I've ever been anything approaching faithful in a relationship.

I want Adam to want me all to himself the way King Edward did.

Whoever he is.

'Nicki, I care. OK? If you're asking if I'm angry . . . what would be the point?' Adam indicates left. 'It was a shock, I'm not denying that, but . . .' He sighs. 'We've been together for twenty years. It'd be too much to expect that you'd *never* be tempted by anyone else.' After a pause, he adds quietly, 'I have been.'

'Really?' I hope I don't sound too eager. 'Tell me. Who? Did anything happen?' I'd give anything for it to turn out that Adam's as bad as me. I would forgive him anything.

'Nothing's ever happened, no,' he says decisively. So decisively it makes me wonder. I don't think he'd lie, but . . . how tempted was he? How many times?

I'd forgive you. Whatever you'd done. Words I say to Sophie and Ethan often. Words no one has ever said to me.

That must be real love, mustn't it? Knowing you want to share the rest of your life with someone whatever they've done, knowing they're perfect for you whatever mistakes they've made. I hope that's how Adam feels about me.

'And nothing happened between you and this Gavin guy, did it?' he asks.

'If nothing had happened, I wouldn't be on my way to the police station to humiliate myself,' I say, nearly gagging as I contemplate the ordeal that lies ahead.

'I mean nothing physical.'

'No. Nothing physical.'

'Good. If you'd slept with him twice a week for the last six months, that I'd find harder to forgive, but you said yourself – when you think about it now, it seems like a kind of madness came over you.'

'Yes.'

'I can understand that. I'm not saying I'm thrilled it happened, but . . . I don't know, maybe it's unrealistic to expect no obstacles ever in a marriage.'

'Maybe,' I say, wondering what exactly Melissa told Lee. She doesn't know about Gavin or King Edward, thank God, but she does know about two one-night stands I had when Adam and I were first married, two incidents that now seem so trivial and far away it's as if they happened to someone else – or perhaps they didn't happen at all. The case for their being real is no more persuasive than an episode of some old soap opera I watched decades ago.

I have to hope that if Melissa or any member of the Redgate family says anything to Adam, it will be in general terms.

So Nicki's told you, has she?

Yeah, she's told me.

My mother would be talking about the two one-night stands, and Adam would be talking about Gavin. No one would be indelicate enough to go into detail, surely.

'I read something once,' I tell Adam. As soon as I've said it, I regret it.

'What?'

'You'll think I'm trying to make an excuse.'

'No, I won't. Even if I do, it might be quite a relief. I'm not sure I can take extreme hair shirt for much longer.' Adam grins at me. When I look at his face, I see that he is upset – more so than he's willing to admit. He's trying to protect me from his pain, because he can see mine growing in me and it scares him.

'I read that people who have judgemental, controlling parents . . . that they kind of . . .' How I wish I'd kept my mouth shut. It's a daft theory. Adam will laugh. 'That they sexualise bad behaviour, in their minds. They grow up being criticised for everything they do, because it's not what the parents would ideally like them to do, and . . . it's hard to live with the daily attacks of a parent determined to improve you. Hard for a child – even an older teenage child – to cope with that kind of onslaught when their only crime is just trying to be themselves.' *Even an adult child*. 'So their minds sort of warp, to defend against too much pain. They twist their perceptions so that they get pleasure from the idea that they're being bad and that people would disapprove. They sexualise wrongdoing. They become the people who get kicks out of illicit affairs. But . . . it's just a theory. One that's obviously hugely convenient for sinners like me.'

'Sounds plausible, I suppose,' says Adam. 'Look, on the

subject of difficult parents . . . I know yours can be irritating, but you didn't mean what you said, did you? About never seeing them again? I hope you didn't.'

'No.' *Yes.* But without Adam's support, I won't be brave enough. So, no.

'Good. Because they're Sophie and Ethan's grandparents.'

I laugh weakly. 'Yeah. Lucky old Sophie and Ethan. You don't think they picked up that anything was wrong, do you? Between us?'

'No. Definitely not.'

We've left them with a babysitter – the teenage daughter of a neighbour. I had to fight the urge to say, 'If by any chance someone rings up or calls round saying they're a member of my family, don't let them in. Don't let them speak to the children.'

'My mother will probably tell them, first chance she gets,' I say to Adam. '"Hi, kids. How's school? By the way, your mother's a cyber-slag. She's lucky your dad didn't throw her out on the street when he found out, to forage for scraps."'

Adam winces. 'Oh, come on! Noreen would never do that to Soph and Ethan. Your family don't really believe you killed Damon Blundy. And I don't think Noreen would actually have told me anything about Gavin, if push had come to shove.'

Has he not been paying attention? 'Adam, Melissa went to the police and encouraged them to suspect me of Damon Blundy's murder. My parents and Lee will have been behind that for sure. No way Melissa'd do it of her own accord.'

'I can see them thinking you needed a bit of sense shaking into you, but I don't believe they honestly think you're capable of murder.'

'I am capable of murder,' I tell him. 'I just haven't committed it yet, that's all.'

~

The police have sent a woman to take my statement: Sergeant Charlotte Zailer. Tall, skinny, dark hair, bright red lipstick.

Sharp dark eyes that make me wonder what she's thinking about me, even before I've said anything. She looks as if she's thinking plenty.

Her breasts are large for a skinny woman. It was the first thing I noticed about her when she walked into the holding cell Adam and I were placed in when we arrived. It's probably not called a holding cell. The man who escorted us in here called it a meeting room. Still, it's not a room I'd wish to spend any time in.

I don't normally pay much attention to other women's breasts, but Sergeant Zailer's are hard to miss. Given what I'm about to reveal, the sight of them, even covered up, makes me feel paranoid. I am certain Adam is thinking the same thing. Perhaps we'll laugh about it together later.

'Mr Clements, perhaps you could encourage your wife to tell me what she came here to tell me?' says Sergeant Zailer. 'I can't wait forever.'

'Nicki . . .' Adam murmurs.

'I don't need encouragement.' I needed to prepare myself, that's all. And now I have. 'Now that Adam knows the truth, there's no reason why you shouldn't. You'll disapprove of me, but I don't mind that. I'm used to being disapproved of.'

'I already disapprove of you,' Sergeant Zailer says as if it's a stroke of good luck. 'You lied to two of my colleagues, didn't you? You said your car was missing a wing mirror on the morning that Damon Blundy was murdered. We know that's not true. We've got CCTV of your car with both mirrors clearly still attached.'

'Yes, I thought of that several days too late. I know it's pathetic, but the mirror thing was the best I could come up with. God knows how I could make such a stupid mistake. I could have told literally *any* other lie and it would have been more convincing: I'd left my phone at home; I remembered I'd left the hob on – anything! Once I realised I'd screwed up, I hoped the CCTV might be so grainy that my mirrors wouldn't stand out, but . . .' I shrug.

'Well, I'm sorry your lie didn't work.' Sergeant Zailer smiles.

She looks and sounds as if she might actually mean it. Unless it's a tactic. It must be a tactic. 'Is that why you rang up and asked to come in? You realised your story'd fall flat, so you decided to tell the truth?'

'No. I've just told you, I was pinning all my hopes on excessive graininess of CCTV film.' I smile back at her. 'I decided to tell the truth because my mother threatened me.'

'Nicki,' Adam says urgently. I don't know what he thinks can be done. The words are out and can't be taken back. I don't want to take them back. 'She didn't *threaten* you.'

'She did, actually.' To Sergeant Zailer, I say, 'My husband refuses to believe my mother would stoop so low, but she did threaten me. She said if I didn't tell Adam the truth, she would. So I told him – and having told him, there's absolutely no reason not to tell you, especially when telling you has the added advantage of making it clear I'm not a murderer.'

'Go on,' says Sergeant Zailer.

I sigh. Even prepared as I am, this is not going to be pleasant. 'I behaved suspiciously on Monday morning on Elmhirst Road – I'm not denying that. I did a U-turn rather than drive past a certain policeman, but . . . my reason for doing so had nothing to do with Damon Blundy, dead or alive. It was the policeman I wanted to avoid.'

'Why?'

'Because I was embarrassed and ashamed about something I'm *still* embarrassed and ashamed about – although now I can bear to face up to it, whereas on Monday morning, I didn't feel I could. I just . . . saw that policeman, panicked and had to get away from him as quickly as I could.' I clear my throat, but the lump in it is still there. 'I suppose the difference is that now I have no choice but to face up to it. All right. I had a cyber affair with a man called Gavin. Well, a man who told me he was called Gavin – I doubt it's his real name. One feature of this . . . relationship, if you can call it that, is that I sent him photographs of myself. Some were more explicit than others.'

'Go on.'

I glance at Adam. How must he feel, hearing all this a second time, in front of a stranger?

'I'm OK,' he says. 'You can tell her. Don't worry about me.' He turns to Sergeant Zailer. 'I love my wife and I'm not going to let a brief stupid lapse turn me against her.'

Really? How about a brief stupid lapse of nearly half a century – my entire life, in fact?

'Your relationship's none of my business, Mr Clements. Go on, Nicki.'

I can't. I can't say the difficult part. Maybe if I start earlier in the story, it'll be easier. 'Gavin put an ad on a website called Intimate Links. Do you know it?'

'I've heard of it,' Sergeant Zailer says.

'If you've never looked at Intimate Links, this might sound a bit strange, but a lot of people advertise for very specific things. Particular fetishes, for example. There's a lot of dom-sub stuff: foot worship, guys wanting mother-baby role play, doctor-patient fantasies . . . When I used to look regularly, there was a man who posted the same ad every day asking for a woman who would make insulting remarks about his wife while having sex with him. I always wondered about that one – I mean, why specifically *that*? Anyway, sorry, that's irrelevant. These ads often have particular physical requirements: this or that type of body – skinny, obese, shaved, unshaved. A lot of the adverts are very direct. Gavin's was. He specified certain . . . physical things, things that applied to me. Blonde, petite and . . . other more intimate things. His advert read as if he was describing *me*.'

Because he was. He was King Edward, using a different name to reel you in.

Adam reaches for my hand. I understand him less now than I ever have.

I say, 'I'm sure this sounds very sordid, and maybe it is, but there's also something liberating about being able to abandon social niceties and read what people really want. And to read an ad written by a man who tells you in advance that he will be completely transfixed by your body when he hasn't seen it yet . . . To write back and say, "That's me you're describing," and to get a reply within ten seconds that says, "Then I want you" . . . There's something refreshing about that, believe it or not.'

'I can believe it,' says Sergeant Zailer. 'Nicki, there's no need to be defensive. I'm not judgemental about other people's sex lives. Really. Mine would probably shock you more than yours shocks me. To be honest, if I'm shocked by anything, it's the resilience of your marriage. I think it's great that you and Adam are sitting here holding hands while you're telling me all this.'

'I know Nicki loves me,' says Adam. 'She didn't love this Gavin person. That's why I can get past it.'

Yes, that's true. I love Adam. I didn't love Gavin. I thought I loved King Edward, but I was wrong.

'Our emails became very graphic very quickly,' I say. 'It was . . . I'm not making an excuse, but it felt as if my brain had been taken over by a kind of fever.'

It always does. Every time. You like the fever, don't you? You need it.

'I wasn't me; I was this . . . lust-crazed maniac. I had no idea what this man looked like, but it made no difference. It was the things he said about my body and what he'd like to do to it that got me hooked on him.'

'So he didn't send you photographs?'

'No. I never asked him to, and he never offered. I liked him being no more than words on a screen. No personality, no history, just . . . words, and sexual demands. That suited me. It made me feel less guilty – less like I had another man. He could have been some kind of computer program.

'The photographs – the ones I sent him – became a regular thing. I tried to make them as varied as possible, which was hard because the subject matter was always the same: my breasts. Sometimes in the bedroom mirror, sometimes an aerial shot, sometimes in a toilet cubicle of a restaurant.' I take a deep breath. Adam squeezes my hand. 'And once – only once, on 5 June this year – in a supermarket car park, in broad daylight, with other people around. I thought no one was close enough to see. I took off my shirt and my bra and took a picture of myself topless. With my phone. It wasn't very good, so I took another one, and then another. That was what I always did, until I had one from that particular batch that I thought was good enough to send to Gavin. I don't know how I could have forgotten where I was, or the danger of being seen, but I did. I got so caught up in what I was doing: mentally, physically. I suppose it's a bit like having sex in public – people do that, don't they?'

Sergeant Zailer nods.

'Taking those photographs . . . that's how it felt, like being in the middle of a sexual encounter. I got carried away. The risk of being seen by someone was part of it, yet at the same time I didn't seriously believe there was a risk. And then I heard knocking on my car window and I looked up and there was a uniformed policeman standing there, staring at me in horror.' Saying these words out loud makes me feel as if I'm being shaken. 'I panicked. It sounds melodramatic, but I thought my life was over: I'd be arrested and charged with flashing; I'd be on the front page of the local paper; my kids would be ridiculed at school; Adam would leave me; I'd have to go to court and get a criminal record for exposing myself in public . . . I lost it completely, became hysterical.'

'Not a pleasant experience,' Sergeant Zailer commiserates. Is she mad? Why isn't she pointing at me and laughing? 'You were unlucky. Silly, but unlucky.'

'No, I was very lucky. He let me off with a warning, even promised not to tell anyone. Poor man, he looked more embarrassed than I was. He was quite kind to me, once he saw how upset I was.'

Rather in the way that Sergeant Zailer is being kind to me now. And Adam.

There are some good people in the world. I need to devise a way of existing that acknowledges this. I can't, mustn't, base my whole life on hiding, on defending myself.

'It could have been so much worse,' I say. 'Anyway, that encounter with the policeman brought me to my senses. I broke off contact with Gavin and resolved never to put myself or my family in that position ever again. Then, on Monday morning, I was driving along Elmhirst Road on my way to my children's school and I saw the same policeman and just . . .' A shudder I can't control passes through me. 'I couldn't help it. It felt like a catastrophe, like something out of a horror film – he was going to be there, waiting for me, round every corner I turned, for the rest of my life. I couldn't drive past him, couldn't bear the thought of him seeing me. It brought it all back: the humiliation of that moment, the fear. I couldn't do it. I did a U-turn, and that's the only reason you know I exist. Not because I had anything to do with Damon Blundy's murder – because I got my tits out in a car park once and got caught.'

'We all do stupid things, Nicki,' says Sergeant Zailer. 'You should have told DS Kombothekra and DC Waterhouse the truth when they interviewed you. It would have saved you a lot of stress.'

'Well, no, I shouldn't have, because I didn't want them to know the truth,' I snap. 'I didn't want *anyone* to know the truth, and I'm pissed off that you all do, thanks to my parents, brother and supposed best friend.'

'Nicki, there's no need to—'

'What do you mean?' Sergeant Zailer asks over Adam's protests. She agrees with me that there's a need.

'Melissa Redgate, who used to be my best friend – she married my brother, Lee. I saw her on Tuesday afternoon. We discussed Damon Blundy's murder. I think she thought I'd killed him – simply because I told her about it, and she thinks I'm the sort of person who must have done every bad thing it's possible to do.'

'I don't believe for a minute that Melissa thinks you killed Blundy,' Adam mutters. It makes me wonder whether, in a bargaining situation, I would sacrifice his determination to think well of me if in return he would agree to assume the worst about my enemies. *Probably.*

I ignore him and fix my eyes on Sergeant Zailer. 'Melissa thinks I *might* have killed Damon Blundy. She must have decided to share all my secrets with Lee, who rang our parents, hence my mother ringing to threaten to reveal my sordid history to Adam. Oh, my mother also asked me if I'd murdered Damon Blundy, in a tone that implied she believed I had.'

Sergeant Zailer produces a sheaf of papers from the folder on her lap. 'I'm going to show you some papers, Nicki. One of them's an ad from Intimate Links, from 2010. The others are your comments on Damon Blundy's newspaper articles.'

I take them and start to leaf through, hoping my hands aren't visibly shaking. Of course the police would read the comments sections beneath all Damon Blundy's articles in search of nutters threatening to kill him for causing them offence, but how the hell did they get hold of an ad I posted on Intimate Links three years ago?

Unless it was in Damon Blundy's house. Which would mean . . .

My heart starts to race, up into my throat. I can't breathe or swallow. My mind blurs around the edges.

'Nicki? Are you all right?' says Sergeant Zailer.

'Can you get her some water?' asks Adam. He's taken the papers and is reading the advert. *Oh God.* Even the word 'nightmare' feels inadequate – it doesn't begin to describe the situation.

I have to deny I wrote and posted that ad. I've no option. If Adam finds out I lied to him even while making my impressive confession, he'll leave me.

'I don't need water,' I say. 'I'm fine. I recognise Damon Blundy's *Herald* columns and my comments, but what's this ad?'

'You didn't put it on Intimate Links in 2010?'

'No. Who said I did? I categorically did not.'

'Are you a fan of BBC4?' Sergeant Zailer asks.

'Yes. And people close to me know that about me.' I see a change in Sergeant Zailer's eyes and know that I guessed right. The police didn't find my ad at Damon Blundy's house. 'Melissa drew your attention to that advert, didn't she? Told you I must have posted it? Or was it my brother, Lee? One of them, for sure.' Pretending to be thinking hard through my shock, I say, 'Which means . . . But Lee wouldn't have written that ad, no way. Melissa must have written it. She must have written it as if it was by me.'

'I don't think she'd do that, Nicki,' says Adam.

'She'd do anything,' I snap at him. To Sergeant Zailer, I say, 'Are you *sure* the ad was posted in 2010? She couldn't have posted it since Damon Blundy died and backdated it?'

I know Melissa did no such thing. Her bringing my Intimate Links ad to the police could mean more than that she suspects me of killing Damon Blundy . . .

'You commented on Blundy's columns a lot,' Sergeant Zailer pushes my thoughts off track. 'Always to support his point of view most enthusiastically. I can't find a single instance of you arguing against him.'

'I usually agreed with him.'

'It was more than usually,' said Charlie. 'Between October 2011 and February this year, you agreed with nearly every column he published. You only missed two or three. Did you know him personally?'

'No. Never clapped eyes on him, never spoke to him. I just happen to think he was a very clever man, and right about most issues.'

'Why did you only start commenting in 2011? Damon Blundy's had a column in the *Daily Herald* since 2009.'

'Surely Nicki's allowed to—'

'I started when I started to read him. I don't remember

the exact date. I didn't know how long he'd had his column for. I just discovered him one day, when I was wasting time online.'

'Why did you stop commenting in February this year?' Sergeant Zailer asks. 'Didn't you say that was when you answered Gavin's advert?'

'Yes, it was,' I say as smoothly as possible. 'And yes, the two are connected. I stopped commenting on Damon Blundy's columns because I'd had enough of getting attacked by his many enemies every time I spoke up for him. Suddenly, there was a gaping hole in my online time-wasting, so I looked on Intimate Links and got . . . drawn in.'

'Do you still have your email correspondence with Gavin?'

'No. When I decided to tell Adam the truth, I deleted every-thing – from my deleted box too. I might have decided to come clean, but Gavin hasn't, as far as I know. I thought it was only fair to protect him.'

'What was his email address?'

'I don't remember,' I lie. 'And if I did, I'd pretend I didn't. Sorry, but Gavin's married and wants to stay married. Not everyone's as understanding as Adam.'

'No, they're definitely not,' Sergeant Zailer agrees.

'Why did Melissa show you that Intimate Links advert?' I ask her. 'It's . . . too much. It's more than doing her duty as a good citizen. Why didn't she just tell you I asked her to lie about a car mirror and leave it at that?'

'I don't know. What's your theory?'

'She must have wanted to make *absolutely certain* that you'd believe I posted that ad, and that Damon Blundy replied to it, and we had an affair, and I ended up killing him. I don't know why she'd want that so much, unless . . .' I break off. I wish I'd never started. I don't really mean what I'm about to say.

Don't you? Then why are you trembling?

'Unless what, Nicki?' Sergeant Zailer asks.

'Unless she murdered him herself,' I whisper.

~

'I need you to drop me somewhere,' I say to Adam. We've hardly spoken since we left the police station. He's shocked that I accused Melissa of murder.

Except I didn't. I was thinking aloud, that's all. A thought crossed my mind and I blurted it out. Despite having done so, it's still there – I didn't succeed in banishing it. If Melissa believes I had an affair with Damon Blundy, and if she persuaded Lee to believe it too; if the two of them made the effort to bring my Intimate Links advert to the police's attention . . .

No. No way they murdered Damon Blundy. Why would they? I'm the one they've got it in for. If they were going to kill anyone, they'd kill me. My parents have always wanted me not to exist – me as I am and have always been. Adam would protest if I said this, but it's true. If you want, endlessly, to change someone's attitudes, behaviours and personality, it means you want that person as they are to be discontinued.

'You're not coming home?' Adam asks.

'I need to go to Kate Zilber's house. There's something I need to ask her.'

'About the kids?'

'No.' I'm too embarrassed to say that I need a new best friend and I'm hoping Kate will be it, but I can tell him part of the truth. 'I'm being followed. By a man with streaked hair and a blue BMW. He hangs around the school gates at the end of the day. Well, he used to – before he knew I'd clocked him.'

'*What?*' Adam does an emergency stop on Spilling's Main Street. The car behind beeps its horn. 'A man's following you and I'm just hearing about it now?'

'I've only known since Tuesday. He must have followed us to the station and then the car-hire office. He followed me to Melissa's. I came out and there he was, across the road. Smoking. I haven't seen him since.'

'Why didn't you tell the police? And what's Kate Zilber got to do with it?'

'I told you – he used to hang around at school. I assumed he was one of the dads, there to pick up his kids, but Kate says there's no parent who fits that description. I believe her. She'd know if there was. I asked her to ask some of the other parents if they'd noticed him, or his car registration. I was so shocked when I saw him outside Melissa's on Tuesday, I didn't think to look at it.'

'You didn't answer my first question,' Adam says impatiently. 'Why didn't you mention any of this to Sergeant Zailer?'

'Because . . .' I breathe. 'Grim though they are, I don't want to get my family into trouble. Not that that'd happen necessarily. Is it illegal to hire someone to tail your sister, or your daughter? It probably isn't.'

Adam rolls his eyes. 'Nicki, you're not seriously suggesting—'

'Who else?' I twist in my seat to face him properly. 'Who else would bother to pay a stooge to follow me around – me, an irrelevant housewife that no one's heard of? Only my parents and my brother have ever taken an unhealthy interest in my day-to-day behaviour. Of course they're behind it.'

'I think this is dangerous paranoia, Nicki.'

'I know. Because you don't understand how it felt to be me, in my childhood.' I hide behind a bright fake smile. 'It's OK. Actually, it's character-building. I didn't get where I am today by being understood.'

They didn't break me. You can't either.

Defeated, Adam shakes his head. 'All right,' he says quietly. 'Kate Zilber's house. What's the address?'

'Gunstool Road. Number 31.'

'So what's the plan? Why do you want to try and find out more about this guy, his car registration? I thought you said you hadn't seen him since Tuesday.'

I'm good at answering neutrally and fully without revealing how I feel about the question I'm responding to. 'I haven't. So either he's being more subtle now that he knows I'm onto him, or he's stopped following me. Either way, I'd like to know who he is and who hired him. I'd like to find out for myself.'

'Is there any point in me trying to—'

'No.'

Adam drives me to Kate's house in silence. All the way there, I imagine telling him the true story of my childhood. It's my fault he doesn't understand, my fault he doesn't know. I could have told him when we first met. I didn't. Even Melissa didn't get to hear the worst parts. I let her think my family situation was a normal one: the standard rebellious-teenager-clashes-with-parents scenario. I still think I made the right choice. Thanks to the safeguard of silence I put in place, no one has ever listened to me tell them how bad it was and, immediately afterwards, said, 'That's not so bad. I've heard worse.'

I tell Adam I'll be back no later than ten, then watch him drive away and out of sight before I ring Kate Zilber's doorbell. Her house is double-fronted, detached, with a bay window on either side of the door. In front of each one, there's an identical landscaped garden patch, a continuation of the house's symmetry.

Kate comes to the door wearing grey yoga trousers and a white sleeveless top, no shoes. My smile withers when I see her hard face. I've never seen her look like this before: completely different from the woman I know. 'I'm sorry, Nicki,' she says.

'Why? What's happened?'

'I can't have you round for the evening. We can't socialise. Your children are at my school. You're a parent; I'm the head-mistress. Let's keep it professional, OK? Again – I'm sorry. I shouldn't have invited you round. It was a bad idea.'

'Kate, what the hell's going on? I was a parent yesterday, when you invited me round. Since when do you care about professional? You're constantly telling me which of your staff you'd like to sack.'

'Nicki,' she says gently, 'you should go.'

'I'll go as soon as you've explained your change of heart.

Luckily for you, I no longer want to socialise with you either – I tend to prefer socialising with people who don't suddenly disown me – but I'm not an idiot, and I want an explanation.'

'The police contacted the school about you,' Kate says. Behind her, in the house, I see encaustic tiles on the floor, a pale blue rug that looks like seagrass or something similar. There's a spicy smell – curry or Mexican food.

'About Monday morning? Yes, I know – Izzie told them I was on and off the phone to her for much of the morning.'

'This is in connection with the murder of that journalist, isn't it? Damon Blundy?'

'Yes. Which, as Izzie made clear to the police, I can't possibly have been responsible for.'

'I'm not accusing you of murder. But . . . you're clearly mixed up in a murder, and you told me on the phone that some weird man's following you—'

'Wait, wait!' I put up a hand to stop her. 'I'm only mixed up in Damon Blundy's murder to the extent that I drove along his road on my way to school—'

'Nicki,' Kate silences me with her loud head-teacher voice. 'Listen. Spare me your innocent-until-proven-guilty speech. This isn't about what you've done or haven't done. Frankly, I couldn't care less. I just don't want to get close to anyone right now who's going to bring any kind of trouble or stress into my life. I'm up to my eyes as it is. This is about protecting myself. Sorry if that sounds selfish. And I'm sorry if you're in a difficult place at the moment, but – again, forgive me for being honest – you're not the kind of friend I need. I thought you were. I thought you'd be fun—'

'Oh, I am, believe me,' I say, nearly choking on what feels like a red spiky ball at the back of my throat. 'I'm great fun when I'm not being wrongly suspected of murder or trying to shake off strange men following me.'

'I understand that you're angry, but I'm trying to be honest. I need friends who are going to lift me up, not drag me down.

I really am sorry. And, just so's we're clear, this doesn't affect Sophie and Ethan – all right? Try taking them out of my school and I'll ring the police and un-alibi you!'

Unbelievable. She's actually trying to save face with a joke. Yes, let's have a good laugh about me being trouble and best avoided.

I can't bring myself to say anything in response. I turn and walk away from her house as fast as I can.

~

An hour later, I'm sitting outside a pub – the first one I came to after my escape from Kate's street – with a double gin and tonic, and my phone on the table in front of me. I can't think, can't do anything, can't stop crying. The only advantage to being in the state I'm in is that no one wants to share my table, so I've got plenty of space.

Kate was supposed to listen to my long, weird story and tell me what to do. I was relying on her. It's a danger, when you can't rely on anyone close to you – you tend to get desperate and pick random strangers instead, put them on pedestals they haven't earned and decide to rely on them.

Most people don't do that, though. Only idiots like you.

OK, think, Nicki. You have no one to turn to apart from your own stupid self. What are you going to do?

As far as I can see, one of two people must have murdered Damon Blundy – his wife, Hannah, or King Edward. Except that adds up to more than two possible people, since King Edward could be anyone.

What if King Edward is Adam?

No, that's absurd. Adam was at work when Damon Blundy was murdered. Wasn't he? Just because he's an IT genius and he defends my parents, that doesn't mean anything. He likes to give people the benefit of the doubt – that's a good thing. He's a good man, one who wouldn't fake an online affair lasting more than two years with his own wife. In order for him to have answered my Intimate Links ad in 2010, Melissa would have had to have told him I'd mentioned the site to her, and that she was suspicious. No, she wouldn't have done that. Not then. She still felt too guilty then about moving in with Lee.

Adam could have grown suspicious all by himself, I suppose. All the time I spent on my computer and on my phone . . .

Where was Lee when Damon was murdered? Was he at work, like Adam?

I shove the thought violently out of my mind. My brother is not King Edward. *Unthinkable.*

Melissa's ruled out, since King Edward I know – knew – is unambiguously a man.

What if he was a man hired and instructed by a woman? By Melissa. A man with a blue BMW and blond streaks in his hair, who maybe didn't follow a hired car all the way from Spilling to Highgate but knew Melissa's address anyway . . .

My stomach heaves like a fragile ship on a churning, storm-tossed sea, threatening to overturn.

I mustn't let myself speculate in all directions. It will drive me crazy.

Crazier.

If I ring Adam's work and try to find out if he was there on Monday morning or not, what does that say about me?

The blindfold. I've been assuming it was so that I wouldn't see his face and say, 'But you're not Damon Blundy.' It never occurred to me that it might have been to stop me saying more than that: 'You're not Damon Blundy. You're . . .'

Who?

I pick up my phone and start to draft an email. There's a voice in my head telling me not to, that it's the worst thing I could possibly do, but it's not a persuasive voice. It's panicky, insecure, reciting lines it learned by rote a long time ago that have since become meaningless.

I have a close relationship with somebody who knows the

truth – someone whose real name I don't know, true, but still: a man I shared my honest thoughts and feelings with for years. He *was* a man. He wasn't Melissa – how could I suspect that, even for a second? He shared his thoughts and feelings with me too, in a way that neither of us ever has with anyone else.

He cares about you. He's a killer, but he loves you. He's obsessed, and when you're obsessed, you'll do anything.

You'll do anything, also, when nothing matters to you more than finding out the truth.

I touch the letter keys on my phone's screen with the tip of my index finger. 'Dear Gavin/King Edward,' I write. 'We need to talk. Can we meet, as soon as possible? N x'

I press 'send'.

~

The man you were with at the Chancery Hotel . . . it wasn't me, or anyone you know. He was a stranger.

Words that will hurt for the rest of my life. Hurt of a kind that most people never feel.

I managed to remain coherent in order to find out as much as I could. I emailed back immediately. 'What do you mean, he was a stranger? If you sent an acquaintance of yours to have sex with me – a process he failed to see through to its logical conclusion, incidentally – then you must know his name. I'd like to know it too.'

As I pressed 'send', I was thinking, 'I could ring the police. I've been raped. This is rape, what's happened to me. Even though . . .' And then I remembered myself on that bed, and how I'd felt at the time. I realised how pointless it would be to think in terms of the police. They'd probably never find him – King Edward would protect him – and even if they did, he'd be sure to mention in court how much I'd enjoyed it. And Adam would find out, and my children would find out . . . No, it was unthinkable.

Another email arrived from King Edward within five minutes.

'Nicki, are you crazy?' it said. 'You honestly think I'd send a stranger – a real stranger? You think I'd do that to you? Wow, I'm pretty cut up about that. KE7.'

'You told me he was a stranger,' was the most I could manage in response.

'You're right, I did,' King Edward wrote back. 'Please forgive me – I'm not thinking clearly at the moment. I'm all over the place, to be honest. Nicki, it was me. Of course it was me. The man you've been writing to since June 2010 and the man in that hotel room are one and the same. KE7.'

'Then what did you mean when you said he was a stranger?' I had detached myself by this point. I knew what my next logical move was each time, and I made it, but I'd switched off my feelings. I knew, though, that when I switched them back on, I would find that nothing King Edward had said or would say, or could ever say, would make me feel any better.

His next email nearly stopped my heart. 'I am not, and have never been, Damon Blundy. That's what I meant by the stranger line. You've believed that you've been having a love affair with Damon Blundy. You haven't. The man in that room was me – a man whose name you still don't know, a man who's still hiding from you. A stranger. I was being melodramatic. Of course I'm not really a stranger.'

I didn't believe a single word he said, and knew I never would again. I remember going through the possibilities in my head:

1) King Edward was Damon Blundy, but the man at the Chancery Hotel wasn't.
2) King Edward was the man at the Chancery, but he wasn't Damon Blundy.
3) King Edward was neither Blundy nor the man at the Chancery.
4) King Edward was Blundy and the man at the Chancery.

There were probably more options to choose from, but I

decided I'd rather run a deep bath and drown myself than try to figure them out.

Another email arrived, when I failed to respond to the last one. 'I lied to you, Nicki. I'm so, so sorry. I know you won't forgive me. That's why I couldn't email you for days afterwards. I felt too guilty, if you want the truth. I hate myself as much as you must hate me. Please believe that. I don't know why I ever thought it was a good idea to pretend to be someone I'm not. Please be reassured that everything else I've ever written to you has been sincere and heartfelt. As for our time together in the hotel, I'm sorry about not seeing things through to their logical conclusion. You know my code – I tried to explain it to you. Quaint though it might sound, I don't want to cross my line in the sand and be fully unfaithful to my wife in terms of all things physical. I need to be able to live with myself. I hope you understand. I suffer from poor impulse control, and if I cut myself too much slack, I'm afraid of what might happen. KE7.'

'Fully unfaithful' – that was the phrase that made me want to stab him in both eyes. And that was when I wrote back and said it: the stupid, ridiculous, reckless thing that led to Damon Blundy's murder.

He is no less dead . . .

That, also – that same angry email – was when I told King Edward never to contact me again. If what he'd done to me was love, then I was going to find the opposite of love, I said. I'd go straight back to Intimate Links and answer an ad that wanted nothing more than sex, nothing more than a body to use; it would be less soul-destroying.

And so King Edward created Gavin.

If I'd only ignored his last email, there'd have been no Gavin, no humiliating encounter with a policeman in a supermarket car park, no involvement in a murder case.

No murder at all?

Very possibly.

It serves me right that I've been dragged into the police investigation. If it weren't for that last email I sent King Edward in February, Damon Blundy might well still be alive.

~

My phone buzzes on the table. I grab it.

A new message.

I gasp when I see the name in my inbox. I wrote to Gavin's address – mr_jugs@hushmail.com – but it's King Edward who's replied from the address that's been engraved in my mind since 2010: kingedward7@hushmail.com. Same subject heading as in my email to Gavin: 'Meet?'

Should I have been suspicious because they both wrote to me from Hushmail accounts? I assumed the majority of cyber-sex sinners used Hushmail as a matter of course. From the name, it sounds as if it was set up for that sole purpose.

My heart hammers in my chest. I drop my phone, pick it up again.

You knew Gavin was King Edward.

Of course I knew, but now the last sliver of doubt is gone.

I open the message.

Hi Nicki,

It would be unreasonable of me to refuse your request, wouldn't it? After everything I've put you through. Am I unreasonable? Not to that extent, no. Yes, we can meet as soon as possible. At the Chancery Hotel again. Make the arrangements and tell me when. Like last time, I will arrive at the appointed hour. You'll be waiting for me, as you were last time. In **all** respects, as you were last time. Yes, even the blindfold, which, once again, you must promise not to remove at any point during our meeting. You must also promise, like last time, not to speak a single word.

You said in your message, 'We need to meet and talk.' I will talk. You will listen. I'm confident that, once you've heard everything I have to say, you will know what you want and need to know. You will know who killed Damon Blundy. (I know you think it was me. You're wrong.)

Am I unreasonable? I suppose I am. Those are my conditions. I hope you will agree to them.

Trust me, Nicki, I won't harm you. I love you.

KE7

Ding Dong, Hypocrisy Is Alive and Well

Damon Blundy, 16 April 2013, *Daily Herald Online*

Yesterday, former Labour MP Paula Privilege, in admirably non-partisan fashion, blogged about misogyny in connection with the death of Margaret Thatcher. By all means, said Saint Paula, criticise Thatcher's harsh treatment of the unions if you wish, and her war-mongering in the Falklands (sic), but don't call her a witch, because that language is sexist and debasing of women. I was amused to learn that this was Saint Paula's opinion, in the light of something she'd tweeted to her 68,000 Twitter followers on 8 April, the day Baroness Maggie died. After reading her blog post that railed against the use of witchy imagery in connection with the unfairer sex, even if they happen to be one's political opponents, I trawled back through Saint Paula's tweets to see if she'd deleted the one that revealed her true feelings on the matter. These, I think, can be summarised neatly: 'It's wrong to compare women to witches, unless I do it, in which case it's OK.'

Here's what Saint Paula tweeted on 8 April:

Paula Riddiough @politixpaula
Finally, room on the broom! For strong but compassionate women in politics. Never celebrate death. Always celebrate hope for the future.

She hadn't deleted the tweet, and must either have forgotten about it by the time she wrote her blog post a week later or else she assumed no one would notice the disparity. For the culturally excluded among you, *Room on the Broom* is a bestselling picture book by Julia Donaldson, author of such children's classics as *The Gruffalo* and *Tiddler*. The broom in question belongs to a witch. I shall spell it out for the hard-of-believing-a-leftie-can-ever-put-a-foot-wrong: Saint Paula's tweet unequivocally implies that Margaret Thatcher was a witch and that, by dying, she has made room for superior women like Paula herself in the political sphere. But the meaning goes further than that:

Paula's tweet suggests that the compassionate women who might take Thatcher's place would also be sitting on the broom. All women in politics are witches, are they, Paula? What, even the ones who <u>empathise with Argentinian dictators</u> partial to purloining islands that don't belong to them?

I couldn't resist embroiling Her Saintliness in a Twitter debate on the subject:

Damon Blundy @blunderfulme
@politixpaula Saw your room on the broom tweet. Read your blog today. So which is it – OK or not OK to compare women to witches?

Paula Riddiough @politixpaula
@blunderfulme Not okay. Good point, I hadn't spotted that. I apologise, and will delete tweet.

Damon Blundy @blunderfulme
@politixpaula Your instinct, on hearing of death of one of UK's greatest women, was to tweet misogynistically, in a way you profess to find unacceptable. Hypocrite!

Paula Riddiough @politixpaula
@blunderfulme I'd be a hypocrite if I tried to defend my original tweet. I've apologised for it and have now deleted it.

Damon Blundy @blunderfulme
@politixpaula Hypocrite. Your misogyny pours forth, soon as you hear of the death of someone you disapprove of. Never call yourself a feminist again.

Wasim Khalid @waswashere
@politixpaula @blunderfulme Paula, ignore him. He is the cunt to end all cunts.

Damon Blundy @blunderfulme

@politixpaula @waswashere Christ, the misogyny on here's unbelievable. I thought I was a sexist shit. Feel like Emmeline
Pankhurst compared to you lot!

Paula Riddiough @politixpaula

@waswashere I will take your advice and ignore him!

Wasim Khalid @waswashere

@politixpaula Haha, yeh, he's a bitter twat! You are one amazing
lady, btw!

Damon Blundy @blunderfulme

@politixpaula @waswashere More misogynistic language! Paula,
any views?

Paula Riddiough @politixpaula

@blunderfulme I don't condone sexist language, but he's right
about one thing: you're bitter. And we're done here.

Damon Blundy @blunderfulme

@politixpaula A Twitter spat with a bitter twat? No better spat. No,
that's where it's at. (To misquote Julia Donaldson.)

Paula Riddiough @politixpaula

@blunderfulme Very good. I'm so very impressed by how clever
you are.

Damon Blundy @blunderfulme

@politixpaula I notice you haven't criticised @waswashere directly
for his appallingly misogynistic language. Can't bear to criticise a
fan? Hypocrite.

Paula Riddiough @politixpaula

@blunderfulme Do fuck off, Damon.

Damon Blundy @blunderfulme
@politixpaula Once there was a dish and her name was Riddiough./She had the blinkered mindset of a left-wing twit/But Riddy was a bird . . .

Damon Blundy @blunderfulme
@politixpaula . . . who inflamed imaginations./She talked pure rubbish but she looked well fit.

Paula Riddiough @politixpaula
@blunderfulme Once again: fuck off, Little Johnny Tory.

Wasim Khalid @waswashere
@politixpaula @blunderfulme You tell him, sweetheart!

Damon Blundy @blunderfulme
@politixpaula @waswashere He's calling you sweetheart now, Paula – any thoughts? Bit sexist, no?

Paula Riddiough @politixpaula
@blunderfulme A former MP took a look online./She spotted the rage of a right-wing swine./Why are you trolling me, tedious louse? . . .

Paula Riddiough @politixpaula
@blunderfulme . . . Go and spout bile in your Hicksville house.

Damon Blundy @blunderfulme
@politixpaula That's terribly kind, but I can't for a bit./I'm busy exposing a hypocrite.

Damon Blundy @blunderfulme
@politixpaula (A hypocrite? What's a hypocrite?)/A hypocrite? Why, Riddiough is it.

Coffee and Biscuits @coffeebiscuits
@politixpaula Hicksville? Charming! Fine way to talk about your former constituency!

Damon Blundy @blunderfulme
@politixpaula She has terrible friends with risible views/And visible cleavage on Channel Four News . . .

Damon Blundy @blunderfulme
@politixpaula . . . Why am I hounding her? Well, she cried, 'Witch!'/And her favourite phrase is 'Tax the rich.'

Alleviate Suffering @thealleviator
@politixpaula @blunderfulme Jesus, what a pair of exhibitionist narcissists! Fuck the both of yous.

(I love that contribution from Alleviate Suffering at the end there. It quite made my day.)

I can't help wondering if Saint Paula was one of the blood-curdling, death-celebrating lefties who downloaded 'Ding Dong, the Witch Is Dead' onto their iPods after Margaret Thatcher ascended to the great cabinet in the sky last week. I'd bet my mortgage-free Hicksville House that she was, and I challenge her to deny it.

8

Thursday 4 July 2013

'I love this one. It's the only one out of about a hundred that shows us as we really are. The others were all ridiculously glamorous, and that's *so* not us.' Paula Riddiough took the framed wedding photograph from the mantelpiece in her lounge and placed it in Simon's hands, which weren't ready. Why did he need to hold it when he'd had a perfectly decent view from where he was standing? He couldn't allow himself to worry about dropping it or else he would.

'Fergus looks so bemused,' said Paula fondly 'As if he's thinking, What's happening? Who are you, and why are you pointing a camera at me?' She laughed.

'What I was actually thinking, after the four hundredth photograph, was, Any minute now this protracted smile will ossify on my face and I'll need a chisel to get it off,' said Fergus Preece, who stood immediately behind Paula and Simon. He'd been sitting down, but had leaped up at the mention of the words 'wedding photo', keen to take part in the viewing of an object that lived in his house and that he could presumably look at every day if he wanted to.

Odd. Though Simon had to admit that his own attitude to wedding pictures would be regarded as odder by most people. He and Charlie had only a couple of photographs of their wedding, which Chris Gibbs had taken. Neither had ever been framed. In one of them, Charlie was yawning and laughing at the same time. Simon had no idea where the pictures had ended up. His best guess was the drawer in the kitchen where the phone chargers lived, and the snarled cling film that had been there for years and was completely unusable. Every time Charlie tried to throw it away, Simon fished it out of the bin, rinsed it under the tap and replaced it in the drawer, determined one day to find a straight edge that would enable him to detach useful lengths of film from the roll. Not that he and Charlie ever generated leftovers that needed to be covered up; the idea that cooking might involve more than putting something in the microwave was one that neither of them was prepared to entertain.

'Photographers – a strange breed,' said Fergus Preece. He was a short man with a tanned face, white hair and a large stomach that created portholes between the buttons of his shirt. Simon knew that Paula was thirty-nine, and guessed that Fergus was fifteen years older, perhaps more.

Like their marriage, the living room of their home blended the historic and the contemporary. There were many ornately framed portraits on the walls, all of which looked like antiques and made Simon think of words like 'ancestry' and 'lineage', but the large red, green and white rug covering the stone-flagged floor had a modern, jagged pattern on it that was as ugly as it was cleverly designed: the effect was rather as if someone had dropped red and green glass onto solid ice from a great height. Simon wouldn't have believed it possible to render such a thing in wool if he hadn't seen it first-hand.

He wondered how soon he could replace the wedding picture on the mantelpiece between and in front of half a dozen framed photos of Paula's son, Toby. This mantelpiece had a two-tier display system; indeed, the whole room suggested that Fergus and Paula were passionate about partially covering things with other things. All three sofas and the two chairs had throws draped over them, and on one there was a large golden-haired dog asleep on top of a smaller black and white dog. Simon could see that they were different types, but didn't know the name of either; he'd never had a pet and knew nothing about dogs apart from that Dalmatians had spots.

There were blinds at the windows with only their central

portions visible behind the swags and pelmets of the curtains.
Wherever there was a cushion, there was a smaller one leaning
against it, if not two. Near the door, there was a nest of three
rectangular wooden coffee tables with intricate carvings on their
legs, tucked in one beneath the other. They looked too old and
heirloomy for the slamming down of mugs of instant Nescafé.
On the surface of the top table were magazines in a fan-like
arrangement, covering other magazines. Simon could see the
beginnings of many titles: *Country Li*, *Vog*, *Bucki*, *Horse &*,
Psycholo. Only one title was fully visible: *Private Eye*.

The colour scheme was one Simon couldn't have lived with
for more than a couple of days without wanting to set fire to
the room: as many shades as possible, as bright as possible, all
jumbled up together. One of the throws was an almost luminous
tangerine orange. The cushions were red, turquoise, lime green.
Bright pink for the curtains, yellow for the blinds. Confronted
with a colour clash on this scale, one could hardly blame the
ancestors on the wall for their haughty, disapproving expressions;
sallow-skinned and muted, they were the outsiders in the room,
and Simon identified with them more than with any living person
present.

He put the wedding picture back on the mantelpiece. Paula
didn't seem to notice. She was ogling her husband appreciatively.
'You should hear Fergus on the subject of photographers,' she
said. 'He can't *bear* them, so they're banned from the house.
Making my husband happy is my new full-time job. I take it
very seriously – as seriously as I used to take my political career.'

'She does,' Fergus agreed enthusiastically. 'She's *extremely*
conscientious.'

Paula giggled for several seconds longer than was necessary.

Mentally, Simon turned his back on the innuendo and the flir-
tatious laughter. He didn't see why people couldn't behave like
grown-ups, especially when visited by the police. If Simon had
owned an eight-bedroom farmhouse and 120 acres of
Buckinghamshire, he would have conducted himself very

differently. He hoped his straight face and lack of response had made it clear to Preece and Paula that he was here for a more serious purpose than to snigger at dirty jokes, though it was evident from their forthright, gregarious demeanour that they were used to setting the agenda, not having it set for them by a man whose only noticeable asset was half of a mortgaged terraced house.

'Being a devoted wife is *so* much less stressful than politics,' Paula said so loudly that Simon flinched. 'God, I'm glad I'm out of all that! I escaped at exactly the right time. Life for MPs is only going to get harder. These days, people *want* to hate politicians. I'm sick of hearing about lack of trust, disillusion-ment, hand-wringing, what can be done about it, blah, blah, blah. The electorate doesn't want politicians it can believe in – God forbid anyone should be forced to abandon their cyni-cism! What everyone wants is a group of convenient patsies, to be sneered at and blamed. They'd find a way to hate whoever was in charge at the first tiniest suggestion of a policy that didn't read as if it was drafted solely with them in mind.'

'This is my wife's idea of leaving all that nasty politics stuff behind.' Fergus chuckled. 'You can see how detached she is, can't you, DC Waterhouse? Oh, she couldn't care less! That's why she's on Twitter all day long: Cameron this, Clegg that.'

Paula smiled. 'I'm afraid I have a serious Twitter addiction,' she said. 'And, of course, I'm still interested in politics. I always will be.' She lifted her thick dark brown hair with both hands, then let it fall, tilting her head back. Simon felt as if she were offering him, with this gesture, the opportunity to notice how stunning she was. For once when Charlie asked him, as she did about every woman he met, 'How attractive was she?', Simon would be able to answer without equivocation. Paula Riddiough was the most beautiful woman he'd ever seen close up. Superhumanly attractive, even in scruffy jeans and a shirt that looked like a man's and was clearly several years old. It was a bit like standing in a room with an alien; Simon didn't feel he belonged to the same species, and was keen to get away from his feelings of inadequacy as quickly as possible. First, though, he had questions to ask. Starting with Paula's marriages past and present had been a mistake. Simon hadn't realised it would lead to sentimental reminiscences and the showing of photos. He was keen to make up for lost time. 'Shall we make ourselves comfortable?' he said. 'There's quite a bit more I'd like to ask.'

Paula shrugged. She walked over to the sofa with the sleeping dogs on it and perched cross-legged on its thick, square arm, looking as if she might levitate. Fergus followed. He positioned himself more conventionally on one of the seat cushions, between his wife and his dogs.

'Ask away,' said Paula.

Simon was momentarily distracted by her multi-coloured toenails: red, pink, green, blue, silver – on both feet, but with the colour order varying. 'Where were you on Monday morning between eight thirty and ten thirty?' he asked.

'Walking the dogs on Hankley Common in Surrey. We'd stayed with friends there the night before. Do you need their contact details?'

'That would be helpful, yes.'

'Stephanie Coates and Eva Patterson,' said Fergus. 'The Old Butchery, Elstead. They're in the phone book.'

Simon made a note of it. 'Thanks. Ms Riddiough, I'm going to need to—'

'Mrs Preece,' Paula corrected him with a smile.

'I'm going to need to ask you some quite personal questions. Are you sure you wouldn't rather talk in private?'

'We are talking in private, and please call me Paula. Fergus is my husband and this is our home. I'm happy for him to hear everything we say. I'm guessing your first question's going to be, was I having an affair with Damon Blundy?'

'Why do you think I'd want to ask you that?' said Simon.

Paula grinned. 'Everyone I've met since my very public war with Damon has asked me. A lot of people thought we'd be a match made in heaven: both good-looking, both shameless self-publicists. It was hilarious. We obviously hated each other, but no one let that put them off! They insisted on seeing sexual tension where there was none.'

'So, are you going to answer the question, then?'

'I thought I had, but if you want me to do so more explicitly: no, I did not sleep with Damon Blundy. Ever. We weren't having an affair.'

'Yet you met him at least twice,' said Simon. 'In 2011, on 26 October and on 11 November.'

'I met him *only* twice.'

'On those two dates, correct?'

'I can't remember. Didn't you contact my assistant, Gemma?'

'Yes. Those were the dates she gave me.'

'Then those were the dates.' Simon heard a steel edge in Paula's voice that he hadn't heard before. Fergus Preece might as well have been a spectator at a tennis match; he was turning back and forth to look at his wife, then at Simon, as each one spoke. He would injure his neck if he didn't watch out.

'I don't think you were entirely honest with me,' Simon said. 'You told me you couldn't remember exactly when you and Damon Blundy met, but I don't think you'd have forgotten arranging to meet him on 11 November 2011. Particularly since the time of the meeting was eleven minutes past eleven a.m.'

'Oh yes!' Paula laughed. 'So it was. Well, you're wrong, as you can see, because I did forget. Completely forgot until I heard you say it.'

Simon gave himself a few seconds, wondering where to go next. Confident outright denial was the hardest kind of dishonesty to deal with. 'I'm trying to imagine the conversation you and Blundy must have had,' he said. 'One of you must have suggested continuing the elevens theme from the date to the time. Sounds like a memorable conversation to me – a memorable diary appointment. How often is it possible to make an arrangement like that? Once a year, maximum? This year, it's not possible at all, is it? There's no thirteenth month.'

'That's a good point,' said Fergus. 'Let's see, a set-up like that wouldn't work again until . . .' He broke off, scratched his head. 'Hmph,' he concluded.

'The first of January 2101,' said Paula. 'We'll all have followed in Damon Blundy's footsteps by then and shuffled off to oblivion. A dispiriting thought.'

Simon was determined not to be sidetracked. 'You only met Damon Blundy twice, you say. Once was at eleven minutes past eleven on the eleventh day of the eleventh month of the eleventh year of this century, and you expect me to believe that that detail slipped your mind?'

Paula inclined her head, raised her eyebrows and gave Simon a look more patronising than anything the Snowman had ever produced. 'DC Waterhouse, when I was an MP, more details slipped my mind than didn't, if they weren't work-related. The job filled my head, to the exclusion of all else. My poor son never had anything he needed for school; I never had clean matching socks, or paid a bill on time; nothing ever got done in the house; I neglected my husband . . .' She shrugged as if to say, 'Point proven.'

'You didn't neglect several other women's husbands,' Simon couldn't resist pointing out.

'Yes!' Paula chuckled. 'I did. The affairs were a by-product of the stress I was under from work, and, yes, I *totally* neglected those men. There was none of me left for a relationship, let alone several concurrent relationships. I was in danger of seriously burning out and I couldn't see it. I was a fool until Fergus saved me, DC Waterhouse. A very clever fool with a PhD, but no less a fool. I can't *tell* you how much happier I am now.' Fergus reached over to squeeze her thigh with his thick-knuckled fingers. Paula stroked the back of his hand, smiling down at it as if it were a favourite pet that had leaped up onto her lap. Meanwhile, the larger of her two real pets had started to snore.

Simon could see that nothing he might say would rile Paula.

She had every corner of her polished act sewn up. He still didn't believe her.

'All right, so tell me about you and Damon Blundy,' he said. 'I know he used his column and blog to attack you, and I know you fought back sometimes. Why the two meetings?'

'Both were at my instigation,' said Paula. 'His columns about me really upset me, and they upset Toby, my son, even more – that was the part I couldn't live with. People at school were either teasing him or commiserating with him for having the worst mother in the country. I emailed Damon to ask him ever so kindly and politely to desist, and he replied saying he wasn't prepared to discuss it via email. If I wanted to talk to him, I had to meet him, he said. He told me when and where. There was no consultation process; he issued me with an order. I turned up, tried to be as diplomatic and reasonable as I could. We got on better than I expected, actually, and when I left, I thought we'd agreed that he would lay off. There was only one problem.'

'He didn't lay off?' Simon guessed.

'Got it in one. If anything, his attacks on me escalated – on his blog, on Twitter. So I repeated the process: emailed him again, asked him to stop, *again*. He pretended not to have noticed that he hadn't stopped. Made me present him with evidence. Then he summoned me to another meeting. This time, he decreed that it had to be on 11 November at eleven minutes past eleven a.m. It was part of a very weird attempt to humiliate me. Probably makes no sense to you, but . . . that's what he was trying to do.'

Simon could see what she meant. It sounded plausible, therefore he didn't like it; it played havoc with his theory that only lovers or prospective lovers would arrange to meet at that particular time.

'It entertained Damon to make me behave in a ridiculous way. I shouldn't have turned up – I should have told him to stick it up his arse, and write whatever he liked. It's a common definition of madness, isn't it: doing the exact same thing and expecting it to have a different result? He told me that if I arrived at ten past eleven, or twelve minutes past, he'd get up and leave. If I wanted to speak to him, I had to be bang on time. Absurd!' Paula ruffled Fergus's hair. 'If only I'd met Fergus sooner. You wouldn't have let me pander to Damon Blundy's ego, would you, darling?'

'I'd have dealt with him,' said Fergus. 'I've never known a man to behave in that way. I don't know what he thought he was up to.'

If Paula and Blundy had been romantically or sexually involved, wouldn't she be visibly upset and shaken? If they'd been enemies, as she claimed, wouldn't she sound angrier when she described how he'd tormented her? Wouldn't she gloat about his death? Simon found her unruffled good humour disturbing.

'So what happened at the second meeting?' he asked.

'Same as at the first. Damon was charming. He apologised for having broken his word last time, he promised again not to eviscerate me in his column – and it was all lies. He did it again and again and again. Until he died.' Paula looked down at her wedding and engagement rings. She adjusted them, twisting them round on her finger. 'At least I wised up after the second time. I didn't bother appealing to his compassionate side again – I'd worked out that he didn't have one.'

'He was a brute,' said Fergus. 'Wasn't he, Loophole?'

Simon didn't immediately realise that Fergus was talking to the larger of the two dogs, now awake, whose ear he was stroking. Loophole? Strange name for a pet. Still, at least it wasn't Fergus's pet name for Paula, as Simon had initially imagined. 'Does anyone call you Riddy?' he asked her.

'Not any more,' she said. 'It was my nickname at school. Why?'

'The password for Damon Blundy's laptop was "Riddy111111".'

'Was it? Doesn't particularly surprise me. The man was obsessed with me.'

'Funny thing is, now Toby has the same nickname at his new school,' said Fergus. 'Riddy! Complete coincidence, too – no one at Ashfold knows that Paula used to be known as Riddy.'

'Ashfold?' said Simon.

'Oh, here we go!' Anger flashed in Paula's eyes. 'Yes, Ashfold – the independent fee-paying prep school. Why did I move my son there from a state school? That's my business and none of yours. Toby couldn't stay at his old school after we moved in with Fergus. If you must know, I decided Damon was right about that one thing – nothing else. But . . . if I can afford the very best education for my son, it's my duty to provide that, isn't it?'

'Your son's surname is Riddiough, then?' Simon asked. 'Not Crumlish like his father?'

'You've done your homework. I'm flattered.' Paula smiled. 'My son's name is Toby Crumlish-Riddiough,' said Paula.

And you sent him to a state school in Combingham, and expected him to survive his first day?

Riddy111111. Was it possible the Riddy in Damon Blundy's password was Toby? 'How did Damon Blundy know your school nickname?'

'Good question,' said Paula. 'One of his hobbies was digging around looking for any dirt on me he could find. He probably unearthed one of my old classmates and got it from her.'

'Or he had your son in mind,' said Simon. 'Did you have Toby with you on 11 November 2011 when you met Damon?'

'No. Of course not. Why would I take my son to what was likely to be a deeply unpleasant meeting?'

'Did you ever refer to Toby as Riddy in Blundy's presence?'

'No. And . . . Damon wouldn't have been interested enough in Toby to make a password out of him,' said Paula. 'Damon's one of those childless men for whom children barely exist. When I tried to explain to him how much his attacks on me were hurting Toby, he laughed and said, "Buy him a packet of Maltesers and he'll be fine." And he had the nerve to call me a bad mother and say I only cared about my career and my sex life! If you added up all the times I've had sex since Toby was born and set that total against the number of times I've read *Tiddler* and *The Gruffalo* and *The Gruffalo's Child* – my favourite books in the *world*! – I promise you sex would be the loser!'

'Paula's a brilliant mother,' Fergus announced loudly.

'Thank you, darling.' She ruffled his hair again.

A brilliant mother to whom, Simon wondered, Toby or Fergus? There was something maternal about the way she was gazing fondly at her husband.

'Thanks for your patience, both of you.' Simon stood up. 'I'll get out of your hair now, but I'll probably be back.'

'Anytime,' said Paula. 'I'll walk you to the front door. Don't want you getting lost on the way. It's a bit of a maze. Are you coming too, Loophole? Sweet *girl*! Darling, you couldn't stick the kettle on, could you? I think we deserve a cup of tea for getting through our first ever police interview!'

Simon could have done with a cup of tea, but at no point had one been offered.

He, Paula and the dog walked to the front door in single file. Every wall had a mountain of miscellaneous items piled up against it – bicycles, Wellington boots, a watering can, two tins of paint – not Dulux's Ruby Fountain 2, Simon noticed. Here were two kegs of beer, a wheelbarrow, several clear plastic containers with royal blue plastic lids. All of these things narrowed the usable space by about half. This was the domestic equivalent of a clogged artery.

At the front door, Paula said, 'I need to come and see you. In Spilling.'

It was an admission. Unambiguous.

'To tell me what you couldn't say in front of your husband?' Simon asked.

'How about Monday, ten a.m.? Or Tuesday afternoon – I've got another appointment in the Culver Valley on Tuesday morning, so I'll be around anyway. No, I tell you what: let's make it Monday at ten past ten. I think that would be appropriate, don't you? And then I'll stay over somewhere, for my Tuesday meeting.'

'I'd rather say ten o'clock,' said Simon uncomfortably.

'And I'd rather say ten past.' Paula raised one eyebrow provocatively. 'If only to prove to you that two people can meet at a daft time of day and not be having a clandestine affair.'

~

Charlie smiled when she heard Simon's voice say, 'What?' He sounded hassled. Normally he didn't answer when she rang him; he preferred to let her give up, then call her back.

'Guess what I've just found waiting for me on my desk,' she said.

'What?'

'Copies of the pathologist's report, the crime-scene report—'

'Damon Blundy?' Simon talked over her.

'—confirmation of several alibis: Rabbi Fedder, Verity Hewson, Abigail Meredith, Richard Crumlish, Lee Redgate, Nicki Clements, the neighbour whose daughter's earlobe he wrote about cutting off. Yeah, Damon Blundy. Nice that someone thought to include me, isn't it? Whoever it was kindly swept all *my* work to one side. Some of it fell off the desk onto the floor.'

'Proust,' said Simon.

'Or Sellers in a bad mood. Do you know what's up with him?'

'Yeah, and I wish I didn't. He deserves his bad mood and worse.'

'Tell me,' said Charlie eagerly.

'Later. Tell me about the pathologist's report.'

'It's everything you know already. Blundy's airways were blocked by a combination of the knife and the tape. He suffocated, after first being knocked out with the knife sharpener. The knife was sharpened at the scene. No identifiable fingerprints in the room apart from Blundy's and his wife's. Some unknown prints too, but you'd expect that.'

'So tell me again who's alibied for sure: Rabbi Fedder, Nicki Clements . . . ?'

'Doormat and Despot,' said Charlie.

'So that leaves Keiran Holland, Bryn Gilligan and Melissa Redgate without a decent alibi.'

'And Hannah Blundy.'

'Maybe Reuben Tasker too, depending on what he's telling Gibbs now.'

'What about Paula Riddiough?' Charlie asked.

'She was with friends. I've no doubt her alibi'll be watertight, whether she murdered Damon Blundy or not.'

Charlie smiled to herself. 'You've met her, then?'

'I'm outside her house now, in Buffler's Holt.'

'That sounds like an arcane sexual practice.'

'Paula Riddiough denies she was having an affair with Damon Blundy,' said Simon. 'She's lying.'

'How do you know?'

'The elevens thing. The fact that he chose to make it his password.'

'I'm not sure that alone—'

'I am,' Simon cut her off.

Charlie wasn't in the mood to be trampled underfoot. 'And *I'm* sure you're wrong, unless Blundy had two bits on the side,' she said. 'I think Nicki Clements was the one having the affair with him, and I've got solid reasons for thinking so. All you've got is a meeting arranged at an aren't-we-clever time of day.'

'Let's hear it, then,' said Simon.

'The tit photo Nicki Clements was taking when Meakin snuck up on her was to send to a man she'd met online, on Intimate Links – a man called Gavin. She told me she answered his ad in February. Also in February, she suddenly stopped commenting on Damon Blundy's columns. I think that's when they broke up. She went looking online for a new lover and found this Gavin person. And before you say that's pure speculation – yes, I know it is, and that's why I did a bit of digging around, to put my theory to the test. I dug up some interesting facts. Nicki and her family moved from London to Spilling in December last year. Damon Blundy made the same move on 5 November 2011—'

'That's only six days before 11 November 2011,' Simon interrupted. 'So Blundy travelled from Spilling back to London for his meeting with Paula Riddiough, six days after moving in the opposite direction. Would he do that if he weren't having an affair with her?'

'Simon.' Charlie laughed. 'Spilling's an hour and a half from London by train. Of course he'd nip in for a meeting if there was someone he needed to meet, whether he was shagging them or not.'

'Really?' Simon sounded doubtful. 'I wouldn't want to revisit the place I'd just moved away from. Not immediately.'

'Yes, well . . . you're a freak and a hermit, aren't you? Can we concentrate on Nicki Clements? Why did she decide to move to Spilling? It wasn't for work reasons – she wasn't working then and isn't now.'

'Husband's work?'

'Ah! Thought you'd say that. No. Her husband, Adam, had an army IT job in London, and they reassigned him to the Culver Valley, but *he asked* for the transfer. I've spoken to them, confidentially. Adam told them he wanted to transfer because his wife had her heart set on relocating round here.'

'That doesn't prove anything,' said Simon. 'The Culver Valley's a beautiful place. Who wouldn't want to live here?'

Charlie was surprised. She'd never heard him say anything like that before. She'd had no idea it was how he felt; normally, apart from needing things to be tidy wherever he was, he seemed oblivious to his physical surroundings.

'It proves as much as a meeting at eleven minutes past eleven does,' she said. 'But if you want more proof . . . I rang round a few local estate agents to see if any of them remembered Nicki Clements. If you're planning to move to a different part of the country, chances are you'd ring an estate agent in your target area and tell them what you were looking for, right? And it was just about recent enough for someone to remember, I thought. Unfortunately, no one remembered anything, but it didn't matter. Two separate estate agents still had Nicki Clements's wish list stored on their systems. Guess what she told both of them she was looking for?'

'Go on.'

'A four-bedroom house in Spilling within ten or fifteen minutes' drive of Elmhirst Road, but not *on* Elmhirst Road and not too near to it.'

'You're kidding? No way!'

It wasn't often that Charlie managed to impress Simon. When she did, she often felt for days afterwards as if she were glowing from within. It was pathetic, she knew. 'Seriously,' she said. 'Now, what possible explanation could there be for that, apart from that Nicki was having an affair with Blundy and wanted to be close enough but not too close – not dangerously close to where he lived with his wife.'

'If I wasn't so sure Blundy was having an affair with Paula Riddiough . . .' Simon's voice was barely audible. It was more like listening to thoughts than words – ideas powerful enough to make themselves heard, but only just. 'He was obsessed with her. Read his columns. He went on about her constantly. Like him, she's famous, spectacularly good-looking, an egotist who loves to be in the public eye – the perfect match for him. Look, you said it before, and maybe we shouldn't dismiss it: what if he was having two affairs? Paula Riddiough *and* Nicki Clements. That'd give three women a motive to kill him – both of them and Hannah, his wife.'

'It's possible,' said Charlie. 'I think I could believe anything about Damon Blundy, he was so outrageous. You need to get the phones and personal computers of all these people looked at: Paula Priv, Nicki Clements, Damon himself—'

'Blundy's is getting the treatment as we speak, I hope.'

'—Melissa Redgate, Keiran Holland, Reuben Tasker if you

think he's a serious contender – perhaps he was sleeping with Damon Blundy as well.'

Silence. Then Simon said, 'That's an interesting idea. Paula Riddiough and Reuben Tasker . . . Paula, Reuben . . .'

'What? You think Blundy might have been bisexual and having affairs with both of them?'

'No. Not at all.'

There was no point waiting for an explanation of why, in that case, Simon had found the idea interesting, not unless she wanted to sit with her phone pressed to her ear for a week. Simon never explained until he was ready.

'You know what bothers me most about all this?' he said. 'The timing. Everything's so close together. Blundy first writes about Paula Riddiough in October 2011. He meets her twice – once in October and once in the first half of November. He also moves from London to Spilling in the first half of November, and meets his future wife, Hannah, at the end of November. Around the same time – September, October, November 2011, Blundy's busy making enemies of Reuben Tasker, Keiran Holland, Bryn Gilligan, and Nicki Clements decides she's going to start commenting regularly on Blundy's columns. It's a lot to be happening in such a short time, involving so many of our key players. We need to find out what connects these people that we don't yet know about.'

Charlie smiled at her phone. 'That's what life is – things happening, constantly. I'm not sure what you're suspicious of, exactly.'

Simon made a dismissive noise. Work frustration always made him more unreasonable; he expected Charlie to know what was in his head without his having to tell her. 'Paula Riddiough married Fergus Preece in January this year,' he said. 'She only met him in August 2012. On 11 November 2011, she was still unhappily married to Richard Crumlish. In November 2011, Damon Blundy was single and available. If he and Paula fell in love, why didn't they marry each other?'

'Because they weren't in love, and you've just made that up?' said Charlie. 'They hated each other. If you loved someone, would you constantly flay them in your newspaper column?'

'*That's* what Paula Riddiough and Reuben Tasker have got in common,' Simon said. 'I knew there was something. They both publicly attacked Damon Blundy. Because he attacked them.' Simon's voice was getting louder. Charlie wished she could work out what he was excited about.

'Can I ask you something personal?' he said.

'I would think so, yes. We're married, so . . . go ahead.' *And I'll try to forget the extremely impersonal question you've just asked me.* Sometimes it was hard not to lose hope.

'Why do you stay with me when I hurt you?'

'What?' Charlie pushed her chair back from her desk. 'You don't hurt me. Not deliberately. What do you mean?'

'Hurt's the wrong word. But . . . before, when I rang and asked you to find out about Melissa Redgate's driving . . . I knew I had no right to ask. I wanted a fight, so that it could end.'

'So that what could end? Our marriage?' *One day, that's what he might mean. Not today, if I'm lucky.*

'No, the fight,' said Simon.

'You wanted a fight so that the fight – the same fight – could end?' *Never assume you know what Simon Waterhouse means. Even if it seems obvious.*

'I think so.' He sounded uncertain. 'I do that, don't I? I provoke you, knowing you'll kick off, because I want to be forgiven. That appeals to me. Not starting a fight in the first place – that doesn't have the same appeal.'

'Hmm.' Charlie wondered about taping all her conversations with Simon from now on, to play to a shrink at some future date. 'Well, I didn't kick off, did I?'

'Having fights and forgiving each other afterwards – that's what normal couples do,' said Simon. 'I think I like it because it makes me feel we're more normal.'

'Really? I'm not sure we'll ever be normal, but who cares? I'd rather be married to you weirdly than to someone else normally.'

'You're missing the point. What if Paula Riddiough and Damon Blundy loved each other and wanted to be together, but for some reason couldn't be? They can't have a proper relationship, so they attack one another in newspapers and online so they can have at least one thing that real, proper couples have – the ability to hurt and forgive each other, endlessly. It's not true closeness, but it makes them feel closer.'

'OK, *now* you've hurt me,' said Charlie quietly.

'No, I didn't mean . . .' Simon broke off. 'Don't take it the wrong way.'

'Don't *give* it the wrong fucking way! You've just basically told me you like hurting me and being forgiven because we're not truly close and it's the best you can hope for.'

'I was talking about Paula Privilege and Damon Blundy.'

'But not only about them. Before, you said—'

'I'm not having a row with you now, Charlie. I just meant . . . those emotional highs and lows – attack, forgive, attack, forgive – they're a form of passion, aren't they?'

Charlie said nothing.

'I need you to find out some more things for me,' said Simon.

'No.'

'Find out if Adam Clements, Nicki's husband, has got an alibi for Monday morning. Also, you know I said find out about Melissa Redgate's driving and if she's got a car? Don't ask Melissa herself – ask Nicki Clements. Let me know how she reacts. And then—'

Charlie missed the end of his sentence. That'll happen if you hang up on someone, she thought. *Oh well.*

She clicked on the Safari icon on her computer screen and typed, 'Intimate Links,' into the search box when it appeared. She'd had an idea. Well, two, really. She could advertise for a new husband: must be a genius detective, appallingly insensitive, badly dressed but, crucially, sexually uninhibited.

And . . . Or . . .

She could write and post an advertisement that would make sense to no one but Damon Blundy's killer, or to someone who knew something about the murder. Would Proust or anybody at the nick find out she'd done it? Hard to say. It was unlikely that it would attract any useful information, but it was worth a try. And to do it without Simon's permission . . . that would be nearly as much fun as advertising for a hornier husband, and less marriage-threatening.

The 'Men Seeking Women' section of the site was the right place to put her advert, she decided. Hannah Blundy, Melissa Redgate, Nicki Clements and Paula Riddiough were all women. If they were looking on Intimate Links at all, chances were this page would be where they'd look.

Would they be looking, though? It was impossible to know. Nicki and Melissa had both looked in the past . . .

It was the longest of long shots, but Charlie felt like giving it a try. She felt like doing something different. And – yes – something she shouldn't do – risky and utterly forbidden.

Fuck Simon.

Charlie clicked on the 'Compose a Personal Ad' button and a new box appeared. In the subject heading, she typed, 'Looking for a Woman with a Secret,' and found herself grinning. She was going to enjoy this.

~

'Was your father really a professional gambler?' Gibbs asked Reuben Tasker, casting his eye over the 'About the Author' paragraph on the jacket flap of *Craving and Aversion*. 'I mean, was that his day job?'

They were in the attic room at the top of the house, where Tasker wrote his books. It was a warm day, but up here the heat was stifling. Gibbs wished nevertheless that Tasker would put on a shirt. The sight of his bare chest was off-putting. Still, he was clean, not obviously stoned, and so far, if you didn't include his initial refusal to open the door, he had been courteous and articulate.

There was nothing in his writing room apart from books and, immediately beneath the dormer window, a desk with a hard right angle of a chair positioned in front of it. No cushion. The remainder of the space was devoted to emptiness that most people would have filled with a couple of chairs, or a large TV that doubled as a PlayStation. On the desk, a computer and a printer stood side by side. There were no lamps, no pictures, no rugs, no plants. Just cork tiles on the floor, white walls with brown patches here and there from water damage, and Tasker's writing station. Gibbs had seen more homely prison cells.

A glaring neon light, attached to the ceiling, was on. The window was still completely covered with sheets of black paper.

'My father's gambling wasn't a day job so much as a night job,' said Tasker, standing in front of a wall of his books in at least seventeen languages. 'I can remember him going out to work as Mum put me to bed, and getting back as she gave me breakfast. That was before he left us, when I was eleven.'

Gibbs glanced down at the author biography again. 'For . . . "an Afro-American jazz singer who was arrested for the abduction and murder of a child in 1983, then released without charge a week later"? Really?'

'Really.' Tasker folded his arms as if expecting to be challenged. 'She had nothing to do with the boy's murder, though Mum and I wished she had. Everything in my novels is true. Even the fiction's true – truer than the truth, sometimes.'

'I'm not doubting you. I just . . . I've never read an "About the Author" like this one.' Before Olivia, Gibbs had never read an 'About the Author', period. Recently, in her company, he had been reading quite a few bits around the edges of books, though not many actual books. Liv tried to force novels on him occasionally, but the titles were usually enough to put him off: *Leopards with Pink Umbrellas*, *The Cartographer's Biographer* . . . Gibbs couldn't understand why an author would give a book a title that bored people before they'd even opened it. It was daft.

'You were arrested for shoplifting aged thirteen, gave a false name, then escaped from the police station?' he asked Tasker. 'You lived for three weeks on your mother's boss's boat and he never found out?'

Tasker nodded. 'I often wonder why other authors' biogs are so dull,' he said. 'Interesting things happen to everybody, so why not mention them if you're writing something about your-self that's going to be read all over the world? The least inter-esting thing about me is that I'm forty-seven and live in King's Lynn with my wife, so I don't bother mentioning it.'

'You could spice up the biog for your next book by adding that you killed Damon Blundy,' Gibbs suggested. *Unprofessional. Fuck it.*

'Except it wouldn't be true. Blundy was murdered on Monday morning, wasn't he? I was here, at home, with Jane.'

'Doesn't Jane have a job?'

'She works for me.'

'Doing what?' Gibbs asked.

'Admin. Fending people off, mainly. Answering endless emails that if I answered them myself, I'd never get a word written. Not from readers,' Tasker clarified. 'If someone's read one of my novels, I always write back myself – even if they've written to say it's the worst book they've ever read, which some do. Jane deals with my agent, the festivals, the media, the account-ants, my travel and hotel arrangements if I've got an event coming up – all the practical stuff.'

All the boring stuff. His wife was his skivvy, working to promote his product. Instead of developing any interest of her own, personal or professional, she had chosen to devote her life to making Tasker's life easier. How likely was she to say, 'No, Reuben, I'm not going to lie to the police for you and pretend I was with you on Monday morning?' Not very, Gibbs concluded.

'Here.' Tasker handed him a copy of *Craving and Aversion*.

'This is my novel that won the prize. Damon Blundy thought it was a pile of pretentious shite. You might agree, or you might not. Either way, I'd be interested to hear what you think.'

Gibbs muttered an awkward thank you. Liv had read it, after it won the Books Enhance Lives Award. In her opinion, it was 'spectacular', and Gibbs should ignore Damon Blundy, who was a philistine. Gibbs had told her it wasn't Blundy's scorn that would put him off so much as the possibility that Tasker was a sadistic murderer. Liv had rolled her eyes. 'He's just a suspect, Chris,' she'd said. 'One of many. And anyway, you've got to separate the art from the artist. But you know, thinking about it . . . it strikes me as highly unlikely that the author of *Craving and Aversion* is a killer of any kind. Really, you should give it a try. Don't look like that! I'm not asking you to marry the man.'

Marriage. Why did it matter so much? To Gibbs, Liv, his wife, her husband? It was no more than a word accompanied by a certificate.

It should and often does mean nothing. And yet, still, it means everything.

'Where and when did you and Jane meet?' Gibbs asked.

'What does it matter? Somewhere, sometime.' Tasker sounded bored. Disappointed – as if he'd hoped for a more interesting question. 'I was probably stoned. No, I was definitely stoned,' he corrected himself. 'Though that's something I've knocked on the head.'

'What, the cannabis?' Gibbs was surprised. 'You're not using any more?'

Tasker looked annoyed. 'You didn't know? See, this just proves how mud sticks. I've blogged about it, I've done interviews, but once you've been written off in the public eye for doing a thing, or being a thing – no matter what that thing is, whether it's weed smoker or paedophile – there's never any possibility of rewriting. You're branded for all eternity. Thanks to Damon Blundy, I'll be known for the rest of my life as "Skunkweed addict Reuben Tasker".'

'How do you feel about Blundy's death?' Gibbs asked.

A faint smile appeared on Tasker's face. 'I feel – and I can't tell you how sincerely I mean this – that I'm not going to worry about it unduly. Lots of people suffer horribly who don't deserve it. I'm going to reserve my sympathy for those people.'

Gibbs had heard this sentiment expressed many times before. He could understand it, and imagine feeling that way himself, but from someone else it always sounded wrong. Was it really so hard to be sorry that someone had died violently, however much you disliked them?

'I suppose I should be grateful to Damon Blundy for one thing,' said Tasker. 'If he hadn't started writing about my drug habit, I doubt I'd have had the motivation to give up. All the attention made me paranoid. Suddenly, all over the bloody media, people were talking about whether I deserved to keep my award or not, given that I'd written my novel under the influence of illegal narcotics. It was insane. I had hate-mail on Facebook, and to the house – one woman whose son died of a heroin overdose wrote to tell me she'd burned all my books in her back garden. Mad!'

Gibbs waited.

Eventually, Tasker said, 'But . . . well, when you read enough tweets and online comments and letters about how you're a drug addict, it's kind of hard to avoid the conclusion that you're a drug addict and that maybe that's not ideal. Jane had been worried about my health, and my concentration, for a while – I'd always told her I was fine and not to be stupid, before. Obviously, I knew I smoked weed every day – I used to tell myself it made my books better, which was bullshit. I mean, I'm writing a book now and it's no worse off for the lack of skunk.' Tasker smiled. 'It's probably better. I can think more clearly. Truth is, I was a drug addict who wanted to spend all day every day stoned and I came up with a convenient justifica-tion: I needed it for the words to flow – because, conveniently, I happened to be a writer too. It was bullshit.'

'And now, thanks to Damon Blundy, you're drug-free,' said Gibbs.

Tasker's smile turned to a grimace. 'Yeah, well . . . let's not give him too much credit. He wouldn't have cared if I'd died in a ditch with a syringe hanging out of my arm. All he cared about was scoring points against Keiran Holland.'

Gibbs wanted to turn the conversation back to Tasker's relationship with Jane, though he wasn't sure why. He hoped he wasn't becoming obsessed with marriages at the stranger end of the spectrum. 'So when you gave up the drugs, your wife must have . . . supported that decision.'

Tasker looked momentarily confused. 'Yeah, I suppose so,' he said.

'You don't sound sure.'

'Jane's supportive whatever I do. She was just as supportive when I was caning it fourteen hours a day. She's a stand-by-your-man kind of woman.'

'Is that a bad thing? You sound as if you're criticising her.'

'No,' said Tasker in a listless voice. He clearly didn't want to talk about his wife. Gibbs knew the feeling.

'Why didn't you open the door when I rang the bell?' he asked. 'And why the black paper on the window?'

'Oh, that.' Tasker shook his head as if he'd remembered an annoying detail.

'It's that fucking school across the road. When I'm writing, I look out of the window a lot. Well, I'd like to – in an ideal world. But I don't like looking at that school.'

'Why not?'

'Noisy, bratty kids everywhere – would you want to see that?'

No. Gibbs wouldn't have bought a house that was opposite a school. Tasker, however, had. 'Do you hate children?' *Is that why you have none of your own?*

'No,' said Tasker. 'I don't hate schools either. Only the one across the road. Jane and I are thinking of moving so that I don't have to look at it any more.'

'I'm not sure I understand,' said Gibbs diplomatically.

'*I'm* sure you *don't* understand,' Tasker said accusingly, staring over Gibbs's shoulder at the window. 'The black paper makes no difference. I can't see out, but I know what's there.'

'Why wouldn't you let me in before?' Gibbs asked.

'I did. I rang Jane. She came and let you in.'

'You know what I'm asking. Are you going to answer or not?'

Tasker made a helpless gesture with his hands. 'I've been judged by every newspaper in the land, thanks to Damon Blundy. I've had hate-mail. I had one death threat. There are a lot of crazy people out there, looking for a convenient target. How do I know whoever's at the door isn't going to chuck acid in my face?'

'You'd rather risk your wife's face?' Gibbs asked.

There was a knock at the door of the attic room. Unbelievably, Tasker nodded at Gibbs as if to say, 'You can let her in.'

It was easier to do it than to object. Gibbs opened the door to Jane Tasker, praying she hadn't overheard the last part of the conversation. 'Can I come in?' she asked.

'It's your house,' said Gibbs.

She stayed where she was, on the top step, outside the room.

'You can come in,' Tasker called out to her.

She started to move at the sound of his voice, like a remote-controlled device at the press of a button.

'What do you want?' he asked her. He looked confused, as if her being there puzzled him. As if he'd rather not deal with it, but recognised that he had no choice.

'I just wondered if the two of you wanted a cup of tea?' Jane blushed as she asked the question, and slid the palm of her right hand over the palm of her left as if trying to wipe something off it. 'DC Gibbs?'

'No, thanks.' Jane had offered him a cup of tea when he'd first arrived, before he and Tasker had come up to the attic.

'Not for me,' said Tasker.

'OK, but . . .' Jane didn't move. Now she looked flustered,

while Tasker was acting as if she'd already left the room. Gibbs had watched as his eyes slid off her and over to the black squares on the window. Jane was peering at him, as if trying to guess what he might want her to say next. Eventually, she said, 'What about . . . something else? Can I get you anything? Water, maybe?'

'No, thanks,' Gibbs said again. 'I'm fine.'

'No.' Tasker was distracted. 'Maybe later. Thanks.'

'Oh! All right, later.' Was that excitement in her voice, at the prospect of being able to bring refreshments in the near future? Impossible. Wasn't it?

'Well, then . . . shall I go?' Jane asked. 'Will you call me when you're ready for a drink?'

No response from Tasker. Gibbs felt awkward. It wasn't up to him to answer. The silence around him thickened.

'Reuben?' said Jane hopefully.

Still nothing.

'Mr Tasker,' Gibbs prompted him.

'Pardon? Sorry, I was just . . .'

Yeah, I know. You were staring at some sheets of black paper that you stuck to your window earlier.

'Did you want something, Jane?'

'Shall I go downstairs, and you'll call me when you're ready for hot drinks?' asked his wife. 'Or shall I wait here?'

Tasker looked uneasy. 'I don't know,' he said. 'It's up to you.' He sighed. 'I mean . . . go downstairs. If we want a drink, we'll come and sort ourselves out.'

Jane looked bereft.

Gibbs watched in horrified amazement, trying to work out how he'd explain this scene to Simon later.

She acts like the faithful servant of a man who doesn't realise he has a servant, and doesn't want one.

'Tell you what,' said Gibbs. 'I'd quite like a cup of tea. I'll come with you to make it.' He moved forward so that he was standing between Jane and her husband, so that she had no choice but to turn and head downstairs. 'Back in a minute or two,' Gibbs told Tasker.

'Do you really want tea, or do you want to get my wife alone and ask her if I'm a murderer?'

'Both,' said Gibbs.

'Reuben didn't kill anyone,' Jane said vehemently. 'He and I were here on the day Damon Blundy died. Together, all the time. Why would Reuben kill the man who was responsible for his book sales tripling? You can't buy publicity of the kind Blundy created for Reuben. Have you read Reuben's books?'

'Jane, stop.'

'The *Scotsman* called his latest "unforgettable".'

'Why would I kill the man responsible for tripling my sales?' said Tasker angrily. 'Let's see – because he kept saying my work was shit, perhaps? I didn't kill him, but that doesn't mean I wouldn't have had a valid motive if I had.'

'Of course,' Jane agreed eagerly, as if she hadn't less than a minute ago suggested that her husband ought to be grateful to Damon Blundy. 'Right.' She clapped her hands together, making Gibbs jump. 'Tea!'

He followed her down the stairs. In the kitchen, there was a lopsided blue bookcase next to a red Aga that looked as if it had seen better days. Gibbs spotted a copy of Verity Hewson's memoir, *A Hole in the Stone*, alongside biographies of more famous people: Julie Andrews, Margaret Thatcher, Stephen Fry. 'I see you've read Damon Blundy's ex-wife's book,' he said. 'Well, maybe you haven't read it, but you've got it.'

'Hmm?' Jane filled the kettle with water. She seemed more relaxed now than she had upstairs.

'This one.' Gibbs pulled it off the shelf. 'Verity Hewson was Blundy's first wife. This is about their marriage.'

The effect upon Jane was remarkable. She gasped, put her right hand in her mouth and bit down on her index finger. Gibbs watched the skin whiten around her teeth. Even when she spoke, she kept her hand close to her face, as if protecting it. 'The writer of that book was . . . Oh my gosh. I've had that book for years. Since long before Damon Blundy first wrote about Reuben. I never read it. Normally, I'll gulp down any biography, but that one was just too . . . nasty.' She started to shake her head. 'Oh blimey. I never made the connection. I'd better . . .'

She moved to take the book from Gibbs, then stepped back. Her eyes filled with tears. 'I don't know what to do,' she said.

Do? Gibbs didn't understand. 'Why is it such a shock?' he asked. 'What does it matter that you've got a book by Damon Blundy's ex-wife and haven't read it?'

'Reuben'll be angry.'

'Don't be daft. Why would he be?'

'He'd *hate* the thought of me having a book about Damon Blundy – even just owning it and not reading it. He hates the books I read anyway. Lowest common denominator, he calls them. Affectionately, but he means it. I tried to read *Middlemarch* once, so that he wouldn't think I was stupid, and he told me not to bother – I wouldn't enjoy it. It wasn't "my" sort of book. Look, can you . . . ?' Jane froze, her face twisted in anxiety.

'What?' Gibbs asked her. He wanted to get out of this house and away from the Taskers. He felt as if something cold had passed through his soul. Was this how his and Debbie's guests felt when they visited?

'Will you take the book away with you and get rid of it?' Jane asked him. 'I don't want it. If it stays here, I'll have to tell Reuben about it – I can't lie to him – and then he'll be even more disappointed in me than usual.'

'He's usually disappointed in you? Why?'

Jane glanced up towards the ceiling. 'I shouldn't talk about it,' she said. 'I feel disloyal.'

Gibbs was wondering how best to encourage her to confide a bit more when she said, 'I don't *know* why. I do everything I can to make him happy. I don't see what more I can do! Nothing works.'

'Were the two of you really here together for the whole of Monday morning?'

'Yes. And that's the truth.'

'Why does Reuben hate the school across the road?'

Jane's eyes widened. 'You know about that? He told you?' She sighed. 'I don't know why. I can't work it out. He never used to hate it. It's recent.'

'How recent?' asked Gibbs.

'This year. January, February . . . Early this year – that's when he started complaining about it, but this sudden *hatred* that just makes no sense – that's really *very* recent.'

'When did it start?' Gibbs asked her.

'The first time he said he couldn't bear it any more and we were going to have to move was . . .' Jane stopped. Her pink face reddened. 'Oh,' she said. 'I've only just realised.'

'What?'

'It was last Monday lunchtime that he said it. Just after we'd seen on the news that Damon Blundy had been murdered.'

9

Sunday 7 July 2013

I close the door of the box room behind me, lean against it and exhale slowly, until there's no air left in my lungs to expel. Even then I try to squeeze out some more, until I start to feel faint. Only then do I allow myself to breathe in.

Alone in a room, at last. I told Adam and the children not to disturb me, that I won't be able to concentrate on emailing Ethan's class teacher if they do. I felt sick saying it. It's so much harder to lie when you're known to have lied. To people you love, anyway. You feel as if your false words are shining in neon all around you.

I never found it hard to lie to my parents. That felt good – like killing a monster.

And now there's a different monster trying to wipe out my new family – the family I love without reservation, the one Adam and I have made together – and I'm too afraid to kill it. I can't destroy it without destroying myself, because it's inside me. It's part of me: the part that's whispering, *Email King Edward. Tell him yes. Agree to the blindfold and the silence and everything – all his conditions. You need to find out who killed Damon Blundy, don't you? How else will you find out? The police will never work it out – they can't possibly. They don't know what you know, and you'll never tell them. What you told them already was hard enough.*

If only I could resign myself to not knowing . . . I would vow never to email King Edward again, never to be unfaithful again. To save my family. That's what I want to do. It's what I *must* do.

In my right hand, I'm clutching the piece of paper that's my official reason for being in this room: Ethan's failed test from school, for which he got zero out of a possible ten marks. I'm supposed to be drafting an email to his teacher about it, asking her to explain to him where he went wrong, and reassure him that he mustn't worry about having misunderstood.

Do that first. Something normal, domestic. That'll make you feel better.

Adam wasn't suspicious when I announced that I needed to lock myself away upstairs to draft a letter to Miss Stefanowicz. He genuinely seems to have forgiven me – incredible in itself – but also to trust me, which is even more surprising. I wouldn't trust me. I *don't* trust me. I never have; it's just that I trust most other people even less.

All weekend, I've waited for Adam to lose his temper with me, or turn silent and moody. It hasn't happened.

Can it really be that easy?

'It wasn't real, Nicki,' he said to me last night, when I asked him for the two hundredth time how he was able to be so calm about my betrayal. 'It was a fantasy – involving another person, but still a fantasy.'

Not real.

Adam doesn't think Gavin – King Edward – matters, but he mattered to me. And my heartfelt confession was so small a portion of the truth that it was no better than any lie I've ever told.

What if Adam finds out the full story? Would he forgive me again? Would that be enough to kill his trust in me? Perhaps he doesn't care if I'm faithful to him or not. He loves me, I know that, but perhaps not passionately enough any more to be thrown into a state of anguish by the idea of me sending photographs of my body to another man.

How can he bear knowing that I did that? How can I bear him being able to bear it?

Maybe King Edward loves you more.

A killer.

No. He says he didn't kill Damon Blundy. He knows who did. It wasn't him.

And you believe him?

I sit down, switch on the computer, put Ethan's test paper down next to the mouse-mat. When the home screen appears, I go straight to Yahoo Mail – my good-wife-and-mother email account.

I'm about to open a box for a new message when the phone beside the computer starts to ring. I pick it up quickly, before Adam can get to the downstairs extension. When you lie a lot, you learn to get to the phone and the letterbox first, always, just in case.

'Hello?'

'Nicki, it's me.'

Melissa. My hand, holding the phone, starts to shake. I want to hang up.

'Nicki? Are you still there?'

'What do you want?' *Yes, I'm still. I'm deathly still, listening to the voice of treachery. Alarmingly, it sounds exactly the same as the voice of my once best friend.*

'I'm sorry I had to talk to the police. I hope you understand that I did *have* to.'

First Kate Zilber, now Melissa . . . Who will be the next betrayer to beg me to understand how hard it was for them?

King Edward, if you let him.

'Are you ringing for a reason?' I ask Melissa.

She says nothing. I've known her long enough to be able to read her mind. She's weighing up whether to return to the subject of whether I can understand and forgive her. In the end, she decides she might get a better result if she moves on. 'Lee and I spent the weekend at your parents' house.'

'My condolences.'

I don't want to be speaking to Melissa, so I tune out and look at Ethan's failed test instead. There are five questions on the sheet of paper. The first four are straightforward, almost impossible to get wrong: what is your name? How old are you? Where do you live? When is your birthday? Ethan has answered all these questions correctly. The fifth question isn't a question; it's an order followed by a threat. It says, 'Do not answer any of the above questions. If you follow this instruction, you will get ten marks. If you do not follow this instruction, you will get zero marks.' At the top of the sheet, there's another order: 'Make sure to read through all the questions before answering them.'

'Nicki? Are you listening?'

'Yep.' *Not very attentively, no. Something about a reservoir and beautiful scenery. I don't care that you went walking with my parents and my brother. I don't care that you had a lovely time.*

Ethan's failed test I care about. Because it's not fair that he got no marks. Even if he'd done as he was told and read through all the questions before he started, there is nothing on this sheet to indicate that question five carries more weight than the other four. Nowhere does it say, 'The final question is the one you must pay the most attention to.' Faced with four questions that demand answers versus one that isn't even a question and says, 'Ignore all the other questions,' how is a child supposed to know that number five takes precedence? There's no indication that it does, or should. If anything, the weight of evidence is strongly on the side of answering questions one to four, since they're in the majority.

Ridiculous bloody idiot teacher.

'I . . . I found something.' Melissa sounds nervous. I've missed part of what she said. *Good.*

'Hmm?' I open a new 'Compose Email' box, for the purpose of writing a letter of protest to Miss Stefanowicz. Ethan should get eight out of ten marks – two each for numbers one to four and none for number five – and I'm going to see that he gets them. And an apology. With one hand I start to type, 'Dear Miss Stef . . .'

'At your parents' house,' Melissa is saying insistently, 'I found two books.'

'Yes, Mum and Dad can read. That's one thing that can be said in their favour. They like books.'

A message flashes up on the computer screen, in a box, then disappears before I can read it properly. 'Request to the server,' I think it said, or something like that.

I look over my shoulder, my heart thumping, half expecting to see the man with streaked hair. Mercifully, he's not here. No one is watching me.

No one's watching you in this room. What if someone's using your computer to watch you?

'Request to the server' – what could it mean? Nothing like that's ever happened before. Has Adam hacked into my Yahoo account? Has anyone?

'No, not published books,' Melissa says. 'Two notebooks. Lee's handwriting. They were with your things, in—'

'No. Shut up.' Melissa's words have dragged me from my state of paranoid dread to an even worse horror. 'I don't want to talk about those notebooks.' I can't bear to remember. I haven't thought about those notebooks for years.

I feel as if I might throw up.

'Nicki, I'm worried. Why—'

'I'm not discussing those . . . things. If you say another word about them, I'll hang up.'

'All right!' Melissa sounds as panicky as I feel. Is she crying? 'Nicki, why didn't you tell me the lunatic asylum story ever? Why did I hear it first from Lee? We were best friends, and you bitched about your parents all the time.'

'I had a strange premonition you'd one day ask not to be confided in,' I say in a brittle voice.

'Lee told me it was horrible for him, but . . . well, it must have been pretty horrible for you too. I can understand why you might not have wanted to talk about it.'

Interesting. For the first time since getting involved with my brother, Melissa cares about how I feel.

Because she's seen the notebooks. And she's wondering . . .

It's too late. I've wanted to talk to her, about everything, for so long, but not any more. I can't.

'I'm sorry, I have to go,' I say, and hang up before she can answer.

On the computer, I open a new tab and go to my Hushmail account. I've still got all the emails I sent to King Edward, and his to me. He's the only person who knows the lunatic asylum story, the only person I've ever felt able to tell – because of the distance between us, probably, and the degree of anonymity. Even then, I sent it to him as a story, and told it through Lee's eyes, making sure I wasn't the emotional focus of the story.

Feeling things is too hard. I'd rather be a body without sensations, without consciousness. Living, dead – who cares?

Stop it, Nicki. Be strong. You have a husband and two children downstairs who need you. And—

I cut off the thought in my mind, but it springs back: it's not only my family who need me. Damon Blundy needs me too. For a while, I thought I loved him. I thought the man I loved was him. Is that a good enough reason for me to be determined to do all I can to bring his killer to justice?

I don't care. I'm determined, whether I should be or not. Whoever murdered Damon will pay – I'm going to make sure of that.

I find the old email I sent King Edward and open the attachment: my story, the one I wrote specially for him before I knew he was lying to me about his identity. I wrote it, but I've never read it – not even before I sent it. Writing it was hard enough.

If I can make it all the way through to the end, I can handle anything.

I start to read.

Once upon a time, there was a twelve-year-old boy who had a seventeen-year-old sister. The sister lied to their parents all the time, about almost everything. If she hadn't, they would have allowed her no privacy. They'd have forced their way into her soul, and whatever they found in there, they'd have torn it to shreds in their determination to improve her character.

Despite her best efforts to deceive her parents, the boy's sister usually ended up getting caught in her various lies. This resulted in daily rows that the boy had to listen to whether he wanted to or not. Even if he went into his bedroom and closed the door, he could hear his father yelling, sometimes for hours, and his sister crying. The noise always came from the same place: his father's games room, in which he played snooker and table football and darts. The games room was across the hall from the boy's bedroom, no more than a few feet away. His father always made sure to close the games room door, but, at that distance, even twenty closed doors wouldn't have protected the boy from the sound of the fighting.

His sister would always cry and say sorry to her father for lying, but she didn't mean it, because she would then lie again the next day, and get found out, and then there would be another row, and more yelling and weeping. After a few years of listening to these episodes, the boy decided that his sister's distress was genuine, but had nothing to do with contrition. Rather, it was that she found it unpleasant to be shouted at for hours at a time about how she'd let herself and her family down. Her father didn't restrict his shouting to the subject of his daughter's lies. He also yelled at her for wearing too much make-up, not spending enough time on her homework, making too many phone calls, getting up too late at weekends, liking the wrong music, having the wrong opinion about every subject, wearing the wrong jewellery, choosing the wrong boyfriends, the wrong clothes, the wrong friends, putting the wrong posters on her walls and many other things. Every choice the daughter made was the wrong choice, and every opinion she expressed was the wrong opinion.

The boy found his father's tirades distressing to listen to. They made him shake. Sometimes he would press himself against the far wall of his bedroom, beneath the window. Sometimes, though he was always terrified to open his door while an episode was in progress, he would force himself to do it so that he could escape downstairs. His father's shouting and his sister's crying could still be heard clearly from downstairs, but it wasn't quite as deafening. However, downstairs there was other crying to contend with: the boy's mother's crying, which usually took place in the kitchen.

The boy couldn't understand why his mother always stayed as far away from the trouble as possible. Surely as a grown-up she could do something to make the noise stop? Yet she never did. As soon as the shouting started, she behaved as if her husband and daughter were members of a different family. She wouldn't even go upstairs if she needed something from her bedroom, not until the yelling had stopped and her husband had finally accepted her daughter's ninety-seventh apology. Then and only then would she wash her face at the kitchen sink, dry it with a tea towel, put on a bright smile and wade back into family life as if nothing had happened.

The boy tried not to blame his mother because he could see that she was weak like him, and scared like him. He didn't blame his father either, because his father, as he kept telling the rest of the family, was a man of high principle who couldn't help it if lies made him angry. The boy learned that lying was the worst thing ever. It made sense to blame his sister, who couldn't possibly have failed to notice that she rarely got away with her attempted deceptions. Why did she bother? Why didn't she admit defeat and start telling the truth?

One day, the boy plucked up the courage to ask her. He was beginning to wonder if she secretly enjoyed the fights with her father. She smiled and said, 'Of course I don't enjoy them. Would you enjoy being screamed at for three hours a day about what a terrible person you are?' The boy said he wouldn't, and that therefore he would resolve never to lie again. 'Often you lie when there's no need,' he told his sister. 'Mum and Dad would have let you go to that concert if you'd asked them. You didn't need to pretend it was a school trip.' His sister laughed. '"Let" me?' she said. 'Maybe they would have. I lie to them because they deserve to be lied to. They don't deserve to have power over me. They've persecuted me since the day I was born.'

'No, they haven't,' said the boy, because, like most people, he didn't recognise persecution that wore a mask of loving parental concern.

The fights continued. The boy grew more anxious and withdrawn.

His sister stopped crying during her father's tirades, and instead turned herself to stone. She taught the boy how to make earplugs out of tissue paper, so that he wouldn't have to listen if he didn't want to when the trouble started.

Sometimes a glimmer of hope was offered by a visiting relative from a different part of the country. Whenever this happened, the boy prayed that there would be a terrible eruption while the relative was in the house and that the relative would leap up and declare, 'This is intolerable! Something must be done! No one can be expected to live like this!' Instead what happened was that extended family members turned into versions of the little boy's mother, perching tensely on the edges of chairs, waiting in silence for the trouble to subside. Sometimes bright, false conversations were had, as the boy's mother and the visiting relatives conspired to cover up the noise.

What made life even more confusing for the boy was that his mum and dad were always scrupulously kind and fair to him, because he was always honest and obedient. That's how he knew they were good parents. He wondered why they never acknowledged that it must be difficult for him, growing up in a war zone. Why didn't it cross his father's mind, or his mother's, that all the shouting was as frightening and unpleasant for him, the blameless child, as it was for his sister?

One weekend morning, his mother shook him awake while it was still dark outside. She was fully dressed and crying. 'Get up,' she whispered. 'We have to go out. You can't stay here on your own.' The boy asked where they were going, but his mother didn't answer. 'Just get dressed,' she said. 'It doesn't matter what you wear: no one's going to see you. Go and sit in the car, as quickly as you can.' The little boy understood that he was to have no breakfast, and that to ask would be a mistake. His mother didn't care about feeding him this morning, or about making sure he brushed his teeth. Something awful was about to happen, if it wasn't happening already – something worse than what the boy was used to.

He dressed and went downstairs. His mother was waiting for him by the front door. She opened it when she saw him coming, and gestured for him to go outside. He stepped out onto the drive and saw that his father and sister were already in the car: his father at the wheel and his sister behind him, in the back. He climbed in and sat beside his sister. His mother got in too, and his father started the engine. They set off. No one spoke, and the little boy's sister didn't look at him, not even when he started to cry. She kept staring straight ahead, at the back of the driver's seat. This frightened the boy more than anything else. His sister had always been kind to him – always. Most people in her situation would detest a brother like him – the favoured good child who never put a foot wrong as far as his parents were concerned – but not his sister; she had never allowed herself to fall into that trap. So why wasn't she comforting him now, as they drove along in silence, in the only-just-dawning daylight, with him crying? Why was she staring straight ahead as if she were in a coma?

The boy eventually asked where they were going, because the dread that was welling up inside him had grown too large and needed to escape. His father replied, 'We're going to a lunatic asylum, where your sister will be staying for a while.'

The boy's sister didn't flinch; the news hadn't come as a shock to her as it had to him. Evidently she had been told where she was going before setting off.

'Someone who keeps lying in the way that your sister lies must be sick in the head,' said the boy's father. 'Your mum and I have tried as hard as we can to make her see the error of her ways, but we're not experts when it comes to mental illness. And that's what a compulsion to deceive is – it's a mental illness. So we've decided to let the doctors at the lunatic asylum deal with it. They have all kinds of techniques and special methods that are meant to be very effective. Like electric shock treatment – where they strap you to a table, tie you down and give you electric shocks that make your whole body light up. It's very painful, but it works, apparently, when it comes to curing sick minds. That's if the patient strapped to the table doesn't catch fire – that happens sometimes, if the electricity current isn't carefully monitored. I'm assured it's never happened at this asylum, though, so we don't need to worry about that.'

The boy was crying hysterically by this point. 'Can you see what you're doing to your brother?' his father said to his sister.

'I can see what *you're* doing to him,' she replied.

'Can you see that you're ruining his life? That's why we have to put you in the asylum.'

The boy's sister rolled her eyes and said, 'I'll escape. I'll fuck whoever's in charge and persuade them to let me out.' She was seventeen and had been sexually active for a year or so. Her brother knew this because it had been the subject of many of the closed-door rows in his father's games room recently. His sister had been caught with boyfriends – sometimes in her bedroom, after she'd snuck them in when her parents were asleep; once at a friend's house.

'Be facetious if you want to,' her father told her, 'but you'll soon see. No one escapes from places like the one we're taking you to. You'll be handcuffed for most of the time. Your legs will be chained together so you won't be able to walk.'

The boy whimpered at the thought of this happening to his sister. She turned to him then and put her hand on his arm. He looked at her and she shook her head. 'It's not true,' she mouthed at him. 'It's a lie. Don't worry.'

Their mother, watching her daughter in the rear-view mirror, said, 'She's telling him it's not true, it's a lie.' She sounded terrified. The boy understood why she felt compelled to inform on her daughter so quickly and efficiently; he understood that he would have done the same in her position.

'Oh, I promise you it's true,' his father said, sounding gleeful about the prospect of incarcerating his only daughter in a lunatic asylum.

After an amount of time that the boy couldn't measure, the car turned off the main road and onto a lane that was straight and wide at first, but soon started to narrow and bend. There were thick hedges on both sides. From this point onwards, the boy saw no cars apart from the one that contained his unhappy family. The lane straightened out again. Daylight had dawned by now, and the boy could see that there was a large house with shuttered windows coming up on the left, behind a stone wall. The shutters were a sickly shade of green.

'Here we are,' said his father, stopping the car in front of two large stone gateposts. Carved into one of them was the name 'Bardolph House'. The boy felt ill. He couldn't bear the idea of leaving his sister in this place.

His father got out of the car. As he did so, two men appeared from between the gateposts. One was bald and older, the other young and very dark, with a low forehead and wire-rimmed glasses. They were both wearing long white overalls. One was carrying a clipboard. The boy heard a strange noise come from his sister. When he looked at her, he saw that she'd turned pale. She hadn't believed what her father had told her until she saw these two men, but now she believed it.

The father opened the car's back door and ordered his daughter to get out. He was carrying a suitcase that he'd retrieved from the boot. 'Come on,' he said. 'There's no point putting it off. It has to be done. Hopefully, if the treatment works, you'll be able to come home – perhaps in a few weeks if you're lucky. On average they say it takes about six months for a complete cure.'

'No. Please,' said the boy's sister. 'I'll never lie again. I swear.'

'You always say that,' said her father, 'but you always let me down, don't you?'

The two men in overalls were standing on either side of the boy's sister, holding one of her arms each as she struggled and begged to be released. Her father had taken the clipboard from one of them and seemed to be filling in a form that was attached to it. Her mother sat silently in the front passenger seat, saying and doing nothing, though the boy knew, even though he couldn't see her face, that she was crying.

The two men in white overalls started to drag the boy's sister towards the house. She continued to howl for a while. Then she went limp and quiet, as if she'd died, and allowed herself to be dragged. Perhaps she fainted. The boy hoped she was still alive. He opened his mouth to say something to his mother – he wasn't sure what – but found that bile came out, thick and sour, instead of words. Still, his mother did and said nothing. The boy imagined climbing behind the wheel and driving away. It was too late to rescue his sister, but he could rescue his mother.

Except he couldn't. He was a twelve-year-old boy who couldn't really do anything.

After a few miserable empty minutes, he saw something that he didn't understand. The two men in overalls were heading back towards the car, carrying his sobbing sister between them. His father was walking alongside them, holding the clipboard in one hand and the suitcase in the other. As they got closer, the boy's father hurried ahead. The boy heard the sound of the car boot opening and something heavy being thrown into it. Then he heard a thud as the boot was slammed shut, and his father appeared by the open back door of the car, minus the suitcase and the clipboard. This made no sense to the boy; the clipboard belonged to the lunatic asylum – why would his father think he could make off with it as if it were his own? Stealing was as wrong as lying, the boy and his sister had always been taught. Had their father changed his mind about that?

The two men who weren't his father shoved the boy's sister back into the car. She was shaking as if an electric current were ripping through her, and wiping her face with her hands. Her father produced two envelopes from his jacket pocket and handed one to each of the men. Then he got into the car and the family set off for home.

'So,' said the father to his daughter, 'you begged for another chance and now you've got one. Are you going to lie to me again?'

'No,' she said.

'Is that a solemn promise?'

'Yes.'

'Good,' said the father. 'Because if you go back on your word, next time there'll be no joking around. Next time it will be the real thing. Bardolph House is a hospice, not a lunatic asylum, but there are lunatic asylums, real ones, and plenty of them. Don't think we wouldn't go through with it just because we didn't today.'

The boy, the brother, didn't understand. Somehow, he mustered the courage to ask about the two men: who were they, if they weren't real lunatic asylum workers? His father told him that they were friends who had agreed to help him out.

The boy hoped that his sister would stop lying after that, but she didn't. She lied as much as she ever had. Mercifully, though, there were no more trips to lunatic asylums, and somehow, after that awful day, the closed-door games room tirades didn't seem quite so frightening. They seemed normal. The boy's mother stopped crying when they happened. Instead, she listened to the radio in the kitchen and got on with preparing the dinner or the breakfast. The boy started to listen to music, through headphones, and found that he was able to think about other things, even knowing that the yelling was going on in the background.

The grown-up boy still sees his sister regularly. They both still see their parents regularly. Since the sister moved out of her parents' home, aged eighteen, there has been no yelling. Her brother has no idea that she only keeps in touch with their parents for his sake. If asked, he would probably say, 'They fought like cat and dog when she was a teenager, but it's all fine now.' His sister, being an expert liar, would probably say the same thing.

By the time I've finished reading the story, I'm calmer than I was before. Calm enough to switch back to my Yahoo account. In the subject box of my draft email to Miss Stefanowicz, I type the words 'Your test failed – my son did not.' Then I sit and stare at the screen and allow myself to think, really think in detail, about my family – not Adam, Sophie and Ethan, but the one I did not choose to be a member of: Mum, Dad and Lee – for the first time in my adult life. For some reason, I'm no longer scared of the thoughts.

Silently, I ask myself the long-avoided question: why didn't Mum protect me? Why didn't she ever beg or calmly ask or yell at Dad to leave me alone? How could she bear to see him persecute me day after day, when I feel like smashing Miss Stefanowicz's head against a wall repeatedly for failing Ethan on one test? Do I love Sophie and Ethan more than Mum loved me as a child? Do I care more about their suffering than she did about mine? Or was she so scared of Dad that she was too afraid to question his treatment of me?

He wouldn't have accepted that it was persecution. In his mind, it was good parenting: 'You will bring yourself into line with how I want you to be or I will make you suffer.'

What about Lee? Why did he never come hurtling out of his bedroom screaming, 'Leave my sister alone'? I know Lee loved me.

Do you? What about what he did behind your back?

Lining the shelf beside the computer are a dozen or so family photographs, framed. They're mainly of me, Adam, Sophie and Ethan, but there are two of Lee – both of him as a very young child. It's strange, given that we're still in contact, but I have completely blocked Lee-the-grown-man from my mind. I've done so all my adult life. When we get together – when I can't avoid seeing him – I arrange it so that I don't really see him. I don't meet his eye, don't look in his direction. He must notice it, but no one else would. Whenever I can, I try to get Melissa on her own, see her when Lee's not there. I behave in this way so that I can continue to keep my innocent baby brother alive in my imagination: the one in the photographs on the shelf, with the red tricycle and the royal blue zip-up jumper.

The one who hadn't yet betrayed his sister.

I save my draft email to Dimwit Stefanowicz and sign out of my Yahoo account. I'll tell Adam and the children I wrote and sent the email, and do it first thing in the morning.

Now for King Edward.

I log into my Hushmail account, open his last message to me and read it again. Then I click on the 'reply' button and start to type:

Hello, King Edward,

I agree to your conditions. If you let me down again . . . well, let's just say you'd be foolish to risk it.

Nicki

Delete that last part. Delete it. Only someone lacking a brain altogether would threaten a dangerous murderer.

I press 'send'.

Too late now. *Good.* I have to do something. The police aren't going to solve the case. If teachers at the best independent primary school in the Culver Valley set tests that make no sense, if parents drive their own children to hospices and pretend they're lunatic asylums . . . No, I don't trust the police to catch Damon Blundy's killer. I don't trust anyone who isn't me.

I picture myself lying in the dark, on a bed in the Chancery Hotel, naked and blindfolded. Will he touch me? Does it still count as infidelity if I'm doing it to catch a killer?

What if I take a knife with me – a sharp one? Lie on top of it to hide it.

Purely hypothetical questions. What-ifs.

Once I've heard King Edward tell me the truth about Damon Blundy, what if I find myself yearning to kill him, to stab him through the heart? What if I don't have the strength to resist?

Paula Privilege on the Couch

Damon Blundy, 30 April 2013, *Daily Herald Online*

What is a poor (or even a rich) woman to do when, week after week, the newspapers contain no mention of her name or her sex life? Much to the chagrin of Saint Paula of Privilege, she can't sue the *Sun* or the *Mail* for failing to run scurrilous stories about her in the absence of new material, and even I, her most vocal adversary, have neglected her of late in favour of my old friends <u>Keiran Holland</u>, <u>Reuben Tasker</u> and <u>Bryn Gilligan</u>, each of whose separate but thematically linked <u>dedication to irrationality grows stronger by the day</u>.

Here's the story, for those of you who missed it: Tasker published a new, much less pretentious and rather gripping horror novel last month, <u>Riven</u>, that garnered some <u>favourable reviews</u>. If I were his editor, I'd encourage him to dispense with the supernatural element of his writing, since his chief talent is for describing gruesome horrors inflicted on one human being by another; meanwhile, the representatives of the spirit world sip ghost-blend coffee out of Styrofoam cups in the wings and mutter, 'We're pretty much redundant here, aren't we, guys?'

If Bryn Gilligan is reading this, he won't approve of the above paragraph. Young Bryn took to Twitter recently to <u>argue</u> that Tasker's novel <u>should not</u> have valuable column inches squandered on it, and that readers should not waste time reading it, when he, Bryn Gilligan, is no longer allowed to sprint competitively. Yes, you did read that correctly. Gilligan seems to believe, in a worrying lost-his-marbles kind of way, that because he suffers, Tasker must also deserve to. (Is this my fault, for drawing a parallel between them? Probably.) Gilligan is still engaging with his Twitter critics on an hourly basis, trying to persuade them that if they had been him, they too would have taken performance-enhancing drugs. When they declare themselves unconvinced, he tweets, 'BLOCKED,' at them and then, as far as I can tell, neglects to block them and continues to try to win them over.

I <u>pointed out</u> to Gilligan that what he ought to want, rather than equal-footing pariah status for him and Tasker, is the opposite for both of them: acceptance, and a modicum of compassion. Gilligan didn't respond, but Keiran Holland did, God help me. Holland <u>retaliated</u> with two lists, each of which he tweeted at me one item at a time, like an online drone attack. The <u>first</u> was of literary masterpieces composed by writers partial to mind-altering substances. The <u>second</u> was of critical and commercial flops written by the square and sober. These lists would have been a devastating critique of my position if only I'd argued, even once, that opium addicts were incapable of writing well and/or that all novels written without a narcotic boost were indisputably fantastic. Perhaps I'll devote my next column to two lists of my own: one of brilliant sporting wins by those on steroids, and one of people who have never taken illegal drugs and can't even run for a bus.

But wait! There I go again, writing about men without cleavages when Saint Paula has gone to the trouble of making herself extra-specially newsworthy to get my attention. In <u>an interview with *J'aime* magazine,</u> Our Lady of Self-Promo has revealed that, while married to diamond geezer Richard Crumlish, she had several extra-marital flings in addition to the three about which we've all already said, 'So what?' Two more, to be precise. To which I say, 'So what? x 2.' I do wonder how Paula's newly ensnared landowner-farmer second husband feels about it, though. Is Fergus Preece the kind of man who will happily and with a heart full of hope spend all his free time parcelling up bottles of Clearasil to send to leopards? One thing's for sure: he'll need either to be extremely open-minded or exceptionally gullible if he's going to go the distance with the People's Pussy.

Of her five illicit entanglements, Paula says cheerily, 'I'm sorry that I wasn't able to be happy with Richard, or to make him happy, but do I regret my affairs? Not one bit. I am pleased and proud to have shared happy and fulfilling moments with some of the loveliest men on the planet. The thing is, I find other human beings fascinating and irresistible. I just really love and care about people. I'm not perfect by any stretch of the imagination, but I have a warm, giving spirit, and every relationship I've ever had with a man has meant a lot to me. Each one of my romantic and sexual experiences has been life-enhancing and has made me a better person.'

One can't help wondering if the category of 'people' that Saint Paula claims to love and care about includes any women – in particular, the betrayed wives of her five dalliances – and why her giving spirit wasn't tempted by the prospect of giving all those husbands back to their rightful owners at the earliest available opportunity. Could it be that there was a taking spirit on the payroll at the same time? Mere hair-splitting on my part, of course, since all that matters in the final analysis is that Saint Paula has been rogered to a state of better personhood. I suppose it's cheaper than psychoanalysis. Talking of which . . .

'I'd love to get her on my couch,' said Mrs Me, who, as careful readers will remember, is a psychotherapist. 'I'm not sure she's the hypocrite you think she is. Not intentionally, anyway. Most people haven't got a clue what's really motivating them. Riddiough might well believe that her addiction to infidelity is a kind of offshoot of a more general joie-de-vivre and affection for humanity.'

'But that's obviously bollocks,' said I (for that is my clinical specialism: things that are obviously bollocks).

Mrs Me agreed. 'That's why I'd be interested to get her on my couch,' she said. 'To find out what's really going on.'

It's pretty self-evident, isn't it? We know that Saint Paula's grudge against her own aristocratic and wealthy parents drove her to embrace left-wing politics and inferior schooling for her son. Since there could be no rational motive for her making these choices, it's safe to assume that her sole aim was to stage a very public vote of no confidence in her own privileged upbringing. Privilege is highly addictive: prized and sought after by those who've never had it, and almost impossible to object to when one has it in abundance, unless one's antipathy for those bestowing it is strong enough to overwhelm all such self-interested considerations. (Don't even think about mentioning altruism or the greater good as possible motivations, dear reader. Have you forgotten the sorry tale of the five betrayed wives? Saint Paula cares not a jot for anything but the gratification of her own ego. In that respect, she is like nearly all of the rest of us.)

The question we must ask ourselves is this: in what circumstances might regular adulteries that undermine and eventually destroy one's marriage feel more gratifying to the ego than cherishing and protecting one's family unit? What kind of psyche could ruthlessly strip innocent women of their husbands, drive away a once-devoted spouse who also happens to be heir to a colossal diamond fortune, create a broken home for one's only child (who already has the misfortune of attending a broken school) and still emerge from all this with 'Yay for me!' as one's dominant narrative?

Could it be that Saint Paula gets an enormous power kick out of undermining the institution of marriage? Every man she seduces into betraying his wife represents a victory over the father who made her feel powerless. And all of those foolish, trusting wives who soldier on in ignorance prove to Paula that she is cleverer and better than they are; they are all too stupid to spot that they're married to utter bastards, and therefore deserving of everything they get.

If I'm right, this would explain why, having successfully kept at least some of her secrets for years, Our Lady of Privilege should suddenly decide to boast in print about these transgressions. Would it be anywhere near as much fun if she didn't get to publicly humiliate all her victims, male and female? Take that, Baron Daddy and Baroness Mummy!

I'm cheating a bit – superimposing therapy guff I've picked up from Mrs Me onto what I know of Saint Paula's personal circumstances, but that's perfectly legitimate, if you think about it. It's rather like a doctor being able to diagnose measles because he's seen measles many times before and knows what they look like. (A livid scarlet bas-relief in the shape of Dr Andrew Wakefield that covers a Welsh child's entire body, for the non-medical among you who are wondering.) Yes, I know that Andrew Wakefield is not officially a doctor any more – in the same way that Bryn Gilligan is no longer officially a winner.

IO

Monday 8 July 2013

'Culver Valley East was your constituency,' Simon said to Paula Riddiough. 'Hicksville, as you now call it.'

She had arrived at Spilling Police Station at exactly 10.10 a.m., as promised, dressed in an expensive-looking grey suit, with her hair pulled back and wound into a neat bun behind her head. She looked as if she expected to be given the keys to 10 Downing Street in front of hundreds of cameras, and had winced at the sight of the unglamorous interview room when Simon had opened the door and ushered her in.

'I referred to Spilling as Hicksville *once*, and I've been apologising to bloody-minded former constituents ever since,' she said. 'It was a stupid thing to say, especially on Twitter, and I only said it because I knew it would annoy Damon Blundy. He lives here, but . . .' She stopped and corrected herself. '*Lived* here. But London was his one true love. London was where he belonged.'

'How do you know?' asked Simon. 'Did he write that in one of his columns? I've not seen it, if he did.'

Paula shrugged, unconcerned. 'He must have done. I can't see how I'd know it otherwise.'

'Why did he move to Spilling in November 2011, if he loved London so much?'

'Why do you think I'd know the answer to that question, DC Waterhouse?' She smiled without warmth. 'Do you think Damon might have discussed his house-buying plans with me, in between writing his column one week about what a terrible mother I am and another one the next week about my home-wrecking tendencies?'

'I think he moved to the Culver Valley because you were its MP,' Simon said. 'Because you were based here some of the time, weren't you? He wanted to be in your part of the country. He was in love with you.'

Paula laughed. 'If he was, he had a funny way of showing it. And surely if he wanted to be in *my* part of the country, he should have moved to North or East Rawndesley? Or Combingham, where I lived, and without which no Labour MP would stand a chance of getting elected in the Culver Valley, ever.'

'Spilling was still nearer than London – and you spent most of your weekends in the Culver Valley, didn't you? Not in your London flat.'

'Yes. It's important for MPs to really live in their constituencies, not just pretend to live in them.' Paula sounded bored. 'Maybe you're right. Maybe Damon was so consumed by his hatred of me that he wanted to move closer to me so that he could hate me close up. I have no way of knowing, I'm afraid.'

'The two of you met for the first time on 26 October 2011. Damon fell for you. Maybe you fell for him too?'

'I truly didn't.'

'He rented in Spilling at first, while he looked for a house to buy,' Simon told her what he suspected she already knew. 'Why was he in such a hurry to get to the Culver Valley, if not to be closer to you?'

'I've just answered that question, DC Waterhouse. If anyone was twisted enough to want to move closer to the primary object of their loathing, Damon was probably that person. So . . . maybe you're right. But we weren't having an affair. If we were lovers, why did he decimate me in column after column? Why did I retaliate?'

'Disguise,' said Simon. 'If you're tearing each other apart in the papers every week, no one's likely to suspect you're having an affair.'

Paula rolled her eyes. 'Look, when I met Damon in October 2011, my marriage to Richard was all but over. Damon was single. There was nothing to stop us falling into each other's arms if we'd wanted to. Why would we fall passionately in love, then decide to slag each other off in public while secretly having an affair? Why would we both marry other people? I have to say, this conversation doesn't fill me with hope about your skills as a detective.'

'Who said anything about passionately in love?'

To Simon's annoyance, Paula remained unruffled. 'Sorry, I took the passionately-in-love part for granted, in your affair scenario,' she said. 'I wouldn't have a relationship of any kind with a man unless I was passionately in love with him. And to answer your next question – have I been passionately in love with lots of people, in that case? – no, I don't think I have, looking back. But if you'd asked me at the time, while those relationships were going on . . . hell, yes. I *always* believe it's the real thing. I'm a romantic. I always have been.'

You're a clever liar with an answer for everything.

If she'd been in love with Blundy, why wasn't she a wreck? That, as far as Simon could see, was the main problem with his theory. Even if he was right about the affair, it didn't make Paula a murderer.

He resisted the urge to kick the leg of the table. No matter how many successes he notched up, he always feared that the current case would be his first failure. He suspected he always would. Charlie reassuring him that he always got there in the end wasn't the consolation she imagined it to be; it only piled on more pressure.

'Can we move on from mine and Damon's imaginary sex life to his murder, which is more important?' Paula asked. 'Do you think you're going to find his killer?'

'I know I will.'

'Oh good. Because . . . don't let this go to your head, but I've heard that you're an excellent detective. The best that Hicksville has to offer.'

Heard where?

'You want Damon's murderer caught, then?' Simon asked.

Paula flashed him a smooth smile. 'I'd want any murderer caught.'

'You mentioned having another appointment in Spilling – tomorrow?'

'Yes. This will be a good test of your powers of detection. My appointment tomorrow is the chronological opposite of my meeting with you today. No, wait. It's the *horological* opposite. If you're as good as I've heard, you'll work out what that means before I leave the room.'

Simon ignored her challenge. 'Your alibi's impressively solid,' he said. 'Your friends confirm that you and your husband were with them last Monday morning. I knew they would.'

'So did I. Because it's the truth.' Paula looked up at the clock on the wall. 'Horological,' she repeated. 'Relating to clocks. Any ideas yet? You're not very fast, for a super detective. Maybe you're not so super after all.'

'I'm good enough,' said Simon.

'Good is different from excellent, though, isn't it? You must know the saying "All it takes for evil to prosper is for good men to do nothing." Damon used to say, "If you take that at face value, it's true, but ninety-nine per cent of people who wheel out that line aren't advocating good men doing *good* deeds. They're advocating good men doing the kind of evil acts that evil men do – which turns them into equally evil men."'

'When did Damon say that?'

'Oh, I don't remember,' Paula said airily.

She's toying with you . . .

'Stop playing games,' Simon snapped, standing up so that he didn't have to have her face in front of him. He walked over to the corner of the room, leaned against the wall. 'Damon Blundy's dead, and your husband's miles away. Tell me the truth. That's why you're here, isn't it? This meeting was your idea, not mine.'

Paula narrowed her eyes. 'There are things I *could* tell you

. . . They might even help you. Can you give me a cast-iron promise that if I share this sensitive information with you, Hannah Blundy will never find out?'

'About your affair with Damon, you mean?'

Paula raised an eyebrow. 'That's not a fair question, DC Waterhouse. We're still discussing the terms and conditions for my telling you. Don't jump the gun. I'll ask again: can you promise me that you won't tell Hannah what I tell you?'

'No. Hannah's Damon's wife. I think she's got the right to understand why her husband was murdered.'

'Very noble,' said Paula. 'There's only one snag: what I know would crush Hannah in a way that's impossible to convey without spoilers. There are some injuries – psychological injuries – that no one could survive. This would be one, believe me. You don't care about Hannah. I do. And what I know would lay waste to her. Beyond repair.'

'You care about Hannah Blundy? I didn't realise you knew her.'

'She was a good wife to Damon – loyal and loving. He loved her. So, for his sake as well as for hers, I won't do that to her, not even to help you solve your case. Damon would rather his murderer went unpunished than have Hannah destroyed.'

Was this the same Paula Riddiough who, only a few minutes ago, had portrayed Damon Blundy as her enemy? Simon didn't like the way his brain was doing three-hundred-and-sixty-degree turns inside his head. He felt as if he wasn't in control, and he hated that feeling more than anything. 'You know Damon well enough to make that claim, and yet you weren't having an affair with him?'

Paula rolled her eyes. 'Oh, you can do better than that. Can't you? Don't you know anyone well that you're not having an affair with? Your mother, your colleagues, your best friend?'

'Don't you think Hannah might want to know the truth, however painful it is?'

'If she would, she's a fool.'

'You need to tell me what you know,' Simon said coldly. 'You might only care about what Damon would have wanted, but I care about catching a murderer.'

'I understand that, and it's why I made you the offer I made,' said Paula. 'Give me your word that you won't tell Hannah and I'll tell you what I know.'

Never would dishonesty be more justified, Simon thought. 'All right,' he lied.

Paula snorted. 'Well, that was unconvincing,' she said. 'And we seem to have reached stalemate, or check mate, or whatever you'd prefer to call it. I can see only one possible way out.'

Simon waited.

Paula pressed her index finger against the middle of her top lip. *Thinking.* Then she said, 'If it were to turn out that Hannah had killed Damon, everything I've said about not wanting to hurt her would leap out of the window.'

'Isn't that a bit hypocritical? Given what you said before about good men doing evil things to evil men and, in doing so, becoming evil themselves?'

'No,' Paula said with confidence. 'My point, or rather Damon's point, was that there's no such thing as a good person. There are only kind and unkind acts. Would it be unkind of me to stop caring about Hannah's feelings if it turned out she'd murdered Damon? I'm not sure. I think it would be understand-able. Unless you'd want to encourage me to protect a murderer from the law? Do you think Hannah did it?'

'I can't discuss the investigation with you,' said Simon.

'*Could* she have done it? If she's got a rock-solid alibi, there's no harm in telling me, is there?'

'Everything relating to the investigation is confidential.'

'You're about as flexible as a metal barrier, aren't you? Still . . . if I had to guess, I'd say you *do* suspect Hannah. Me too.' Paula stared out of the window.

Simon had sat where she was sitting. He knew she could see nothing but the red-brick wall of the job centre. 'There are a few things I could charge you with, if you don't tell me what you know,' he said.

She laughed. 'You think I care about getting a criminal record? My parents would be devastated, but me? I'd be all over the papers again. The only columnist who thought me interesting enough to write about once I left politics is dead, remember? I do love the spotlight.'

'I think you loved Damon Blundy,' Simon said on impulse. 'I think you're devastated by his death, and trying very hard to hide it.'

Paula's expression was sympathetic. 'Then you think wrong. Any ideas yet about my horologically opposite appointment tomorrow?' She glanced up at the clock again. 'Tick, tick, tick . . . No pressure.'

'Would Damon do the same for you, if the roles were reversed?' Simon asked. 'If you'd been murdered, and he had information that would destroy Fergus, would he withhold it?'

'Excellent question. Yes, he would.'

Simon saw a shadow at the back of his mind, mouthing words. Trying to tell him something, but he couldn't hear, or see clearly, or . . . No, it was gone. As so often, he could feel the presence of several pieces of a good idea, but he couldn't put them together.

'What made you ask me that?' said Paula.

'I'm not sure.'

'Your subconscious is an intelligent guesser.' She smiled.

'It's hard to know what to ask when you're being told a combination of lies and truth,' Simon said. 'I think you're being deliberately inconsistent. You want me to catch whoever killed Damon. That means you want to help me. But not too much – because of the secret you still need to keep. It's not only your affair with Damon Blundy, is it? That's not what would destroy Hannah. It's more than that.'

Paula sat forward in her chair. 'All right, here's something that might help you. If Hannah didn't kill him, I think I might know who did.'

'Who?'

'A woman called Nicki Clements. She was obsessed with Damon – head over heels, even though she'd never met him. Whenever he wrote a column or a blog post, she commented. Each of her comments was a long, passionate hymn of praise to the wondrous Damon Blundy.'

'Did she praise him when he said unpleasant things about you?' asked Simon.

'Oh yes, all the time. Whatever he wrote, Nicki Clements just happened to share his view, and launched into a rant against his opponent. Usually quite effectively, it has to be said. She's clearly a bright woman. I didn't much like it when the opponent was me. Most of the time – when Damon's target was infant male circumcision, or Barack Obama, or the burka – most of the time I agreed with every word she said.'

'And, therefore, with every word Damon Blundy said?'

'Well . . . yes, I suppose so,' Paula admitted grudgingly. 'As long as it wasn't anti-me, or political. Damon said some sensible things, despite his determination to be ridiculous whenever possible.'

'Barack Obama?' said Simon. 'That sounds political.'

'I meant domestic political – Labour-versus-Tory stuff. I'm not a fan of the terror tactics used in America's never-ending war on terror. Damon thought Obama was a hypocrite: trying to look like a good guy while acting like a bad guy. Cardinal sin, that, in Damon's book.'

'You used the expression "head over heels" to describe Nicki Clements,' said Simon. 'That phrase refers to romantic love.'

Paula laughed. 'Er . . . well, yes, obviously. I think it's a fairly well-known expression.'

'How do you know Nicki Clements had romantic feelings for Damon? Couldn't she have been an ardent supporter of his writing and his opinions, without there being any more to it?'

'Trust me, she was in love with him,' Paula said.

Offhand, Simon couldn't think of many people he'd met that

he'd trusted less. 'How do you know? Is there any proof of that?'

'Read her comments!'

'I have. She was undeniably a fan of Blundy, but I've read nothing that suggests love.'

'Oh, come on! The protective tone, the hurt when people misjudge him . . .'

'Protectiveness can take a platonic form,' said Simon. 'People want to protect friends as well as . . . Don't they?'

'She was in love with him,' Paula said flatly. 'I can't believe you can't see it.'

'I can't see it, no,' said Simon, feeling at last that he was on firmer ground. 'But I believe that you can.'

'What do you mean by that?'

Simon looked pointedly at the clock on the wall. *Tick, tick, tick* . . .

It was the perfect moment to end the interview.

~

'And then I pressed "Post advertisement" and the deed was done,' Charlie told Simon, Liv and Gibbs. She decided not to mention that so far she'd had not one single reply that wasn't spam of one kind or another.

Simon, who had heard the story already, was furious. 'You're telling more people?' he said. 'Do you want to get sacked?'

'Liv and Gibbs won't say anything, will they? Morally compromised as they are. As we *all* are.'

The four of them were having dinner at Passaparola. These days, Charlie and Simon had dinner with Liv and Gibbs more often than with Liv and Dom. Charlie had never been keen on her official brother-in-law, and increasingly Dom, a lawyer with a thick skin and a high opinion of himself, seemed to need to be the centre of attention. He'd taken to prefacing nearly all of his I-know-better pronouncements with the words 'Here's the thing', followed by an audible colon.

'For once, nothing's leaked out to the press,' said Simon. '*Nothing* – and you go and do this.'

'And still nothing's been leaked to the press,' said Charlie. 'So. Relax.'

Liv clinked her fork against her glass. 'Chris and I have something important to tell you,' she said.

Charlie held her breath.

'Now, *please* don't be sad for us because we're *absolutely fine.* OK? We've decided that from now on, we're going to proceed on a new basis: just very good friends. *Best* friends!' She beamed. 'It won't change anything as far as you're concerned. We can still all meet for dinner. But . . . we've decided not to continue with the romantic side of our relationship.'

'You're splitting up?' Charlie had dreamed of this day for years. Now that it had come, she felt oddly deflated. But . . . Gibbs had been sucking up to her like mad, and Simon had said he'd been the same with him. Charlie had been sure a large favour was about to be asked of them. Why would you butter people up in order to tell them your relationship was over? It made no sense.

'We're no longer an item in that sense, no, but we'll still see each other just as often,' said Liv. 'Won't we, Chris?'

Gibbs sighed. 'If you say so,' he muttered. Charlie turned her attention to him, away from her sister. He looked embarrassed and slightly impatient. Not distraught, not in shock . . . Charlie glanced at Simon, who shook his head almost imperceptibly to let her know he agreed with her: something here didn't add up.

Whatever they were playing at, it was Liv's idea, Liv's crazy plan, and Gibbs was going along with it.

'Why are you going to see each other just as often?' Charlie asked. 'Isn't the one advantage of a break-up that you can finally be rid of the person?'

'Chris and I love each other,' said Liv. 'We'll always be part of one another's lives, just in a different way.' She reached over and squeezed Gibbs's hand.

'I don't believe you,' said Charlie. 'You're lying. What I can't work out is why.' She turned to Simon. 'What do they have to gain by pretending they're not sleeping together any more?'

'Dunno.' He shrugged. 'I suppose they'll tell us if and when they want us to know. In the meantime, we can talk about something else. Charlie spoke to another estate agent today,' he said to Gibbs. 'From Bateman Yoke.'

Gibbs stared down at the table.

'We're not lying!' Liv insisted.

'I don't think Simon's that interested,' Charlie told her. It was a good tactic. Deprived of the attention she'd been counting on, Liv might be forced into revealing the truth. 'He'd be very interested to hear what's *really* going on with you and Gibbs, though, and so would I,' Charlie said, ramming the point home.

'I've told you what's going on – we've broken up, but we're still best friends.'

'Liv, if they want to change the subject, there's nothing you can do,' said Gibbs. 'We've done our bit. Right?'

She pursed her lips. 'Well, I just thought . . . No, you're right. We've told them. It's . . . fine!'

Charlie watched the complex sequence of eye signals that passed between them. At that moment, she'd have given her right arm and perhaps a few toes too to know what the hell was going on.

'Tell me about this estate agent from Bateman Yoke,' Gibbs said.

Charlie opened her mouth, but Simon beat her to it. 'He wasn't one of the ones Nicki Clements asked to find her a house near Elmhirst Road last year – which is probably why she contacted him on 7 March this year and asked him what price she should ask for her Bartholomew Gardens house if she wanted to sell it as quickly as possible. She sounded upset, he said, and she didn't seem to care about making a loss – just seemed desperate to get out of Spilling as soon as she could. The guy said he'd go round and do a valuation, but before he had a chance, Nicki had rung him back and said she'd changed her mind and didn't want to move. She cancelled him.'

'Are you thinking the first call was immediately after she broke up with Damon Blundy?' Gibbs asked.

'That's my guess,' said Charlie. 'They had an affair; it went wrong; she wanted to get away from him, having only moved to the Culver Valley to be near him. Then a day or so later, her mood changed – she started to feel stronger and realised it was bad enough that she'd moved for him once. Twice would be pathetic.'

'So Damon Blundy and this Nicki woman were having an affair, and they'd split up by 7 March?' Liv said. 'That sounds about right.'

'What? What do you know about it?' Charlie asked her. *You manipulative liar.*

'I know that by April this year Damon Blundy was having an affair with Paula Riddiough.' It was a few seconds before Liv noticed the effect her words had had. 'What? Why are you all staring at me weirdly? Oh, come on, *everyone* knows about Damon Blundy and Paula Privilege!'

'Whatever you know, why the fuck haven't you told me?' said Gibbs, red in the face.

'I've been preoccupied. We both have, with our . . .' Liv stopped and bit her lip.

'With your fake break-up?' Charlie suggested helpfully.

'Let's not get sidetracked,' said Simon. 'Liv, tell us.'

'I'm sorry, I thought we all knew,' she said shakily. 'All my Twitter friends know. Blundy and Paula had a big row on Twitter after Margaret Thatcher died – insulting and mocking each other in rhyming couplets, copying the exact metrical structure of *The Gruffalo* by Julia Donaldson.'

'And *Tiddler*,' said Simon.

Liv looked shocked, then giggled. 'How do you know about *Tiddler*?'

'I didn't until recently. Until I read the Twitter argument between Paula Riddiough and Damon Blundy.'

'He likes to be thorough in his research,' said Charlie. 'Plus, he loves books about fish.'

Simon's face tightened, as she'd known it would. '*Moby Dick*'s not about a fish,' he said. 'A whale isn't a fish.'

'Tiddler's *heavenly*,' Liv gushed. She was in a remarkably sunny mood for someone who had recently terminated a passionate love affair. 'Morally, it's the opposite of "The Boy Who Cried Wolf". Making up stories isn't bad – it's the only thing that can save you. That's the message.'

'Interesting that your idea of "heavenly" is a book that makes the case for lying,' Charlie muttered.

'Can we get back to Blundy and Riddiough?' Gibbs snapped.

'If you followed their Thatcher witch fight, you can't have failed to notice how it ended. Don't you remember?' Liv asked Simon.

'Not word for word, no.'

'We don't all spend our days browsing Twitter,' said Charlie.

'There's a bit in *Tiddler*, near the end, where Tiddler says, "I was lost, I was scared, but a story led me home again." The other fish all say, "Oh no, it didn't," and Tiddler says, "Oh yes, it did." Immediately after their spat on Twitter – maybe ten minutes later – Paula Riddiough tweeted Damon Blundy and said, "I was lost, I was scared, but a Tory led me home again." Blundy tweeted back, "Oh no, he didn't", to which she replied, "Oh yes, he did!"' Liv looked at Gibbs, who was staring at her open-mouthed. 'I read that and I thought, "They *must* be having an affair."'

'It's not there any more,' Simon said to Gibbs in the voice Charlie feared, the one that always signalled his failure to notice she was alive for the foreseeable future. 'Is it? Am I going senile?'

'Of course it's not there *now*,' said Liv. 'The incriminating tweets vanished seconds after they appeared.'

'You sure about this, Liv?' Gibbs asked her. 'You didn't imagine it, or . . . misremember?'

'One hundred and fifty per cent positive. I follow both of

them. I watched those tweets as they happened. I've still got DMs from that day, probably – friends who saw it too. I was suspicious even *before* the nicey-nicey bit at the end. Damon Blundy had no kids and regularly wrote about how he couldn't stand children and everything relating to them – how did he know *The Gruffalo* and *Tiddler* well enough to be able to parody them at such speed, unless he was involved with Paula Riddiough? Everyone knows they're her favourite books – well, everyone who follows her tweets, like I do. And then, when the row was followed by that lovey-dovey bit, it seemed obvious. I waited for it to blow up into a huge thing – screengrabs, the works – but no one said anything, not on general Twitter. I think a hell of a lot of people'd be scared to antagonise Damon Blundy, knowing how he goes after anyone he's got it in for.'

A waiter was approaching. 'No,' Simon barked at him without looking in his direction. 'Not now.' The waiter retreated, looking grateful to have been warned away from a potentially toxic area of the restaurant.

'Oh, and there was a smiley face too,' said Liv.

'What?' Simon and Gibbs both pounced at the same time.

'Yes, after what I've already said – "Oh no, he didn't", "Oh yes, he did!" et cetera – Blundy sent her a tweet that was just a smiley face. No words.' Liv paused for dramatic effect. She was starting to enjoy the expert-witness role. 'And . . . I'm not absolutely sure, but I *think* the face might even have been winking,' she said.

II

Tuesday 9 July 2013

The Chancery Hotel hasn't changed since I was last here in February. I expected it to be different. I wanted it to be. Or maybe I only want me to be different – no longer the same fool who arrived here full of hope and excitement five months ago, thinking she was about to consummate her illicit love affair with one of the UK's most famous newspaper columnists.

Still the same.

The grey and red lobby décor, the flower photographs on the walls . . . Separated from reception by a glass partition, there's the same skinny rectangle of a bar, where you'd be foolish to sit and have a drink if you didn't want the bar staff to overhear your entire conversation, not to mention the ticking and squelching of your internal organs. The room can't be more than three feet wide. No one's in there today; I can't imagine that anyone ever sits at the bar, on one of the twelve high red-topped stools arranged in a perfectly straight line. Who would want to be stared at by people like me, waiting to be checked in?

There's only one receptionist on duty, and the most tedious man in the world is in front of me. He seems determined to ask about everything a guest at a hotel might conceivably ask about: Wi-Fi, breakfast times, gym times, the business centre, newspapers, alarm calls, does his room have a minibar. I suppress the urge to scream at him, 'How can you want and need so much?' He even has an annoying name that he has to spell out letter by letter because it's so unusual. U-s-k-a-l-i-s. He pushed in front of me on the hotel steps and actually jogged to reception in order to get there before me, the creep.

While I wait, I keep turning round to see if anyone walks through the hotel's main door. All the way here from King's Cross Station – a fifteen-minute walk – I sensed that someone was following me, but there was no sign of anyone. No streaked-haired man, no blue BMW, no one who stopped walking when I did and lowered their eyes.

I tell myself I'm being paranoid. No one's followed me here. No one knows where I am and what I'm doing apart from King Edward. I told Adam I was going to London to try and sort things out with Melissa. I even told him which hotel I'd be staying in and that I didn't know exactly when I'd be back; perhaps I'd need to stay overnight. 'I'm not going to her house,' I said. 'I want to be absolutely sure I don't run into Lee. I want to invite Melissa to *my* territory to talk, instead of being on hers like I usually am – where she can kick me out whenever it suits her. This time, I'm going to set the agenda and do any kicking out that needs to be done.'

Adam believed me. I believed myself. It sounded plausible because it's the truth. I'm going to make it true. When I get to my room – if I ever get there, if Mr Uskalis ever stops wittering on – the first thing I'm going to do is ring Melissa and invite her to meet me and talk, but only if she's willing to pack a suitcase and leave Lee at the same time, having told him she wants a divorce. She will, of course, refuse. I can then text Adam and tell him she's refused to meet me, but that I'm going to stay at the hotel and have another try later.

I am a truly great liar. Legendary.

Finally, the tedious guy has released the receptionist. 'I've reserved a room,' I tell her.

'Thank you for your patience. Sorry I kept you waiting. Name?'

'Kate Zilber. Z-i-l-b-e-r.' I think about Gavin's – King Edward's – disdain for Damon Blundy, his suggestion that Blundy was evil. Is that why he chose his name to hide behind when he was behaving badly, for the same reason I've chosen Kate's?

As a kind of revenge? I've given the Chancery Hotel all of Kate's details and none of my own.

'Yes, we've got you here,' the receptionist says. Superior Double for one night?'

'That's right.' When I hand over my credit card as an advance against my minibar costs, she doesn't look at the name on it, just hands me the machine to key in my PIN.

I sign where I'm told to sign – Kate's name – and I'm given the key to room 419. The hotel lift is nearly as narrow as the bar: it would accommodate no more than two people. Its four mirrored walls don't make it look any bigger, only crazier: dozens of clones of a hollow-eyed, paranoid woman with unbrushed hair.

I didn't bring a hairbrush, make-up, perfume. I didn't even have a shower this morning. I don't care what I look like or how I smell. I'm not here for romantic or sexual reasons, not this time.

Once I've rung Melissa and texted Adam, I will email King Edward and give him my room number and a time, as agreed. I look at my watch: 12.50 p.m. Yesterday, he said anytime after two. I'll tell him three o'clock. That will give me enough time.

To leave the door slightly ajar with the 'Do not disturb' sign displayed. To take off my clothes, climb into the bed, tie the blindfold securely in place and wait.

He's not going to kill me. He wouldn't do that. He's done terrible things to me, and he's maybe killed Damon Blundy, but he wouldn't kill me.

Tomorrow evening, I'll be at home again, with Sophie and Ethan. And Adam. If I can just get home safely, I'll never cheat on him again – never. I won't flirt, won't look on Intimate Links, won't do anything I have to lie to anybody about.

The lift doors open at the fourth floor. I pull my phone out of my bag as I walk along the corridor to room 419, suddenly feeling an urgent need to remove any trace of myself from the Intimate Links website. Deleting my 'I Want a Secret' ad won't undo anything that's happened, but symbolically it will help me, make me feel I've disconnected from something horrible.

Will my advert still be there, buried beneath all the more recent ones? Maybe they delete them automatically after a year or so.

In my room – also red and grey – I throw my rucksack on the bed, trying not to think about the bed itself. I've brought nothing with me apart from my phone, the blindfold, spare underwear and a toothbrush and toothpaste.

I'm not going to have sex with him. He won't insist on it. He could easily make it a condition of his telling me the truth about Damon Blundy's murder, but he won't. I don't care if he wants me not to utter a word, like last time. He'll soon find out that I intend to speak as much as I want to.

He cares about me, about what I want.

Then why has he deceived you twice, in such a damaging way?

All right: I've no idea if he cares or not, or what caring even means to a man like King Edward. Do I trust him? No. But I want something from him: information.

If I have to have sex with him in order to find out who killed Damon Blundy, I'll do it. I've had sex I didn't want plenty of times – never against my will, always by choice, to make the other person happy. This time, it would be for my own satisfaction, because I need to understand how exactly my life ended up entangled in a murder investigation.

On my phone's screen, I bring up the Intimate Links site and go to 'Personals'. In the search box, I type, 'Secret'. There's no way it'll still be there after all these years.

Several results appear. None of them's my advert. They're all too recent. I click on the most recent one, from 4 July, last Thursday. It's headed, 'Looking for a Woman with a Secret'. I start to read it, at first because I find it puzzling. The writer claims to want neither a long-term relationship nor casual sex.

I gasp when I see the words 'pale blue and brown jukebox'. Damon Blundy had a blue and brown jukebox. He wrote a column about it, and mentioned it in a couple of his other columns. What's . . .

Oh God. Oh fuck.

This isn't a personal ad; it's a description of Damon's murder. A knife – sharp, sharpened at the scene, but he wasn't stabbed . . .

Oh Jesus Christ.

I wish I hadn't read it, wish I didn't know how precisely Damon Blundy was killed, because now that I know how, I know why.

You knew already. Don't lie to yourself. Lie to other people if necessary, but not to yourself.

As soon as you worked out what 'He is no less dead' meant, you knew . . .

A man's been murdered because of something I said.

I almost know who killed Damon. *Almost.* Trouble is, there's more than one person it might be. The likelihood of the police working it out, any of it, is zero unless I tell them everything I know.

I can't do it. Or rather, I could, but I know I never will. If there were a murder trial, it would all come out, be made public. It would be in all the papers. No, I can't let that happen, no matter what.

I reread the 'Looking for a Woman with a Secret' advert five times to check I haven't missed anything. Beads of cold sweat have appeared on my upper lip. I feel as if I might faint.

It's for me. This ad is directed at me. It must be – there's no one else who could make any sense of it. Its author has been waiting for a response for five days.

I press 'reply'.

Keiran Holland @KeiranBHolland
Happy publication day to my better half @IonaDennis73!
#proudhusband
07:50am - 27 June 2013

Damon Blundy @blunderfulme
@KeiranBHolland If her book sells more than 500 copies, I'll treat
you to lunch at the Ivy.
07:58am - 27 June 2013

Keiran Holland @KeiranBHolland
@blunderfulme You really are the lowest of the low, aren't you,
Damon? You're turning your venom on my wife now?
08:02am - 27 June 2013

Damon Blundy @blunderfulme
@KeiranBHolland No venom, just opinion. Just so we're
clear – are you accusing me of treating your wife badly?
#onemanhypocrisyepidemic
08:04am - 27 June 2013

Anne McSorley @lilorphanannie
@blunderfulme You are a nasty, rude man, Damon Blundy!
@KeiranBHolland
08:10am - 27 June 2013

Damon Blundy @blunderfulme
@KeiranBHolland Who's treated your wife worse, you or me? Let's
recap . . .
08:15am - 27 June 2013

Damon Blundy @blunderfulme
@KeiranBHolland You: make vows to wife to love & cherish
forever. You: shag Paula R on the sly for months, leave wife for
her, go back only . . .
08:19am - 27 June 2013

Damon Blundy @blunderfulme

@KeiranBHolland . . . when dumped by PR, lie to world and wife
by pretending you always loved wife more & it's not just a
rebound take-me-back.
08:21am - 27 June 2013

Damon Blundy @blunderfulme

@KeiranBHolland Me: never met your wife or made any vows to her.
Owe her nothing. Suggest on Twitter that her tedious book won't sell.
08:24am - 27 June 2013

Damon Blundy @blunderfulme

@KeiranBHolland Which of us has treated @IonaDennis73 worse,
Keiran – you or me?
08:25am - 27 June 2013

Damon Blundy @blunderfulme

@IonaDennis73 Iona, who has hurt you more, me or @KeiranBHolland?
08:26am - 27 June 2013

Bryn Gilligan @sprinterbryng

I'm no fan of Damon Blundy, but he's right to say Keiran Holland's
a hypocrite.
08:42am - 27 June 2013

Bicester Mister @bicestermister

@sprinterbryng Fuck off lying cheating asswipe. No one cares
what you think.
08:44am - 27 June 2013

12

Tuesday 9 July 2013

'He's a novelist,' Simon shouted into his phone, hoping he'd be heard over the wind and the rushing of the river. 'He writes supernatural-horror kind of books. He lives opposite your school, on Gaywood Road. I just wondered if you'd ever had any contact with him.'

'None whatsoever,' said the improbably named headmistress whose voice he could barely hear. Nastia Grekov was obviously of Russian ancestry, or something similar, though she sounded very English. Having a name that sounded identical to the word 'nastier' when you worked in a school couldn't be easy, thought Simon.

'I'd never heard of him until I got your message,' she said. 'Do you mind telling me what this is about? Do I need to worry about this man?'

'No, not at all.' Having heard the answer, he was impatient to end the call. He was supposed to be meeting Hannah Blundy at her office five minutes ago, was standing outside it, and had been about to press the buzzer when his phone had started to ring.

'You say "not at all" and yet you're a police detective, and you say he writes horror, so . . . I'm a little concerned,' said Mrs Grekov. 'What can you tell me to put my mind at rest? Has Mr Tasker committed a crime? Is he suspected of a crime? I'm responsible for the welfare of several hundred—'

'Your pupils aren't in any danger,' Simon told her, hoping to God that he was right. A few more abstract reassurances and he was able to extract himself.

Why did Reuben Tasker hate the school opposite his house

so much? And only since Damon Blundy's death, according to Gibbs, who had spoken to Tasker's wife, Jane, about it. It surely must have something to do with the murder, but how could it possibly be connected?

Simon pressed the buzzer. The '21' beside the door was so subtle that, even with the sun shining directly on it, Simon almost missed it. Hannah Blundy's psychotherapy practice was obviously doing well if she could afford space in this large white stucco-fronted townhouse, the middle one of a wide, regal, terraced block of three on the riverfront in Silsford.

'Yes?' a crackly voice emerged from the intercom on the wall. Hannah's?

'DC Simon Waterhouse, to see Hannah Blun— Hannah Yeatman.' At work, she called herself by her maiden name. Simon didn't understand why anyone would allow themselves to end up in a situation where they had two names. Having one was bad enough; he'd always hated saying his own out loud.

The crackly voice said something he couldn't make out. It was followed by a deeper buzzing noise, which Simon took to mean that he should push his way in. He had to apply his full weight to the shiny black front door in order to get it to move.

Inside, he expected to see a person, or something that hinted at the presence of a person or people nearby, but there was nothing – no visible reception area, no sound of voices or movement. Simon was standing in a wide, elegant hall with mustard-coloured walls and one of those zigzag-patterned wooden floors, dark and shiny. Ahead of him were two doors, one on either side: one ajar and one closed.

He moved forward and looked into the room that was open. It looked like a waiting room, waiting for people to wait within it. There was a display of glossy magazines on a rectangular table with wooden legs and a thick marble slab-like top, three armchairs that looked as if they'd been designed for a royal court, a backless pink sofa that reminded Simon of a rolled-out tongue, and two tall, rubbery-leafed plants in large terracotta pots.

Surroundings so ostentatiously flawless made Simon suspicious. The inside of the building smelled of new paint and new carpet. He pictured waves of crimson blood flowing down the curved staircase in front of him, rushing towards him like a curling red ribbon.

He shook his head to banish the image. 'Hello?' he called out. 'Anyone in? Hannah?'

A pair of legs appeared at the top of the wide staircase in front of him. 'Sorry!' It was Hannah's voice.

Simon was embarrassed by how relieved he was to hear it. The building had a bad vibe. He wouldn't have liked to be in it alone.

'Sorry,' Hannah said again. 'I had a patient on the phone and couldn't disentangle myself easily. Come on up.'

Simon followed her to her office on the first floor and did a double take as he entered the room.

Incredible. Someone had covered the whole floor with a painted Chinese landscape. It was mainly blue and white, with touches of pale green and pale pink here and there. Like an intricate china-teacup pattern, but on the floor.

'Amazing, isn't it?' said Hannah. She was smiling, but her eyes were red and swollen, her face pale. 'My friend did it for me. She's a genius.'

On the far wall, above a filing cabinet, there was a framed quote that must have been chosen for its psychological relevance:

> Deep-rooted fears –
> Should not fears have deep roots? –
> And terrifying love
> Send their pale shoots above
> The surface where no other growth appears.

'Do have a seat there, near the water,' Hannah said.

At first, Simon thought she meant the painted river on the floorboards. Then he saw the carafe on the table between the sofa and the window, with an upended glass resting on its neck, acting as a lid. He walked over to the sofa and sat down, trying not to mind that this was probably where Hannah's patients sat. Or – even worse – lay.

'I hope it wasn't too inconvenient for you to meet me here.'

'It's fine. Are you back at work?'

'No. I just . . . Being here's preferable to being at home alone,' Hannah said. 'Damon never came here, so . . . it's just easier.'

'So, you're not seeing anybody? Apart from me, I mean – no appointments?'

She shook her head.

'Are you sure?' Simon tried to sound as relaxed as possible. 'No one came to see you this morning? I don't mean a patient, necessarily.'

Hannah's mouth tightened. 'If you know – which you seem to – then why ask me?'

'Could you answer, please?'

'Paula Riddiough came to see me,' said Hannah quietly. 'She's obviously told you all about it.'

Simon considered denying this, then realised that if he did, he'd have to explain. He'd worked out, ten minutes after Paula Riddiough had left his office yesterday, that the horological opposite of a meeting that begins at 10.10 a.m, ten minutes past the hour, is a meeting that ends at ten minutes *to* the hour. Appointments with psychotherapists were famous for ending at ten minutes to the hour. Not that Simon knew from personal experience, but he'd heard references to the fifty-minute hour.

'Did you contact Paula to arrange this meeting, or did she contact you?' he asked.

'She contacted me.'

'And you agreed to see her?'

'I was curious.'

'And? What did she want?'

Hannah flinched. Never had it been more obvious that someone didn't want to talk about something. *Why?*

'She wanted to tell me that she didn't kill Damon. I told her

I didn't for a moment imagine she had. Without drawing breath, she asked me if I'd killed him.'

Simon frowned. 'She can't have thought you'd tell her even if you had,' he said, more to himself than to Hannah.

'You know, I think she did.' Hannah sounded angry. 'Her tone was horrible. Kind of matey-confiding, as if she were saying, "Go on, admit you murdered your husband – it can be our little secret." I think she hated him so much she'd have liked to make a new friend of his murderer.'

'Did Damon ever talk to you about Paula?' Simon asked.

'Often. We had lots of fun slagging her off. He thought she was a waste of space.'

'Culver Valley East was her constituency when Damon moved from London to Spilling in November 2011.'

Hannah recoiled.

Feeling uneasy, and a little bit guilty without really understanding why, Simon asked, 'Do you know why Damon decided to move to the Culver Valley?'

'He was tired of London, I suppose,' Hannah said abruptly. 'I'm not sure. Is this why you came, to ask me about Paula Riddiough?'

'It's not the only reason. Why are you so reluctant to talk about Paula?'

Hannah said nothing. She stared at Simon as if it were his turn to speak and she were the one waiting.

'Why did you lie when I first asked if you'd had any appointments?' he asked.

'I didn't *lie*. I . . . Look, Paula hated Damon and he hated her. I'd rather not think about her, discuss her, have her in this room. Can we change the subject, please?'

'You don't want to discuss her with me, but you were happy to slag her off with Damon?' said Simon. 'How come?'

Hannah looked away.

'Something's changed, hasn't it? Today. When Paula came to see you—'

'Look, I don't want to talk about Paula Riddiough, and I *won't* talk about her,' said Hannah forcefully. 'All right? If that's the only topic you plan to cover, you can leave now. It wasn't pleasant, being asked if I'd murdered Damon, in a tone that suggested she'd approve if I had.'

'I can understand that, but—'

'I can't see why she'd care enough to insist on meeting me in person, but she did. I can't think why Damon would make part of her name into his computer password, but he did. Now, do you have any questions for me that aren't about Paula Riddiough?'

She cared enough to want to meet you in person because she was in love with your husband. And he was in love with her, hence his password based on her name. And you know it, don't you? You're doing everything you can to avoid acknowledging the truth, but you know.

After giving Hannah a few seconds to compose herself, Simon asked, 'Does the name Nicki Clements mean anything to you?'

'No. Who is she?'

'A regular contributor to the comments threads beneath Damon's columns online. It's been suggested to us that she might have been obsessed with him. He never mentioned her name?'

'No,' said Hannah.

'I need to ask you something,' Simon said. 'You'll want to say no, but . . . I think it could be important. And I promise you, anything I see that's not relevant to the investigation will go no further than me.'

'Hold on,' Hannah cut him off. 'What are we talking about here?'

There was no point putting it off, though Simon was tempted. He hated asking questions to which he knew the answer would be 'no'. 'I'd like to look through your client files,' he said. 'Do you make notes on what you talk to them about?'

Hannah nodded. 'I do. And I'm sorry, but there's not a chance in hell that I'm going to let you see them.'

'It's possible that the person who killed Damon made an

appointment to see you at some point. He or she might even be a regular client.'

Hannah frowned. 'That's a strange assumption to make, isn't it? What makes you think that?'

Simon wasn't prepared to tell her the truth, so he said nothing. He was certain he was right.

'Sorry,' said Hannah. 'Confidential. My work is pretty much all I've got now, so my professional integrity's not up for grabs.'

Simon struggled to suppress his mounting frustration. Somewhere in this room was the information he wanted . . . In that filing cabinet, probably. 'Got any clients called Nicki?' he asked.

'No.'

Would she use her own name, though? 'How about Melissa Redgate?'

Hannah flinched. Her hand flew to her neck and started to make grasping motions, as if she were reaching for a necklace that wasn't there. 'Melissa,' she whispered. 'Did she kill Damon? Oh my God. Oh my God!' Her eyes widened. 'Those words, "He is no less dead" . . .'

'What? What, Hannah? You've thought of something – what is it?'

She pressed her lips together and shook her head.

'Hannah? You've got to tell me what you've—'

'The filing cabinet.' She leaped to her feet, her face a mess of pink and white blotches. 'Third drawer down. I've got to . . . I'm sorry, I need some air.'

Simon didn't follow her. He listened to her footsteps on the stairs. A few seconds later, he heard a door slam. Was he in the building alone? 'Filing cabinet, third drawer down,' he repeated to himself.

He is no less dead. Than what? A 'less' implies a 'than'. Was Simon about to find out the answer, from one of Hannah's patient's files?

He opened the drawer and saw that it contained surnames

'P to S'. He found the file with the name 'Melissa Redgate' on it and pulled it out. Heart racing, he started to flick through it. When he got to the fourth page, he stopped and read more carefully.

He swore under his breath. This was it. Here it was, all neatly written down.

It made sense. Hannah's shocked reaction, though . . . She hadn't known, hadn't made the connection, not until Simon had nudged her into thinking of her patient 'Melissa Redgate' as a possible murderer.

Simon read and reread the words. The identity of Damon Blundy's killer was still a mystery to him, but he was getting closer. An important part of the solution to the overall puzzle had fallen into place. Simon now knew what Hannah knew, and what the woman whose file he was holding in his hands knew. He knew why Damon Blundy had been killed in the way that he had.

~

Charlie felt her phone buzz in her pocket. She sighed to herself. This was going to be interesting. There was no point asking Fortunata to keep the noise down; Charlie had tried before and failed.

'Hello?' she raised her voice.

'You're in Mario's,' Simon said immediately.

'Do you know any other cafés where the owner sings loud Italian arias all day long, making all the customers want to strangle her?'

'What are you doing there?'

'Waiting for Melissa Redgate. She refused to come to the nick, for some reason.'

'I want to ask you something,' said Simon. 'About Liv and Gibbs.'

'I'm trying not to think about them. How *dare* they sit there and tell us a barefaced lie about their stupid affair when we've spent years helping them bloody well get away with it? I bet

Sellers knows the truth. He and Gibbs are blood brothers, aren't they? Or, to be more accurate, sleaze brothers.'

'They're lying, but Gibbs doesn't want to,' said Simon. 'He hates it. Liv loves it, though – in the restaurant the other night, she'd have spent the whole evening talking about the pretend separation if we'd been willing to indulge her.'

'We're agreed they haven't really split up, right? I mean, no *way* have they split. So why, suddenly, does Liv need us to believe they have?'

'A new fantasy?' Simon suggested. 'This is what I'm getting at. Liv enjoys making things up. She enjoys fantasy. Gibbs prefers the reality, which is why he'd rather tell us the truth, whatever it is.'

'It's the same as it always was. It must be: they're shagging, and lying to their spouses.'

'No, something must have changed between them to spark off this break-up story.'

'I can hardly hear you,' Charlie said loudly in the hope that Fortunata would take the hint. 'OK, so what's the change? They're not leaving Dom and Debbie, are they? What are the other possibilities?'

'Who cares? I only care about the difference in their characters: fantasist, realist. Gibbs'd leave Debbie and move in with Liv at the drop of a hat, wouldn't he? She'd only have to say the word.'

'True,' Charlie agreed.

'He wants a real life with her, but she doesn't. She wants to preserve her real life with Dom, and have her secret life with Gibbs, *and* lie about it!'

'So . . . what does that mean?' Charlie asked.

'It means I'm starting to understand something I didn't before.'

'About Liv and Gibbs?'

'No. Well, yes, but no. By the way, I know why Damon Blundy wasn't stabbed.'

The line went dead. Behind the counter, Fortunata switched

from *Madame Butterfly* to *Tosca*. Charlie held her phone over her mug of tea and thought about dropping it in.

'Sergeant Zailer?'

She looked up. 'Are you Melissa?'

The woman nodded. She was short and plump, with dark brown shoulder-length hair, big brown eyes and a pronounced dimple at the centre of her chin. She had a handbag draped over her shoulder and was clutching an orange plastic bag with both hands. From the way she held it, Charlie deduced that it contained something important. It looked, through the semi-transparent bag, like books.

'Have a seat. She'll come over and take your order – in between the verse and the chorus.'

Melissa didn't sit down. She eyed Fortunata nervously, wincing when she hit a high note. 'Shouldn't we go somewhere quieter?'

'How about the police station?'

Melissa looked shocked, as if Charlie had suggested a brothel. 'I told you, I don't want to go there. Once was enough. I agreed to meet for a chat, not an official interview.'

Charlie nodded. She had no idea what Melissa imagined the difference was, but she didn't intend to set her straight – not before she'd found out what was in the orange bag. 'Then here's as good a place as any. And they do the best cakes,' she said, pointing at the crumbs on her plate.

Melissa sat down opposite her, a defeated expression on her face. Charlie thought she recognised the personality type: obedient, afraid of authority, a tendency to repress resentment – something that grows ever harder, the more of it you do.

'So, let's start chatting straight away. I hear you don't have an alibi for last Monday morning.'

'I do,' Melissa said. 'I was working. At home. It's not my fault that I work from home. Plenty of people do and they aren't all murderers.'

'Between eight thirty and ten thirty a.m. you had no phone calls, sent no emails, no texts?'

'No, I didn't. I was doing paperwork. Involving paper, not online. How do you know all this, anyway?'

'From speaking to colleagues,' said Charlie. 'Sorry, is this not the kind of chat you wanted to have? What did you want to talk about?'

'Nothing. You asked to meet me, remember?' Melissa slid the orange plastic bag off her lap and onto the floor under the table. The harsher Charlie was, the further away the contents of that bag were going to get. *Time to be diplomatic.*

'Fair enough. We have to ask these things, you know. I kind of got the impression you'd brought something to show me?' Charlie smiled.

'No,' said Melissa flatly.

Liar.

Mentally, Charlie kicked herself for being too confrontational too soon. Why had she made such a stupid mistake? Blaming it on Melissa was too easy, but . . . there was something about the woman sitting across the table from her that made Charlie's skin prickle. She didn't like her.

Because she trespassed, like Liv. She married her best friend's brother. Psychology 101.

'I hope you don't mind if I ask you a couple of other questions, unrelated to alibis,' said Charlie.

'That's why I'm here. I'm happy to help if I can. Ask away.'

'Do you own a car?'

'A car?'

'Yes.' Charlie mimed steering. 'Four wheels, gearstick, dashboard . . .'

'What's that got to do with anything?' Melissa asked.

'I honestly don't know. Look, I told you on the phone, I'm not a detective – I'm a flunky, working her way through someone else's list of questions.'

Fortunata chose this moment to appear with a curly-paged notepad and a pencil. 'You want something?' she demanded loudly.

Melissa shrank back.

'Another latte for Charlie?'

'Go on, then. Cheers.'

'And for Charlie friend?'

'Diet Coke, please,' said Melissa.

Once they were alone again, she said, 'Yes. I have a car. What a strange question.'

'Do you share it with Lee, or is it just yours?'

'We have a car each. Lee has a Vauxhall Insignia, and I've got a Mazda RX-8.'

'What kind of driver are you?' Charlie asked her. 'Would you happily drive on a motorway on your own at night? Do you only do short, local trips unless Lee's with you?'

'No.' Melissa looked as if she suspected some sort of practical joke was in progress, and she was its victim. 'I drive alone on motorways at night all the time. When my mum and dad got divorced, he moved to Truro. I often drive there to visit him, on my own, often getting back at two or three in the morning. I drive in all weathers, through the centre of London in rush hour if I need to. I'd drive in light snow too if Lee would let me – he's the more cautious driver of the two of us, by far. Is that enough information for you?'

'I think so,' said Charlie.

'You really don't know why you've been told to ask me that?'

'Not a clue. What's in the orange bag under the table?'

Melissa looked away quickly, as if by avoiding Charlie's eye, she could avoid answering.

'Melissa? You brought something with you. You must have wanted to show it to me.'

'I've changed my mind. I don't think it's got anything to do with Damon Blundy's murder.'

'But at first you thought it might have? Please show it to me. If there's even a tiny chance it could shed some light, I need to see it.'

Melissa's eyes had filled with tears. 'Well, you know where it is if you want to look at it,' she said.

Charlie stood up, walked round the side of the table and picked up the bag – all so that Melissa would be able to say to herself, *I didn't give it to her – she took it.* Crazy.

Emptying the bag onto the table, Charlie saw that she'd been nearly right but not quite. Not books, but two white thin-spined notebooks. Lined paper. On the cover of one, in blue biro that had driven grooves into the thin cover, 'The Lies' was written in childish handwriting. On the other, someone had simply written, 'LIES', in capital letters.

Charlie opened the first and started to flick through. '"Pretended to be doing fun run for charity, got Mum and Dad to sponsor",' she read aloud. '"Promised never to go on Danny McKillop's motorbike, went on it today without a helmet." What *are* these?'

'Pages and pages of lies,' said Melissa. 'Two notebooks' full. I found them at Nicki's parents' house when Lee and I were there over the weekend. I . . . This is going to sound terrible, but I searched Nicki's old bedroom while I was there. Lee and his mum and dad went out for a walk, and . . . well, I've been so worried about this Damon Blundy thing – the thought that Nicki might actually have . . .' Melissa closed her eyes for a few seconds. 'I knew Quentin and Nora still had a lot of her old stuff in the attic, so I thought I'd have a look at it. Not to find anything directly connected to Damon Blundy's death, obviously – Nicki didn't know Damon Blundy when she was a child . . .'

'Then why?' Charlie asked. 'What were you hoping to find?'

'I don't know,' Melissa whispered tearfully. 'Something that would help me understand Nicki better, maybe. Her psychology, why she lies. When she was a teenager, her parents nearly had her committed. Lee won't talk about it much, but apparently they got as far as actually taking her to the place, the asylum, but at the last minute they just couldn't do it.'

'*Committed?*' For lying to her parents when she was a teenager? Everyone did that.

Melissa nodded.

'So . . . you found these notebooks?' Charlie started to flick through the pages again. It was a record of lies told – an archive of lies, each one in a separate box, with a straight blue-ink line above and below it, each one accompanied by the date, and a number that bore no relation to the date. 'In which Nicki listed all the lies she told her parents. How odd. Why would anyone do that? And what are these numbers, after the lies – 150, 250, 300 – what do they mean?'

Melissa said nothing. She looked shifty.

'Please, Melissa, if you know what any of it means or why Nicki did this, you've got to tell me. What you're thinking right now could be right: if she's crazy enough to collect her lies in notebooks and keep them, she might be crazy enough to—'

'No. That's not . . .' Melissa looked desperate. 'It's not Nicki's handwriting,' she said. 'It's Lee's.'

'Lee? Her brother?'

'And my husband, yes.'

'Are you sure? Lee kept a written record of his sister's lies? Why would he do that?'

'I don't know. And the notebooks were with Nicki's things, not Lee's, but that's definitely his writing.' Two tears spilled over and snaked down Melissa's face. 'I'm too scared to ask him about it. I tried to mention the notebooks to Nicki and she slammed the phone down on me. I'm scared I might have traded in my best ever friend for . . .' Melissa bit down hard on her bottom lip. She seemed to have decided against whatever she'd been about to say.

'Can I hang on to these notebooks?' Charlie asked her. 'I'm sure they have no bearing on the investigation into Damon Blundy's murder, but . . . I'd like to put them in front of people who know more about it than I do.'

'Keep them,' said Melissa. 'I wish I'd never found them.'

Was she worried it was her husband and not his sister who belonged in an asylum? Charlie would be, in her shoes. Who keeps lists of lies?

The table started to vibrate. 'Your phone's ringing,' said Melissa.

It was bound to be Simon, ringing with more ambiguous teasers to drive Charlie insane. 'Sorry,' she said. 'I'll switch it off. I . . . Oh.'

It wasn't a phone call. It was an email, to Charlie's 'Confidant' account, the one she set up to post her 'Looking for a Woman with a Secret' ad on the Intimate Links website. 'Can you excuse me for a second?' she asked Melissa. She didn't notice the response, if there was one.

In the loo at Mario's, mercifully free from Fortunata's singing, Charlie opened the email that had arrived from 'Nicki', whose email address was 'nickibeingnaughty@hushmail.com'. She started to read.

Interesting and . . . Oh shit. Too interesting. And potentially lethal.

She texted Simon: 'Just had a reply to my Intimate Links ad from "Nicki". Meet me CID room asap + team. C.'

Charlie hurried back to the operatic section of the café. 'I'm sorry, I've got to go,' she told Melissa. 'Something urgent's come up. Do you know someone who goes by the name of King Edward?'

'Know personally? No. I mean, I've obviously heard of King Edward the king – the Mrs Simpson one. Do you mean him?'

She was either serious or the subtlest smart-arse in the world. 'No, I mean a real-life man who uses the alias King Edward. Possibly an associate of Nicki's.'

Melissa shook her head. 'I've never heard of him,' she said.

Sophie Hannah

From: Nicki <nickibeingnaughty@hushmail.com>
Date: Tue, 9 July 2013 14:10:21
To: <confidant2013@gmail.com>
Subject: Re: Looking for a Woman with a Secret

First King Edward, then Damon Blundy, then Gavin and now Confidant – your fourth assumed identity. Did you really think I'd fall for another one?

I'm assuming it's you I'm writing to – the man I know as King Edward VII. I doubt the police would be stupid enough to post the details of a crime scene on a dating website. The only other person it could be is Damon's wife, Hannah.

You don't understand how it could be her, do you? You think that the knife, and the way you used it on Damon, and what it means, is a secret that only you and I know. Well, you're wrong.

Still, I don't think Hannah killed him. She didn't have a motive – or rather, she didn't know she had one. I took care to make sure she didn't find out about me and Damon (not that there ever really was a 'me and Damon', of course).

I think it was you who killed him, King Edward. Even though you say in your ad that you think the killer's a woman. Me, presumably? Are you trying to scare me, make me think you might try to frame me for Damon's murder? I had no reason to kill him, though, did I?

You, on the other hand, had a glaringly obvious motive: you were jealous. By pretending to be Damon for so long, you allowed me – encouraged me – to fall in love with someone who was neither entirely Damon nor entirely you. I fell in love with your emails and his newspaper columns – the sensitive private 'Damon' and the brash public one, combined. That was the man I became obsessed with – the fascinating, contradictory, complicated creation I fell for. Only one problem: he didn't exist apart from in my head.

Didn't you foresee that once you'd made me fall in love with Damon, you'd be jealous of him? Why didn't you just make up a name – one that didn't belong to anyone real that I might latch on to?

And you had a second reason for killing Damon, too: to prove that you weren't him. After the way you'd tricked me, you knew I'd never trust a word you said ever again. You'd told me that you weren't Damon Blundy, but why would I believe you? I did, eventually, but it took a while. For a few weeks, I continued to believe you might be Damon pretending not to be Damon. Once I knew you were willing to lie to me so flagrantly, anything could have been true. You could have been lying when you said you *were* him or lying when you said you *weren't* him – how did I know?

That's why you murdered him in the way that you did. Only King Edward, you believed, would choose that precise way of committing murder. It was your way of proving to me that you, King Edward, exist independently of Damon Blundy. You sacrificed his life to show me how much I mean to you. I get that. But I can't love, or forgive, Damon Blundy's killer. I loved him, even though I didn't know him. And part of what I loved about him *was* the real him. I read nearly as many of his words as yours, remember.

He wasn't a bad person. As Gavin, you were wrong about him. Damon was the best kind of good: the kind that's willing to sacrifice its own appearance of goodness in the eyes of the world, and the ego-boost that goes with that, in order to make a real difference. Damon Blundy wasn't a good man, no – he was a great man. He stuck up for people. He forced hypocrites and mediocrities to face unwelcome truths so that they had the opportunity to become their best possible selves. Hardly anyone understood this about him.

You probably waited for the details of how you murdered him to appear in the papers, and when they never did, you placed your 'Looking for a Woman with a Secret' ad – to make sure I found out how he'd been killed. What did you hope would happen then? Did you expect me to take a brutal murder as definitive evidence of your love for me, and give you another chance? Or did you simply want me to know that you, King Edward, are a person in your own right?

Which person, though? Who are you, King Edward? I'm waiting here, in 'our' hotel, only because I need to know the answer to that question. Where are you? I expected you to be here by now.

Please don't let me down again. I've emailed your King Edward account and the Gavin one to say I'm in room 419, the Chancery Hotel, Bloomsbury – same as last time. I'll wait as long as I have to. Please come.

Nicki

Sent from my BlackBerry 10 smartphone

13

Tuesday 9 July 2013

King Edward is late. Nearly an hour late. I've had nothing from him in the last hour apart from a text message saying, 'Wait. Don't move. I'll be there as soon as I can. Turn your phone off, prepare the room and wait.'

I am prepared. In bed, blindfold on. The curtains are drawn; the door is ajar; the 'Do not disturb' sign is in position.

My heart ticks in my chest. It's the only sound I can hear, since I turned off the too-noisy air conditioning. It makes me think of the old clock in Lee and Melissa's kitchen. *Tick, tick, tick . . .*

Last time I lay blindfolded in a Chancery Hotel room waiting for King Edward to arrive, I told myself that if he strangled or abducted me, there would be a small silver lining: Melissa would have to tell everybody, when they said, 'But surely you know *something* about what Nicki might have been up to, since she's your best friend,' that she'd forbidden me to tell her my secrets. She'd have been forced to admit – to the police, to herself – that her moral prissiness might have cost me my life.

The way your recklessness cost Damon Blundy his?

I wonder what Adam, Sophie and Ethan are doing now. Adam's probably preparing dinner. Sophie might be on the Internet, Googling singing or talent competitions, planning her quickest route to becoming someone like Una Healey from the Saturdays. Ethan's patiently explaining to Adam why he has to be allowed to move tables at school, because Nikhil never stops talking about how much he loves Jessica, and it's boring. Or else he'll be playing on *Minecraft*. I don't know what that is, only that it obsesses my son. Yesterday, he said to me in a tone of great excitement, 'Mummy, there are more than three hundred chickens guarding my world!'

I wish I were at home with my family. I was wrong to think that Bartholomew Gardens and Spilling could never be home. This room, this hotel, contains all the 'not home' that exists in the world. If I get out of here alive, I'm never coming back.

I hear a creaking noise coming from nearby. My body stiffens. Is it him?

I lie still. One by one, the seconds stretch out and then contract, my imagination racing to the end of each one and back again.

'Don't move,' says a man's voice. 'Say nothing. Don't touch the blindfold. Keep your hands where they are, by your sides.' There's a *thwack* as the door closes.

I've never heard the voice before. *Nobody I know from my real life. Thank God.* Though I never allowed myself to fear the worst, I'm relieved to know for sure.

I'm pleased to have heard King Edward's voice, finally. When he and I met here in February, we'd made a pact of silence. He didn't utter a word.

I keep completely still. I'm willing to stay silent for the time being because I want to listen. What's he doing? I can hear movement. Some kind of tape, a cutting sound, whimpering . . .

Was that a woman? Has he brought a woman with him?

Tape. Damon Blundy had a knife taped to his face. His wrists and ankles were taped together, round his chair . . .

What's King Edward going to do? Now that he's here, my conviction that he won't hurt me has grown stronger. So has my fear, which has turned into terror. I don't think I could move even if I decided I wanted to.

The whimpering stops – not a clean stop, but a muffling. More tape-pulling sounds, and cutting.

There's definitely someone else in the room. King Edward's put tape over her mouth. I inhale hard, filling my lungs with as much air as I can.

'Don't worry, Nicki,' King Edward says. 'You're afraid I'm going to hurt her, but I'm not. I'm not going to hurt anyone. If you want her to, she'll walk out of this room alive and unharmed once we're done here.'

'Done doing what?' I ask, my voice so hoarse I almost don't recognise it. 'Tell me what I want to know – everything.' I pull off my blindfold and see him as a moving shadow in the semi-darkness. And a chair, with someone in it . . .

'Put that back on,' King Edward snaps. 'You agreed to my conditions.'

'And you told me you were Damon Blundy, you stupid piece of shit! Give me one good reason why I should keep any promise I ever made you.' I would have, if he hadn't brought a woman with him. Her presence – the danger she might be in – has broken his hold over me.

I reach for the metal chain dangling from the lamp attached to the wall by the bed, and pull.

At first, his face is like pieces of a jigsaw assembled in the wrong order: flashes of familiarity not quite adding up to a recognisable picture. Then my brain catches up and it makes sense. I know who this man is. I know what he's capable of.

Pain. Unimaginable agony.

I know I'd be safer if he were someone else, anyone else . . .

He's moving towards me with the tape in his hand.

I open my mouth to scream.

Bryn Gilligan Commits Suicide and Confesses to Murder

Tuesday 9 July 2013, *Daily Herald Online*

Disgraced sprinter Bryn Gilligan, 28, took his own life today. His body was found by his mother, Jennifer, 56, when she returned from her health club to the home she shared with her son in Norwich. An ambulance worker who attended the scene claimed to have seen a suicide note in which Gilligan confessed to the murder of *Daily Herald* columnist Damon Blundy.

Blundy, a prominent supporter of Gilligan's right to race again, was found dead in his home in Spilling on Monday 1 July. Police are investigating his death. DS Sam Kombothekra of Culver Valley CID said, 'It would be premature to comment at this early stage.' DS Kombothekra wouldn't confirm or deny that Gilligan had left a note containing a confession.

Gilligan's suicide came after a heated exchange on Twitter during which detractors accused the former athlete of being 'worthless', 'scum' and 'a waste of skin'. Norfolk Police said Gilligan had swallowed several tablets of a powerful painkiller before lying down on the kitchen floor, where he was found.

When his mother tried and failed to wake him, she contacted emergency services. 'Bryn's laptop computer was on the kitchen table,' she said. 'On the screen was a tweet from a stranger accusing him of having "zero integrity". I think it was that tweet that pushed him over the edge, so that person's got blood on their hands.'

Mrs Gilligan said, 'I blame heartless online bullies for my beloved son's death. Bryn knew he'd made serious mistakes, but he deserved a second chance. Everyone deserves another chance, don't they?'

Gilligan was banned for life from competitive sprinting in 2010, after it was revealed that he had taken prohibited performance-enhancing drugs over a period of years. In September 2011, his appeal to have the ban lifted was rejected by the Court of Arbitration for Sport.

'That was the beginning of his downward spiral,' said his mother.

'He had nothing to look forward to, so he lived via the Internet. And the Internet was full of people who kept telling him they hated him. How could they hate him? They didn't even know him. And now, thanks to them, and thanks to the likes of Keiran Holland, who had a powerful voice in the media and had nothing but condemnation for Bryn, I've lost my only son.'

Gilligan isn't the first victim of online bullying to commit suicide. His mother said, 'Twitter and Facebook have to do something so that this doesn't keep happening. It's my son this time, but next time it'll be someone else's son or daughter.'

As yet, there has been no response from Twitter or Facebook to the news of Gilligan's death.

14

Tuesday 9 July 2013

'There you are,' said Charlie, as Simon landed in the CID room like something dangerous that had been thrown from a distance. He'd disappeared briefly.

'Sorry,' he muttered. 'This Bryn Gilligan shit's causing no end of aggro.' Sam, Gibbs, Sellers and Proust moved out of his way as he marched towards Charlie. 'Get someone from London who knows what they're doing to room 419 at the Chancery Hotel straight away. King Edward's going to kill Nicki in that room if we don't get there first. Once you've done that, get down there yourself. I'll follow as soon as I can.'

'You can't just—' Charlie started to protest.

'I have to. I need to explain to the others, and with this Gilligan business too, I'm needed here. Look, you're the only one of us who shouldn't be having anything to do with the Blundy murder – there's no reason why you can't go to London.'

'"Shouldn't be having anything to do with the Blundy murder",' Proust repeated. 'Is that a euphemism for "Shouldn't be posting details of the crime scene on a dating site without permission", I wonder?'

'It worked, didn't it?' Charlie snapped at him. To Simon, she said, 'Yeah, me not being CID means you shouldn't ask me to do *anything*. It doesn't mean you get to send me to London whenever it suits you! Who's King Edward?'

'Did he murder Damon Blundy?' Gibbs asked. He sounded nearly as desperate as Charlie felt.

'Go,' Simon told Charlie. 'You won't miss out. I'll tell you everything later. I haven't got time to explain it all now.'

'Oh, fucking . . . All right! I'm going.'

'Faster,' Simon shouted after her.

Charlie swore to herself all the way back to her office. Dictatorial, infuriating arse-wipe! Didn't he realise how arrogant it was to be unwilling to share any information at all simply because you don't have the time to give your usual detailed presentation, in the order that most suits you? Simon wouldn't dream of revealing only the who without the why, the how, the how-the-hell-did-you-work-that-out? And, as he'd so kindly pointed out, Charlie wasn't part of his team. Whenever he felt like excluding her, she had no official right to object.

How would it have compromised the case in any way if he'd answered her question before sending her packing? How long would that have taken? First name, last name: three seconds, maximum.

Bastard. He could have given her a name. Unless he wasn't certain yet. Maybe he wanted to talk it through with . . .

Charlie's phone buzzed in her pocket, interrupting her speculations. It was a text from Simon. A name. Followed by the words 'explanation to follow'.

'Wow,' Charlie whispered to herself. 'So that's who King Edward is.' She thought: 'If Damon Blundy were still alive, he would write *such* a brilliant column about his own murder.' It didn't make sense, but she knew what she meant.

She understood why Simon had texted the name after refusing to tell her. He hadn't wanted to blurt out the identity of King Edward in front of the others; they were going to get the explanation first and then the name. Wherever possible, Simon liked to do things in the correct order.

~

'Right,' said Simon, putting his phone back in his pocket. 'Are we all agreed: Bryn Gilligan didn't murder anyone?'

'I am,' said Sam.

'Me too.' Sellers glanced nervously at Proust as he spoke. 'It's clear what mood Gilligan was in when he wrote that letter. Suicidal, playing the martyr. He obviously trawled the Web for unsolved murders, picked a few at random and decided to confess, since he was confessing to Blundy's anyway.'

'Why would he do that?' asked Gibbs. 'Why confess to four murders you've not done?'

'Three reasons,' said Simon. 'One, it's a statement: "You all think I'm such a bad person? All right, then, have it your way. I must have killed Damon Blundy, mustn't I, if I'm the monster you all think I am? And even if I didn't, I might as well say I did, since you couldn't think any less highly of me." The spirit of "You bastards made me do this." And maybe also an element of "You're all determined to believe I'm a pathological liar? Fine, then let me confess to a murder – see if you'd rather believe I'm evil or believe I'm a liar. Which is it, since I can't be both?"'

'I need an aspirin already and he's only just started,' Proust muttered to Gibbs, who was standing next to him.

'That's Blundy's murder covered, but why add three others to his slate?' Sellers asked.

'For reason number two,' said Simon. 'Contrary to what all the vindictive dicks on Twitter and Facebook believed, Bryn Gilligan genuinely wanted to be a better man. He wanted to prove he was a good guy. He must have known there was a strong chance his confession'd leak to the press, and that we'd establish pretty quickly that it wasn't true. I think he wanted everyone to find out he'd tried to take the blame for four crimes he didn't commit. The more he confessed to, the more heroic he looked. He wanted the world to know he was prepared to make the biggest sacrifice of himself that he could – to atone.'

'Oh, to *atone*?' said Proust in his red-flag voice. 'This detective lark is easy, isn't it, when you don't have to worry about logic, motive or evidence? It's as easy as joining some words together.'

'But it wouldn't make anyone think better of him, would it?' Gibbs asked Simon. 'Perverting the course of justice in four serious crimes, on top of doping before races – it makes him look like even more of a twat. To me, anyway.'

'That's not how he'd have seen it,' said Simon. 'In his eyes, confessing to four murders he hasn't committed is bringing himself lower than even his worst enemies ever wanted him brought. Throwing himself onto the burning pyre. Turning his ambition, which once made him want to soar to great heights, in the opposite direction: a gruesome drive to claim the depths—'

'Is this a free-form poem, Waterhouse? Is the end in sight?'

Simon felt his face heat up. He resolved to stick to simple language. 'Just one thing to add,' he said. 'Maybe he—'

'One thing to add to reason number two?' Proust cut in again. 'If only we had a printed order of service.'

'No, this is a fourth possible reason, one I've just thought of: he liked the idea of newspaper headlines saying, "Bryn Gilligan Not Guilty of Any Murders, Despite Confessions." If we look into it and find he didn't do any of the four, he gets to be found innocent four times. Might make a nice change after being found guilty for the drugs thing, having first insisted he was innocent. Kind of like a reversal. The general public gets a vague sense of "Oh, that guy wasn't guilty after all."'

'And the cruelly overlooked third reason?' Proust asked wearily. 'He wanted to practise his cursive handwriting, and it takes longer to write four names than one?'

'Third reason: he knows what it's like to do something stupid and be vilified for it. He knows exactly how shit that feels. By trying to take the blame for these four murders, thinking he might succeed in getting them attributed to him, he's protecting the four real murderers from similar vilification. He's going to kill himself anyway, so he's got nothing to lose and plenty to gain. He's noble – the patron saint of sinners.'

'See my earlier point,' Gibbs said. 'A twat.'

'No, you don't get it. He doesn't want to help them to escape justice so that they can kill more people. He wants to help them so they'll think, I've got a real chance here – to live a better life, stay out of trouble.'

'Got that, everybody?' Proust was looking only at Simon. 'Bryn Gilligan has more motivations than Starbucks has branches on UK high streets. Also like Starbucks branches, some of them appear to be miles apart.'

'Have you never met anyone with several contradictory impulses at once?' said Simon. 'I'm not saying his thoughts were consistent, or that he was full of great ideas. He'd decided the way forward was suicide, remember?'

'Instead of creating morbid fantasies on behalf of a dead cheat, let's examine the facts,' said Proust. 'On the one hand, we have a letter in which Gilligan, who had both motive and opportunity, plainly confesses to murdering Damon Blundy as well as a few other people, and on the other hand, we have Waterhouse telling us that he didn't because of atonement, sacrifice, saintliness and noble pyres. I know which I find more persuasive.'

'King Edward VII murdered Damon Blundy,' said Simon. 'I can prove it, and I will. Give me a chance.' *Don't bait him. Stay humble.* 'Can you explain to me why Bryn Gilligan killed Damon Blundy in the way he did – with the knife taped to his face, sharpening it at the scene, the photo of himself in a protective bodysuit emailed to Blundy? Giving us the computer password so we'd see the photo? Why did Bryn Gilligan do all that, do you think?'

'Oh, let's see. Contradictory impulses?' Proust glared at Simon. 'He wanted to stab Blundy, and yet, being in possession of a complex and nuanced mind, he also didn't want to stab him. So he suffocated him with a knife and some parcel tape by way of a compromise.'

'You don't believe that.'

'All right, I don't know why he did it that way!' the Snowman snapped. 'All I know is I've got a letter here confessing to murder, and I'm taking it seriously. Your turn next: who's King Edward VII, and why did he kill Blundy the way he did?'

'King Edward VII,' Gibbs murmured. 'I've heard that name – recently. I mean, outside this room.'

'I don't think you have,' Simon contradicted him. 'If you'd heard it, you'd remember who said it.'

'What? People always remember everything immediately, do they?' Gibbs shook his head and exchanged a look with Sellers.

'Sir, you mentioned before that Gilligan had motive,' Sam finally managed to get a word in. 'I'm not sure that's true. 'Damon Blundy was his chief defender.'

'Gilligan threatened Blundy with legal action for calling him a liar and a cheat, though,' said Gibbs.

'And went on to regret it,' Simon said.

'Or so he claimed,' said the Snowman. 'Did he ever apologise publicly to Blundy for the threat to sue?'

Simon shook his head. 'He told me he wanted to, but didn't want to be seen to be making peace with Blundy because of Blundy's general persona and attitude. Gilligan thought he was vicious, enjoyed ripping people to shreds a bit too much. He didn't really want to communicate with him at all. I think, in an ideal world, he'd have chosen a gentler and less offensive defender.'

'Certainly one less swaddled in parcel tape,' said Proust. 'Wouldn't we all? I don't believe for a moment that Bryn Gilligan murdered these three other people in –' he looked down at the papers on his desk '– Nottingham, Glasgow and Taunton, but I think he killed Damon Blundy, as he says he did. We find out he's alibied for the other three, what do we say to ourselves? *Poor deluded man, confessing to murders he didn't commit . . .* Then we assume he mustn't have killed Blundy because we know he didn't kill the others. That's what he was hoping for – I'd put money on it.'

'He's about to top himself,' said Simon. 'Why would he bother with such Machiavellian calculations?'

'If he's worried that, in his absence, we might pin it on him for convenience's sake and he won't be there to defend himself;

if he wants his name cleared after death – which was an element of one of your theories, as I recall. Want to keep that one all to yourself, do you?'

'Look, we'll get nowhere by squabbling,' said Sam. 'Simon, you said you could prove King Edward VII killed Blundy. How?'

'Can we please learn this man's name immediately, so that we don't have to keep referring to him as King Edward VII?'

'Let me talk you through it,' said Simon. 'I want to get it straight in my own head anyway.'

'I don't need to be talked through a perishing *name*, Waterhouse. He's got a name, hasn't he? I mean, he is a man? Not a lizard in luminous slippers?'

'He's a man, yes,' said Simon.

'Then spit it out,' Proust growled. 'Afterwards, by all means, follow up with whatever parable takes your fancy.'

'Chris –' Simon looked at Gibbs '– you didn't hear the name King Edward VII. You saw it.'

Gibbs frowned. 'Written down?'

'Printed. On a sign. A sign none of us has seen, only you. Well, I've seen it on a website.'

'What sign?'

'Think about sheets of black paper stuck to a windowpane, to cover up the view,' said Simon.

'Reuben Tasker's attic window,' said Gibbs. 'But there was no . . .' He stopped. His eyes widened. 'The school.'

Simon nodded. To Sam, Sellers and Proust, he said, 'The school opposite Reuben Tasker's house, the one he could no longer stand the sight of, is called King Edward VII.'

'So . . . that's why . . .' Gibbs broke off, rubbed his face with his hands. Unable to reach a conclusion as quickly as he'd have liked to, he diverted to a question: 'So where does that get us? Tasker killed Blundy – right?'

'Nicki's reply to Charlie's "Confidant" ad tells us a lot,' said Simon. 'Given everything else we know, I think it's safe to assume a few things: Nicki posted an ad on Intimate Links in 2010 – "I

Want a Secret". A man calling himself King Edward VII replied. At first, he maintained his anonymity, as you would if you were cyber-cheating with a virtual stranger. Why trust them with your true identity? Then, I'm guessing, they got closer, came to trust each other more, and Nicki probably told him who she was: her full name, where she lived, details about her life. She wanted him to reciprocate – a signal that this increased trust was mutual. Wouldn't that be a natural way of moving to the next level in an adulterous online relationship?'

'Yes,' said Sellers.

'Right. But King Edward didn't want to tell Nicki who he was. Why not? I'll come back to that. He also didn't want to refuse to tell her who he was, so he told her he was Damon Blundy. This happened round about October 2011 – that's why Nicki started commenting on Blundy's columns like someone who was head over heels in love with him, as Paula Riddiough said – because she *was* in love with him. Or, rather, she thought she was. At that point, the man she'd fallen in love with, through his emails, was King Edward. They mustn't have met in all that time. Once he'd told her he was Damon Blundy, she started to read Blundy's columns. She researched him, read every word he'd ever blogged and tweeted, no doubt. Blundy was an attractive alpha male with a strong personality.'

Simon paused for long enough to realise that no one was interested in interrupting him any more. *Good.* 'Before too long, although King Edward was the man Nicki was corresponding with, he was no longer, straightforwardly and for his own sake, the man she loved. Now she loved Blundy too, although she didn't realise there was a "too" involved. It's interesting, if you think about it: Nicki fell in love with one real flesh-and-blood man at the instigation of another and yet . . . still managed to fall in love with a man who didn't really exist. The man she fell for was a fictional fusion of the two: King Edward's private emails to her combined with Damon Blundy's public persona.

'Between October 2011 and February this year, Nicki was in

no doubt that the man she was emailing – King Edward – was Damon Blundy. She continued to comment on his columns. In February, they broke up. She stopped commenting and answered a new Intimate Links ad: Gavin.'

'But her email to Charlie – to Confidant – implies that King Edward is Gavin,' said Sellers.

'He is,' said Simon. 'I don't know why Nicki and King Edward split up, but *he* knew, didn't he? King Edward knew – not only Nicki's innermost thoughts and feelings, after their years-long correspondence, but also what she was likely to want after breaking up with him. That's the character he created in Gavin.'

'The Internet's brought us a plague of invisible men.' Proust smacked his hand against his computer screen. 'I dread to think how many fake online identities *you've* spawned, DC Sellers, and how you've deployed them.'

'Dongcaster's the one he's most famous for, sir,' Gibbs said.

'For fuck's sake, can we pay attention here?' said Simon. 'If Charlie and I split up, acrimoniously, and I knew she was likely to go straight to a particular website to hunt for a new man, I'd know exactly what kind of ad to write to reel her in – one that sounds as if it's been written by a man who's everything I'm not.'

'If she finds such an advert, ask her to forward it to me,' said Proust. 'I'm sure we'd all enjoy working with him.'

'King Edward reeled Nicki in *again*, as Gavin – again pretending to be someone he wasn't,' said Simon. 'OK, at this point, she still believes Damon Blundy's the man she's broken up with. That's why she contacts an estate agent and instructs him to sell her house, too cheaply if necessary, as soon as possible. She only moved to Spilling because Blundy lived there and she believed he was her secret lover – she wanted to be closer to him. Once they've split, she wants to get out of Spilling and away from him as quickly as she can. Except then she has a change of heart, doesn't she? She rings the estate agent back and says, "Forget all that – I don't want to sell my house after all." Why?'

'She decides she doesn't want to let Damon Blundy drive her away, because it's weak?' suggested Sam. 'Spilling's her home as much as it's his – why should she leave?'

'Or she found out, soon after deciding to sell, that King Edward wasn't Damon Blundy,' said Gibbs. 'If he's not Blundy, then the guy who broke her heart, assuming that's what happened, doesn't live near her. She has no idea who he is or where he lives, so no need to move.'

'That's what I think it was,' said Simon. 'Sam, when you and I interviewed Nicki on the day of the murder, she told us she didn't know Blundy. If she knew him and didn't want to admit it, she'd lie, obviously, but that wasn't all she said. She also said, "I couldn't have known him any less if I'd tried." Why add that? Most people wouldn't. She sounded bitter when she said it.'

Sam nodded slowly. 'To us, it sounded like a more emphatic "I didn't know him", but to her, it meant "What an idiot I am – believing I was romantically involved with a man who'd never even heard of me."'

'Spot on,' said Simon.

'You said you were going to come back to why King Edward didn't want to tell Nicki who he was, and you haven't,' said Proust. 'Who is he, by the way?' he added with exaggerated casualness.

Simon decided he'd made them wait long enough. Almost. 'A man who, sitting at his desk one day browsing the Intimate Links "Women Seeking Men" page, found an ad he wanted to respond to. He couldn't use his own name, so he needed a pseudonym. He probably got up from his desk at that point, walked around the room a bit, like I am now, because it helps me to think clearly. He looked out of the window at the school opposite his house and thought, King Edward VII – that'll do nicely.'

'Reuben Tasker,' said Gibbs. 'I fucking knew that guy was dodgy.'

'Well? Waterhouse?'

'Yes.' Finally, Simon gave Proust the name he was after. 'Reuben Tasker. That's why he started to hate the school and wanted to block out its sign – after his long relationship with Nicki ended, he didn't welcome the reminder. It would have hurt him every time he saw that name.'

'And then after Blundy died, he hated it even more,' said Sam, his voice rising in excitement. 'That has to be significant.'

'It is,' said Simon. 'Before last Monday, the name King Edward VII was a painful reminder of a love affair gone horribly wrong. Since the murder, it's reminded Tasker of something he's even keener to avoid thinking about: the fact that he killed Damon Blundy.'

~

'No, *you're* wrong, love,' PC Claire Whelan told Yolanda Shaw, the receptionist on duty at the Chancery Hotel. 'You've got a Nicki Clements staying in room 419. Just look, will you?'

'You can say it as often as you like, it doesn't make it true,' said Yolanda. 'I *have* looked – you saw me. There's a guest in room 419 whose name bears no resemblance to the one you've just given me.'

'Well, that's not what I've been told.' PC Whelan pulled her phone out of her pocket. 'All right, what's the name of your person, then?'

'How do I know you're a real policewoman?' asked Yolanda, irritated by the attitude.

PC Whelan passed her ID card across the desk. 'Satisfied?' As though Yolanda were an unreasonable nag and not a responsible member of hotel staff concerned about guests' privacy.

The ID looked legitimate. *Damn.* Now Yolanda had no choice but to tell her. 'There's a woman called Kate Zilber in 419.'

'I need the key to that room,' said PC Whelan. She held out her hand, nearly whacking Yolanda in the face with it, and made repetitive flicking movements with her fingers as if to say, 'Come on, hurry up.'

'No,' Yolanda told her. 'I'm sorry. Why do you need the key?'

'With respect, I don't have to explain myself to you.'

A man in the waiting area, no more than four feet from the reception desk, lowered his copy of the *Daily Telegraph* and said, 'However, if you did explain, you'd stand a better chance of getting the key, so . . .'

Yolanda recognised the man whose check-in process earlier in the day had taken fourteen years. She'd nearly started crying, he'd asked so many questions. Mr . . . Some weird name beginning with a 'U'. Undalis or something. No, Uskalis. U-s-k-a-l-i-s. Nice of him to intervene on her behalf, but what was he doing reading his paper in reception when he had a far more comfortable room to go to? Now that she'd noticed him, Yolanda realised he'd been sitting there for a long time.

'Thank you, sir,' said PC Whelan. 'I think I know how to do my job.'

'I'm not sure you know how to do it very well,' said Uskalis. His voice sounded different. Not only his voice, but his manner too. 'In your position, I'd have had the key in my hand in a matter of seconds,' he said. 'You still haven't got it.'

Yolanda, bolstered by his support, decided to hold out for as long as she could. He was quite right. This policewoman was rubbish at dealing with people. With all the training courses these days for anyone who had to deal with the public, how did she get away with being so brusque and rude? 'Can I speak to someone and check you're who you say you are?' she asked PC Whelan.

'You've seen my ID.'

'Why do you need to get into Nicki Clements's hotel room?' asked Mr Uskalis.

This was getting weirder by the second. 'There is no Nicki Clements,' Yolanda told him. 'Her name's Kate Zilber.'

'Actually, her name's Nicki Clements,' said Uskalis. 'Is she in some kind of trouble?'

'I've been told she is,' said PC Whelan.

'What kind of trouble?'

'I've no idea. The message I picked up wasn't exactly clear.'

'Trouble should be good enough, right?' Uskalis turned to Yolanda. 'One of your guests is in danger. Are you going to let us in?'

'Sir, even if I let the police in, I can't let you in. I can't let one guest into another guest's room, and I'm afraid I can't take your word for it that this woman's name's Nicki Clements when she told me it was Kate Zilber.'

Uskalis stared coldly at her. 'And I'm telling you it's *not* Kate Zilber. I know who Kate Zilber is. She's a primary-school head-mistress from the Culver Valley who snorts cocaine in her car before the school day starts, when she thinks no one's looking.'

'Sir, with respect—'

'Oh, I've had enough of this,' said PC Whelan. She turned and made for the door.

Before Yolanda had a chance to say anything more to him, Mr Uskalis ran after her.

~

'King Edward – Reuben Tasker – didn't want to tell Nicki who he was because he didn't enjoy *being* who he was,' said Simon. 'He told Gibbs he got himself off drugs because Damon Blundy's portrayal of him as a pathetic addict got to him. But I checked – I rang his literary agent. Tasker only stopped taking drugs last summer, August 2012, so when he first told Nicki he was Damon Blundy, in October 2011, he was still using. And prob-ably hating himself for it, and wishing Blundy would stop drawing the world's attention to his addiction via his *Daily Herald* column. Tasker's online fling with Nicki was a chance for him to pretend to be someone better. Someone he admired and wished he was.'

'Damon Blundy?' Gibbs sounded incredulous.

'Wait, wait,' said Sellers. 'Aren't you stretching it a bit?'

'One hundred per cent Lycra.' Proust yawned. 'Not even a

Lycra-truth blend, this theory we're about to hear. Buckle up, boys.'

'Tasker hated Blundy,' said Gibbs. 'Slagged him off all over the show, for criticising his novels unfairly.'

'Yes, but you're missing the crucial aspect here,' Simon told him. 'Who do we all secretly admire most? Who do we wish we could be, deep down, though we'd never admit it? The people who disdain us and scoff at us! Those so sure they're superior to us that they don't mind saying so in a public and witty way. Also, the people who've got something on us – they've got the power to destroy us. How desperately we'd rather be them, in their privileged pedestal position, than us. Think about it! Think of the envy you'd feel. Remember Tasker published a book this year that Blundy said was much better than his last one? What if he wrote that better book consciously trying to eradicate the pretentiousness Blundy had accused him of? I'd say there's more than enough evidence that he admired Blundy and might well have wished he was him. There was a similar dynamic in operation between Blundy and his lover, Paula Riddiough – but let's leave that for now.'

'Now and forever,' Proust amended. 'If Riddiough didn't murder Blundy, I don't need to hear about their sex life. Nor do I care why Reuben Tasker pretended to be Blundy. I only care that he killed him and that Sergeant Zailer's on her way to arrest him.'

'Do we know for sure that he did?' Sellers asked. 'In Nicki Clements's reply to the "Confidant" ad, where she thinks she's replying to King Edward, she says Hannah Blundy might have murdered Damon.'

'That's easily explained,' said Simon. 'Hannah's a psychotherapist and Nicki was her patient until February this year, when she broke up with the man she believed was Damon Blundy. She called herself Melissa Redgate, but it wasn't Melissa. Melissa lives in London – why would she go and see a therapist in the Culver Valley? Nicki, on the other hand, was too curious to stay away from the woman she thought of as her rival. Again, as with Reuben Tasker and Damon Blundy, it's the attraction-to-adversary syndrome. You're drawn to your opposite number – the person who might, in various ways, represent your doom.'

'In your case, can that be me, Waterhouse?'

'Imagine the power kick: Nicki gets to tell Blundy's wife all about the affair, every detail – mentioning no names, of course – and Hannah has to listen and make understanding noises and try to help *Nicki*. It's the perfect revenge, from Nicki's point of view, on the wife who's got Damon in her bed every night.'

'Though in fact the last laugh's Hannah's, since King Edward turned out not to be Damon,' said Gibbs.

'I've known, or at least suspected, that Nicki was Hannah's patient for quite a while,' Simon said. 'When you and I interviewed Hannah, Sam, she mentioned a former patient who was paranoid about letting anyone drive her anywhere – remember? Train and taxi drivers, pilots of planes. This patient was neurotic and imagined these strangers would drive her to some terrible destination. I started to wonder if it could be Nicki Clements the first time she mentioned the auction.'

Gibbs and Sam exchanged a puzzled look. 'Auction?' Sellers asked.

'The one Nicki and Melissa went to in Grantham – in Nicki's car, complete with wing mirror,' said Simon. 'But why were they in Nicki's car at all? Melissa has a car too. I asked Charlie to find out if she had any driving hang-ups. A lot of people do, especially women – won't drive on motorways or without their husbands, that kind of thing. But no, Melissa's used to driving in all conditions – so why didn't she and Nicki go to the auction in her car instead of Nicki's?'

Proust covered his eyes with his hands and groaned.

Simon ignored him. 'Let's imagine for a minute that they had: Melissa drives from her home in Highgate to Nicki's in Spilling to pick Nicki up. At least a two-hour drive. Then together they drive to Grantham, which is half an hour from Spilling. Then back to Spilling after the auction to drop Nicki off, and then Melissa drives back to Highgate – two longer journeys and two short ones. Instead, what happened was that Nicki drove to Highgate to pick Melissa up, then to Grantham, then back to Highgate to drop Melissa off, and then Nicki drove back to Spilling. Four long journeys, instead of two long and two short. Eight hours' driving – *eight hours!* – when it could have been only five. As a plan, that makes no sense, unless Nicki has a phobia of being driven by anyone but herself. And, I think, her husband,' Simon added as an afterthought. 'He's probably the only one she'll agree to be driven by. He drove her to the train station last Tuesday, when she wanted to go to London to see Melissa and couldn't take her own car because we needed to inspect its wing mirror, or lack of.'

'You offered her a lift home after we interviewed her,' said Sam. 'She refused.'

'Didn't want to be driven by us,' Simon said. 'She had no choice when we turned up at her house and insisted she accompany us to the police station, which was why she was such a hysterical mess at first. Partly why, at any rate. So she refused a lift home and set off running instead. She'd told us she had other things to do in town, but I followed her. Instead of heading towards the shops, or going to the taxi rank by the Corn Exchange and getting a cab, she ran in the direction of her house. It couldn't have been lack of cash. There's a cashpoint opposite the Corn Exchange.'

'The train to London,' said Sam. He appeared to be too startled by what he'd realised to say anything else.

Simon knew what he meant. 'Yes, the trains that were supposedly not running on Tuesday afternoon, forcing Nicki to hire a car. I checked: the trains on Tuesday ran exactly according to the schedule – no problems at all. But Nicki didn't want to travel by train because of her phobia, so she had her husband drop her at the station, then walked to a car-rental place.'

'Her husband doesn't know about her phobia?' Gibbs asked.

'According to the case notes in Hannah Blundy's office, he knows she hates travelling by train and avoids it when she can, but not the real reason why. Apparently if he's with her on the train, or plane, she doesn't get quite so frightened. On Tuesday, she'd have had to take the train to London alone. I'll tell you something else about Nicki Clements, and this I *really* can't prove, but I know I'm right,' Simon added recklessly. 'Subconsciously, she wants to get in trouble for things associated with her car. She smashes off her wing mirror, tells us she's been driving around without one when it's not true and we can prove it easily with CCTV. Why doesn't this occur to her? She takes topless photos of herself in her car, and lets herself get caught. Why does she take that risk? She might be phobic about being driven, but deep down she doesn't trust herself to drive either. Chronically low self-esteem. She fears she's not fit to take charge, to make decisions—'

Proust laid his head down on the table in front of him with a bang. He left it there.

'She fears being punished for wrongdoing involving her car, but she invites such punishments with her behaviour,' Simon went on. 'Like a lightning rod, she attracts the trouble that she dreads. It sounds contradictory, but it isn't. There's not much space between what we fear and what we fantasise about.'

'All right, so Hannah Blundy was Nicki Clements's therapist, and Nicki's got low self-esteem,' said Sellers. 'So what?'

Simon nodded. He too was eager to get to the point. 'King Edward – Reuben Tasker – murdered Damon Blundy in the way he did because of something Nicki said to him. The only people who know about that thing are Nicki, Tasker and Hannah Blundy – because, as her patient, in the process of telling her the whole sorry tale, Nicki told her. From Nicki's point of view, since Hannah lived with Blundy and had easy access to him, and in theory could have found out that her patient "Melissa" was shagging her husband, even though she wasn't, it looks as if Hannah might be a suspect. Though Nicki was clever enough to nominate King Edward as her prime suspect.'

'So . . . what was this thing Nicki said that inspired a murder?' Gibbs asked.

'No, what Nicki said didn't inspire the murder itself,' Simon clarified. 'King— Sorry, *Reuben Tasker* killed Damon Blundy for the reasons Nicki outlines in her reply to Charlie's "Woman with a Secret" ad – jealousy, mainly. Having presented himself to Nicki as Damon-Blundy-the-love-object, Tasker then couldn't forgive the real Damon Blundy for being the illegitimate beneficiary of Nicki's love.'

'But you said—'

'What Nicki said inspired *only the way Tasker did it*: the knife, essential to the murder, but not used in the way a knife is normally used. The words on the wall, "He is no less dead." When I told Hannah Blundy that Damon's killer might be one of her regular patients, it clicked for her suddenly: she remembered a story she'd heard from the patient calling herself Melissa Redgate, a story she'd made a note of in a file and then forgotten all about. It wasn't exactly the same – it wasn't licking poison off a knife, and it was in the mental compartment she'd labelled "Work" rather than "Personal", so she didn't make the connection at first.'

'Waterhouse, enough.' Proust lifted his head from the desk. 'What did Nicki Clements, calling herself Melissa Redgate, say to Reuben Tasker-slash-King Edward and then repeat in the presence of her therapist, Hannah? Take pity on us. What was this all-important utterance that inspired a murder?'

'It was a flippant remark. She drew a kind of . . . well, an analogy, I suppose. Between sex and killing.'

15

Tuesday 9 July 2013

I recognise him from the Internet: Reuben Tasker, the author. Writes supernatural novels. I've read half of one. It won a prize.

'Look at me,' he says.

I can't tell him I'd rather look anywhere but straight at him. He's put tape over my mouth. I'm scared to move. He's kneeling astride me, holding a pair of scissors in one hand. If I make him angry, he could stab me.

Behind him, in the corner of the room, there's a woman sitting in a chair, crying. She also has tape over her mouth. She could run to the door while Tasker's busy with me, but she doesn't move.

Why not?

'Look at me, Nicki. Don't keep turning away. I want to see your face. I haven't seen it for a long time.'

I should have made a run for it while I could. Now he's sitting astride me. In order to escape, I'd have to push him off. Can't. He's too heavy. He might have a handsome face if he had different eyes, but not with these: two round, dark insects determined to burrow into me. I try to blur my focus so that I won't see him clearly, try not to dissolve in fear and lose my grip.

Why Tasker? Why did you have to be this man, King Edward – a man whose imagination dreams up tortures and punishments so intricately gruesome that no ordinary person would think of them if they tried for a year?

If he can invent horrors like the ones I read in his book, he can hurt me. He's likely to hurt me. How would it feel to be stabbed with scissors?

In the eye. In the neck . . .

'Open your eyes.'

I come to. I must have blacked out for a moment.

If I'm going to die, I don't want to miss the last part of my life. I'd rather die with my mind working.

Think. Not Sophie and Ethan. Too hard, too painful. Think about anything else.

Craving and Aversion – that was Tasker's book. I gave it up. Too frightening. Damon hated it. He got into a fight about it with Keiran Holland and I decided I'd read it. I was on Damon's side – I was always on his side against anyone, and especially against that stupid windbag Holland – but I wanted to be able to write something intelligent in the comments about why Damon was right.

Gave up. Couldn't write anything.

I make a noise that means 'Take the tape off my mouth', moving my face to show what I mean.

'No. Not until I'm ready. Keep still.' He sounds sad, not angry. Sad, holding scissors.

What can I do? There has to be a way out. Nicki Clements, super fibber, can blag her way out of anything. I try to remember what else I know about Tasker, in case there's something I can use. All I can dredge up, from something I read online, is that his father was a professional gambler who ran off with a singer. No help at all.

I used to do my best to keep up with Damon's various obsessions, Googling all the people he ranted about. It was exhausting: infant male circumcision, athletes banned for taking drugs, pretentious novelists, hypocritical MPs.

I didn't pay much attention to Tasker. Damon wasn't interested in him in his own right. He'd only written about him to illustrate a point he wanted to make about Bryn Gilligan. Oh, but wait . . .

'Keep still, Nicki.'

I can't. Can't stop shaking.

I've remembered something else. The woman, the singer Tasker's father eloped with – she was accused of murdering a young boy, before they caught the actual . . .

Oh my God. The boy, the murdered little boy.

His name was Gavin. Was that why King Edward chose that name? It never occurred to me to make the connection.

Of course it didn't. You had no reason to think about Gavin in connection with Reuben Tasker.

'What's the matter?' He knows I've thought of something. Wants to know what it is.

I move my face again from side to side, chin in the air. *Let me talk, you fucker.*

He puts the scissors down next to him on the bed and tears off the strip of tape. I cry out in pain.

'Sorry,' he says. 'Nicki, the last thing I want to do is hurt you. That's not why I'm here.'

'Who's the woman?'

'My wife, Jane. You said you wanted to know who killed Damon Blundy. She killed him.'

His wife. His wife murdered Damon Blundy? *Impossible.*

I open my mouth to speak, but nothing makes sense – nothing I've heard and nothing I might say. 'No. You killed him.'

'That's not true, Nicki. Can I kiss you?'

'No.' My stomach flips over.

'All right, I won't if you'd rather I didn't. I don't want to do anything you don't want.' He looks at my naked body as he says it, taking his time. Lingering with his eyes.

I try to imagine that I am wearing clothes, lots of them: underwear, dark woolly tights, a skirt, a shirt, a thick jumper . . .

'I want to leave this room,' I say.

'Well, you can. But you said you wanted me to explain about Damon Blundy.'

'I don't need your explanation. I know you killed him and I know why.' If Hannah Blundy didn't kill Damon, Tasker must have. His wife wouldn't have done the thing with the knife. Why would she? It would mean nothing to anyone apart from me and King Edward. 'I know what "He is no less dead" means,' I tell him.

'Do you?' He smiles.

I'm not going to give him the reward he's after: the satisfaction of hearing the solution to the puzzle that means so much to him. All the trouble he went to: organising his cryptic murder scene, then typing it out in painstaking detail in his 'Looking for a Woman with a Secret' ad for me to find.

Yes, King Edward. I know what 'He is no less dead' means. After you emailed me to explain your strange views on adultery – that it doesn't count and isn't wrong if you only kiss and stroke and rub and lick and suck and bite, then run away in time to salve your conscience – I told you in no uncertain terms what I thought of your hypocrisy. I used one of my bizarre analogies that you're so fond of. I wrote back and said, 'You're free to behave as you like, obviously, but if you want to know what I think of your ethical position on infidelity, I think it's the stupidest, most self-serving piece of crap I've ever heard. If a married man writes to a married woman secretly for years telling her she's the love of his life, that's cheating. If he meets her at a hotel and they both remove all their clothes and touch each other in every conceivable sexual way bar one, that's cheating. To pretend it isn't is so dishonest it's pathetic. It's as pathetic as forcing a man to lick fatal poison off a knife and then, once he's dead, saying, "But I didn't stab him, Officer. The knife didn't actually penetrate his skin." So what? He's just as dead, isn't he? You're still a fucking murderer.'

'You're a murderer,' I hear myself say.

'No, Nicki. I didn't kill him. I'll admit the way of doing it was my idea, but I wasn't there when it happened. I was at home, writing. Jane was the one who killed him.'

My eyes move to the woman in the corner. She's nodding. Nodding and crying. She won't be able to breathe through her nose for much longer if she doesn't stop crying. *Fuck.* I don't want to watch a woman die. Thinking about it gives me a sharp pinch of fear in my heart.

'You made her do it, Reuben,' I say gently. 'It's not her fault. Take the tape off her mouth – let her tell me.'

If he gets off me, I can try to run. I still have a life, at the moment. A husband, two beautiful children . . .

You can't run and leave her here with him. He doesn't care if she lives or dies.

I think about what Gavin wrote in an email: 'The only person I know whom I can never forgive is my wife . . . It was my inability to forgive her that drove me to the Intimate Links website.'

Tasker's shaking his head. I can't remember the last thing I said to him. I must stop my mind from wandering. 'Jane's a free agent,' he says. That's right: I asked him to take the tape off her mouth. 'Yeah, I said, "Do this, do that." She didn't have to listen. I was upset – I didn't mean what I said. I wanted to see if she'd do it. She'll do anything I say, won't you, honey?' His words speed up as his eyes start to flit around the room. As if he's lost me and is frantically looking for me, even though I haven't moved. He tips forward suddenly, nearly losing his balance before he rights himself. His breath touches my skin like warm poisonous gas. 'She took it too literally. I was depressed. A chance encounter between a policeman and a friend of mine had ruined a promising relationship.'

'My relationship with Gavin, you mean?'

'You met a policeman and you dumped Gavin. You wouldn't tell him why.'

'I want to hear Jane tell me what she did,' I say. 'Please, Reuben. Let her speak.'

'No. I want *us* to speak, not her. You and me, Nicki. We need to decide what to do about her. She killed Damon Blundy – I bet you think the person who killed Damon Blundy ought to pay for their crime, don't you? He wasn't evil – that's what you said – so the person who murdered him must have been. Jane's willing to accept whatever punishment we decide on. She's come here by choice. I explained everything to her. She's OK with it. Look, she's not restrained in any way; she's just sitting there. She could get up and leave if she wanted to.'

'If you want Damon's killer punished, ring the police,' I say.

Tasker lunges for the scissors, holds them up in the air. 'No police,' he says.

'All right. OK, no police.' My heart is pushing to exit my body through my mouth. 'It's up to you.'

I watch as his breathing returns to normal. He puts the scissors down again. 'Sorry,' he mutters. 'Look, you want to hear Jane's story? Be my guest.' He climbs off me and walks over to the chair in the corner. Rips the tape off his wife's mouth. Her face twists in response to the pain. A nondescript face. 'Tell Nicki what happened,' he says.

'I killed him. Reuben's telling the truth. I . . . I thought he wanted me to. He was so . . . clear about what should happen. Every detail.'

'Tell me,' I say. Slowly, as she starts to talk, I raise myself up to a seated position, reach for the bed's coverlet and wrap it around me.

'I . . . had to send Damon Blundy an email, as if it were from him. From Reuben. Had to say I wanted to set up a staged murder scene, for research for my next book, and could he help by posing as the victim? "You'll be meeting my wife, Jane, not me" – that's what I put. Reuben said to put that. "Jane's my research assistant." Reuben said Damon Blundy would like the idea. He told me to say that he could make a good column out of it.'

'I knew Blundy wouldn't be able to resist,' says Tasker. 'For all his self-proclaimed brilliance and cleverness, he let Jane tape his hands together behind his chair, tape his ankles to the chair. And then it was too late. Wasn't it, Jane?'

Her nods are like the mechanical vibrations of an inanimate object. 'I felt terrible. He was nice to me. He must have been watching out of the window when I arrived. He came out to greet me, helped me carry all my things into the house.'

'The man was an idiot, Nicki,' says Tasker. He's not interested in Jane. He's watching me, all the time, for my reaction.

'Oh, he couldn't possibly have suspected what I was going to do,' says Jane. An anguished expression contorts her face. 'Until . . . well, he screamed when he saw . . . But no one came. I thought someone might come, but his wife must have been in the basement, which was two floors down. I heard a radio on my way out of the house, quite loud. No one tried to stop me, you see. And, I mean, Damon liked me, before I started in earnest. I liked him. He was nice. We had a nice chat about Reuben's new book and his research. Damon seemed pleased to be helping – quite sincere, I thought. He zipped up my suit – my protective suit.'

Suit. The word makes me think back to the 'Confidant' email. 'What about his computer password?' I say. 'Why would he give you that?'

'I threatened to stab him to death if he didn't,' says Jane, her brow creased in anxiety. She sounds as if she's confessing to accidentally having put some whites in with a coloureds wash and ruined a favourite shirt. 'Once he was taped to his chair securely, I could do whatever I wanted to him. He shouted out, but no one heard. Then I knocked him out with the knife sharpener, painted the words Reuben had told me—'

'Wrong order,' Tasker snaps. Jane shrinks back as if he's physically struck her. He turns to me. 'I had to give her a numbered list of instructions, right down to deleting all her emails-as-me from Blundy's inbox, all his in response from his "Sent" box and both from his "Deleted".' To Jane he says, 'After you knocked him out, you sharpened the knife and then taped it over his mouth.' He sniggers. 'That was kind of the crucial part. I'm surprised you'd choose to forget that bit.'

I want to throw up.

'Actually, I'm not surprised,' Tasker contradicts himself. 'It's typical of you, darling wifey.'

Jane says and does nothing. Just carries on crying.

'Why are you so hard on her?' I ask.

'When she's good enough to kill a man to make me happy, you mean? I agree.' Tasker walks over to the window and pulls open the curtains. Bright sunlight outside. Unbearable: people free and light out there, going about their business. 'I really thought this one might do the trick, but it made no difference. You know what they say: once the rot's set in.'

'What did Jane do that you couldn't forgive?'

He's coming towards me. Too fast. He grabs the scissors and holds them out like a knife to keep me away, as if I'm moving in on him. 'How do you know about that? She didn't do anything!' I've made him angry.

'Gavin told me. Remember? In the email where he said he'd forgive me anything.' I force a smile. 'I hope that's true.'

The rage doesn't leave his eyes, but his mouth forms a smile to mimic mine. 'Jane's never *done* anything I can't forgive. It's what she hasn't done that's the problem.'

'What?' she wails. 'What haven't I done? There's not one single thing I haven't done for you! Name it!'

I recognise that sound. I've never heard it, apart from inside myself: boiling fury, silenced for years.

Tasker doesn't look at her. He keeps his eyes on me. 'She's never read any of my books,' he says. 'Can't stand violence. Even the misery memoirs she reads, she skips the nasty bits – don't you, wifey? Pretty pointless, really, when the nasty bits are the whole point of that particular genre.'

I watch Jane. She's frozen. Her skin is grey. *A Pompeii volcanic-ash woman.*

Adam and I went to Sorrento for our honeymoon. We went on a day trip to Pompeii. The coach was too hot, and we didn't take enough water, and all the shops had sold out – there were too many tourists. We wished we'd stayed in Sorrento, lounging by the swimming pool.

I'm going to see Adam again. If Tasker were intending to kill me, he'd have done it by now. He doesn't want to hurt me; he wants to talk. I'll talk to him for as long as it takes, until I think of a way out of this room.

'I didn't think I'd be able to kill a man, because of the violence involved,' said Jane quietly. 'Reuben's right – I can't read about it. In books, it's presented in a way to make you care, though, isn't it? Books make you feel *upset* about violence. In real life, there's no one in charge behind the scenes steering your feelings in a particular direction. You just do it, and it . . . it's not so bad.'

'Remember your ad, Nicki?' Reuben asks. '"I Want a Secret"? You said you wanted someone who would leave no stone unturned in his determination to find out every secret thing there is to know about you. You promised to reciprocate.'

'Yes. I remember.'

'That's how I knew you were the one for me. You'd have read my novels – every one, cover to cover. How can you claim to love someone who puts their whole heart and soul into their work and completely ignore that work? How can you think that any amount of admin and cooking and cleaning and *fucking* can compensate for such a blatant lack of interest in the person you're married to?' His anger's building again.

'Why didn't you say something?' asks Jane. It's strange: she doesn't seem to be scared any more. 'If I'd known it mattered to you that much—'

'But you didn't, did you, darling wifey? I didn't *say something* because if you don't do it of your own accord, it's worthless. What's the point? Nicki read what Damon Blundy wrote, didn't you, Nicki? She commented on it on the *Daily Herald*'s website. Religiously. That's love, Jane. Nicki knows how to do it properly.'

He turns to face her finally, scissors still in his hand, pointing at her. 'I should kill you now, save you a life prison term.'

'Do it if you want to,' Jane says quietly. 'I don't care.'

He takes a step towards her. Raises his hand above his head.

'No! You murdering . . .' I leap up and throw myself across the room at him. We land in a pile on the carpet, by Jane's feet.

Brown shoes. I struggle to push Tasker off me, but he's too strong. He's on top of me, crushing me. His eyes are glazed, then manic.

'Looking for a secret,' he says. 'Tell me a secret, Nicki.'

'I haven't got any that you don't know.'

'Not true. Tell me a secret.'

'You *are* my fucking secret! There's nothing else.'

'Tell me a secret. You might as well. I'm going to have to kill us all – me, you, Jane. Why wouldn't I? What have I got to look forward to?'

'All right, I'll tell you a secret,' I say quickly, my mouth dry. *Dry as a day in Pompeii.* 'But if I do, you don't kill anyone. Promise.'

He laughs. I can hardly breathe with the weight of him pressing down on my chest. 'Hope to *die*,' he whispers in my ear. 'Tell me your secret, Nicki.'

'My brother,' I say. 'He spied on me, all through my childhood. From when he was about nine until I left home.'

Tell him the worst part. All children tell tales. That's nothing special. Tell him the part that you've numbed yourself into never thinking about because it was the only way to stop the wound bleeding forever.

'He did it for money,' I say. 'It was a business venture for him. My parents paid him. Every time he found out about something I'd done wrong, he'd tell them and they'd pay him more or less, depending on how serious it was, what I'd done.' Bile rises in my throat. I swallow it. 'He used to write them all down in notebooks, with the date next to each one and how much he'd earned, always in pennies. He'd stick gold star stickers and draw smiley faces next to the particularly large amounts. I never suspected. I used to wonder how my parents managed to catch me out so often. I used to talk on the phone in front of Lee, when they were at work, when it was just me, Lee and the au pair of the moment. It never occurred to me that he'd tell. He was my little brother, just a sweet little boy. I loved him, and he loved me – I *know* he did. He wasn't pretending. And then one day, I found these weird notebooks in his bedroom – he'd left them out by mistake. I asked him about it and he . . .' I break off. I've said enough. Tasker wanted a secret and I gave him one. The most agonising secret of all.

'He what?' Tasker holds the scissors under my chin. Touches my neck. Cold metal. 'He what, Nicki?'

'He told me. About being an informant for my parents. And he cried. Cried and cried and cried. I ended up having to comfort him. When I was a student, he sent me a cheque. No covering note. He didn't need to explain. I knew what it was. All the money he'd earned from snitching on me. He wanted to settle the debt.'

'That's a good stor—' Tasker stops. I feel his body tense on top of mine. 'What's that?' he says. 'I heard something.'

I'm about to tell him I heard nothing when the door swings open with a metallic click. Two women stand in the doorway, with a man behind them. That's . . . It's Flash Dad, but with no streaks – with black cropped hair, like . . . Oh my God, like Mr Uskalis, the boring man at reception earlier. They're the same person. I was looking out for someone following me; I didn't notice Uskalis because he rudely pushed in front of me. *Clever.*

I recognise one of the women too: Sergeant Zailer, from Spilling Police Station. She's holding some handcuffs. Putting them on Tasker. She's saying the best words I've ever heard: 'Reuben Tasker, I'm arresting you for the murder of Damon Blundy . . .'

She won't tell Adam. Or that awful DC Waterhouse. I can explain everything, persuade her. She's understanding, Sergeant Zailer. She'll listen to me. I'll tell her: I will never, ever cheat on Adam again. Not physically, not online, not in any way. I've learned my lesson this time – how could I not?

I will be good. I was good for more than three weeks, so I know I can do it, but only if Adam doesn't find out any more than he already knows.

The best of both worlds – that's what I need. Usually when someone wants the best of both worlds, it's some kind of swizz, but this isn't. I don't want to keep Adam in the dark so that I can continue to deceive him. I want to be so much better from now on – a good wife and mother. How can I do that if I have to live with a man who looks at me every day with eyes full of memories of Bad Nicki and everything she did wrong?

I need the best of both worlds. *Please.* For the best of reasons. Sergeant Zailer will understand. I'll make her understand.

16

Thursday 11 July 2013

'Why didn't you tell me you'd hired someone to follow Nicki Clements?' Simon asked Paula Riddiough.

'Jared Uskalis, my slavishly devoted private detective?' She smiled.

They were in the Rose Lounge at the Sofitel St James in London. It was the only place Paula had been willing to meet him, the place where she and Damon Blundy had first met. She'd also flirtatiously insisted on meeting at twelve minutes past twelve rather than twelve o'clock. Simon hadn't been happy about her attempt to embarrass him by recreating the exact conditions of the beginning of her and Blundy's affair, but he'd had no choice. He needed to talk to her, to hear her tell him that his theory about her and Blundy was right. His ego needed it, after he'd been wrong about Reuben Tasker. No matter how many times Charlie said, 'But it *was* Tasker! It was his idea. He planned it and ordered his slave wife to do it!' Simon's despair was left untouched. For the first time in his professional life, he'd told his team the name of the killer and that person had turned out not to have committed the murder. All the pointers had seemed to point to Tasker, and Simon had allowed himself to be seduced by the neatness of it. He'd forgotten to think about the things that didn't quite fit: Gibbs waiting outside on the pavement because Reuben Tasker, for some reason, couldn't or wouldn't come down and let him in. No, it was his wife, Jane, who had to put herself out to open the door . . .

Jane Tasker: the wife Gibbs had described as being like a

servant working for a man who didn't need or want one. Waiting to do Reuben Tasker's bidding, as if nothing else could give her a purpose in life. Terrified when she found out she owned a memoir by Damon Blundy's ex-wife in case Tasker was furious. Giving him an alibi, or so it had seemed. Simon had even thought, Oh, she obviously lied about that, without thinking that Jane too might have been involved in the murder, let alone that she'd done it herself, while Reuben stayed at home and wrote Chapter Fourteen of his latest novel.

It was the minutest details that stung the most.

Simon had been wrong about something else too: he'd assumed the cryptic crime scene was the killer's way of communicating with the police. With him, specifically – the great Simon Waterhouse. Instead, all the clues had been for the benefit of Nicki Clements. Reuben Tasker had taken for granted that the details of how Damon Blundy had been killed would appear in the press and that Nicki would realise who must have killed him.

Simon had been so sure that the message was for him. Humiliating though it was to admit it to himself, he now felt ignored and irrelevant.

'I didn't tell you I'd hired Uskalis to follow Nicki because I couldn't,' said Paula. 'Not without revealing a suspicious level of interest in a woman I didn't know.'

'Yet *now* you're willing to reveal the suspicious interest that you took in Nicki Clements,' said Simon.

'Yes, I am.' Paula flashed him a 'lucky you' smile. 'As I told you before, Nicki's comments on Damon's columns made it clear she was in love with him. I wondered if they were having an affair. Since I'm rich, I could afford to find out.'

'You wondered because you were jealous,' said Simon. 'You were Damon's other woman, and you hated the thought of him having someone else on the go at the same time.'

'Actually, no,' said Paula, sipping her tea. Unlike Simon, she'd spilled none in her saucer. Not a drop. 'I wanted to dig up dirt on Damon, so that I could publicly embarrass him. Not with

an affair – in itself, that wouldn't have made a dent – but . . .
well, as far as I could tell, Nicki Clements was just a nonentity
housewife. She's hardly A-list. Damon wouldn't have wanted to
be caught screwing a nobody.'

Simon narrowed his eyes at her. 'Very good,' he said. 'That's
my cue to say, "Didn't you once hope to be the first female
Labour prime minister?" and get distracted by the hypocrisy of
champagne socialism – talking about equality while secretly
sneering at ordinary people. I'm sure you are a snob, but you're
playing it up to distract me from the lies.'

Paula's smile remained static.

'You offered me a deal when you came to the police station:
if I'd agree not to tell Hannah Blundy, you'd tell me everything.
I'm ready to take you up on that deal.'

The frozen smile turned into a broad grin. 'Really? A wise
decision. All right, then, scratch what I just said. You're right.
I was lying.'

It seemed too easy. 'You admit to the affair with Blundy?'
Simon asked.

'Yes.'

'And you trust me to keep my side of the bargain and not
tell Hannah – just like that?'

'Yes. You won't tell her. You wouldn't want to destroy her,
and from what you've told me, it's clear Damon's and my affair
had nothing to do with his murder.'

Simon gulped down the rest of his tea. Drips from the bottom
of his cup fell onto his shirt and tie, which was partly why he
was keen to be finished drinking from it. Every time he splashed
himself with tea, he noticed Paula making an effort not to laugh.
'You had Nicki followed because you thought she was in love
with Damon,' he started again. 'You knew she was because you
were. Her comments on his columns were *exactly what you'd
have written*. Uncannily identical. You spotted that it wasn't
just any old defence Nicki was providing but a defence motivated
by love.'

'Yes,' said Paula. 'Correct. I trusted Damon one hundred per cent not to cheat on me, but . . . sometimes reading Nicki's comments was like reading the contents of my own heart. It was spooky. So, yes, a *teensy* bit of doubt crept in. Plus in December last year, she moved to Spilling – that gave me a bit of a jump. I knew because she changed her location on her *Herald* comments profile. And, as I say, I've got plenty of money, so there was no reason not to put my mind at rest by having someone tail her for a while. It reassured me enormously: it became clear that Nicki and Damon never went anywhere near one another. I came to the conclusion she was just an obsessive fan. And then she stopped commenting—'

'But you kept up the surveillance.'

'Yes.' Another bright, brittle smile from Paula.

She doesn't mind feeling embarrassed as long as she doesn't look it. Doesn't mind being eaten up by grief as long as the world can't see it.

'Essentially, I was paying for peace of mind,' she said. 'I didn't want to have to start worrying again. I'd have called off my dogs eventually, I promise. In my defence . . . once she moved to Spilling, Nicki's drive to her children's school took her past Damon's front door twice a day. I wasn't only worried that they were getting it on behind my back; I was also afraid she might firebomb his house or something. That level of obsession?' Paula made an exaggerated *Oh, help* face. 'Anything can happen, can't it?'

'So you and Damon were enemies in public, lovers in private?'

'Yes. Before we met, we were genuine enemies, but when we clapped eyes on each other in the flesh . . .' She giggled. 'Well, that rather put paid to all the hate. It wasn't long before we were making love not war.'

'And that's the truth that would devastate Hannah Blundy?' Simon asked, making no attempt to hide his scepticism.

'Yes,' said Paula.

'There's nothing else?'

'What else could there be?'

'You and Damon carried on attacking each other in public. Why? As a smokescreen?'

'Yes, a brilliant one that fooled the world.' Paula laughed. 'I slipped up only once – I tweeted something to him thinking it was a private message, but it was public.'

'"I was lost, I was scared, but a Tory led me home again"?' Simon quoted.

For a second, Paula's smile slipped. Her eyes shone, and she blinked hard a few times. Then she pulled her face back into the right order.

'That's right,' she said. 'It's a line from—'

'I know what it is. Damon replied, didn't he? Did he also believe it was a private exchange, or didn't he care? I think you were the one who insisted on the secrecy, the one who came up with the plan that would devastate Hannah if I told her about it.'

Paula said nothing.

'When you deleted your incriminating tweets, Damon followed suit and deleted his, but he wouldn't have done if you hadn't. He wanted to marry you, didn't he? When the two of you first met in October 2011 – here, in this room – you and Richard Crumlish were on the verge of officially separating. Damon was single. There was nothing to stop the two of you getting together – openly, not illicitly. Damon wanted to. You didn't.'

'Carry on,' said Paula. 'I'm enjoying this shaggy dog story.'

'I know another couple who are having an affair, in a similar situation,' Simon told her. 'He'd leave his wife for her like a shot, but she won't leave her husband. She's always claimed it was because she didn't want to hurt anyone, but it's not that – it's a strong preference for fantasy over reality. He, the man, wants a happier reality. He's practical, a realist. She's a big kid at heart, with her head in the clouds, and wants to keep it there. Whether she realises it or not, she believes that if you let your ideal, fantasy man become your day-to-day reality, it'll spoil the fantasy. The only way to keep the fantasy alive forever is to get yourself fixed up with a less inspiring reality from which you'll regularly want to escape.'

And then you pretend to split up and you announce your separation . . . why? Simon didn't have even the stirrings of a theory in relation to Liv and Gibbs's fake break-up. Perhaps the mistake was to assume it was fake. Could it be true: they'd stopped sleeping together, reinvented themselves as platonic best friends? Charlie said definitely not.

Dragging his mind away from the puzzle, Simon said to Paula, 'I think you're similar to her, this other woman I know. You prefer fantasy to reality. You want to keep what you value most highly *out* of your real, everyday life. Hence Hannah for Damon, and Fergus Preece for you. That's the devastating truth you're determined to keep from Hannah: not that her husband was sleeping with you, not boring old normal adultery, *but that he was using her to please you from the second he laid eyes on her.* He needed a wife in place in order to satisfy the requirements of the woman he really loved: you.'

'Have you finished?'

'No,' said Simon. 'Damon met Hannah in late November 2011, less than two months after he first met you, and he appeared to fall in love with her immediately. He married her in March 2012. You were strict with him, weren't you? I bet you refused to let him lay a finger on you until he'd found himself someone to marry. You said, "Find a wife and make her happy, so that you stay married to her, and *then* I'll be your . . . other woman."'

Paula laughed. 'You make it sound so delightfully *quaint*,' she said.

'It took you slightly longer to find Fergus. There was probably a list of characteristics the two spouse stooges needed to have. You and Damon drew it up together. I'm trying to think what Hannah Blundy and Fergus Preece have in common. Fergus owns all that land, but Hannah's not a landowner, she's not rich—'

'You're a cynical sod, aren't you?' said Paula, smiling. She took another sip of tea. 'Well, I suppose I'll have to give you ten out of ten. You're basically right, though *not* about the criteria we used to choose a husband for me and a wife for Damon.' She sighed. 'Look, we knew what we were planning was grossly unfair to whichever man and woman we picked. Neither of us had any illusions about our moral rectitude. Damon hated hypocrisy more than anything and . . . well, I've come to hate it too. But we didn't want to do any more harm than we needed to in order to protect our relationship. I knew our perfect love – and it *was* perfect – would only survive if we remained separated by circumstances. You can't still be some- one's perfect woman once they've pulled strands of your hair out of the shower plughole enough times! Even *I* can't, and look at me.' She pointed at her face. 'I'm the most beautiful woman I know, but so what? The second time I met Damon – our all- the-elevens date, when we stopped skirting around the issue and admitted we were soulmates – he told me he'd divorced his second wife for snoring. Between you, me and the gatepost, DC Waterhouse . . . *I* snore. You see what I'm saying?'

She leaned forward in her chair. 'Damon was as madly in love with me on the day he died as he was on 11 November 2011.' Her eyes were shining again. 'That's only because I stood my ground and said no – no marriage, no living together, no sex till he was safely married to someone else. Even after that, when we had our trysts, I'd never agree to share a room with him overnight. You can't risk it if you really care about making a good impression. Morning breath, stinky armpits . . .'

Stinky way of looking at the world, thought Simon.

'Judge me all you like,' said Paula, 'but I bet you've never been in love with someone who'd divorce you for snoring. And before you conclude that Damon was a monster and I was his brainwashed victim . . . well, it actually worked both ways. Damon was a perfectionist, but I'm very easily hurt. I find it difficult to recover from any kind of wound. I told Damon; I was very upfront about it. I said, "If I'm ever hurt by you, we're done for." When I first met Crummy – my ex-husband, Richard Crumlish – he promised me the earth and more. I thought he was wonderful; he thought I was a goddess. Everything seemed perfect. And then he hurt me in a relatively minor way and that was it for me. I pretended to forgive him, but secretly, from that moment, I was keeping my eyes peeled for someone new.'

'What was the hurt?' Simon asked.

'I needed a lift home from Central London late at night. He told me to get a cab – he couldn't be bothered to get dressed and come out. It wasn't as if I couldn't afford a cab, but he'd always been happy to give me lifts before. I thought, "So, that's it, then. You care about me less tonight than you did last time I needed a ride home. The golden age is over." And, frankly, who wants to bother with the dull beige age, which is where all marriages can't help ending up, however hard they try.'

'But . . . Damon Blundy attacked you week after week, in his column,' said Simon. 'Didn't that hurt?'

'Ah.' Paula closed her eyes for a few seconds. 'Yes, it did. But you see, with Damon things moved in the opposite direction, the best direction, always. He hurt me *first*, before he knew me. Then he met me and fell in love with me and . . . well, to use my colours metaphor again, it went from black to gold. For him, it was like that too – I loathed him and then I forgave him: black to gold. And so . . . we did it over and over again: savaged each other publicly, as hurtfully as we could, then made up for it later in private. When the person you love cures the pain they caused by being as loving as they were hateful, it's an incredible high. The love wouldn't be anywhere near as powerful if it weren't the longed-for antidote to the hate. Like having a can of Coke after a long and thirsty game of tennis. Tastes better than any other can of Coke you've ever had. Marriage, by contrast, is like starting with a fizzy can of Coke and waiting around while it gets flatter and flatter.'

Simon nodded. Romantic sadism. An intimate, intense agony that only the loved one could take away. Ought he to worry about how easily he understood it, how little Paula's explanation fazed him?

'So what were the criteria?' he asked. 'For . . . spouses?'

'Oh yes, the good-deed part of our plan,' said Paula.

Good deed? Simon waited. It struck him as unlikely that Paula and Damon Blundy's conspiracy would have an altruistic strand to it, but he decided to keep an open mind.

'It was vitally important to me that we didn't just use people. Damon, of course, said, "Great, I'll grab a bimbo waitress at the Groucho and propose to her."' Paula rolled her eyes in mock despair. 'I said, "No. You'll find an intelligent, *un*attractive woman whom you can love and respect as a person. And you *will* love and respect her – not in the way you love me, not a grand passion, but in a *married* way. The best that a marriage can be – that's what I want you to make with whichever woman you choose, so bloody well choose someone who you think deserves it." This is going to sound weird and spiritual – I *am*, in fact, a bit spiritual, though I keep quiet about it to avoid mockery – but . . . love's something you get better at with practice. Loving Hannah, every day, behaving in a loving way towards her – that was Damon's spiritual practice.'

Paula laughed suddenly. 'I never put it to him in those terms – he'd have told me to pull my brain out of my arse – but I managed to make him understand the basic principle. Men who treat their wives badly treat their lovers badly too. Always, always – maybe not straight away, but eventually. And the opposite's equally true: if you treat your wife well, you'll treat your lover well. So, if you're ever looking for a mistress, make sure you don't choose a woman who speaks ill of her husband. Choose someone like me – I *adore* Fergus. Not romantically, and very differently from how I adored Damon, but I still love him to bits. And by putting that love into practice every day, I'm getting better at being a loving person – and that benefits—'

Paula broke off with a sharp intake of breath. 'That benefitted Damon,' she said, altering the tense.

'I can see why you don't want Hannah to find out,' said Simon. 'It's worse than the average extra-marital affair.'

'More upsetting,' Paula corrected him. 'I'm not sure about worse.'

Simon was. 'I won't tell Hannah, but for the record? I don't think it's acceptable, what you and Damon did. You did a bad thing. Telling Damon the woman he chose to marry had to be unattractive? I bet you said you'd do the same, didn't you – find a physically unattractive man?'

'What's wrong with that?' Paula asked. 'What would have been the point of Damon and I inciting each other's sexual jealousy? We knew we'd be jealous enough as it was – it was always part of the plan that we'd sleep with the people we married. It wouldn't have been fair not to.'

Simon said nothing. He stared at her for as long as he thought he could get away with. Then he asked, 'Don't you feel guilty?'

'No. Which doesn't mean I think we behaved entirely well, but . . . we behaved a *bit* well. As well as we could, given our goal. If we wanted our love to last forever – and we did, and it *will* – we had to do what we did, exactly as we did it. Nothing else would have worked. Everyone treats other people instrumentally in their quest for personal happiness, apart from maybe a few self-sacrificing old monks. But most people do.'

Simon put a five-pound note down on the table and stood up to leave. He was thirsty – tea always had that effect on him. 'Thanks for telling me the truth,' he said to Paula.

'I make Fergus extremely happy,' she called after him.

As he walked through the Sofitel's lobby, Simon imagined himself telling Hannah Blundy what he'd found out. Should he? It was the answer she'd been waiting for, but would it make her happier to know? Was happiness always the most important consideration? What good would it do her to find out the truth?

Outside the hotel, Simon blinked in the light and enjoyed the feeling of the fresh air in his lungs.

He knew it was useless. No matter how much he argued with himself, he would end up telling Hannah what he knew. The truth mattered. If he were in her shoes, he'd rather know.

Time to ring Charlie, who would disagree with him and try to change his mind.

Acknowledgements

I am profoundly grateful to the talented team at Hodder, as always, and to my ace agent Peter Straus. Huge thanks to Emily Winslow, who read an early draft of the novel and made incredibly helpful suggestions for improvement, and to Dominic Gregory and Rosanna Keefe, for the Clark Kent/Superman discussion. Thanks to Chris Gribble for 'The Cartographer's Biographer', which simply had to be included, and to Dan, Phoebe and Guy Jones for putting up with another year of my distracted dishevelment. Thanks to everyone who entered into the 'Why is sports doping worse than stoned writers?' debate with me: Morgan and Klair White and Mic Wright, to name but three. Special thanks to my husband Dan for drawing the issue to my attention in the first place, and for always being ready to think the unthinkable and say the unsayable.

I am very grateful to Naomi Alderman, whose use of the term 'telling error' in a tweeted conversation gave me a title that I love, and who contributed some valuable psychological insights.

I would like to thank all the controversial newspaper columnists and bloggers whose work I enjoy reading, and who jointly inspired the character of Damon Blundy in this novel; there are too many of them to name (and, to be honest, some are people that one is not allowed to admire if one doesn't want to get moaned at on Twitter). Speaking of which, this book was heavily inspired by Twitter, the online home of much kindness, much cruelty, and endless pockets of hitherto unimaginable absurdity. Twitter reminds me, daily, that even my most deranged characters are unrealistically well-balanced compared with many actual people. Thanks to my lovely readers who take the time to tweet, email and write to me about the books – I really hope you enjoy this one! And thank you to all my international publishers, who have enabled Simon Waterhouse and Charlie Zailer's strange partnership to travel far and wide (not to mention Liv and Gibbs' equally strange relationship).

Thanks to Carcanet for permission to publish an extract from 'Deep-Rooted Fears' by C.H. Sisson. The poem appears in his Carcanet collection *Antidotes*.

Last but far from least, I would like to thank the uniquely awesome Dan Mallory, whose inspiring friendship and endless enthusiasm for discussing books and human beings with me has added a new dimension to my life.

In the best books, the ending often comes as a shock.
Not just because of that one last twist in the tale,
but because you have been so absorbed in their world,
that coming back to the harsh light of reality is a jolt.

If that describes you now, then perhaps you should track down
some new leads, and find new suspense in other worlds.

Join us at www.hodder.co.uk, or follow us on
Twitter @hodderbooks, and you can tap in to a
community of fellow thrill-seekers.

Whether you want to find out more about this book,
or a particular author, watch trailers and interviews, have
the chance to win early limited editions, or simply browse
our expert readers' selection of the very best books,
we think you'll find what you're looking for.

And if you don't, that's the place to tell us what's missing.

We love what we do, and we'd love you to be part of it.

www.hodder.co.uk

 @hodderbooks

HodderBooks

HodderBooks